CITY OF WIND

STEEL AND FIRE BOOK 4

JORDAN RIVET

Staunton Street Press
HONG KONG

Contact Jordan Rivet via email at jordan@jordanrivet.com

Cover by Deranged Doctor Design

Edited by Red Adept Editing

Maps by Jordan Rivet

City of Wind, Steel and Fire Book 4 – First Edition: December 2016

For Whitney and Jeff
who fight together

CONTENTS

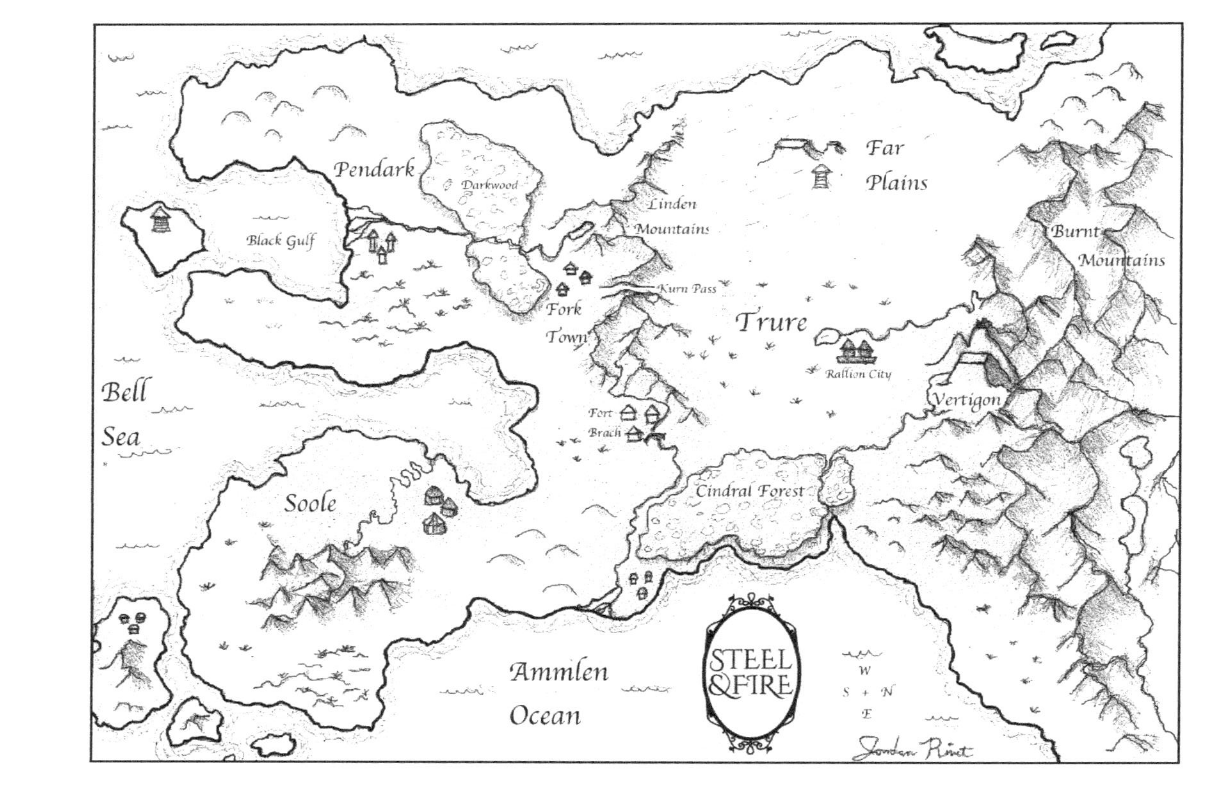
Far
Plains
Pendark
Darkwood
Linden
Mountains
Burnt
Mountains
Black Gulf
Kurn Pass
Fork
Town
Trure
Rallion City
Vertigon
Bell
Sea
Fort
Brach
Cindral Forest
Soole
Ammlen
Ocean
STEEL
&FIRE
W
S
N
E
Jordan Rivet

1

SWIMMING

Dara stepped into the murky water. She shivered, wishing they'd waited until summer to try this. She took another step—and her feet slipped out from under her. She landed with a terrific splash, drenching her clothes and dousing her eyes with saltwater. Nearby, Siv doubled over laughing.

"Shut up."

"Dara," he gasped between chuckles. "You're one of the best athletes I've ever met. I don't get why you flail like a greckleflush the minute you encounter water."

"Easy for you to say," Dara said, scrambling to her feet. "Your grandfather rules a city with a great-big lake."

"Didn't you ever play in the streams in Vertigon?"

"Those are three feet deep."

"Still." Siv splashed a few feet farther from the shoreline and beckoned for Dara to join him. "I expected more of you. What would Coach Doban say?"

"I'm sure Berg has a healthy respect for open water," Dara mumbled, cheeks heating. Her dueling friends were another story. Kel would find her underdeveloped swimming abilities particularly amusing. Of course, Siv teased her enough for the lot of them.

"Come on, Dara, it's shallow for another twenty paces. You're not even swimming yet."

Dara trudged after him, the cold water quickly rising up her bare legs. She wore her old trousers rolled above the knees. Wyla had given her some clothes in the Pendarkan style to wear when she was out in the city, but she didn't want to get those wet. Firelord knew she owed Wyla enough.

The water of the Black Gulf rippled around her, cloudy with silt and unknown detritus. The volcanic rock that gave the gulf its name was rough on her bare feet. The chilly water was refreshing, though. Pendark grew warmer every day. It would be as hot as a Vertigonian summer soon, and winter had barely come to an end.

Dara and Siv weren't the only pair taking advantage of the sunny afternoon to go for a swim—or wade, as Dara wasn't certain she'd be going out far enough for it to count as a swim today. Children splashed in the shallows, fully clothed, and a few older boys raced each other to the beach from a large black rock sticking out of the gulf. Others lounged at the water's edge or dug in the mud for spiny creatures that always seemed to skitter out of their reach. A handful of adults floated on their backs farther out, allowing the gentle roll of the waves to carry them along. Dara wondered if any of them worked in the Watermight practitioner's manor overlooking this stretch of sand. Orange flags flew from its black stone walls. Siv's pen-fighting friends had assured him the Waterworker, who controlled half of Pendark's port, didn't care if people used his beach. Dara was wary of getting too close to any of them. She had her own Waterworker to worry about.

"Okay." Siv stopped when the water reached their waists. "Let's practice dunking first."

"I'd rather just learn to swim with my head above water," Dara said.

"That's cheating. Besides, you'll never swim really fast like that. You wouldn't want everyone to be able to beat you in a race, would you?"

Dara opened her mouth then closed it again. So she was a bit competitive. It wasn't fair for him to use that against her. Still, if it was the best way . . .

She sucked in a breath, squeezed her eyes shut, and dropped into the water. Underneath, a cool rush surrounded her, caressing her skin, blurring sound. She felt weightless and surprisingly calm. Her pendant necklace shifted against her chest, the stone warm compared to the water. This wasn't so bad.

Then something slimy brushed her ankle. She gasped, swallowing a huge mouthful of salty water. She scrambled to her feet, coughing and spluttering.

Siv splashed closer and patted her on the back as she gasped in air.

"Easy there. You're supposed to keep your mouth closed."

"Oh." She coughed. "I didn't know."

Siv chuckled. "You were down there a long time. I was starting to worry you meant to set a record on your first go."

"Maybe on my second," Dara said, still wheezing. The saltwater burned like Fire in her throat. "Something touched me," she said. "Something slimy."

"Probably just seaweed," Siv said. "Although I've heard there are krellfish and the occasional salt adder in these waters."

Dara's eyes bulged, and she felt a sharp kick of panic, but Siv stopped her before she could charge back to the shore. Or leap into his arms.

"I'm kidding. No salt adders." He narrowed his eyes. "Someone's jumpy today."

"Let's get this over with," Dara said. "What's next?"

"Try floating on your back. Once you get used to the feeling, it's really relaxing. Watch me."

Siv flopped backward and drifted on the surface, looking up at the clear blue sky. His bare chest floated high enough out of the water to reveal the thin scars crossing his ribs. White puckered scars from stab wounds dotted his sword arm, and a faint line slashed across his temple. All the blade wounds were old. He had a supply of fresh bruises patterning his body, but Dara was used to those as a duelist. Training could be a rough activity. She was glad to see his more grievous wounds were healed and his strength had returned. If anything, he was more muscular than ever. Kres March kept his pen fighters to a rigorous training schedule, even on the road.

"Liking what you see, eh?" Siv said, and Dara started.

"What? Oh, uh, I was studying your technique."

"Sure you were. My technique." Siv grinned and winked at her. Water dripped from his short beard and ran over his chest as he stood. Dara cleared her throat. Right. Technique. Swimming.

"Let me get you started." Siv advanced toward her through the water, eyes bright, and her heart stuttered a bit. "Just take a deep breath and lie back. Try not to move, and let the water do the rest."

He put his hands low on her back and guided her down. She eased back, letting her feet leave the bottom. Siv held her firmly, and she straightened out as much as she could.

"That's it. You're still relying too much on me. Let the water hold you up." He removed one hand, and she balanced on the other, the water lapping her body and filling her ears. She could sense the water buoying her up. She was getting the idea. But she liked the feeling of Siv's hand firm against her back, and she didn't want him to let go just yet.

Something touched her face. She jerked up, imagining toxic salt adders, and flailed out of balance before she realized Siv had just been brushing a strand of hair from her forehead.

"Sorry. Bad timing," Siv said, catching her as she found her feet once more. "You're just so damn pretty. I couldn't resist."

Dara faced him, pressed close against his chest with his arms around her. Her cheeks flushed, and warmth from Siv's body seeped into her, keeping the chill of the water at bay. She still wasn't used to him saying things like this openly. Siv wanted to return to Vertigon, but he no longer seemed to care she wasn't a suitable match for a king in need of alliances. Something huge had changed between them. After everything they had been through, it was clear they wanted to be together no matter what. Wanted each other.

She rested her hands on his chest and looked up, memorizing the lines of his face—many of them new thanks to the scar on his temple and the beard lining his strong jaw. His breath was warm on her face, his arms tight around her, their faces inches apart. The moment was so precious, she felt as if it could shatter at the slightest movement. She'd all but given up on this once. She knew Siv had almost given up on it too. But here in the waters of the Black Gulf on the opposite side of the continent from their home, they were free to hold each other where anyone could see.

They weren't free to be together all the time, though. Dara had struck a bargain with Wyla the Watermight Artist in exchange for her help when Dara and her friends chased Siv to Pendark. Dara had committed to helping Wyla experiment with combining Fire and Watermight. She would stay with Wyla in her manor, her thrall for the next three months. Meanwhile, Siv had taken up residence in the blue house on stilts belonging to the pen fighters who'd adopted him. They had both stolen away from their respective districts for this afternoon swimming lesson.

Dara hadn't seen much of Wyla in the five days since she arrived in the city. The Waterworker had been busy since returning from Fork Town, where they'd met. She'd instructed Dara to practice her Fireworking skills using Fire from a supply of Works she'd had brought in. She wanted Dara in peak condition before they began their research. Dara still wasn't sure what form the research would take.

"You look solemn," Siv said. He brushed a hand through her wet hair, tangling it in the process. "Nervous about your mad Artist friend?"

"I don't know if she's mad," Dara said. "She's dangerous, though."

"Are you sure you can't buy your way out of the bargain?"

"With what money?" Dara didn't have a single coin to her name. For the moment, at least, she was at the Waterworker's mercy in every way.

"I'll make you some," Siv said. "A few rounds in the Steel Pentagon ought to be enough to buy your freedom."

"You're not seriously going through with that, are you?"

"Why not? I'm a decent knife fighter. Kres expects me to contribute to the team if I'm going to stay there for the next few months. I can pick up a few gutter matches too. The coins will roll in."

Dara shook her head. Wyla had used her Watermight to set some sort of bond or curse that would freeze Dara's sword arm to the bone if she tried to leave the city. Someone so determined to have a Fireworker for a research assistant would never let her go for a pile of gold. There was no way it was worth the risk.

"You could be killed."

"Only if I lose," Siv said. His hand trailed from her hair to her neck, traced her jaw line. "I don't plan to do much of that. Otherwise, I won't get the gold anyway."

"But—"

"I'm getting you out of here, Dara." He dropped his hand, eyes steady on hers. "After everything you've done for me, I'm surprised you're even questioning it."

"I went through all that to make sure you *didn't* get stabbed through the heart." She tapped her fingers on his bare chest for emphasis. "Don't undo all my hard work."

"Look, even if I didn't owe you my life, I'd still do everything in my power to help you. I'm not going to let you stay in that woman's clutches a minute longer than you have to."

"And what about Sora?"

A shadow crossed Siv's face, pain and guilt in equal measures. "Dara—"

"My parents won't need her as their figurehead forever. You should go back to her."

Siv grimaced. This wasn't easy for him. He'd only known his sister was alive for a few days, but it tore him up inside that he'd left her behind. He wanted to go to her as soon as possible. That was driving him more than any notions of regaining his former power. Dara wished she could convince him to go ahead, even though she didn't like the idea of being away from him so soon. She herself didn't have a choice.

"It's a long journey," she said softly. "You should go."

"I won't leave you." Siv cupped her face in his hands, his eyes boring into her and setting her heart fluttering. "I'm counting on us saving Sora together." Their faces inched closer, his breath brushing her lips. "Besides, we need more fighters to help us. That'll be another good use for all the gold I'm going to win in the Dance of Steel."

"Siv."

"Dara."

"What if you're—?"

"I'll be fine. Sheesh, Dara, are we going to kiss or not?"

Dara blinked, and Siv took advantage of her momentary silence to bring his mouth down to hers. His fingers tangled in her hair again, as if he'd never let go. She found herself twining her arms around his neck, pulling him closer.

The warmth of Siv's arms around her was nothing compared to the heat that swept through her core at the touch of his lips, brushed with salt from the gulf. This was why she had crossed the continent to find him. This was why she couldn't bring herself to send him away. She loved him more than she could stand, and she wanted him so much, she could hardly stand up.

She ran her hands over his face, enjoying the roughness of his beard against her skin. His mouth was soft and firm against hers.

She had been so afraid she would find him too late. She almost didn't believe she had him in her arms at last, no longer pretending they hadn't both been longing to do this for months—even before they were separated. She loved him with a fierceness that surprised her. And for now, at least, she had him all to herself.

Siv pulled his mouth from hers and trailed a line of kisses across her jaw and down the side of her neck, his lips brushing her collarbone. Her breath hitched in her throat, and her fingers tightened in his hair.

Then she hooked her foot around his ankle and yanked his feet out from under him.

He crashed into the water with a splash, pulling her down with him. They still weren't out too deep, and she rested her knees on the rocky bottom with her face safely out of the water. She grinned at him as he regained his footing, still spluttering and coughing.

"Who's flailing like a greckleflush now?" she said.

"Oh, you're going to regret that, Dara Ruminor," Siv said.

He swept her into his arms and tossed her through the air. She landed in deeper water and immediately kicked farther out so he couldn't snatch her up again. He charged after her, and she let him overtake her, laughing in spite of the cold water creeping up to her neck.

"Maybe this swimming lesson was a bad idea," he grumbled.

"You're not a very good teacher," she said. "Too easily distracted."

"Only by you."

She grinned and eased into his arms again. He held her waist and steered her farther out into the gulf. The water got deeper and deeper, but she kept her eyes on his as they advanced. Slowly, Dara's feet left the ground. Siv still held her, his legs churning to keep them afloat.

He kissed her again, slowly and gently, as a wave lifted them up. He stared into her eyes as if they were all he ever wanted to look at for the rest of his life. Dara wrapped her arms around his neck, pressing close as he carried her deeper. The idea that she might lose him again, whether in the Steel Pentagon or anywhere else, sent hot knives of fear through her chest. But, for now, she wanted to enjoy this. Enjoy him.

A whooping sound came from nearby. They had drifted into the path of the young boys racing from the beach to the large rock.

The swimmers churned through the water on either side of them, splashing and shouting. Dara and Siv broke off the kiss to wipe the water out of their eyes. Dara eased away from him a little and kicked steadily, imitating the racers' movements. She still held Siv's shoulders, but she thought she was starting to understand how this swimming thing worked. He moved slowly, letting her guide their progress as they swam together.

"Not bad," Siv said. "You're a fast learner."

"Let's hope I can learn something useful from Wyla in the next few months."

"You won't be here for months if I can help it," Siv said. Dara appreciated his conviction, but he couldn't possibly break the Watermight bond Wyla had placed on her arm to seal their bargain. She'd have to convince him to return to Vertigon without her.

The young swimmers reached the rock and lay on their backs or perched on the irregular outcroppings. The glitter of the afternoon sun on the water made it look as if the rock were rising out of a pool of molten silver.

"Ho there," one of the boys called as Dara and Siv swam nearer. "Did you hear the news from Trure?"

"What news?" Siv called.

"Everyone's talking about it," another boy said. "Them Soolens captured Rallion City."

Siv's face went ashen. Fortunately, Dara was getting the hang of swimming, because she almost had to hold him up now. She squeezed his shoulders, bringing his attention back to their position. He met her eyes, mouth tense. When they had left Rallion City, his mother and sister had been staying in the royal palace with his grandfather, the king.

They swam over to the rock where the group of boys gathered.

"When did this happen?" Siv asked as he climbed up to join them.

"A few days ago, I reckon," said the first boy. He wore a scrap of cloth tied around his forehead, the orange hue identifying him as an errand boy for the Waterworker who owned the manor house by the beach. "That's what the merchants are saying, anyway."

"Have you heard anything about the King of Trure or his family?" Siv asked.

"Nope. Could be dead for all I know."

Dara shivered as a breeze blew across the gulf, chilling her damp clothes. Siv didn't seem to notice.

"Was there anything else?" he said, voice so soft, it was almost lost on the wind.

"My father says the Soolens will come here next," said the largest of the boys.

"That's stupid," said the boy in orange. "The Waterworkers would drown 'em all."

The larger boy leapt to his feet, fists raised. "You calling my father stupid, Tel?"

"Nah." Tel didn't even blink. "Why would they want this big pile of mud anyway?"

"My father says the Soolens do all kinds of crazy things." The larger boy lowered his fists. "They eat rocks and raw fish there, you know."

"I don't know about eating rocks, but they took over Trure." Tel straightened his orange bandana and cast an appraising eye over Siv. Shirtless, he was paler than the olive-skinned Pendarkans. He could easily pass for Truren. "Don't they have a great-big army, with tons of horses and stuff?"

"Trure has the finest cavalry on the continent," Siv said. "No Soolen army should be able to defeat them."

"That's what my father said!" shouted the larger boy.

Siv looked back at Dara. She held his gaze steadily. She didn't know as much about armies as he did, but she didn't understand how the great Rallion City had fallen either.

"It could be a rumor," she said. "Let's see if there's any truth to it before you worry too much."

Siv thanked their informants and climbed back toward the waterline, taking Dara's hand before slipping back into the water. The boys began to argue over whether or not you could die from eating raw fish as Dara and Siv swam toward the shore. She held onto his arm to help keep her head above water. He barely seemed to notice her weight as he tugged her along. He was far too quiet.

When they reached shallow-enough water for Dara to stand, she released his arm and grabbed his hand again, squeezing it tightly.

"I'm sure Selivia and your mother are okay," she said. "Even if Rallion City has been captured, Commander Brach wouldn't hurt the royal family."

"He'd better not," Siv said darkly.

A shadow fell over them as they trudged through the shallows to where they'd left their weapons and shoes. Clouds began to creep into the afternoon sky. The weather changed so quickly here. It could be raining by suppertime.

The city spread before them, a mix of houses on stilts, meandering canals, and rocky islands. Orange flags whipped in the wind, decorating many of the houses near the beach. The flags switched to burgundy around where a narrow jetty jutted out into the gulf. Pendark was still a mystery to Dara. She had three months to get to know it, but with the news from Siv's grandfather's kingdom, she couldn't justify asking him to stay.

"Siv, you should go—"

"No," Siv said. "I'm not leaving you. I can't go back empty handed anyway. I need to gather men and resources if I'm going to be of any use to anyone." He looked to the north as he put his sword belt on over damp trousers. "My grandfather must have sent them to safety long before the Soolens arrived."

Despite his words, the set of Siv's jaw and his uncharacteristic frown showed that he wasn't as certain as he sounded. He must feel conflicted about delaying his departure—even if he was doing it for her sake.

"We'd better find out more details," Dara said. "Maybe you can—"

She stopped as an icy sensation crept through her sword arm. It wasn't exactly painful, but it had nothing to do with the cold water drenching her shirt. There was no mistaking the unnatural chill. Watermight.

"What's wrong?" Siv asked.

"It's Wyla," Dara said. She squeezed her sword arm, trying to get it to warm up. She was afraid to move it too much lest her bones crack.

"She's doing something to you?" Siv's knife appeared in his hand—little use against this threat.

"My arm just went all cold. Wait, it's fading now." She flexed her muscles gently, but the chill didn't subside entirely.

"Is that some sort of signal?"

"Must be. I'd better go back to the manor just in case."

"Let me come with you," Siv said. "I'd like to give that woman a signal."

"No, it's okay," Dara said quickly. "I don't want her to get her claws in you." She shook her arm. "There. The feeling is gone. She probably just wanted to remind me of our bargain."

"I don't like this," Siv said.

"Me neither, but it'll be okay." Dara hurriedly gathered up the rest of her things. "I'll be glad to get started, actually. I don't like waiting and wondering."

"Just be careful." Siv rested his hands on her sword arm for a moment, his touch as light as if her arm were made of spun sugar. "And let me know if you want me to storm the manor. I reckon the pen fighters would help."

"Don't do anything foolish." The cold sensation began to return, pulsing this time. "I'd better get back. See what you can find out about Rallion City."

The sooner she started working with Wyla, the better. The Watermight Artist studied magical substances. She could teach Dara something about the Fire that would be more useful for retaking their lost mountain than men and coin. The Soolens were a threat, but it was Dara's father—and his power—that stood in their way. Despite everything he had done, she still wanted to find a way to stop him without killing him. Wyla could hold the key.

2

THE LANTERN MAKER

Queen Soraline Amintelle hurtled down the spiral staircase. She hiked her skirt up to her knees to keep from tripping, flying down the steps as quickly as she could. Her ankle turned beneath her when she reached the ground floor of the castle. She ignored the twinge of pain and hurried toward the entrance hall.

Her guards ran beside her, their boots thudding in time. Captain Thrashe was on her right, a hand on his saber and a scowl on his scarred, one-eyed face. Kelad Korran kept pace to her left, as relaxed as if he were out for a jog. Both of them were ready to fight, but it was Sora who would do battle today. She'd seen the conflict brewing from the window. She had to stop it before things got out of hand.

She flung the doors open, not waiting for the guards to do it for her. Weak spring sunshine filled the courtyard. The cold bit into her instantly. She'd left her cloak back in the library. No time to delay.

She hurried toward a group of five people in the barren courtyard. Rafe Ruminor, Lantern Maker and Chief Regent of Vertigon, stood tall at the center, unmoving. His very presence radiated tension like heat from a Fire Gate.

Madame Pandan, a Metalworker from Square Peak, radiated actual heat. Her body quivered and blazed as she faced down the Lantern Maker. A grim Worker called Jara the Gilder stood by her side. He'd once been an ally of the Ruminors, but he too appeared to be holding Fire. Sora had learned to identify the signs, even though she couldn't sense or touch the magic substance herself.

Lima Ruminor and Master Corren flanked the Lantern Maker. Corren the Firespinner was a stocky man in a fine embroidered coat. He didn't seem about to burst with Fire, but that didn't mean he wasn't ready to Wield to defend Rafe. Lima's face could have been carved from stone. She wore a permanent scowl these days, which spoiled her otherwise handsome features. Sora wouldn't be surprised if Lima attacked Madame Pandan and Master Jara with her fists.

An assortment of Castle Guards stood back from the Workers, none willing to get too close. Oat and Yuri, two of her loyal men, were among them. It wasn't the first time they'd witnessed a confrontation between Fireworkers. They would be powerless if this kettle reached a boiling point.

Sora skidded to a stop at the edge of the group, a stitch catching in her side. "What's going on here?" she demanded. She didn't step between the Workers. She made a point of appearing unafraid of the Fire, but she wasn't stupid.

"Jara and Madame Pandan were just leaving," Lima said.

"You cannot make us," Madame Pandan hissed. Her hair was in disarray, and even her thick, expressive eyebrows looked wild. Sora hadn't seen her since she escaped the huge surge of power at the Well the night of Sora's eighteenth birthday. Madame Pandan had been the only Square Worker to survive the disaster. It looked as if she wasn't coping well.

"I will do what I must," the Lantern Maker said softly.

"Go ahead and threaten us," Madame Pandan said. "Do violence like a Pendarkan animal."

"You are the only one advocating violence here," Master Corren said. "What do you want?"

Madame Pandan looked at Sora, and it was all she could do to keep from signaling for her to be quiet. Madame Pandan couldn't give away their alliance. The Ruminors still didn't know Sora had conspired against them with the Square Peak Workers. Sora had to get her out of here before she ruined everything.

Madame Pandan turned back to the Lantern Maker. "We want you gone," she said. "We will bring our Fire against you. You can't contain it anymore. The Fire runs loose on the mountain. You cannot stop us."

She nodded at Jara, and their eyes blazed golden. The heat billowing off them intensified. They meant to attack the Lantern Maker right here in the castle courtyard! The spring snowdrifts melted away from them in an ever-widening ring.

Sora struggled with indecision. She could let them try, let them eliminate the threat of the Lantern Maker once and for all. But if they lost, he would obliterate them—and take half the occupants of the courtyard with them.

"Friends," she said quickly, stepping closer. "Will you kindly join me for a cup of tea in the library? I'd like you to hear your complaints."

Master Corren glanced at her, and even Lima was momentarily distracted. The Lantern Maker kept his eyes on the two Workers. They still shivered and shimmered like burning brands. Were they going to do it?

"Master Jara? Madame Pandan?" Sora said. "Won't you come inside?"

"We won't stand for it anymore," Madame Pandan said. "Daz was right. He is too dangerous. He has unleashed the Well. The Spring itself has been disturbed." She met Sora's eyes for an instant. "We didn't know he'd go this far."

The second Madame Pandan's attention left him, the Lantern Maker struck. A blast of Fire erupted between Rafe and the two Workers. Heat rushed outward, and a toe-curling scream split the air.

Sora stumbled back, unable to withstand the burning, blinding onslaught. A hand on her shoulder steadied her. Kel. She blinked rapidly, trying to see through the white-hot blaze.

At first she thought Rafe had shot something at his opponents, like a bolt of Fireworked lightning. But the Lantern Maker wasn't shooting Fire *at* the two Workers. He was sucking it *from* them, somehow drawing a violent flood of power from their bodies.

The two Workers linked hands. Sweat poured down their faces. Madame Pandan screamed louder. Her hands were bone-white, one gripping Jara's hand, the other clenched in her skirt. They fought the Lantern Maker for their Fire, and it stretched like a cloth of gold between them.

Sora didn't dare speak. The Castle Guards retreated to the walls, except for Kel and Captain Thrashe at her back. Their steel would be of no use here. Even Lima looked afraid.

For a moment, it appeared that Madame Pandan and Jara's combined strength might keep the Lantern Maker from seizing their store of Fire. The Metalworker stopped screaming and bared her teeth in a vicious snarl. Then Rafe smiled. The heat swelled. More Fire rushed from the two Workers, straight to the Lantern Maker's hands. His skin glowed. And still he drew in more power.

As the Fire spewed from the Workers' bodies, blood began to flow with it, as if Rafe was drawing away their very lives. Sora took a step toward them, hand outstretched. Madame Pandan crumpled to her knees. Jara's grip was the only thing keeping her from collapsing entirely. Blood dripped from his nose, and he looked on the verge of fainting himself.

"Enough!" Sora shouted. "Stop this!"

The Lantern Maker glanced at her. If he had quivered with power before, now his body positively sang with it. He seemed to grow larger with the incredible quantity of energy roaring hot beneath his skin. Even Lima stepped away from him.

Sora resisted the urge to run from those fiery eyes. "I'm sure we can resolve this like civilized people," she said, voice faltering. "I don't want Fire fights in my courtyard."

Rafe stared down at her. Could he even hear her? He was struggling. Had he tried to take in too much Fire at last? She held his gaze as he blazed like a sun. Madame Pandan whimpered. Jara sucked in raw, rasping breaths.

"Master Ruminor," Sora said, faking a calm she didn't feel at all. "Can you hear me?"

"Renna?"

Sora blinked, not daring to look at Lima as Rafe said their long-deceased daughter's name. "Master Ruminor, it's me, Soraline. Please stop."

Rafe drew in a deep breath. At last, he lowered his hands.

The two Workers collapsed. Sora nodded at Kel, and he hurried forward to check on them.

"Master Ruminor?"

Rafe flexed his hands as if trying to get the blood flowing again.

When he finally spoke, his voice shook slightly, lacking its usual deep, rich quality. "Yes, Queen Soraline?"

She swallowed. "I'd like to speak with you about the repair work in the library, if you please," she said. "Then we must discuss the latest recruitment reports from General Pavorran."

"Reports. Of course, my queen." Rafe turned and strode toward the castle, walking stiffly. Sora didn't breathe until the doors fell shut behind him. She had been sure he was going to blast her with the Fire. She had never seen the power overtake him like that. But there had been far more Fire flowing loose on the mountain since the accident at the Well. Rafe seemed to welcome the rampant outbursts, feed off them. He had almost looked pleased that Madame Pandan and Jara had come to challenge him.

She turned back to the pair, but Kel was already standing up and shaking his head.

"Are they dead?"

"I'm sorry, my queen. I can't rouse them."

Sora slumped. She had been too late after all. They had few allies left. Most of Madame Pandan's friends had died alongside Daz Stoneburner at the Well. She'd managed to recruit Jara the Gilder—all for nothing.

"Send for someone to carry them home."

"Yes, my queen."

She turned to Lima and Corren. Neither of them had followed Rafe into the castle. They seemed to be waiting for her instructions.

"What was all this about?"

"Madame Pandan is unbalanced," Lima said. "We think she was one of the traitors behind the surge."

"She's been punished enough," Master Corren said. He watched the Castle Guards carry the two Workers away, looking slightly sick.

"Madame Pandan isn't the only one struggling with balance," Sora said. "Master Ruminor nearly lost control."

Lima's mouth tightened. "It's good for him to have other tasks," she said. "Reports. That was wise."

"Uh . . . thank you." Sora thought she might crumple like Madame Pandan. Did Lima Ruminor just compliment her wisdom?

"That could have been worse than it was, my queen," Master Corren said. "You kept your head admirably." He nudged Lima and nodded pointedly in Sora's direction.

Lima drew in a short breath, her shoulders stiffening. "We . . . I think you are containing the situation well. The aftermath of the recent surge was not as bad as it could have been thanks to you."

Sora stared at her. Lima was right. It could have been much worse if she hadn't calmed the mob at their gates, but she could hardly believe the woman was acknowledging it. There must be a catch. She waited.

"Rafe is occupied with his Work," Lima said. "It is good to know we can count on you to oversee Vertigon in the meantime."

"Oversee Vertigon?"

"We want you to continue working in your capacity of . . . increased responsibility. Rafe plans to begin the expansion of his domain soon."

"It'll be good for him to channel away some of this excess Fire," Master Corren said. He looked at the far gates, where the two ill-fated insurgents were being carried off, and shuddered. "We can't have disgruntled Workers getting their hands on it."

"The Fire is still surging?" Sora asked.

"It is. Whatever happened down at the Well changed something. I'm not sure if all this extra Fire is a good thing. And if the Spring—"

"Rafe can manage it," Lima snapped. "You will continue your good work, Soraline." As if she couldn't stand to utter anymore compliments, Lima turned abruptly and stalked toward the castle. Master Corren followed, concern still shadowing his features.

Sora stared after them. Was Lima saying she wanted her to act more like a true queen? Because it helped them with *their* work? The thought that she was helping the Ruminors made her feel ill. When her people rose in anger against the Lantern Maker, she had dissuaded them from trying something that would only get them killed. The common people couldn't defeat the Fireworkers. The Workers she had lured to her side had died trying to resist the Lantern Maker. But, in keeping the peace, had she become an accomplice in her usurper's work?

A screeching sound came from overhead. A pair of cur-dragons swooped low, as if that rush of Fire had called them. The creatures had been increasingly restless since the surge. Were they responding to the power flowing unchecked through the land?

Sora remembered the old song Kel had shared with her about true dragons waking in the Burnt Mountains. It had included a line about a spring, hadn't it? Master Corren had used that word before Lima interrupted him. She wondered if she could find the full song in her father's library.

The little cur-dragons circled around the courtyard and flew off again, perhaps returning to their cavern beneath the castle. Sora shook her head. She had more important things to worry about than old legends about extinct creatures. Such as what she was going to do if the Lantern Maker ever really lost control.

She returned to the castle, Captain Thrashe and Kel falling in beside her once more. Kel pulled open the elaborately wrought doors. As Sora entered, he brushed a hand against hers. His face was a study in neutrality. They'd been finding more and more excuses to touch hands of late. And that had definitely been him steadying her shoulder when the Fire burst forth in the courtyard. At first she'd thought Kel was merely supporting her in a difficult time, but she wasn't so sure anymore.

Before she could return Kel's touch, Captain Thrashe turned crisply and fixed her with his single eye.

"My queen, I advise you to take care when running toward Fireworkers in the future."

"I had to get there before any innocent bystanders got hurt."

"Your purpose was admirable," Captain Thrashe said. "But magic wielders are not to be trusted."

"Madame Pandan wouldn't hurt me."

"Madame Pandan is not the danger here." Captain Thrashe looked around the deserted entryway. "You must be wary of the Ruminors."

Sora's jaw went slack. Captain Thrashe was warning her to be careful around the very people he'd helped capture her? He had guarded her since the coup against her brother, along with a small group of Soolen swordsmen. They had come to Vertigon on the orders of Commander Brach, leader of the Soolen army that had invaded Cindral Forest and Trure. Sora knew the Lantern Maker planned to betray his erstwhile alliance with Commander Brach. Perhaps Captain Thrashe had finally figured it out too.

"I will be careful," she said.

Captain Thrashe nodded and turned to march across the entrance hall. Sora watched him, wondering how far his concern would take him. She needed all the help she could get in the powder keg Vertigon had become.

She looked back at the courtyard, where the blast of power had melted the early-spring snow all the way to the walls. She feared they would all come to regret the unleashing of the Fire.

3

THE WATERMIGHT ARTIST

The streets of Pendark bubbled with rumors. Whispers of Rallion City and the Soolen army's unprecedented success mingled with the usual chatter about fish prices and export tariffs. Dara could tell Siv was distracted when they parted ways at the boundary of Wyla's Jewel District. She feared their distance from Rallion City would distort the news and make the situation sound worse than it really was. He already worried enough.

The icy sensation had faded from her sword arm. The bargain confined her to the boundaries of Pendark, but she hadn't been aware Wyla could make her feel things from a distance too. She didn't know enough about the Watermight Artist—or the magical substance she wielded.

Poison-green flags flew from every building in the vicinity, proclaiming Wyla's domain. Her manor was the most impressive structure in sight. A thick rock wall surrounded it, obscuring everything except the peaked slate roof. The wall rose from a rocky island, creating the impression that the manor was more mountain than man-made structure. Or woman-made. Dara was pretty sure Wyla had moved the stones herself using her considerable Watermight strength.

Not that Dara had seen much of that power over the past few days, but judging by the size and wealth of her district, Wyla had plenty.

Dara rapped on the solid iron gate in the outer wall. It screeched open, and the doorman admitted her with a solemn nod. Wyla's bodyguard and right-hand man, Siln, was waiting for her in the overgrown garden courtyard. He was slim and middle aged, with intricate tattoos twining around his arms.

"She wants to see you in her study," he said.

"Now?"

"She said to send you the moment you returned."

Dara grimaced at her clothes, which were still damp from her swimming lesson.

Siln raised an eyebrow. "I would not make her wait."

Dara thanked him and hurried along the garden path toward the house, fighting down a burst of nerves. She'd been waiting for Wyla to send for her, but she still felt unprepared. She'd have preferred to meet her in a less straggly state. At least her Savven blade swung at her hip, its weight and warmth a comfort.

The manor house, like the outer wall, was built of black rock, with thick-paned windows and statues of strange sea creatures decorating the eaves. The plants growing wild in the courtyard gave it an eerie quality, as if the house itself were a living thing. The place filled Dara with unease. She had been allowed to come and go at will so far, but it still felt like a prison.

She jogged to Wyla's large study on the second floor. Ceiling-high bookcases covered two of the walls, containing an eclectic assortment of books and scrolls. An array of diagrams, drawings, and notes papered the remaining wall space. Sturdy tables bore more notes and books, along with a variety of metal objects, Fireworked and otherwise.

The entire space was lit with a priceless collection of Fire Lanterns. At least two had been Worked by Dara's father, taking shape in the workshop beneath the very house where Dara grew up.

These Ruminor Lanterns were a matching set. One depicted a Firewielder conjuring Fireblossoms. The other showed a Watermight Artist spinning whirlpools from her fingertips. Dara wondered what her father had been thinking as he sculpted those flows of Firegold water. He had never talked about Watermight much. That power was almost impossible to store and transport over long distances. Fireworkers had never worried about it threatening their position. But Dara hoped she could learn something about Working magical substances from Wyla that applied to the Fire—and use it to neutralize her father.

The woman herself sat in a large armchair beneath the window, knitting needles clacking away in her lap. Wyla didn't even look at Dara when she approached.

"You wanted to see me?"

"I have been waiting."

"I didn't know you'd need me today," Dara said. "I apologize. We—I went for a swim."

"So I see." Wyla still didn't look away from her work. "In the future, you will be ready when I call. And you will be clean, dry, and presentable. Is that clear?"

"Yes, ma'am." Dara couldn't help snapping to attention. Wyla's presence shivered with power, despite her grandmotherly posture and appearance. She had wrinkly olive skin and white hair cut to her chin. She wore the wide, many-layered skirts favored in Pendark, which ended just below the knee. Many Pendarkans wore sandals in warmer weather, but Wyla favored tall, steel-toed boots.

"My arm—" Dara began.

"Yes. If you'd been in the manor, I would not have had to resort to such methods," Wyla said. "We have work to do."

"Are we going to Wield together today?" Dara asked. She had been looking forward to this, despite her nerves. She was intrigued by the possibility of two magic workers wielding their respective powers in unison.

"Today we will talk," Wyla said. "I don't wish to rush my research. After all, we have three months." She looked up at last, her gaze piercing. "Three months during which you agreed to make yourself available to me."

Dara resisted the urge to clutch her sword arm. "I won't be late again."

"No matter. Take a seat, child," Wyla said. "And tell me again how you came to discover your Spark. I've met others whose skills manifested late, but none of them lived above a Fireshop. I assume you tried to Work when you were younger?"

"I tried," Dara said, pulling up a high-backed wooden chair. She angled her seat so she could catch a glimpse of the clouds amassing outside the window, sweeping toward them on the sea wind. "I wanted to Work more than anything—for a while. My sister could do it, and I thought the Fire was magnificent."

"Your sister? You haven't mentioned a sister."

"She died," Dara said. "Over ten years ago."

"Interesting." Dara noted the distinct lack of sympathy in Wyla's tone. "You would have been around eight at the time?"

"Yes."

"A prime age for the Spark to manifest."

"Yes, but it never did. I used to sneak down to the access point in the shop when my parents were sleeping, but I could never get the Fire to come." She had tried so hard to access the molten magic. She hadn't understood why she couldn't do it, especially after it had come so easily to her sister. She'd loved to watch Renna Work, molding and spinning the Fire above her small hands.

"I wonder if the trauma of your sister's demise contributed to the delay in your own abilities." Wyla tapped her knitting needles against each other for a moment as she considered this. Again, no sympathy for Dara's tragedy was evident in her expression. Only inquisitiveness. "How did your parents respond to your difficulty?"

"They weren't happy," Dara said. "They always wanted me to follow in my father's footsteps."

"Your mother cannot Work either, correct?"

"That's right. But she was always involved in the business." Dara didn't say just how dedicated Lima Ruminor was to her husband's cause. The pressure her mother had put on her to embrace the work of the Fire Guild had long been a sore spot for Dara, but it was nothing compared to when she had seen Lima toss a severed head from a window. All for the sake of her father's ambitions. She shifted uncomfortably, tugging on her rough, salt-washed trousers.

"Hmm." Wyla studied her, seeming to sense the tension these memories evoked. "I believe there is an emotional component to Working the magical substances," she said. "It can factor into the way the Artist develops her skills. Your sense of bereavement and subsequent desire to live up to your parents' expectations could have contributed to your stunted development as well. I shouldn't say stunted. Delayed is better. Your skills certainly seem to have progressed rapidly."

"I had a strict teacher for a while," Dara said.

"Indeed. We will speak more of him another time. I wish to know more about the circumstances surrounding the awakening of your power. This occurred last summer, correct?"

"Yes . . . " It hadn't occurred to her that specific events could have triggered it. She *had* had a remarkably fraught summer. She'd met Siv and discovered her parents were murderous usurpers all around the time that her Spark first appeared. Siv had made her feel special—even powerful—in a way that her parents never had. She wondered if that was part of why her Spark had at last been ready to ignite. Not that she'd share that with Wyla.

"It happened while I was training for a big dueling tournament," she said instead. "The Vertigon Cup. I was trying to win a patron. When I focus on dueling, it's a lot like the focus it takes to Work. Do you think that could have triggered it?"

"Perhaps," Wyla said. "Are you sure nothing else happened then that could have led to the change?"

"Not that I can think of." Dara avoided Wyla's gaze, shifting on her hard wooden seat.

Wyla tapped a knitting needle against her lips for a moment.

"Have I given the impression that I am a forgiving woman?" she said, her voice going dangerously quiet.

"Ma'am?"

"Is there a reason you think you can obfuscate the truth when you speak to me?"

"No, ma'am," Dara said. "Truly, I was training for a big tournament when I first felt the Spark. I'm sure you can verify that the Vertigon Cup is a huge deal for sport duelists."

Wyla frowned. Dara met her eyes, trying to focus on her memories of those months of training, all the hopes that had ridden on her performance. She dared not think about Siv. She'd already seen Wyla create the bond on her arm, which could tell her location and call Dara to her. If Watermight could do such intangible things, could Wyla also use it to somehow look into her thoughts and figure out she wasn't telling the full truth?

At last, Wyla broke Dara's gaze and returned to her knitting. "We will discuss this further. See if you can't think of anything else that might have induced you to begin wielding magic."

"I will try."

"Before we begin our experimentation," Wyla said, "what do *you* wish to know about Watermight?"

Dara pulled at her damp clothes. Dare she ask whether Watermight could influence someone's mind or interpret thoughts? No, it would be better to keep to safer topics. Or more useful ones.

Only one question really mattered if Wyla might one day help her overcome her parents.

"Is Watermight stronger than Fire?"

"Stronger?"

"Can one power defeat the other?"

"You mean in direct combat, I presume?"

Dara nodded. The two Ruminor Fire Lanterns seemed to burn brighter as she waited for the answer.

"It depends on the strength of the Wielder and their area of expertise," Wyla said. "Fireworkers typically learn a trade through apprenticeships: Firespinning, Metalworking, Lantern-making. Everyone can do the basic things, but the longer you spend on one skill, the more difficult it is to learn others, you understand?"

"Yes," Dara said. "Though some people use multiple skills in a single craft depending on what they make." Dara's father had often drawn on other aspects of the craft to help develop his own Works. It was part of what had made his lanterns so unique and sought-after, even as far away as Pendark.

"Waterworkers are less driven by this incessant desire to make things," Wyla said. "Most of our Art is more fleeting, though no less effective, than Fireworks. But Artists do specialize, and they develop skills that would rival even the most powerful Fireworker—sometimes in combat. Thanks to their sanctuary atop a mountain, Fireworkers rarely do battle. We are the ones with experience. Brute strength matters less than you might think."

"How do you fight with Watermight?" Dara asked.

"You've already seen it in action."

"I'm sorry?"

"Come, child. You are a smart girl." Wyla gave her a dry smile. "I'm sure you know that canals don't rise up to drop people on islands under normal circumstances."

"I thought that was you." Dara remembered that desperate moment when she'd almost been too late to save Siv. She'd begged for help as she charged into the canal. *Please. I'll do anything.* Utter desperation had filled her to the brim. Then a rush of water and silver-white power had propelled her forward in time to interrupt Vex Rollendar's attack. "I've been meaning to thank you for your help."

"I didn't do it for thanks," Wyla said. "But we can discuss your payment for that piece of assistance another time." She met Dara's eyes steadily, the promise in them undeniable. Then she resumed her knitting. "That wave would be an example of one way in which one fights with Watermight."

"So you can wash people off their feet," Dara said. "And drown them?"

"It's remarkably effective," Wyla said.

"I can imagine." Allying with a Waterworker who would drown her father wasn't quite what Dara had in mind. She wanted to stop her father's violence, not intensify it. "What else can you do?"

"There will be time enough to discuss combat later," Wyla said. "I have more questions for you."

The last hints of daylight faded from the window before Wyla allowed Dara to go change into dry clothes at last. The interview reminded her unpleasantly of when her mother had made her work on the accounts in the lantern shop for hours. She hoped they weren't going to spend the entirety of the next three months sitting and talking. It would be hard to keep Siv out of the Steel Pentagon if she barely saw him.

For now, she couldn't let Wyla find out how much he mattered to her, even if it would help her understand Dara's Spark better. She hadn't missed Wyla's reminder of the debt she owed. Dara feared she wouldn't like it when Wyla finally decided to exact her fee.

4

PEN FIGHTING

Siv checked the sharpness of his knife for the tenth time and bounced on the balls of his feet. The announcer's voice rang loudly above the arena. The crowds stomped in time to the clashes of broadswords, the rhythm drumming through the dirt under his boots. Siv leaned against the wooden railing, surveying the five-sided arena. The Steel Pentagon. It was almost his turn to fight. His hands were sweating worse than a Truren saddlemaker's at midsummer, but he felt ready. Mostly.

He had neglected to tell Dara he had a big pen fight scheduled for the day after their swimming lesson. He'd let her think she had time to convince him not to do it. The team had originally been scheduled to compete the day after their scrape with Vex Rollendar's mercenaries, but they'd been worn out from their unplanned melee. Kres had ordered a few days of rest before they risked themselves in the pen. But they couldn't delay another match.

Of course, Dara would be mad at Siv for going ahead with this, but she was almost as pretty mad as she was when she smiled. Besides, he needed the coin. He couldn't sit idly by for three months without working toward their return to Vertigon. It was the only way he could justify leaving Sora in the Lantern Maker's clutches for a little while longer. He felt confident that Dara would come up with a way to deal with her father, but they needed armed backup too. Judging by the rumors from Trure, his grandfather was no longer in a position to provide him with men or gold.

Besides, Siv had always wanted to fight in front of a really big crowd.

The one filling the benches overlooking the Steel Pentagon didn't disappoint. They cheered for the competitors with an enthusiasm bordering on bloodlust. Pendarkans loved the heave of competition, the frenzy of violence. He should be sickened, but it was exhilarating. He could hardly wait to show them what he could do.

The previous match ended, and Fiz Timon strutted around the pentagon, waving his broadsword over his head in victory. The weapon looked small compared to Fiz's massive frame. The flaxen-haired man was a colossal fighter—and a decent friend and drinking companion. He accepted a prize purse and acknowledged the adoration of the crowd with a bow. Siv's fight was next.

"Don't die." A hand slapped his back, and Siv turned to find Gull Mornington standing beside him. The grumpy swordswoman hailed from Fork Town. Gull had proved to be a friend too, once she decided not to kill him.

"Thanks," Siv said. "I'm getting better at that every day."

"Let's not get cocky now, Sivren." Krestian March appeared on his other side wearing his signature red baldric and an assortment of knives, both hidden and visible.

"Don't worry about making it a show," Gull said. "At least for your first few fights."

"No need to smother the lad, Gull dear," Kres said. "He can be as showy as he likes in the pen."

"I'll settle for winning for now," Siv said.

"That's my boy."

The final member of the pen-fighting team, Latch, didn't offer any encouraging words, but he gave Siv a reasonably friendly nod from beneath a broad-brimmed hat. Latch was still grumpy about not being allowed to compete. He was here strictly to cheer Siv on—or at least give him reasonably friendly nods.

Siv nodded back and wiped his palms on his trousers again. It was time.

The announcer shouted his assumed name (Sivren "the Slicer" Amen) and informed the audience that this "new talent from the north" had made his debut in a gutter match a few days ago. Siv had defeated the Pendarkan Panviper in an ungainly victory. But as he hopped the railing and jogged out to scattered applause, he could tell this fight wouldn't be so easy.

"Siv the Slicer will face the Pallbearer, a fighter from right here in the Market District. Let's hear it for the Pallbearer!"

Siv's opponent was about ten years older than him, and he looked as if he'd spent every one of those years with a knife in his hand. His blade was nicked and battered, and his vest had a dozen slashes sewn up with bright-red thread. His face had been sewn up a few times too. He raised his arms, and the crowds roared in response, bloodthirsty and eager.

Siv faced the Pallbearer in the center of the Steel Pentagon, which was about forty paces across. Obstacles were scattered around them: barrels, logs, a battered wagon, the pockmarked hull of an old boat. A wide patch of muddy water covered two corners of the arena, but it wasn't clear whether that was an intentional obstacle or a natural feature of the swampy Pendarkan terrain. It all looked more ominous from inside the arena. What had he gotten himself into?

"All ready?" the announcer shouted.

Siv drew his knife, forced himself to breathe deeply. This was for Vertigon, for Sora, for Dara.

"Let us dance!"

The Pallbearer advanced slowly, keeping the edge of the fallen wagon between him and Siv. His scarred brow furrowed, and he studied Siv's stance like a craftsman.

Siv crouched, aware his form wasn't perfect yet. He was probably giving away his intentions with every step. He wouldn't rush the fight, though. Dara was right. He couldn't get himself killed when his family needed him. But he'd have no chance to bring them help unless he could pay for it.

The crowds murmured as Siv and the Pallbearer continued to circle each other, moving cautiously around the pen. They danced around the obstacles, using them for cover, feeling out the space. The spectators began to boo and stamp their feet, impatient for blood. Neither fighter made a move to attack yet. They were both—

The Pallbearer struck, leaping over the wagon and hurling himself toward Siv. The crowds shrieked. Siv barely managed to dive out of the way. He tried to catch his opponent with his foot as he passed, but the fellow was too agile for such tricks. The Pallbearer dodged the trip and plunged forward, knife flashing.

Siv caught his wrist, gaining control of the blade for a moment. The Pallbearer twisted like a viper. Siv couldn't get near his throat. He tried to shake the knife out of the Pallbearer's grasp, but his grip remained solid.

Siv changed tactics and yanked the man toward him. The Pallbearer resisted, knife firmly clasped, pulling against him with his considerable strength. But the muddy earth betrayed him. His boots slid through the mud.

Siv tugged the Pallbearer across the arena, straining and sweating with every step. He'd drag him all the way out the other side if that was what it took. Then his back slammed into something. The Pallbearer stopped resisting. Siv suddenly found himself flattened against the hull of the fishing boat. *Uh-oh.*

The Pallbearer lunged, driving his knife toward Siv's torso, which was now stuck against the boat.

Siv dropped his own knife and grabbed the Pallbearer's arm with both hands, barely keeping the blade from his belly.

They strained against each other, arms locked. Siv was trapped. The smell of old leather, sweat, and fearsome garlic breath assaulted his senses. The spectators roared. They could feel the end coming.

A triumphant gleam lit the Pallbearer's eyes. Siv bared his teeth. He wasn't going to lose like this. Not when people were counting on him.

Siv knocked his head into the Pallbearer's nose with an audible crack. A gasp tore through the crowd.

The Pallbearer staggered back, disoriented. Siv scooped up his knife from the ground and leapt forward. Before he knew what was happening, the Pallbearer leaned a thick shoulder down, not as stunned by the head butt as he should have been. Siv barreled into him with the force of a terrerack bull—and flipped right over his back.

He landed hard, every ounce of wind knocked out of his body. A glint of silver flashed above him as the Pallbearer swung his knife downward.

Siv threw up his hands to block his face, knowing they wouldn't do any good. The Pallbearer's knife stopped mere inches from Siv's neck. He froze, waiting for the end.

Then hot drops of blood dripped onto his face.

The Pallbearer let out a fierce howl and stumbled back. Siv's knife was embedded in his wrist. Right. He'd been holding that when he threw up his hands to protect his face. The knife had angled up—and sliced into his opponent's forearm at the last moment.

Siv scrambled to his feet, not quite able to breathe after being thrown, and punched the Pallbearer in the face. The fellow was definitely the type to keep fighting with a knife sticking out of his arm. The punch felled him. Siv dove on top of his opponent, yanked his knife from where it was lodged between sinew and bone, and put it to the Pallbearer's throat before even managing to suck air into his lungs. Firelord, that was close!

By the time Siv could breathe again, the crowds had erupted. They hollered his name, every man, woman, and child on their feet. The Pallbearer lay in the mud, his hand wrapped tightly around his wrist to hold in the blood. He looked more worried about his injury than his loss. He gave a brief nod as Siv pulled back the knife and staggered away.

A hand landed on Siv's shoulder, and he almost stabbed this new attacker before realizing it was the announcer. His head spun with nerves and adrenaline. Then the man was shouting the results and shoving a clinking bag into his hands and pushing him toward the edge of the pentagon. It was over. And he had won!

Now that his head was catching up with what had happened, Siv wasn't ready to leave the arena quite yet. He had won a real pen match against a skilled opponent. True, he'd been knocked flat, and he wasn't sure he'd ever breathe normally again, but it didn't matter. He had burning won!

He turned in a full circle, hands raised for the crowd. They cheered in response, drumming their feet on the rickety wooden stands.

"All right, all right, Siv the Slicer," the announcer said with a chuckle. "Let's make room for the next dance. Let's hear it one more time for Siv the Slicer, folks!"

The crowds screamed, chanted his name. Faces blurred around him. The hot flush of victory swept through his body like the purest brandy. Oh, he could definitely get used to this.

"Well done, lad," Kres said when he finally stumbled out of the pen. "That's the way to get them to look at you. Not a clean fight, but that slug at the end sealed it for you."

"Not bad." Gull gave him an approving nod. "Don't get trapped on the obstacles like that, though."

"We'll work on it in practice," Fiz said, thumping him on the back so hard, he staggered.

"It's always good to give your audience something to worry about anyway," Kres said. "Now you just have to hold your own in the Dance."

"The Dance?" Siv blinked.

"We're fighting again in half an hour." Kres grinned at the look of consternation on Siv's face. "Don't let every little victory go to your head. We still have the melee."

"Right," Siv said. "I'll be ready." And he thought he would be. He had been perilously close to losing, but what a rush! And the prize purse was bigger than the piddling bag of coins he'd received for his gutter fight. He could make this work. He'd buy Dara her freedom yet.

The pen fighters adjourned to a tent beside the arena while they waited for their next Dance. It had rained during the night, and the tent did little to protect them from the muddy ground. Siv felt as if he'd been covered in mud more often than not since he arrived in Pendark. Still, this place wasn't so bad. Fighters in mismatched and patched clothing milled around the tent, assorted weapons gleaming from their belts and backs. They were a ramshackle bunch, drawn by the money as much as the glory. Siv supposed he was one of them now.

The fighters traded insults and called out for ale and medical attention. A harried-looking young man darted amongst them, pausing to send silvery streams of Watermight from his fingertips into the wounds to clean and seal them. His patients offered coins from their prize purses in return for his help. The Watermight healers were a big part of why more Pendarkan pen fighters didn't end up dead or maimed—and why Siv deemed it worth the risk. Watermight didn't heal instantly, but it would allow the injured to recover more quickly and fully. Siv was lucky he didn't need the man's assistance today, though. Watermight healing didn't come cheap.

Fiz handed around mugs of ale poured from a barrel in their corner. Siv gulped his down in one go, still breathing heavily. The fight hadn't lasted long, but it had been surprisingly taxing. Maybe he should start running laps or something. That would make Dara proud. Or—he supposed—he could skip the ale between matches.

"Watch your center of gravity," Latch said, coming up beside him. "You shouldn't have gone flying over that fellow."

"Made for a better show, didn't it?" Siv said.

Latch grunted. "Just trying to help." He started to walk away, but Siv put a hand on his arm.

"Hey, can you help me practice a way around that move later?"

Latch brightened—well, for him—and Siv reminded himself that Latch was still disappointed he wasn't allowed to fight. He'd joined the team hoping to participate in the Dance of Steel, but Kres had decided he was too valuable to risk. He'd taken it upon himself to protect Latch against all threats—including Siv, if he caused trouble. Still, Siv figured training with Latch was the least he could do. Plus he was sure Latch wasn't telling the full truth about his father. Siv needed to know more about Commander Brach than ever now that the Soolen had occupied his grandfather's capital city. There was no way Brach's army should have been able to defeat Trure so quickly. Latch was still hiding something, and Siv meant to find out what.

The fighters were called back from the tent to ready themselves for the five-a-side Dance of Steel all too soon. With Latch being kept out of the fighting, they were one man short. Kres had called on an old friend to substitute. A few minutes before the Dance was to begin, a man of medium height and slight build sauntered up to join them at the barrier, a rapier slung low on his hip. Scars crisscrossed his olive skin, and he was missing a couple of fingers and part of his ear.

"Ah," Kres said. "At last. Siv lad, meet Dellario Darting, the Darting Death."

"Siv."

"The Slicer." The man's handshake was firm, his palms rough and callused. "Saw your match. Not bad."

"Thanks."

"Your first Dance?"

Siv shrugged, trying not to let on how excited he was about his victory. "I won a gutter match a few—"

"It was just the Panviper," Gull cut in. She leaned on the barrier nearby, inspecting her saber's edge with a critical eye.

"I see." Dellario chuckled. "Well, I look forward to seeing what you can do in the Dance of Steel."

"We've seen him fight multiple opponents before," Fiz said. "Real fights too."

"Indeed?" Dellario studied Siv with renewed curiosity.

"I made it through all right," Siv said. "With plenty of help from the team."

Kres gave him a piercing look. He hadn't been there when Vex Rollendar's men attacked them outside headquarters, but he had been more interested in Siv than ever since then.

"You're lucky to be with Kres's team," Dellario said. "Where are you fr—?"

"All ready, children?" Kres said, taking Siv by the arm and drawing him away before Dellario could finish his question. "The Steel Pentagon awaits!"

The Dance of Steel melees were fought with five weapon types: rapier, saber, knife, broadsword, and battle-axe. Each team had a different strategy for dealing with the mixed fights. Some split into groups to take on the more dangerous fighters first. Broadsword and battle-axe fighters in particular had a nasty tendency to cut off people's heads. It was best to deal with them early on. Other teams sectioned off their opponents, with each team member taking on the fighter wielding their own weapon type. Spectators tended to respond poorly to that strategy, though. Different styles always made fights more interesting, and there was no better place to pit style against style than in the Dance of Steel.

Kres preferred to keep fights interesting. For this Dance, they faced a team that favored the divide-and-conquer method. Kres had carefully coordinated a plan to prevent them from splitting the fight to suit them. Siv felt less nervous after his victory against the Pallbearer, but he didn't want to accidentally get any of his teammates killed. None of them had threatened to kill him all week.

The crowd roared louder than ever when the team strutted into the pentagon. They were clearly popular, and Kres was the most admired of them all. He preened as the crowds shouted his name, bowing to each of the five sides, accepting their adoration. Men shouted marriage proposals and lewd suggestions to Gull. She responded to them all with an equally imperious glare. Fiz had his fair share of fans too, and a few people must have been impressed by Siv's fight, because they shouted his name just as loud as the others'. He waved, remembering that hot flush of victory when he'd knocked the Pallbearer down. He wanted that feeling again.

Their opponents entered the ring to somewhat lesser applause. They all wore jet-black team uniforms, going for a cohesive, intimidating look. They looked like capable fighters, but none of them had Kres's charisma. He continued to bow and preen for the crowd, clearly in his element.

A few fighters on the other team nodded to Dellario the Darting Death.

"I'm a go-to substitute these days," he told Siv as they took up their positions. "You can always count on Dellario. I even fought for these fellows a few times."

"But you might kill them."

"I might." Dellario drew his sword. "Then again, I might not. No reason to be sensitive about it."

"If you say so."

Siv didn't quite believe Dellario's nonchalance over whether he might kill his opponents. All the pen fighters seemed determined not to let the killing bother them. Their fans wouldn't like that. His teammates' casualness made it easier for Siv to quash his nerves, but he couldn't get complacent. Watermight healers couldn't fix everything.

The crowds quieted at last, and the ten fighters faced each other across the pentagon. Siv forced himself to breathe steadily and focus on their strategy. For a brief moment, he wondered what madness compelled him to do this. But people were counting on him. He would do his part to get them home.

"Stay sharp," Gull said.

"Sharp as knives," Kres answered.

The announcer stepped up once more.

"All ready? Let us dance!"

The fight was a whirl of steel and pounding heartbeats. Siv barely formed a coherent thought after it began. All he knew was the thrust of his blade, the flailing of his fists, the felling of his opponents. He felt drunk. Drunk on the roar of the crowd and the speed of the fight and the glint of the steel. He took a blow to the head. Blood streaked down his face and into his collar, but it didn't slow him. He *was* nothing but the whirl of steel, the clench of fists, the pounding of his heart. What a rush! No wonder people got obsessed with the Dance of Steel.

And then it was over. Siv had barely gotten his bearings before every member of the opposing team lay in the mud, groaning or gurgling, one lying still. Kres's team was that good.

The crowds went wild over the decisive victory. They hollered the fighters' names again and again, voices becoming hoarse. Their faces were a roiling mass of flashing teeth and wide eyes.

Bewildered by the raucous cheers, Siv followed his team out of the pen, almost forgetting to wave. His head spun with the effects of the adrenaline, the drunken rush of battle. He thought he'd stuck to the team's strategy, but he was having a hard time remembering anything of the fight itself.

"Well fought, well fought," Kres said. He looked as if his feet might leave the ground at any moment. "Well fought indeed."

"This is our year," Fiz said. "I can feel it!"

Even Gull allowed herself a grin. "Not bad."

After a round of backslapping and congratulations, the fighters scraped the mud and blood off their boots and returned to the tent to gather their gear. People shouted friendly jeers as they strode in.

"Kres is back!"

"Long live Kres the Master!"

Kres accepted their compliments with haughty grace. But he wasn't the only one drawing attention from the other combatants.

"You're a real boxer, aren't you, Siv?" someone called.

"Yeah, nice fist action there."

"Think you found the wrong sport."

Siv frowned. "What are they talking about?"

"You got in a decent slug or two, my friend," Fiz said. He thumped him on the back and went to pour the last of their ale into assorted mugs.

Siv stared after him, rubbing his sore knuckles and trying to picture a moment where he'd actually used them in the fight. He didn't understand it. He could replay every instant of his solo match, but it was different when he faced so many opponents. He couldn't really focus on any of them, knowing that someone else could be coming at him from any direction, ready to drive a blade through his ribs or swipe his head from his shoulders. He said as much to Gull.

"Relax," she said, busy cleaning the blood off her blade. "It's normal not to remember much about your first few Dances."

Siv wondered if he'd been hit harder than he realized. "That fellow with the messed-up nose called me a boxer?"

"You took out one of their guys with a punch to the head, and you were pummeling another when Kres finished him off," Gull said. "It was a bit messy, but the crowds love that sort of thing."

"Right," Siv said faintly. "Messy."

"It's okay. You'll get the hang of it."

"I guess."

"Just be happy they're noticing you," Gull said. "It's easy for new fighters to get lost in the shuffle their first few Dances. If they're already talking, you might do well here."

"Thanks." Siv touched the coin purse in his pocket. He'd have to give a portion to Kres for his room and board, but he'd put the rest away. He would get home yet. "I'm lucky I found the right team to show me the ropes."

Gull snorted. "That's the spirit."

"Come, friends!" Dellario called to the team. "That's enough talk. Drinks are on me!"

"Drinks?" Siv definitely couldn't spend his money carousing, but if other people were going to buy him drinks . . .

"Come along, lad." The slim man dropped a four-fingered hand on his shoulder. "The taverns in this district are wilder than your dreams, I can tell you that. And I can introduce you to a friend or two. Important people. An enterprising young lad can go far in this city." Dellario gave him a sly wink. "I can get you an invite to—"

"Our young friend has had a big day." Kres shouldered in between Dellario and Siv. His red baldric shimmered faintly with fresh blood, and a familiar dangerous light glinted in his eyes. "Let's not wear him out too soon."

"Now, Kres," Dellario said, relinquishing his grip on Siv and stepping back with an even smile. "I didn't mean to tread on your territory."

Kres didn't smile back.

"We'll be returning to headquarters now. Here's your portion of the winnings."

Dellario accepted the coin purse warily. "Much obliged." He glanced at Siv once more. "You're new in the city, friend. You'd do well to keep your options open."

"Run along, now," Kres said. "Friend."

Dellario smiled. "See you again, Sivren." He bowed mockingly to Kres and disappeared into the crowd.

"What was that about?" Siv asked when he was gone.

"Never you mind, lad," Kres said. "You'd do well to remember who brought you here, though. And where you come from." He shot Siv a look and then sauntered off before Siv could ask exactly what Kres knew about where he came from.

5

FAR PLAINS STRONGHOLD

Princess Selivia Amintelle trailed her fingers along the battlements of the Far Plains Stronghold. The sun hovered lazily above the Rock. The towering monolith dwarfed the sandstone walls of the fortress. She could make out the colors of the magnificent cliff paintings on its side when the sun was right, but late-afternoon shadows hid the paintings now.

She desperately wanted to climb the winding stone steps to the base of the Rock and scale the cliff with the help of the ladders attached to its sheer face. Not that her mother would ever let her do that. Perhaps she could sneak out through the back gate of the fortress.

That'll never work. The Stronghold guards were too vigilant. Fighting had been reported on the plains in the days since the occupation of Rallion City. The clashes between the Truren cavalry and the army of Soole were getting closer. Tension filled the Stronghold, quivering in the sandstone walls, whispering through the shadowy corridors. Selivia would never be let out again.

She circled the fortress. The vast expanse of the Truren Horseplains shimmered, yellow and gold, around her. The wind hissed through the grasses in the distance, carrying the first fresh hints of spring.

A tuft of dust bloomed in the distance. Selivia leaned over the battlements to watch the rider approach. It took a long time for him to cross the plain from the horizon, his horse kicking up dirt with every stride. Selivia wished she could ride across those plains with the wind in her face, her scarf streaming behind her. She took off the bright-yellow one she wore today and let it wave in the wind, enjoying the striking contrast with the robin-egg blue of the sky. The rider drew nearer to the walls far beneath her.

Suddenly, a sharp gust of wind snatched the scarf from her hand. It sailed away, carried on the plains wind.

"Blast," Selivia said. "That was my favorite."

"You shouldn't use such language, my lady."

Selivia jumped. "Oh, I didn't see you there, Fenn."

"Perhaps you should come inside, Princess," said Fenn Hurling, her bodyguard, as she came up beside her. "You shouldn't spend so much idle time out here."

Selivia stopped herself just short of sticking out her lower lip and pouting. "What am I going to do inside? Mother won't even let me dye my hair anymore."

Fenn chuckled. "You have your studies."

"I finished my reading for today."

"What about your harp? You haven't practiced in—"

"What's the point?" Selivia folded her arms and slumped against the sandstone wall. "I'm locked in this tower while everyone else is out there doing important things. Who cares if I can play the harp?"

"I love to hear you play, Princess."

"I'm sorry, Fenn." Selivia heaved a sigh. "I know you're trying to cheer me up. But I can't stand all this waiting. There's a war out there, and it has been ages since we had news from—"

"Princess Selivia! There is news!" Zala Toven, her handmaid and language tutor, hurried out onto the ramparts to join them.

"Finally!" Selivia sprang forward. "I hoped that was a messenger down there."

"Yes, he—what happened to your scarf, my lady?"

"I don't want to talk about it." Selivia quickly smoothed down her dark hair, which blew wild in the wind. "What's the news?"

"I'm not sure. Your lady mother wishes to see you."

"It's about time."

Selivia and Fenn followed Zala into the Stronghold. It had been ages since the Soolens attacked Rallion City and the Far Plains garrison rode out to patrol the surrounding prairies. They'd received precious little communication since then. Selivia had thought her grandfather, King Atrin, would keep the Soolens at bay. *She* was scared stiff of him half the time. The Soolens would be too if they knew what was good for them, but they had occupied his city with little trouble. What were they up to now? Her heart raced as they hurried through the austere corridors.

Instead of taking her to her mother's sitting room, Zala led her down the winding staircase that corkscrewed through the center of the Stronghold's main tower. Servants and soldiers ran back and forth on the stairs. The burst of activity was strange after all the sitting and waiting of the past weeks. Many people looked nervous, or even outright scared. Selivia stared as a severe serving woman hurried past her with a bundle of freshly fletched arrows in her arms. Just what kind of news had that messenger brought?

Zala herself, normally a pleasant and unflappable presence, seemed nervous. She clutched the soft brown folds of her skirt as she stepped aside to allow half a dozen armed men to pass them on the stairs. The soldiers smelled strongly of sweat and boot polish, and the creaking of their leather jerkins echoed in the stairwell. Excitement and fear mixed in their eyes.

Selivia noticed Fenn resting her hand on her sword hilt as the soldiers passed. That was strange. These were her Uncle Valon's men. She was in no danger here. Fortunately, the men paid little attention to the princess's female bodyguard, and they continued down the stairs unchallenged.

Zala turned onto a wide landing and led her to the stark war room where Uncle Valon strategized with his officers. Selivia had never been allowed in this room in the daytime before—though she'd snuck in for a peek with her brother once during a childhood visit. The flurry of activity here was more controlled than that in the corridors, but no less urgent. Men in uniforms bent over maps and moved bits of wood across them like mijen tiles. The walls were bare, unlike in the living areas of the Stronghold, where colorful tapestries softened the harsh stone.

Uncle Valon, a bony man with a long, pointed nose, was arguing with a pair of gruff, old officers. They all looked terribly serious. A slim young man covered in dust stood beside them. He must be the messenger.

Before Selivia could take more than three steps into the room, her mother pounced, pulling her to the side. Tirra, the former Queen of Vertigon, was a beautiful woman, but her face had become increasingly pinched and drawn over the past few weeks. Despite Selivia's prodding, she had never given up her somber black gowns even after they learned that her sister, Sora, was alive. The former queen glanced around, apparently worried that someone would overhear, then pulled her daughter a little closer.

"You must prepare to leave at once."

"Leave? What are you talking about, Mother?"

"The Soolen army is marching on our gates. They will be here within the hour."

"They can't actually get in, can they?" Selivia looked around at her uncle and all of his strong military men. Surely the Soolens weren't foolish enough to think they could capture the Stronghold itself. "This is the safest fortress on the continent."

"Your grandfather is a captive," her mother said. "I fear he has told the Soolens of some weakness."

"Can't Uncle Valon stop them?"

"The Soolens have defeated our cavalry again and again." Tirra glanced around and lowered her voice. "Their campaign has been far too successful. Something isn't right."

Selivia could hardly believe it. The whole point in coming to this far-off hunk of rock in the first place was that it was impenetrable. Plenty of the estates spread across the plains were supposed to be more vulnerable. Why were the Soolens coming here? And more importantly . . .

"What are we going to do?"

"You must leave the Stronghold," her mother said. "I cannot risk you being captured."

"But—"

"There is no time to argue." Tirra began ushering Selivia toward the door. "You must forget your name and hide until this is all over. Zala!"

"Yes, my queen?"

Selivia's handmaid appeared at their side.

"You must take her. You know the way?"

"Yes, my queen."

"The way where?" Selivia demanded. Zala didn't seem nearly as surprised about this as she was. Neither did Fenn, who had edged in front of them, blocking them from the view of the men in the war room.

"Somewhere safe," her mother said. "Safer than here."

Selivia feared her mother had gone mad. Where on the continent could be safer than the Far Plains Stronghold? It didn't make any sense!

"You must hide." Her mother rested a hand on Zala's shoulder. "Zala will take you. Do as she says."

"What about you?"

"I am staying here."

"But—"

"My presence may appease Commander Brach for a time."

"I don't want—"

"There is no time." Tirra squeezed her hand tightly enough to hurt. "The army was right on the heels of that messenger. They are moving far faster than we expected. Fenn?"

"Yes, my lady?"

"Watch out for her. Zala's people will shelter you, but be wary."

"Of course, my lady. The princess is safe with me."

Tirra met the woman's eyes for a moment then nodded.

Before Selivia could demand that they quit talking over her, Uncle Valon extracted himself from his discussion and strode over to join them.

"You shouldn't let my niece into the war room, Tirra." He put a bony hand on his sister's shoulder. She stiffened at his touch in a way Selivia had never seen before. The sight made fear flutter through her belly.

"I didn't want her to worry while everyone kept busy with their preparations," Tirra said. "I'm sending her up to her room to take refuge."

"Of course," Uncle Valon said. "You needn't fear, little lady. You'll be safe and well in my Stronghold."

Selivia gaped at him until her mother pinched her hand.

"Uh, thank you," she said and dropped into a curtsy for good measure.

Uncle Valon nodded and strode back to join his men. Selivia's mother waited until he was out of earshot before speaking again.

"No one may know you're leaving," she whispered. "Now that he has seen you, he won't think of you again until you are far away from here."

"What about you?" If her mother didn't trust her own brother, Selivia certainly didn't want to leave her here with him.

"I'll be fine," Tirra said. "Quickly. Stay close to Fenn and Zala.

They will watch out for you."

Selivia flung her arms around her mother's willowy waist and held her tight. She had resolved to be brave during this war. She had spent most of it staring at the plains while other people went into battle. It was time for her to prove that she was as strong as her siblings.

Her mother returned the hug briefly then pushed her toward the door. Tears welled in her eyes, but she brushed them away quickly. She squeezed Selivia's hand one more time then straightened her back and strode over to the map table.

Selivia stared after her mother as she floated among the military men like a beautiful black shadow. Zala tugged urgently on her sleeve. It was time to go.

They hurried out of the war room and down two more levels on the main staircase. Zala paused while a pair of Air Sensors passed them on the stairs, their movements serene compared to the frenzy of the soldiers and servants. As soon as they rounded the bend, Zala led the way through a small doorway to a narrower staircase. They passed a few servants here who were clearly preoccupied with the attack. The Soolens would be here soon.

Selivia kept her head down, but everyone was too busy to pay attention to the princess in the servants' corridor. They headed toward the kitchens. She'd been caught sneaking snacks there a time or two. Hopefully no one would think anything of her presence.

When the kitchen door came into view, Zala ducked into a small room off the corridor. Three satchels full of supplies and three changes of clothing waited for them on the bed. Zala handed the clothes to Selivia and Fenn and began unbuttoning her own dress.

"How long have you been planning this?" Selivia asked.

"Your lady mother and I discussed it on our way to the Stronghold," Zala said. "She asked me to be ready at a moment's notice."

"Where are we going?"

"You'll see. There's no time to talk."

Selivia quickly donned the simple dress, which was free of the ruffles she had adopted with enthusiasm in Trure. It was a light-tan color, not at all like the vibrant outfits Zala usually chose for her. She slipped it on and covered her hair in a dusky-blue scarf, wrapping it a few extra times to conceal her dark curls.

Zala had selected a dress for Fenn too. It was the first time Selivia had ever seen her bodyguard wear one. Fenn wrapped a scarf around her red hair and strapped a pair of belt knives at her waist. Zala handed her a shawl to conceal the weapons. Fenn's bulk would make her stand out no matter what, but with the dress, scarf, and shawl, she could almost be a Truren innkeeper instead of a skilled guardswoman.

Zala changed into a dress that matched Selivia's and put on a light-green scarf, not bothering to hide her pale-brown hair completely. At sixteen, she was two years older than Selivia, and they could almost be sisters if you didn't look too closely.

"Are you ready?" Zala asked.

"Lead the way."

In truth, Selivia wasn't ready at all. Why had her mother suddenly decided she couldn't trust her own brother to keep them safe from a foreign enemy? The Soolens couldn't truly capture the Stronghold, could they? Selivia didn't understand how the invaders had gotten so far in the first place. As her mother had said, something wasn't right.

Despite her worries, she couldn't help feeling a burst of exhilaration as they strode through the kitchens in their disguises. Not a single person offered her a bow or even looked twice at her. True, most of the cooks and scullery maids were busy chattering about the coming siege and taking hasty inventory of their supplies. They might not have noticed if she waltzed through in a ball gown with a whole company of guards.

On the opposite side of the kitchens, they found yet another staircase leading down to the ground level of the stronghold, which was entirely occupied with the soldiers' barracks and armory. They hurried out to the grounds. Men charged back and forth, as nervous and talkative as the cooks had been. Still, no one challenged them.

Their troubles were sure to begin when they reached the gates. The Stronghold walls only had two: the main east-facing gate and the smaller doorway that led out to Stronghold Town, the village that rested to the west between the Rock and the fortress. Both gates were heavily guarded. Selivia doubted the guards would let a trio of "washerwomen" out as the Soolen army bore down on them.

They approached the west gate across the Stronghold's practice yard. Men marched across it in hurried single file, the spring sunshine glittering on their weapons and making their sweaty foreheads shine. The guards posted atop the walls didn't look as though they'd open the gates for the Firelord himself. Zala studied them, her mouth tightening with concern. They would never make it out!

Suddenly, a flash of silver zipped through the air, and one of the guards toppled off the wall. Shouts rose all along the balustrade as more flashes of silver darted through the air. Selivia froze, unable to look away. She was too surprised to feel afraid. She hadn't realized arrows would look quite so shiny when they zipped into a man's heart. Another guard fell from the walls and landed with a wet crack.

Zala seized Selivia's arm and pulled her out of the practice yard.

"Quickly. We're too late." She pushed open the door to a stable bordering the practice yard.

"We're riding?" Selivia asked.

Zala put a finger to her lips. "Horses won't fit through the tunnel."

She led them swiftly past rows of snorting horses toward the back of the stable. Only half the stalls were occupied. The rest of the horses must be out on the plains with the men trying to hold back the Soolen army.

Men continued to shout and scream out by the walls. Some of them must be dying. Shock shot through Selivia as if it were an arrow. How had the bowmen gotten through Stronghold Town so quickly?

Zala didn't seem worried at all. Her hips suddenly took on a swaying, seductive quality as she approached a young soldier standing watch at the back of the stable. He stared at her, eyes widening. Before he could so much as ask her what she wanted, she closed the distance between them reached up to touch his face. Selivia couldn't see what she was doing, but an instant later, the man collapsed into the straw and began snoring peacefully. Zala tucked a small bottle back into her belt.

"Quickly," she said. "That won't work for long." She tugged the soldier aside and heaved open a trapdoor in the floor. A yawning darkness greeted them.

Fenn advanced to the tunnel without hesitation. She hiked up her skirts to get them out of her way and dropped into the darkness.

"All clear," she called softly.

Zala held out a hand to Selivia. "Come along, Princess."

Selivia wanted to stand and gape, but the sounds of the battle outside were growing more frantic. "Are you sure?"

"It'll be okay," Zala said. "I've gone through the tunnels before."

Selivia struggled with sudden misgivings. Did she truly know her handmaiden? Her mother had brought Zala back from Trure to help Selivia learn the Far Plains language. They had bonded quickly over their love of clothes. Zala had excellent taste, and she loved colorful things almost as much as Selivia did. But there was no sign of the frivolous young woman who had squealed and schemed over gowns now.

"You owe me an explanation for all this madness," Selivia said. She went to the opening and sat, her feet swinging over blackness. She had wanted her time at the Stronghold to be more interesting. Well, she had just gotten her wish.

Selivia closed her eyes, imagining that she was a spy in a storybook about to set out on a daring mission. The thought made her brave, and she pushed off the edge and dropped into the tunnel.

She landed on soft dirt. Fenn put a hand on her arm to steady her. They took a few steps into utter darkness together to make way for Zala. Dexterous as a cat, she somehow managed to swing into the opening and pull the trapdoor down with her. She hung at the edge for a moment then let the trapdoor slam as she released her grip and dropped to the ground.

Utter darkness swallowed them. Selivia clutched Fenn's hand, grateful for her soft warmth in the darkness.

"I have a light," Zala whispered. "Let's walk a few paces before we use it in case someone looks down here."

"Which way?" Selivia asked. She was sure the others could hear her heart pounding in the darkness. Footsteps thudded overhead. Was that from the practice yard or the stable itself?

"Follow my voice." Zala had slipped around them somehow, and she was moving west as far as Selivia could tell. "The ground is smooth here," Zala said. "You won't fall."

Selivia and Fenn held hands as they shuffled slowly after Zala.

She spoke every few seconds to let them know she was still ahead of them. Selivia could hardly believe she had been pouting on the battlements less than an hour ago and now she was creeping away from the fortress through an underground tunnel. She wished her mother had come with them. If Selivia wasn't safe in the Stronghold, she didn't think her mother would be either.

A scraping sound echoed up the tunnel behind them. Selivia froze. Was someone following them? The Soolens couldn't have breached the walls already, could they? Her heart thundered so loudly, she could barely hear anything else. But the scraping sound didn't come again. Maybe it was nothing.

Besides, she had resolved to be brave. This was a real, true adventure, the first of her life! She'd been sad when Dara hadn't invited her along on her quest to save Siv after she escaped the palace dungeon. Well, Selivia would show everyone that she could take care of herself too—as long as she had Fenn and Zala with her, of course.

They continued through the tunnel in utter darkness. The only sounds were the shuffling of their feet on the dirt, the pounding of Selivia's heart, and Fenn's heavy, steady breathing. Zala made no sound at all, except when she whispered to let them know she was still ahead.

After what felt like a hundred years, Zala spoke in a normal voice. "I don't think we were followed. There's a bend in the tunnel here. I'll get out my light as soon as we go around it."

Selivia let go of Fenn to feel for the cool stone in front of her so she wouldn't bump into anything. It was rough beneath her fingers, and sand sifted away as she followed the curve of the wall around the bend.

At last, Zala took out an Everlight and released its glow into the tunnel. The light revealed a long, narrow passageway. The stone walls were polished smooth and gleaming, as if hundreds of years' worth of hands had fumbled their way along them. Strange shapes were carved in places, perhaps markers to guide their way through the darkness. Zala herself looked otherworldly, like a witch from a story who had lured them into her underground lair. It was hard to believe this was the girl Selivia had giggled and gossiped with over the past few months, the girl who had been a companion and a comfort in uncertain times.

"Will you please tell me where we're going?"

"The far side of the Rock," Zala said. "My people will shelter us until the war is over."

"I thought your people lived in Stronghold Town," Selivia said. "You always talked about growing up in the shadow of the Rock."

Zala smiled. "The far shadow. The journey will take time. I'm afraid we'll have to travel underground until we reach the center of the Rock."

"The center?" Selivia gaped at her. The Rock was a solid mass. Surely she didn't mean . . .

"There's a network of caves," Zala said, "but most people live outside on the sunset side." She glanced around the grim walls of their tunnel. "We don't like being trapped inside like this."

"Are you telling me the Far Plainsfolk have a tunnel leading all the way into the Stronghold itself?" She looked at Fenn, who appeared as calm as ever. "Does everyone know about this except me?"

"No," Zala said. "This is an ancient secret. You mustn't mention it to anyone on the other side. We will tell them we left days earlier and traveled around the Rock. This is very important, Princess."

"*I* won't tell anyone," Selivia said. "But how do *you* know about it?"

"It's part of my job."

"Your job as a handmaid and language tutor?"

Zala smiled. "It's a little more complicated than that. The important thing is that your mother trusts me, and I intend to keep you safe. The rest will become clear soon."

"Well, let's get going, then!" Selivia said, preparing to march into the unknown at the other end of the tunnel. "I hope you packed something to eat in these satchels. All this adventure is making me hungry."

6

WORKING

Dara stood by a large table in Wyla's study, slowly draining molten power from a basket of Firebulbs. The lights winked out one by one as the Fire seeped into her veins, running hot beneath her skin. Firebulbs were the best way to get the power, apart from Rumy. The cur-dragon's strange version of the substance was still unpredictable, difficult to control. And Wyla demanded absolute control from her new research assistant.

"That's enough for now," she said when Dara finished drawing the Fire from her seventh bulb.

"I can hold more."

"No need. Now, tell me how you feel."

Dara breathed, concentrating. The Fire rushing through her was thrilling, its heat intoxicating, overwhelming. She wanted more, wanted to demonstrate how powerful she could become.

She forced down the thought, reminding herself that her father's desire for more power had ended the Peace of Vertigon and turned him into a murderer. She wouldn't be like that. The Fire was a tool, a material to be crafted, nothing more.

Wyla cleared her throat, rustling the piece of parchment spread before her.

"It's like blood," Dara began. "Liquid and hot, but smooth. Maybe more like oil than blood?"

Wyla scribbled some notes. "And you can actually feel it running through your veins?"

"Yes. I guess that means it's *not* like blood. And I can feel it underneath my skin." Dara let the power pool in her hand and seep out of the cracks in her palm. "I can make it ooze out like sweat. It's strange because it's thicker than water, but I don't know how else to describe it."

"How do you feel? Energized? Drained?"

"It's hard to explain."

"Try."

Dara frowned, paying attention to the sensations, focusing on the details lest the furious rush sweep her away. "I guess it's like how I feel after a particularly tough run," she said at last. "My face flushes, and my heart beats faster, but the sensation goes through my entire body."

"You mentioned that it's hot," Wyla said. "Tell me more about that."

"Well, heat in general is different to me now," Dara said. "Hot things don't burn me, and I can hold a lot of Fire in my body before I ever feel uncomfortable. I can touch coals, and boiling liquids like soup or tea don't hurt if they touch my skin. At the same time, I *know* the Fire is hot, and I can feel it like heat in my body."

"Exactly how hot?" Wyla asked. "Boiling?"

Dara frowned. "I can't tell how it would feel to a normal person. I don't know how much this would hurt you if you touched it." She extended her palm toward Wyla, revealing the pool of Fire cupped in it, glistening like molten gold.

"It would hurt," Wyla said. "But not as much as it would hurt someone without my abilities."

"Really? Can you protect yourself with the Watermight?"

Wyla didn't answer. She often didn't answer Dara's questions. She simply ignored her and picked another Firebulb out of the basket. "Do another, very slowly this time."

Dara obliged, first pulling the handful of Fire back into her skin and then slowly draining the power out of the new Firebulb. Wyla watched closely, eyes glittering like a thunderbird's. The Firebulb went dark. Dara's skin hummed with the additional power.

"Did you do anything to ready yourself before you drew in the Fire?" Wyla asked, quill poised to write once more.

"Ready myself?"

"Such as meditation, or perhaps you steeled yourself against the heat?"

"No, not really." Dara turned the empty Firebulb in her hands, no more than a hunk of metal now. "It's . . . it's something I welcome, not something I steel myself against. I invite it in. I've always wanted to Work the Fire, so maybe that's part of it."

"Perhaps." Wyla didn't sound convinced by that theory. "Now, you have eight Firebulbs of power within you, correct?"

"Yes, ma'am."

"I want you to create one of those Fireblossoms like the one you inserted into the statue in Fork Town. Allow it to spin here in the air between us. Keep it as stable as possible, if you please."

Dara did as she was told. First she formed the basic shape with thin spirals of Fire. The molten substance coiled above her palm, expanded, blossomed. She didn't use all of the power, leaving some to simmer beneath her skin. Next she spun the object. She had figured out this part was easier if she held the Fire in her body first than if she simply Worked with Fire she hadn't absorbed before. She told Wyla as much as she spun the completed Fireblossom between them.

"I've observed the same effect with Watermight," Wyla said. "The powers respond better when they're more closely linked with the Artist or Worker's physiology."

"And you think Watermight Workers and Fireworkers have the same physiology?"

Wyla went as still as a stone gargoyle for a moment. Then she set down her quill and looked up.

"I have never said that."

"It was just a guess," Dara said. "You've talked about wanting to Work the powers together. But you've shown a lot more interest in my background, particularly my delayed abilities. I thought that was why you wanted to work with me specifically. I'm sure other Fireworkers travel through Pendark all the time. But you really wanted *my* help."

Wyla made a soft sound, somewhere between a sniff and a sigh. Maybe she hadn't expected Dara to work this part out on her own.

"Slow the spinning of your Blossom, please," she said.

Dara obeyed. The spiral glowed gold between them. Dara had formed it to look more like a snowflake than a flower, with jagged spires sticking out in all directions. Firelight glowed from the fractal pattern, the effect somewhat muted by the blaze of the Fire Lanterns hanging overhead.

Wyla lifted her hand almost lazily. A thin rim of silver appeared beneath her fingernails, and Watermight oozed from her fingertips. Dara watched closely. She still wasn't sure how Wyla stored and transported her power. Unlike Fire, Watermight was supposed to be difficult to contain. It couldn't simply be sealed up in barrels and shipped around like wine, even though it appeared to be the consistency—if not the color—of ordinary water.

Five streams of shimmery silver poured from Wyla's fingertips, weaving together in a braid, looping and twisting over her hands. The Watermight emitted a faint light, which danced in Wyla's eyes and made her white hair glow. Dara nearly lost control of her Fireblossom, so mesmerizing was the magical substance curling and twining in the air.

Wyla extended her palm and allowed her braid of silver to drift closer to Dara's Fireblossom. The brightness of the Fire didn't dim the silvery-white light at all, as if neither substance could absorb the light of the other. They inched closer. The five threads of Watermight merged, and what looked like a rope of pure silver snaked around the Fireblossom. It looped around the spiral, weaving through the gaps, coiling like a snake, but didn't actually touch it. Then it curled inward around the core of the Fireblossom, a ring of silver encircling the gold.

"Brace yourself," Wyla said.

Before Dara could ask why, the cord of Watermight tightened and made contact with the Fire.

Light flashed between them, silver and gold and white. A shockwave rolled over Dara's skin, not strong enough to push her off her feet, but enough to make her hair stir.

When her vision cleared, purple spots still dancing at the edges, the spiral of Fire and the braid of Watermight were gone.

"What was that?" Dara asked.

"That," Wyla said, "is my problem. Fire and Watermight are incompatible. They consume each other in a flash. This would be useful if the burst of pressure could knock people to the ground or send armies to their knees, but I haven't managed to harness the energy in that way. It's gone like nothing more than a gust of wind."

"Did you think it would be different with me just now?" Dara asked. She still held the extra Fire, burning beneath her skin. As the shockwave passed, it had felt as if the power within her contracted, retreating into her bones to protect itself from the Watermight.

"I wanted you to see what we're working with first," Wyla said. "You see there's a lot of light and a bit of pressure. Nothing too dangerous."

"Yes . . ."

"Good. Then you see you'll be in no danger if you take Fire and Watermight into your body at the same time."

"But I can't wield Watermight."

"I'm not so certain that's true," Wyla said.

"I—really?"

Dara had assumed when Wyla enlisted her as a research assistant that they would be producing Works together, each controlling their own unique power to figure out how they could be connected. But this?

"You want me to try using Watermight myself?"

Wyla didn't respond, busy scribbling notes once more.

"Wyla?" Dara didn't want to irritate the woman, but her brain was turning like a Firespindle as she considered the possibilities. Was such a thing actually possible?

At last, Wyla looked up. "My theory is that the inherent ability to Work the magical substances of this land is the same in all people with the gift. We in Pendark and you in Vertigon learn only one substance. The scarcity of the other in each dominion means no one discovers they are both a Waterworker and a Fireworker at the same time."

Dara shook her head as she tried to take this in.

"Are you saying *you* can Work the Fire?"

"Not me," Wyla said impatiently. "And neither can the other Watermight practitioners in Pendark. That is the problem. I learned the Watermight Arts in my youth. My body is trained to take in that substance alone. The two powers behave differently, you see. Once you become accustomed to one, your body is no longer compatible with the other."

Wyla stood and plucked another Firebulb from the basket. She held it flat in her palm and closed her eyes. A few seconds later, a faint sizzling sound filled the air. She dropped the Firebulb, and it clinked on the floor and rolled away. Wyla showed Dara the faint red outline of a burn on her palm. Dara seized her hand for a closer look. Wyla snorted disapprovingly, but Dara barely noticed. Firebulbs were safe for anyone to use. Wyla must have pulled some of the Fire out to get it to burn. It couldn't be possible.

"My theory," Wyla said, pulling her hand delicately out of Dara's grip, "is that someone with the Spark could learn to Wield both powers. I've tried it with children before and made some progress, but it is very difficult for them to achieve the level of control it takes to Wield both powers at once. It has proved too much for them."

Dara went cold at the thought. Wyla had been experimenting with young Firesparked—or Watertouched—children. She must have forced them to draw on incompatible powers, forced them to control the wild rush of substances that even lifelong wielders didn't fully understand.

But Dara wasn't a child. She met Wyla's eyes. "You think I'll have more control than your other . . . research assistants?"

"You are old enough and disciplined enough to have a great deal of control over your body," Wyla said. "Your history as an athlete only confirms this. You progressed very quickly when you began to learn the Work. However, you are still early enough in your training that I believe you could learn to hold both Fire and Watermight within you at the same time without allowing them to combust." Wyla took a step closer to Dara and seized her hand, exactly as Dara had done before. She turned her palm over, tracing the lines in Dara's skin. "That could be the key to getting the powers to cooperate at last."

Dara pulled her hand out of Wyla's grasp. "And what exactly do you want me to do with the power if I can use it like you suggest?"

"You could confirm my theories, first of all," Wyla said. "I also hope you can articulate your process clearly enough that I could attempt it myself under the right conditions."

Dara glanced at Wyla's hand, thinking of the angry burn marking her palm. She was skeptical about Wyla's theory. And if she somehow managed to combine the powers thanks to her unique circumstances, Wyla would want a whole lot more from her. She doubted she could just walk away.

But what if she really got this to work? What if she could harness the energy in that shockwave and turn it into real power? She hardly dared to admit the way her heart raced at the thought.

She met Wyla's eyes and recognized the challenge in them, the chance to compete. "Shouldn't we see if I can actually do anything with Watermight before we get too excited?"

Wyla smiled. "I hoped you'd be intrigued. Come. Let me show you my power."

Wyla led the way out of her study and down to the ground floor of the manor. She took out a large silver key ring and opened a small door Dara had assumed led to a broom closet, revealing a narrow staircase descending into darkness.

"A light, if you please."

Dara hesitated, nervous at the idea of bringing Fire into contact with Wyla's stash of Watermight. The Waterworker tapped her foot impatiently and motioned toward the stairs.

Dara drew the last of the Fire from the Firebulbs out of her body and spun a temporary light above her palm. She couldn't help forming it into the shape of a lantern. She lifted the conjured light aloft and entered the bowels of the manor, Wyla following closely behind her.

The air grew cold and damp as they descended. Dara estimated they walked at least forty feet into the swampy ground beneath the waterline. They entered a dank room at the bottom, whose stone walls were sealed and reinforced with silver mortar. Watermight couldn't be solidified like Fire, so Dara wasn't sure what this substance was. Some strange hybrid Wyla was keeping away from prying eyes?

They didn't need the light from Dara's Fire once they entered the room. There was more than enough illumination coming from Wyla's personal Watermight supply.

A vast whirlpool was set in the floor of the dungeon-like room. Silvery Watermight swirled in an endless tornado of power. White light glittered from the surface. If diamonds could become liquid and swirl around like wine in a goblet, it might look a little like this.

"You must not speak of this," Wyla said. "I assume you know that already."

"Who would I talk to?" Wyla had kept her too occupied to leave the manor over the past few days. She hadn't seen Siv since their swimming lesson.

"I know you and Vine discuss the Work," Wyla said. "She has spent a lot of time out in the city of late. I don't want her carrying tales to any other practitioners."

"You don't have to worry about Vine," Dara said. "I trust her."

Wyla snorted softly. "You should trust no one."

"Do the other Waterworkers keep their power underneath their manor houses like this?"

"Some. We are protective of our methods. This whirlpool containment system is my own invention." Wyla sounded genuinely proud as she stood at the edge of the pool, the light flickering on her steel-toed boots. "I found it much simpler to build my home over my primary power source than to guard it in another location, as others do. Some are forced to guard their supplies from boats in the Gulf itself."

"They can't just move it?"

"One of the great weaknesses of the Watermight is the difficulty of transporting and holding it, but Watermight is at its most powerful when it can be drawn from the sea and wielded in concert with true water."

Dara studied Wyla's whirlpool. Yes, there was ordinary water mixed in with the silvery magical substance. It came from a spout in the stone wall, perhaps originating from the small stream that ran through the courtyard garden. She guessed Wyla stored the power by keeping it in motion. She must constantly have her senses tuned to this room to prevent it from slipping away. That must take an incredible amount of focus—not to mention strength.

Dara walked around the thin lip of stone surrounding the silver pool. The sight of the swirling power was utterly mesmerizing. She could feel it too. The power. The intensity.

She lifted her lantern of Fire over the pool. The light from the Watermight seemed to fight against the Firelight. She didn't need the illumination now, but she was afraid to draw the power back into her body. She could only imagine what would happen if she accidentally slipped into the pool with Fire in her blood.

"Where does the power come from?" she asked. "Is this a spring?"

"A vent. Most of the power comes from vents on the seafloor, not unlike smaller versions of your Well." Wyla stretched out a hand and called a stream of Watermight to her. It moved differently than the Fire, more sinuous and smooth, but also more ethereal. Fire and Watermight were both liquids, but where Fire was denser than water, the Watermight seemed lighter, as if it was almost at the point of becoming a gas.

"The power spews forth and mixes with the seawater," Wyla explained. "The practitioners must gather it up. If they control a vent, it's easier to capture the power before it slips away."

"How many vents are in the Black Gulf?"

"A dozen are active at any given time," Wyla said. "Many Workers employ less powerful practitioners to keep watch for new ones. But they may try to capture the power from the newly opened vent and use it to claim more territory, so it's a dangerous arrangement. If too many strong practitioners join the contest, it can get ugly. Most of the periods of conflict in our history began with a new vent discovery."

"Do the vents ever run out?"

"Eventually."

"So there's not enough power available for everyone with the ability?"

"There is never enough."

Dara remembered when Zage Lorrid had explained how the Waterworkers of Pendark warred for dominance. His experiences in this city had been why he felt so strongly that the Fire needed to be carefully regulated and distributed amongst many Workers in Vertigon. Dara's father had set out to change that. How soon would the Fireworkers fight amongst themselves now that the regulations had been eliminated? At least the Well produced a consistent amount of Fire. She couldn't imagine what would happen if more power was somehow injected into the mountain.

She shook her head. The Fire was far away in Vertigon. She had more immediate concerns.

"Have the Waterworkers ever tried to use their power to conquer other lands?"

Wyla pursed her lips, the expression reminding Dara suddenly and forcibly of her mother. "The difficulty of solidifying and storing the power has largely kept it within the bounds of Pendark."

"So Watermight can't be used anywhere else? At all?" That was a flaw in Dara's plan to somehow use Waterworks—or an alliance with a Watermight Artist—to neutralize her father.

"With the proper training, you can travel some distance carrying Watermight, but it drains away within a week," Wyla said. "When practitioners have tried to use their power to expand too far, it has only led to defeat and humiliation."

"Hmm." Dara paced along the edge of the pool. A week was far too short. "What about Soole?" She turned to face Wyla. "It's on the sea too."

"I've heard claims of Watermight vents opening off the coast of Soole, but they have never been substantiated. Watermight belongs to Pendark alone."

Dara frowned at the silvery depths of the whirlpool, feeling frustrated. What good was all this, then? What did it matter that she might be able to Work the Watermight if she never got anywhere near her father with it? There had to be something Wyla wasn't telling her.

"How did you get your vent?" she asked.

Wyla smiled, and the flickering light of the Watermight made her teeth glow. "I won't teach you all of my secrets just yet."

Dara studied the older woman as if she were a dueling opponent. It wouldn't be any easy match. The constant struggle over this ephemeral power hadn't made Wyla particularly trusting. But at least she thought Dara could learn a thing or two from her.

"Are you sure you have enough Watermight for me to experiment?"

"For a time."

"I might not be able to do it. I hope it won't be wasted."

"Oh, I expect to make back my investment in you," Wyla said. "Shall we begin?"

7

VINE

Dara was exhausted by the time she finished her daily session with Wyla and returned to the room she shared with Vine Silltine on the top floor of the manor house. The spacious guestroom had a pair of beds, matching washstands, and tall mirrors on each wall. A wardrobe separated two windows overlooking the front courtyard. Staying here was much nicer than sleeping on the cold ground, as they'd had to do too often while they searched for Siv, but she couldn't rest yet.

Dara drew her sword and did footwork in the narrow space between the two beds. Advance. Retreat. Advance. Lunge. She slashed the air in familiar patterns, refusing to neglect her dueling training despite her fatigue. The Savven hummed with warmth. Siv had given her the fine black blade made by Drade Savven, the best sword smith of his generation. It had somehow transformed into a Fire Blade during her confrontation with her father back in Vertigon. She still hadn't fully delved the mysteries of its creation.

Her boots thudded on the wood floor as the Savven flashed before her, unnaturally swift and strong. When she created the Fire Blade, she'd been desperate to save Siv and devastated by the encounter with her father. Wyla believed there was a link between emotions and the Work. Could her pain and heightened emotions have caused the transformation of the Savven? All Dara knew was they were connected now, she and the blade. After Vex Rollendar's men stole it from her, she'd been drawn back to it by the faint impression of a spark in her chest.

Dara's skirts flared as she executed a neat advance lunge. She wore one of the dresses Wyla had supplied in the same poison-green shade as her flags. Dara couldn't help thinking of it as a uniform. Wyla owned her for the next three months, and she had much higher hopes for her than Dara had anticipated. Was it really possible she could wield Watermight? And if she did, would Wyla ever let her go?

Dara lunged, sinking the tip of her blade deep into the wardrobe door. The thud echoed through the room. Despite her worries, she couldn't help being excited about the possibilities. If she could use her Fire along with the fabled Watermight, there might be no limit to what she could do.

She yanked her blade from the door, tossed it on her bed, and sat down to stretch, adjusting her many-layered skirt. She was still getting used to the shorter length, but it kept her hem out of the mud—and away from her feet if she ever had to fight or run in the thing. Besides—not that she'd admit it to anyone—the poison-green looked good against her golden hair.

The door opened, and Vine waltzed into the room. She too wore a Pendarkan dress from Wyla, pale-blue in an equally fine material.

"You're back early today," Dara said.

"I promised Rid I'd dine with him this evening," Vine said. "I've been busy of late, and he's looking forlorn. It was so much easier when I had my own network of informants."

Vine had appointed herself information gatherer and rumor interpreter when it became clear she wouldn't be included in Wyla and Dara's conversations about the Work. For some reason, Wyla wasn't interested in Vine's faculty for Sensing the Air, the magical substance most commonly found on the plains of Trure. Perhaps Wyla had worked with enough Air Sensors before, or perhaps she didn't value the talent. Dara's father had been equally unimpressed by the Air, but Dara wasn't willing to be as dismissive.

"Did you hear anything new about Rallion City?"

"Nothing good, I'm afraid," Vine said, shedding her shawl and her own assortment of weapons. "What do you know?"

"Just what those kids told us a few days ago," Dara said.

"Well, the rumors do seem to be true. Commander Brach

assaulted the city walls and captured the palace. The latest news is that he's holding King Atrin in his own dungeon."

"He must be grumpy about that."

"I would imagine so," Vine said. "He *does* have a vitriolic streak."

Dara snorted. "That's one way to put it." King Atrin had locked her in those very dungeons in a rage after Siv was kidnapped, delaying her search until Vine came for her. But he was still Siv's grandfather, and she didn't want any harm to come to him.

Vine sat on her bed and eased off her shoes. "No one has seen Lady Tirra or Princess Selivia in the city since before the siege began. My sources believe they were sent to one of the plains estates as a precaution. They should be safe."

"That's good news," Dara said. Selivia was her friend as well as Siv's sister. "Any word on what Commander Brach will do next?"

"I'm afraid that's where the rumors devolve into pure speculation." Vine frowned and looked toward the window, which faced the inky waters of the Black Gulf in the distance. "I wish I could communicate directly with my friends in Trure. The Air sometimes consents to carry voices on the wind, but it has been silent of late."

"You can speak to people with the Air? Even as far away as Rallion City?"

"If the Air wills it." Vine sighed. "As I said, it has been quiet these past weeks."

Vine fell silent, and Dara feared she'd lapse into one of her meditative trances again.

"About Brach?"

"Oh yes. If he means to rule Trure, he still has enemies to face. He cut straight to the capital using the Cindral Forest route, but much of Trure is yet to fall under his control."

"Why do you think he invaded Trure anyway?" Dara asked.

"I've wondered that myself." Vine twirled a finger through her lustrous dark hair. It spilled over her shoulders, always hanging loose no matter what she was doing, from dueling to dancing to everything in between. "The Brach family doesn't have prime positioning in the rank of succession in Soole. They are rich and powerful, but Brach would have to murder three-quarters of the nobility to ever become king. Perhaps he decided he'd rather carve out his own kingdom."

"As long as Selivia is safe, I don't mind what Brach does, to be honest."

"You've thrown your lot in with a king in the most spectacular way, Dara," Vine said. "You have to keep yourself informed about what all the kings and kingmakers are up to these days."

Dara shrugged. "I have you to help me with that."

Vine smiled, but the expression soon faded, and her eyes took on a thoughtful look.

"What is it?"

"Oh, well, it's Vex," Vine said.

Dara started up, automatically reaching for the black hilt of her Savven blade.

"You found out where he's staying?"

"I have a list of possibilities," Vine said. "It's a bit tricky as I don't want to attract the attention of his informants. The Rollendars are famously well informed, you know. I asked a cobbler about him this afternoon. His eyes went as round as coat buttons, and then he started asking *me* questions. I got out of there as quickly as I could."

"Vex already knows we're in the city," Dara said. "As long as you didn't tell him where you're staying, it probably doesn't matter." He'd been gravely injured in his attempt to kill Siv, but it was only a matter of time before the crafty Rollendar lord caught up with them. She gripped her sword, thinking of the Fire supply Wyla had purchased for their research. Vex was an excellent swordsman, but she'd like to see him try to capture her again with Fire in her veins and a Fire Blade in her hands.

"I know," Vine said. "But it scared me worse than anything. What if I'd gone into that cobbler's shop and Vex had been there asking for his latest reports?"

"You didn't," Dara said. "And now you know to avoid it."

"Yes, but . . ." Vine hesitated, biting her lip.

"What?"

"I dreamed about that cobbler, Dara," Vine said. "Last night. I thought it was the Air giving me a hint, so I searched for the shop, and there it was, with the same purple flags and the same shoes for sale and everything. Then the cobbler turned out to be a Rollendar informant. I wouldn't expect the Air to send me into danger like that."

"Are you sure it was the Air? You could have walked by that shop before and dreamed of it by chance."

"Maybe," Vine said. "But it was very vivid."

"Have you had dreams from the Air before?"

"Oh, I've dreamt the most wonderful things on my Air retreats," Vine said. "But never with such clarity."

"Maybe the Air somehow knew today would be a safe time to stop by that shop. Now you know to avoid it in the future."

"Perhaps." Vine toyed with the ends of her hair, still looking troubled.

"There's something else?" Dara asked.

"Well, I've been dreaming about Lord Vex too," she said at last. "Nothing as helpful as his location. Just dreams. We're riding through the woods together or chatting over tea or—never mind."

Dara frowned. Vine and Lord Vex had spent a lot of time talking on their journey through Kurn Pass. Perhaps the dreams were vestiges of those days. Hopefully, they didn't mean anything.

"Do you want to ask Wyla if she knows anything about Air dreams?" Dara asked.

"Of course I'd like to," Vine said with a huff. "I'd love to ask her all sorts of things."

"Sorry," Dara said. "I wish she was more interested in you too."

"It doesn't matter." Vine brushed her hair back over her shoulders as if shaking off Wyla's indifference. "How was your lesson? I forgot to ask."

Dara launched into an explanation of everything she had discussed with Wyla over the past few sessions. She held back from revealing that Wyla thought she might be able to use the Watermight herself, focusing on the other insights Wyla had offered about the magical substances, the possible explanations behind her delayed Spark, and their conversation about the physical sensations as she drew in power from the Firebulbs. When she finally stopped for a breath, she realized Vine was chuckling.

"What?"

"That's all very fascinating, Dara," Vine said. "But I meant your *swimming* lesson. With your long-lost love?"

"Oh." Dara blushed and gave a much more abbreviated account of that afternoon. She didn't mention all the kissing, but judging by the knowing look Vine gave her, there was no need.

"It's a shame Wyla keeps you so busy," Vine said when Dara finished. "It's high time you two got to enjoy each other for once."

"It is nice." Dara blushed. "But I still don't know if—"

"Stop!" Vine leapt to her feet.

"What?"

"Don't even say it."

"Say what?"

"You 'don't even know if you'll get to be together.' Honestly, Dara, have you seen how that man looks at you? Besides, if he doesn't make you his queen after all you've been through, I'll kill him myself." She put her hands on her hips, staring Dara down. "And I'll go through you to do it."

"His . . . his queen?"

Vine chuckled. "You know I love you, Dara, but you can be remarkably naïve. What else would you become if you help him take back his throne and you all live happily ever after?"

"I guess it didn't occur to me," Dara said faintly. She had pictured them back in the castle together in her most hopeful daydreams, but even then she'd been wearing her old Castle Guard uniform, not a queen's diadem.

"That is because you are not nearly conniving and political enough, my dear Dara." Vine patted her on the head. "There is a particular order of things. Women who marry kings become queens. And the other way around, of course. I daresay Tull Denmore thought about it all the time."

"I'll worry about that later," Dara said. "Right now, I want to learn what I can from Wyla and make sure Siv doesn't get himself killed in the Dance of Steel."

"There's the grave, earnest Dara I know," Vine said. "He's really competing in that barbaric sport?"

"He thinks he can earn enough money to buy my way out of my bargain with Wyla *and* hire enough men to retake Vertigon."

"Hmm, that may be a touch optimistic," Vine said. "But I suppose it *would* help to have some gold. I'm pondering how to solve our current financial situation as well. If he can make some money in the Steel Pentagon, that would be most welcome."

Dara gaped at her. "You can't be serious."

"Why not? It may be the most useful thing he can do while you serve your time. We won't get far without gold."

"What if he gets killed?"

"You should really have more faith in him. Didn't you teach him everything you know about fighting?"

"With a sword," Dara said. "He fancies himself a knife fighter now."

"Oh well. Nobody's perfect." Vine skipped toward the door. "Let us go collect Rid. We don't want to be late for supper."

"But—"

"Our dear king needs to prove himself too, Dara," Vine said. "You're not the only one who aims to do that with more steel than sense."

8

THE ROCK

Selivia had never walked so much in her entire life. They traveled through the darkness beneath the Rock for three days, the way forward lit only by Zala's Everlight. Selivia couldn't wait to reach the mysterious city of the Far Plainsfolk on the sunset side of the Rock. She'd wanted to see it long before she ever met Zala. She wished she could get there without developing quite so many blisters on her feet, though.

They told stories to pass the time. Selivia's favorites were tales of adventure and romance and exotic lands. For the first time in her life, she was embarking on a real adventure of her own. The first few hours had been terribly exciting, but as the days passed, she wished to see something besides the endless tunnel of rock and the plodding backs of her companions.

She tried to stay positive, but she was worried about her mother. It was especially bad when they stopped to sleep, and the dark hours stretched on with no sound but the stirring of their breath. Selivia didn't want to believe anyone would hurt her mother. She was a lovely person, if a bit sad and cold of late. Selivia had never known her to be rash. If she had risked sending her youngest daughter into these deep, dark tunnels, the danger must be greater than Selivia knew.

She began to doubt her memories as they continued through the darkness, every footstep making dust bloom beneath their slippers. Had her mother really been afraid of Uncle Valon—her own brother? What if she was just paranoid after the death of her husband and the disappearance of her son? What if the Stronghold really was the safest place, and they were getting farther away from it with each underground mile?

Selivia trailed her fingers on the tunnel walls, the cool sensation calming her runaway thoughts. The attack had been real. She remembered those silver arrows flying over the walls with perfect clarity. This wasn't a story. Her mother had protected her. And she had to be brave.

The air felt heavy in the tunnel. Selivia missed the sunshine and the spring flowers. She missed the wind blowing sharply over the plains as she watched the soldiers from the Stronghold battlements. She missed the comfort of her pets and the company of her family. It got harder to stay positive the longer she spent beneath the earth. Would this journey never end?

On the third day, Zala stopped at last and ran her fingers over a marking carved on the wall.

"We're here." She turned, angling the Everlight down so it wouldn't shine in their eyes. Her face looked otherworldly in the shadows. "There's a staircase ahead."

"Finally!" Selivia exclaimed, then she clapped a hand over her mouth as the sound echoed through the tunnel. "Sorry," she whispered.

"Is it daytime?" Fenn asked. "I've lost track."

"I think so," Zala said. "Time passes so slowly when you can't see the sun."

"Will we have somewhere to sleep up there?" Selivia asked.

"We'll be fine," Zala said. "We're going to stay with my family."

"But I don't know your family." Suddenly the fears that had been brewing within her throughout the long, dark walk bubbled up like a pot of tea. "I feel like I don't know you at all."

Zala's face fell. She shifted the Everlight to straighten her scarf, and in an instant, she was Selivia's handmaid again, not the mysterious shadow guide she had become as they fled the Stronghold.

"I thought we were friends, Princess."

"Of course we are," Selivia said quickly. "I just mean you've been keeping important things secret."

"It was necessary."

"Are you . . . are you some sort of spy?"

"I'm your handmaid and tutor. If the Peace had endured in Vertigon, that's all I'd be for as long as you needed me."

"And now?"

"My duty was to stay by your side and spirit you to safety with the Far Plainsfolk if necessary, nothing more."

Selivia frowned, trying to quiet the fears bubbling through her. She wanted to trust Zala, but the past few days in the darkness had been so strange.

"Your lady mother hired me for this," Zala said. "She wanted to keep you from harm."

Fenn shifted, her feet scraping the stones.

"My apologies, Fenn," Zala said quickly. "Anyone who sees you knows you can defend the princess. It makes you a target. But people barely glance at me, even though I can protect her too."

"I'm not offended," Fenn said. "I was aware of your additional role."

"You were?" Selivia asked. Even Zala looked surprised at that.

"I knew you didn't truly grow up in Stronghold Town. I guessed you were from the sunset side of the Rock, and I spoke to Queen Tirra about what you might be hiding. She explained everything to me."

"You know the Far Plainsfolk that well?" Zala asked.

Fenn shrugged, her cheeks going a bit pink. "I spent several years with a lover in Stronghold Town."

"A lover?" Selivia gaped at her stoic bodyguard. "Apparently I don't know *either* of you as well as I thought."

"I'm twenty years older than you, Princess," Fenn said kindly. "I wouldn't expect you to know everything about me."

Selivia bit her lip. It was hard to think of Fenn having another life before she and her brother came to work for the Amintelles as bodyguards. She resolved to learn more about her during their stay in the Far Plains. And to get the full story about this Stronghold Town lover.

Selivia turned to Zala. "If my mother trusts you, then so do I. Only . . ."

"What is it?"

"Well, you're a secret bodyguard. That's so . . . serious." She felt embarrassed. Everyone had big, important roles except for her. "You must have been so bored when I spent so much time talking about dresses and boys."

Zala laughed, the sound echoing around the tunnel like music. "I like dresses and boys. I'm still the same person."

"Good." Selivia looked between the two women who had done so much to protect her. The women her mother had entrusted with her safety. "Well, what are we waiting for?"

Zala led the way around a final bend. The air felt less oppressive here. The ground started sloping upward.

"Do any of your people know we're coming?" Fenn asked.

"That depends on what the Air Sensors have heard. They sometimes receive messages in their meditations." Zala hesitated. She had been reluctant to talk about Air Sensors when she told Selivia about growing up among the Far Plainsfolk before. "Try to stay clear of them. Talking to Air Sensors can be . . . confusing. And be wary of their riddles."

"Riddles?"

"You'll see. Ah, here we are." Zala pointed her Everlight. The slick rock of the tunnel floor ended in a flight of stone steps climbing up through the darkness. "Be careful. The steps are very old."

Selivia wanted to run up and burst into the sunshine, but she kept pace with Zala as they climbed. Despite the age, the steps felt as stable as ancient tree stumps. Sand gathered on them in clumps. Their feet scraped and slid on the grit, crunching with every step.

A rough screeching sounded ahead, Zala pulling open a door. It was as dark on the other side as it was in the tunnel, but Selivia immediately got the sense of space opening up. Zala's silhouette stood sharp against the little Everlight. Selivia and Fenn followed her into the chamber, and the door slammed behind them.

A moment later, light erupted in the space as Zala uncovered an old-fashioned Fire Lantern, adorned with simple golden casings. She moved around the room, pulling covers off ancient Fire Lanterns until six of them illuminated the space.

The chamber felt old. Selivia didn't know how else to describe it. A heavy stone table with stone benches was the only furniture. The walls were covered with paintings of figures in strange clothing and creatures the likes of which Selivia had only seen in storybooks. She hadn't been allowed out of the Stronghold to see the famous cliff paintings up close, but she imagined they were done in the same style as these. She wondered how many people knew there were more paintings hidden inside the Rock.

"Wait here," Zala said. "I'll make sure it's safe outside and come back for you."

She dropped her pack and strode out a door on the opposite side of the chamber. Fenn sat on one of the stone benches, sighing and rubbing her ankle. Selivia was far too excited to sit. She walked slowly around the chamber, kicking through a thick layer of sand, and examined the paintings on the walls. Words in a language she didn't understand were painted above the images. The figures themselves wore flowing garments, like blankets twisted into dresses that left their shoulders bare. They wore crowns of flowers, and their features were strange. The paintings reminded her of the mural on the ceiling of her grandfather's palace in Rallion City, though the style was more ancient somehow.

And the creatures! Selivia loved animals more than just about anything. She missed the pets she had left behind in Vertigon almost as much as she missed her family. The paintings depicted creatures more magnificent than any she had ever seen. There were horses, of course, and some figures rode on the backs of giant lizards like wingless dragons. Fanciful birds spread their wings wide across the walls in a hundred colors, encircling the people in sheltering arms. Painted tarbears, an adorable but long-extinct relative of the velgon bear, frolicked in what looked like a much wetter, greener version of the Far Plains.

All of the animals and people in the images appeared to be friends and partners—until she reached the wall with the second door. Here, instead of running and playing together, the ancient people and creatures faced off against one another. An ugly, bald thing with wicked teeth and black fur lurked beside the door. Could that be a cullmoran? A bird with talons like knives and the face of a snake circled above it. And then there were dragons.

True dragons. Selivia recognized them at once. They were gigantic compared to the people and other animals in the paintings. Their shapes weren't that different from the cur-dragons Selivia had grown up with, but the painter had depicted them with cruel gleams in their eyes and vicious teeth. They spurted flame across the doorframe, and the paint glowed gold in the Firelight. The figure was so lifelike that Selivia wondered if the ancient painter had been alive when true dragons last roamed the earth. They were supposed to be sleeping in the far-off Burnt Mountains. She gave a little shiver. She would *love* to see a real true dragon. They were supposed to be fierce beasts. Selivia couldn't help thinking they had been vilified unfairly. After all, everyone hated greckleflushes, but Selivia thought those made delightful pets.

A scrape sounded behind her. Zala had returned.

"Princess, we can go up. I met a few Air Sensors outside the tunnel. All is well."

"Have they heard any news of my mother or the Stronghold?"

"The Sensors believe the fortress still stands," Zala said, moving to cover the old Fire Lanterns once more. "The messages in the Air are not clear, but the Soolens don't seem to be advancing around the Rock yet. We should be safe."

It hadn't actually occurred to Selivia that the Soolens might try attacking the far side of the Rock too. They could have walked right into their arms.

"Why aren't the messages clear?" she asked.

"The Air blows where it wills," Zala said. Then she grinned. "Come. We're just in time for supper!"

Zala led the way out of the ancient chamber. Sand thickened on the steps as they climbed out of the depths of the Rock. The air was definitely lighter here, and more markings appeared on the walls in the Far Plains language, directing their path.

"I haven't told anyone who you are," Zala explained as they walked. "Is it all right if I call you Sel while you're here?"

"Of course." Selivia paused as an exciting thought occurred to her. "You haven't been going by a fake name in Vertigon, have you?"

"There's no need," Zala said. "But my real family name is Tovenarov, not Toven."

"You shortened it?"

"I didn't want anyone making the connection with my family here. Many of the Tovenarovs are powerful Air Sensors. That makes people nervous outside of Trure."

"Well, I'm glad you're still Zala." *Zala Tovenarov.* Selivia repeated the name in her head a few times to help remember it.

"What will you tell your people about us?" Fenn asked.

"You are mother and daughter, my friends from Stronghold Town," Zala said. "You wanted to escape the violence. More of the Plainsfolk who live in the shadow of the Stronghold will probably arrive within a few days anyway."

"That's easy to remember," Selivia said. She squeezed Fenn's hand. Her bodyguard was still wary, but she was sure they were going to be fine. They had to be.

At the top of the staircase, they found a sandy corridor with doorways and tunnels leading off in other directions. Footsteps and murmurs whispered along them, people moving through the tunnels like ants. Selivia was eager to investigate, but the natural daylight flooding in ahead of them drew her onward.

As the end of the tunnel neared, Zala picked up the pace, leading them through a beam of sunlight and out of the Rock at last. Selivia followed her into the bright light of day—and stopped. They stood on a ledge overlooking a sprawling city. Caves and smaller dwellings peeked out from the sloping cliffside, at their level and a little below it, but most of the people lived on the Far Plain itself. The Far Desert might have been a better name for it. The actual plains grass was sparse here, giving way to rocks and rough golden and russet brush. A strong wind blew in from the west, sending dust and sand through the wide streets. In some places, sand piled as thick as snow in a Vertigonian winter.

"Welcome to Sunset City," Zala said.

"It's beautiful," Selivia whispered.

Most of the buildings were a similar size, and Selivia didn't see anything that looked like a palace or anything official. The houses were single-level dwellings built of sandstone and pale mud bricks. They would have blended in with the landscape if not for the colorful textiles fluttering through the village. Awnings provided shade in front of most of the houses, and colorful curtains kept away the blowing dust.

Zala led the way down a winding path and into the city. Selivia thought she must be so excited to spend time at home after months on the mountain. And what a home it was!

The people wore magnificent fabrics, woven from thick fibers in hundreds of colors. Selivia could see in an instant where Zala got her appreciation for color. She could hardly keep from dancing as they walked among the colorful textiles lining the wide, sandy streets. She spotted a pair of animal tracks she couldn't identify, and only Fenn's hand on her shoulder stopped her from following the trail to see what sort of magnificent creature she'd find at the other end. The streets had a hushed, busy feeling. Most people seemed to be hurrying home for supper, though the sun still hadn't reached the horizon.

Selivia's stomach rumbled. It had been a while since their last meal of jerky and flatbread. She couldn't wait to try the Far Plains delicacies Zala had told her about.

The Far Plains were technically a part of Trure, but their affairs were largely separate from the rest of the kingdom. They had their own language and customs, and the Sunset City wasn't easy to reach. It was much more common for young Far Plainsfolk to seek their fortune in Rallion City and the towns on the High Road than it was for other Trurens to travel all the way out here. Selivia's mother hadn't been here since her childhood, as far as she knew. She must have chosen it for Selivia's refuge because of the remote location. She felt a twinge of worry for her mother but tried not to dwell on it.

They approached a larger house near the northern edge of the city. A broad woven awning out front covered a space bigger than the house itself. The awning featured a beautiful pattern of blues and greens that made Selivia think of the sea—or what she imagined the sea must be like. Assorted tables and chairs formed a rough circle beneath it. A dozen people were sitting down to a meal when Selivia and the others walked up.

"The Air has granted me safe passage," Zala said in the Far Plains tongue. She bowed formally then waited.

A dozen faces turned to her as one. The first person to recover from her surprise leapt to her feet and offered a similar bow. "We thank the Air for your safe return." Then she knocked over her chair as she ran forward and swept Zala into a huge hug. "We didn't think you'd be back so soon. We would have come to meet you. When did you get here? What was it like in Vertigon? Are you hungry? Let me get you something."

The woman didn't stop talking long enough for Zala to answer any of her questions. Selivia gathered that her name was Ananova, and she was Zala's aunt and the matriarch of this family. She ushered them toward the tables and waved for a young man to fetch seats for the newcomers.

The others introduced themselves in a flurry of names and voices that quickly ran together. Selivia understood the Far Plains tongue much better than she had when Zala first came to Vertigon, but her accent needed work. She felt a bit shy about using the language herself. Then someone gave her a plate of pink, rubbery fruit, a cup of tea, and a cold towel to clean her hands. With the first bite of the fruit, which was as sweet as candy, she quickly decided she liked this place and these people and she didn't care if she made a few mistakes. Soon she was chattering away with what turned out to be Zala's cousins from several families, who talked faster than she could ever hope to understand. Fenn seemed less certain they were among friends. She didn't remove her weapons or stray far from Selivia's side. Selivia was far too excited about meeting the Far Plainsfolk to worry too much about her bodyguard. Their reception was warm, and they were happy to see Zala. That was enough for her.

Ananova bustled around them, making sure they had everything they needed. Her hair was the same pale brown as Zala's. She had a warm, motherly quality to her voice—and she talked a lot!

"You must be so tired. The Air will bless your sleep tonight. Are you warm? Have you had enough feather cactus? Let me get you some. How about more tea? Darling! Fetch Sel another cup of tea." She bustled off to see to the tea before Selivia could say a word.

Three of the children in the group belonged to Ananova, including the young man who had fetched their chairs, Ivran. Zala's cousin was slim, with longish brown hair that fell roguishly over his eyes. He was handsome, and Selivia's cheeks went as pink as the feather cactus when he pulled up a chair beside hers.

"I knew she wouldn't last," he said.

Selivia blinked. "What?"

"Zala. She's been gone less than a year. I knew she wouldn't make it out there."

"Make it?"

"In the Other Lands." There was a bitter note to his voice. "She thought she was so smart, going off to Rallion City like that."

"Zala *is* smart," Selivia said. She quickly revised her opinion of Ivran. Something in his sneering smile made him terribly unattractive despite his roguish hair. "What's your problem anyway?"

Ivran snorted. "You mean you haven't figured it out?"

"Figured what out?" Selivia asked.

"I bet you think Zala is your friend, don't you?"

"What are you talking about?"

"Ivran!" Zala waved her cousin over and spoke sharply to him for a few minutes. Selivia couldn't hear what they were saying, but

Ivran rolled his eyes and slumped over to a different seat farther away from Selivia. *That was weird.*

Ananova took the chair her son had vacated. Everyone had shifted around and traded seats a dozen times during the meal.

"You must rest from your journey soon," Ananova said. "Did you get enough sleep on the way over?"

"I'm too excited to be tired." Selivia tried to summon her prior enthusiasm, but she felt wrong footed after speaking with Ivran. "I've always wanted to visit the Far Plains."

"You'll love it here," Ananova said. "If you're finished eating, we must see the sunset. It's the best thing about the City of Wind."

"The City of—?"

"You'll understand why we call it that soon. You'll have enough of the wind. And all this sand! I daresay it's the Air's own tribulation sent to teach us patience." Ananova reached out to adjust the scarf over Selivia's hair, the gesture intimate and motherly. "Come. It's almost time."

The older children picked up the plates and cups and took them into the house. Everyone else gathered outside, looking to the west. Families had stepped out of the houses around them too, preparing for the evening ritual.

Selivia and Fenn stood together at the edge of the group. Some of the Far Plainsfolk looked at them curiously, but most kept their faces turned toward the setting sun.

And what a sunset! Low clouds hung in the sky, giving the sun a dramatic canvas on which to splash its glorious colors. The edges of the clouds were feathered with gold and pink, not unlike that delicious rubbery fruit. The centers of the clouds were a deep purple, flirting with indigo farther from the sinking sun. As the brilliant disk slipped downward, the colors morphed and curled along the clouds. A deeper purple-blue seeped slowly across the sky, rolling over their heads and chasing the sun down to its resting place.

Without warning, Selivia burst into tears. She wasn't sure if it was because of the most beautiful sunset she'd ever seen, or because of Ivran's unkindness, or if finding herself in a land so strange and far away had finally caught up to her. She missed her family, and she didn't know when she'd see any of them again. This place was new and beautiful, but she wanted to be back with the people she loved.

Fenn rested a hand on her shoulder. At first, Selivia thought she was giving comfort, but her bodyguard had tears in her eyes too. They glittered like dark diamonds. Selivia patted Fenn's hand, sniffling a bit. At least they had each other.

Zala joined them, perhaps noticing Selivia's tears and Fenn's somber mood. She had something furry tucked into her arms.

"Would you like to hold this little fellow, Sel?"

Selivia reached for the bundle of fur, blinking away her tears. It was a tiny puppy, its fur a shade of vivid yellow. The little creature was fast asleep, and she'd never seen anything more precious. She wrapped her arms around it and buried her nose in its fur.

"I love him," she gasped.

Zala laughed. "I thought you might. Would you like to take care of him for now?"

"Do you even have to ask?" Selivia kissed the little creature as it slept soundly in her arms. "But what is he?"

"A purlendog," Zala said.

"I've only seen them in books." Selivia examined the puppy more closely. It looked like an ordinary dog, apart from the color and the fact that it had ears like a bat. Oh, and three tails. It opened its eyes, blinking at her sleepily. "It's so yellow!"

"It won't be so bright when it's grown up," Zala said. "They start to look more muted and golden around the age when they learn to sing."

"Thank you." Selivia thought she might cry again. She'd always wanted a purlendog. Their voices were supposed to be more beautiful than the calling of thunderbirds. She held the puppy tighter and pulled Zala into the hug too.

The breeze picked up, whispering through her hair, and for a moment, she was sure she heard a voice on the wind. She caught sight of Ivran lurking nearby and thought about asking Zala about what he'd said earlier. But as the purlendog licked her cheek with its soft blue tongue, she resolved not to be consumed by worry. She may be far from her family, but she was sure she was going to like this place. And Zala was definitely her friend, wasn't she?

9

INVITATION

Siv wiped the blood off his blade and strutted across the pentagon to rousing applause. His latest opponent had been as tough as a hungry velgon bear. Siv had leapt onto his back from one of the pen obstacles to pull off the victory. This arena featured a selection of platforms of different heights, some with false floors that could fall at any moment.

The spectators had enjoyed that leaping move. Siv should add it to his repertoire. He still relied on his fists a bit too much. Most people had abandoned the nickname Kres had assigned him. He was becoming known as Siv the Slugger.

He raised his fists to the crowds, and they shouted his name. He enjoyed the attention, the rush of admiration, the way the shouts rumbled through his core. A man could get used to this.

He should probably work on securing cleaner victories, though. Too often, a frantic intensity overtook him when he fought. Sometimes he finished a match and had no idea what had happened. Oh well. Latch would tell him if he made a stupid move. The surly Soolen had taken it upon himself to train with Siv, even though he preferred swords to knives.

Siv finally exited the pen to make way for the next solo match. Dellario the Darting Death was leaning against the barrier, waiting for him. Siv hadn't seen him since their first Dance of Steel a few weeks ago.

"Got another one, eh?" Dellario said.

"Haven't been killed yet," Siv said.

"So I hear. I've heard your name more than once, in fact. You're making an impression on our fair city."

"I'm trying."

A trio of broadsword fighters strolled past, slowing to compliment his performance. Siv accepted their attentions graciously. Dellario watched with interest.

"A friend of mine was asking about you just the other day," he said when they were alone again. "He saw our first Dance together, and he was impressed. He asked me to invite you to a little gathering he's having tomorrow evening."

"A gathering?"

"More of a party, really. At his manor house." Dellario ran a cloth over his rapier with a calculated casualness. "He'd love to meet you."

"He's a lord?" Siv asked.

"A Waterlord." Dellario took a parchment from his coat and held it out with his four-fingered hand. It listed an address in the Garment District. "Khrillin, one of the most powerful Watermight practitioners in Pendark."

Siv accepted the parchment warily. A prominent Waterworker wanted to meet him? Because of his pen fighting?

"You'd do well not to take his interest lightly," Dellario said.

"Will the others from the team be there?"

"Don't worry about the others."

Siv narrowed his eyes. "They're impressive fighters too."

"But *you* are one of Pendark's most exciting up-and-comers." Dellario winked. "Enjoy it."

Siv wondered if this Khrillin fellow knew Wyla. All the Waterworkers seemed to be at odds with each other. Befriending one of Wyla's enemies could be useful. He didn't like the power the woman had over Dara.

"Maybe I can stop by," he said slowly.

"Excellent." Dellario clapped him on the shoulder, apparently taking maybe to mean yes. "See that you dress well. He'll notice."

Siv looked down at his bloodstained coat. He supposed he could spare a bit of his winnings to buy a nicer one, though it would sting. Despite his victories, it was taking longer than Siv expected to put away money. He had to give Kres a portion of his winnings for room and board, and everything in Pendark was expensive. He hadn't ever had to think about coin back in his princely days. Now that he knew what it was like to be poor, he was beginning to understand why Dara questioned the wisdom of his plan. He needed a faster way to raise funds.

He glanced at the address on the parchment. Garment District, eh? A powerful friend could prove even more valuable than an extra bit of coin, especially if this Khrillin might be able to help him rescue Dara from Wyla. Speaking of which . . .

"Any chance I could bring a date?"

"Of course." Dellario grinned. Out in the pen, the announcer called his name. "But the company at Khrillin's parties never disappoints. You wouldn't be lonely."

"Sure. See you there?"

"Oh, I'm always around," Dellario said. "Perhaps you shouldn't mention it to our friend Kres, though." He tipped an imaginary hat and darted into the pen.

Siv tucked the parchment into his pocket. He was surprised his fighting had attracted so much attention. He *was* feeling pretty proud of his knife skills, all things considered. He hadn't won every solo match, but he always put up a good fight, and he'd only had to pay for Watermight healing for major cuts once. Okay, maybe twice. The other pen fighters liked him too. He almost never had to buy his own drinks, which was good because he was saving every coin.

But a powerful friend could prove more useful than a small pile of gold. He'd have to see what this Khrillin was all about.

He was excited to take Dara to a party in any case. He didn't get to see her nearly often enough. He'd been turned away on his last attempt to visit her. Wyla kept her busy—no doubt working on dangerous magical experiments. The sooner he could free her, the better.

Siv's hopes that Dara would be able to sneak out for a drink and a dance were soundly dashed a few hours later when he was turned away at the gates yet again.

"Miss Dara is occupied," the door guard said. "Come back later."

"You say that every time," Siv said.

"They are doing important work. I won't interrupt Lady Wyla, especially not for some grimy vagabond."

"Grimy vagabond?" Siv shifted his arms to hide the worst of the bloodstains on his coat. Okay, maybe it had been a while since he bought new clothes. But he didn't need to take this from one of Wyla's lackeys. "I'll have you know I'm one of the city's most exciting up-and-coming pen fighters."

The guard snorted and muttered something that sounded suspiciously like "Gutter trash."

"Excuse me?" Siv said.

"Get lost," the guard said. "Lady Wyla won't have the likes of you getting filth on her floorboards."

"This is the muddiest city on the damn continent," Siv said. "I can hardly help a bit of dirt on my boots."

The guard dismissed him with a final sniff. This was an entirely new experience for Siv. He didn't think he was spoiled, exactly, but he'd never had anyone look at him as if he were scum while he'd been royalty. Plus, he thought he was popular here. He had his own nickname and everything!

He retreated a few paces and circled the manor, looking for another way in. He hadn't seen Dara in days, and he was tired of waiting for the Waterworker to let her out. Guards clad in green uniforms patrolled the wall around the house. The manor was close enough to trafficked areas that they didn't even glance at the young man in moderately grimy clothing striding alongside it.

The walls were constructed of rough stones, leaving lots of irregular dents and handholds. Siv spotted a promising section with a few larger ledges. He should be able to climb that. It was far enough away from the guards that he had a chance of getting all the way up before anyone spotted him. The only trouble was that this part of the wall rose directly from a canal. The waters of the channel lapped against the rough stone. No wonder the guards weren't watching this section too closely.

Well, nothing for it. Siv waded out to his knees, then his waist, keeping watch lest the guards glance his way. His boots made a too-loud sucking sound with every step. A few people strolled by, but no one looked twice as he eased into the canal. It was deeper than he'd thought. The water level rose above his belt. He'd have to clean and dry his knife as soon as possible. Fortunately, he'd left his sword back at headquarters.

The ledge he'd spotted from farther away was higher above his head than he'd anticipated thanks to the depth of the canal. He jumped a few times and managed to grab it without making too much noise. He pulled himself up, bracing his boots against the slick wall below the waterline. His feet slipped into a gap where water flowed into the manor house grounds through the wall. A heavy grate blocked the entrance. A Waterworker like Wyla would never leave a large opening in her wall unprotected. Siv used the grate to push himself up.

Climbing the wall was tricky, but he scrambled halfway up before running into serious difficulty. Then a rock he planned to use as a handhold broke off at his touch and plunged into the canal with a terrific splash. He reached frantically for another handhold, managing to wedge his fingers into the gap where the rock had been just before losing his balance.

He froze, spread like a burrlinbat against the wall, hoping none of the guards would come to investigate the sound. Slowly, he eased his right boot up to a new position. His arms trembled as he struggled to support his weight on his fingertips, and his breathing grew heavy. He swung his left hand up to another ledge and prepared to move his left leg further up the wall.

"What on earth are you doing?"

Siv flailed, barely managing to put his foot down before he lost his grip entirely.

"Mother of a cullmoran," he swore.

"There's no need to talk like that, Your Majesty. I'm merely curious."

Siv glanced over his shoulder. Vine Silltine stood on the canal bank, looking prim and clean in a Pendarkan dress. Her friend Rid, who had appointed himself her dedicated lackey, stood behind her, gaping at Siv's inelegant position halfway up the wall.

"I'm visiting Dara."

"The manor has a door, you know," Vine said.

"The guards won't let me in," Siv said, trying to keep the strain from his voice. "Is Dara really that busy?"

"Wyla does seem to enjoy her company," Vine said. "They are usually finished by this time of day, though. Dara has been wondering why you haven't come to see her lately."

"I've tried! They won't let me—"

Siv's foot slipped on the wall. This probably wasn't the best time for this conversation.

"Can you get the door guard to let me in?"

"If they've turned you away before, I'm not sure I can sway them," Vine said. "I have very little influence amongst Wyla's people." Vine sounded genuinely confused by that. She was usually great at getting people to do her bidding.

"Climbing it is, then," Siv said. Now that he knew his attempts to visit hadn't been communicated to Dara, he was more determined than ever to get inside. Wyla had no right to keep them apart.

"I'll see to it that the guards don't look this way," Vine said. "The Air is quite limited here, but I ought to be able to coax it to draw their attention elsewhere. If not with the Air, I will find other ways to occupy them."

"Much appreciated," Siv grunted. He resumed his climb, knowing his tenuous grip wouldn't hold him much longer.

Vine and Rid disappeared around the corner, and Siv focused on the wall. Whatever Vine did must have worked, because when he finally heaved himself over the wall, he didn't see any guards on the narrow catwalk at the top. He stopped to catch his breath, surveying the manor house grounds. A stream issued from the wall directly beneath him, fed by the canal outside. It flowed gently through a wild garden of exotic vines and trees. A few buds peeking through the greenery suggested there would be plenty of flowers when spring began in earnest.

A large tree grew beside the wall a few paces on. He quickly scrambled into its branches, afraid Vine wouldn't keep the wall guards occupied for long. A snap split the quiet of the garden. Uh-oh. The branches weren't as strong as he'd thought. He plummeted into a thorny hedge.

When he could tell which way was up again, he lurched out of the brambles, muttering curses far worse than the one Vine had overheard. But he was in.

He crouched low and approached the black stone manor house, which rose like a castle in the center of the garden courtyard. Grotesque statues of ancient sea creatures decorated the eaves. For a moment, Siv swore their eyes glowed silver. He shuddered. This place was damn creepy.

He remembered Dara saying her room looked toward the gulf,

so he snuck around to the southern side of the large manor. Unfortunately, Dara's Waterworker was quite wealthy, and dozens of windows filled this side of the building. After a moment's consideration, he collected a pocketful of rocks and began systematically tossing them at the windows on the top floor and immediately diving out of view. No one responded at the first window. At the second, a serving woman appeared at the glass. Siv hid behind a tree until she left the window. No one came to the third window. At the fourth, his rock struck true, and Dara's face appeared a second later.

Siv stepped out from his hiding place and waved, hoping no one else was looking out of the windows on this side of the house. It had been far too long since he'd seen Dara. The sheer angle of the wall was the only thing that kept him from trying to scale it to reach her at once.

A huge smile split Dara's face the instant she noticed him. It made the whole climb up the wall worth it. Disapproval and maybe exasperation followed the smile, but he didn't care. She was happy to see him.

Dara waved for him to stay where he was and disappeared from the window. Siv settled down behind a wild hedge filled with tiny green buds to wait. A few minutes later, the crunch of gravel announced her arrival. She hurried over to the hedge and sat down so she couldn't be seen from the house.

"What are you doing here?" she demanded.

"Hello to you too."

"I met Vine on my way down the stairs," Dara said. "She saw you climbing the wall. Why didn't you come through the front door?"

"And forgo such a grand romantic gesture? Not a chance. Besides, the door guard wouldn't let me in."

"Did it have anything to do with the fact that you're covered in mud?"

Siv blinked and realized for the first time that water and canal slime coated him from his ribs to his toes. Right. At least some of the bloodstains from his fight earlier in the day had been washed away. Dara had definitely seen him in worse states than this.

"Not only did I scale a wall, but I waded through a canal to see you," Siv said. "I reckon your Waterworker doesn't want to share you."

Dara grimaced. "She has been keeping me busy."

"Well, I want to steal you away for a little while tomorrow night. There's a party at another Waterworker's manor house, and we're invited. What do you say?"

Her eyes narrowed. "Which Waterworker?"

"Khrillin. I don't know anything about him. A pen fighter invited me. Here's the address." He handed her the dampened parchment, relieved that the ink had only run a little.

"The Waterworkers aren't exactly friendly with each other," Dara said. "I'm not sure Wyla would let me go to another one's house."

"So don't tell her."

Dara shot him a look, but he could tell she was tempted. It must bother her that the Waterworker was dictating who she visited after hours.

"What could it hurt?" Siv said. "It's just like a parlor gathering. We probably won't even talk to the Waterworker himself."

Dara frowned down at the parchment. "Why did he invite *you*?"

"Apparently, he's impressed with my fighting. I'm quite impressive these days, you know."

"Yes, Vine told me."

"She's heard of me?" Siv grinned. "I must be more famous than I thought."

"I'm not so sure that's good news," Dara said. "Isn't it only a matter of time before someone recognizes you?"

Siv shrugged. "Vertigon is a long way from Pendark. And my presence here is highly improbable. I doubt anyone would make the connection, *especially* because I'm fighting in the pen."

"Maybe," Dara said. Concern furrowed her brow. Siv reached up and rubbed a thumb across her forehead as if he could wipe away her worries. She looked up at him. Damn, she was cute.

"So how about it?" Siv asked. "The Garment District is within the city boundaries. You deserve a night off."

"All right," Dara said at last. She grinned. "I just won't tell her I'm going out with a pen fighter. Apparently, they're disreputable."

"Yes, we can be a terrible influence on respectable young sorceresses such as yourself." He brushed his hand down her cheek, enjoying the way she leaned into his touch. He accidentally left a smudge of mud on her face, but he didn't think she'd mind.

"How is your work with Wyla going anyway?"

"Not as well as I'd hoped," Dara said. "She says I might be able to use the Watermight, but I haven't made much progress. The most I can do is cup it in my palms for a few seconds longer than a normal person can. She's not pleased."

"Maybe she'll get bored of you and release you from your bargain early."

"I doubt it," Dara said. "I feel more . . . aware of the Watermight every day. I think the potential is there. It's just a matter of figuring out how to actually access it."

"You're getting as eager as Wyla."

"I don't know about that," Dara said. "This is her life's work. Still, the possibilities are intriguing. I wish I were doing better." Her attention drifted away from him, and Siv tugged on her chin to draw her eyes back.

"Just be careful," he said. "I reckon Wyla's more dangerous than all the pen fighters in this city combined."

"You're probably right," Dara said. "Not that you should be taking pen fighting lightly. I'm glad to see you still have both eyes and all your limbs."

"I'm as healthy as a velgon bear on the first day of spring." Siv leaned in for a kiss, deciding to demonstrate what else was still in good working condition. She responded with enthusiasm, arms wrapping around his neck, body pressing close. Kissing Dara was a rush far better than any pen fight. He'd never touch another knife or hear another crowd roar his name if it meant he could kiss her every day.

She pulled away after a little while. "I'd better get back inside." He was pleased to hear that she sounded a bit hazy.

He brushed his lips along her jaw, still not relinquishing his hold on her. "Pick you up tomorrow night?"

"I'll meet you at the nearest bridge at sundown."

"Mmm," he muttered, leaning in again. Her heartbeat quickened beneath his hands. It was impossible not to touch her when they were this close. He couldn't get enough of her.

"Don't wait too long," Dara said the next time her mouth was free. "I might not be able to slip away."

"I'd wait for you all night." He went in for one last kiss. A long one.

Dara finally wriggled out of his arms, standing to brush the dirt and leaves off her skirt at last. She was wearing a poison-green dress in the Pendarkan style. He so rarely got to see her in dresses, and she looked adorable. He almost pulled her down for another kiss.

"You'd better get out of here before you get caught," she said, playfully pushing his hand away.

"One more," he said, feeling a bit hazy himself.

"I'd rather not have to explain this to her."

He sighed. "As you wish." He wanted to do a whole lot more than kiss, but their position hidden behind a hedge in a powerful Waterworker's back garden wasn't ideal. Plus, he was covered in muddy canal water, and he might not smell that great after a day of trying not to get skewered in the pen.

"See you tomorrow at sundown."

10

THE PARTY

Dara got to the bridge later than planned the following evening. Wyla had kept her longer than usual, and Vine had insisted on fixing her hair. Then she'd had to stop and chat with Rid in the entryway. He'd been doing odd jobs for Vine, but he often seemed lost in this large, foreign city. Fortunately, he didn't comment on Dara's festive attire.

Vine had procured the dress. She'd heard about the fanciful parties at Khrillin's manor in the Garment District, and she knew Dara's ordinary outfits wouldn't be appropriate. She traded two of the uniform-like dresses Wyla had given them to pay for Dara's party dress.

"I'm going to trade it back in the morning, so do try not to spill anything on it," she said when she handed over the gown.

"As long as no one tries to stab me, it should be fine."

Vine sighed. "Don't jinx yourself, Dara, especially given the winter we've had."

"I'll do my best to remain safely anonymous and unstabbed."

She really would hate to mess up the dress. She'd never seen its like. The bloodred dress ended just below the knee in the Pendarkan fashion. It had a deeper neckline than Dara ordinarily wore, and multiple petticoats made the skirt flare out from her waist and swish around her legs when she walked. Her golden hair flowed loose over her shoulders in waves, with a single section braided across her head. It all felt incredibly decadent. Dara feared the red gown would draw too much attention, but Vine assured her she'd fit right in.

Vine herself was positively bubbling with envy over the occasion to dress up, but when Dara had suggested she come along, Vine waved her off.

"I have a new lead on Lord Vex. I plan to do some reconnaissance tonight."

She had found no link between the mysterious Waterworker and Lord Vex. Dara wouldn't like to run into a sword-wielding Rollendar tonight, especially in a dress she couldn't afford to stain with blood.

"Are you sure you'll be safe?"

"I'll have Rid with me," Vine said. "Besides, I don't want to get in the way of your alone time with a certain handsome young man."

Dara finally escaped the manor and strode toward the bridge alone. She'd made the difficult decision to leave her Savven blade behind lest it draw unwanted attention. She had concealed several small Firebulbs in a pouch attached to her belt in case she needed to defend herself or Siv. In truth, she was hoping for a night off from magic and weapons and intrigue.

Siv was leaning against the railing when she reached the bridge at last, wearing a fine gray coat trimmed with black thread. *He* carried a sword, but then he had been invited because he was a popular pen fighter. He'd be expected to sport a bit of steel. His companion for the night wouldn't have the same excuse.

Siv noticed her striding toward him when she was about ten paces away. He stood bolt upright, and the blood drained from his face. Dara whirled around, her hand going to the Fire at her waist. She couldn't see any threats coming up behind her. What had made him react like that? When she turned back, Siv wore a strange grin.

"What is it?" Dara said quickly. "Did you see something?" She scanned the street behind her again but saw no sign of trouble.

"Just you," Siv said hoarsely.

"Huh?"

"Burning Firelord, Dara Ruminor, have you seen yourself?"

"What are talking about?"

"Where did you get that *dress*?"

"Oh. Vine found it." Dara brushed her fingers over the

bloodred fabric. "She said it would help me fit in at the party. I don't want to draw unnecessary attention."

"Vine Silltine has funny ideas about what blending in means," Siv muttered. He fell silent, and a good thirty seconds passed before he seemed to realize he was staring directly at her neckline. She supposed it *was* rather deep. He cleared his throat elaborately and offered her his arm. "My lady?"

Dara looped her arm in his, grinning.

"You look nice," she said. "New coat?"

"I found it in a secondhand shop on the outskirts of the Garment District. Need to look the part of an up-and-coming pen fighter. I also walked by the manor house we're visiting tonight. It's even bigger than Wyla's."

"Sounds like it'll be quite the party."

"I certainly hope so." Siv smiled down at her, and nearly walked into a mud puddle in his freshly shined boots before Dara reminded him to watch where he was going.

"You'd better stay alert tonight," she said.

"I will. And I won't drink too much, if you're worried about that," Siv said. "Don't need to with you on my arm."

Dara smiled in spite of herself. If she'd known it would have this effect on him, she'd have bought a red Pendarkan dress a lot sooner.

The Market District separated Wyla's domain from Khrillin's Garment District. They paid a few coppers to take a canal boat from the edge of Wyla's territory. Siv insisted on helping Dara into the flat-bottomed boat. It was crowded at this time of the evening, and they squished together on a bench in the bow. Two men propelled the boat forward with long darkwood poles.

A strong wind blew over the city from the Black Gulf, carrying the salt smells of the sea and the swampy aroma of the canals. Murky brown water slid beneath them. Once, a strange creature poked a multi-eyed head out of the water. It disappeared again before Dara could get a good look.

The city had once been a natural river delta. Dozens of little islands had been carved up and divided many times over the years. Canals and bridges created a maze of pathways amongst the districts. Flags representing whichever Waterworker held the power helped to distinguish each region.

"I've heard some boats use Watermight to go faster," Siv said. "Their operators charge a premium."

"I can imagine," Dara said. "The Waterworkers don't do as much practical Work as we do in Vertigon. They use their power sparingly."

"Zage used to say that was the problem with having it all concentrated with only a few Waterworkers," Siv said. "They get greedy and jealous."

"And violent," Dara said.

"Let's hope we don't have to see any of that before we get out of here."

Dara didn't answer. She appreciated that Siv wanted to free her from Wyla's service early, but the more she got to know the woman, the more she doubted that would be possible. And Wyla still hadn't decided how Dara was to repay her for that Watermight-assisted wave. Dara suspected Wyla was waiting until she knew whether or not her theories were correct before exacting her final price.

Tonight, Dara intended to forget all about that. She tucked her arm under Siv's and leaned her head on his shoulder, enjoying the sights and sounds of the Pendarkan evening. He rested his cheek on her head, his breath ruffling her hair.

The canal boat soon left Wyla's poison-green Jewel District and meandered amongst the fluttering red flags of the Market District. The main island boasted a lively bazaar selling food and imported goods for the residents of the city. The district was mostly for local commerce. The vast warehouses storing goods bound for northern lands were located in the port districts closer to the sea.

In addition to the main island, barges carried floating markets through the canals of the Market District. Hundreds of lights swung from their decks, and clusters of smaller boats surrounded them like litters of nursing cur-dragons. Their boat barely squeezed past, the operators directing it with much swearing and bluster.

They made it past the traffic jam around the market barges and continued through the waterlogged city. They were traveling northwest, away from the coast. A group of taller towers Dara hadn't had a chance to investigate rose in the distance. Lights burned from windows at the very top like candle flames.

"That's the Royal District," Siv said. "The King of Pendark lives in the tallest tower."

Dara sat up, leaning around Siv to get a better look. "He doesn't have much power here, right?"

"He's not a Waterworker. His district has more tall buildings, but it isn't any bigger than the others. His territory looks more impressive than it is." Siv frowned, watching the towers in the fading light. "He keeps the peace as well as he can, I guess."

"Do you miss being king?" Dara asked, careful to keep her voice down so the other passengers wouldn't hear.

"No . . . or at least, I don't think so. I liked some things about it, I'm not going to lie, but it was a lot of responsibility." Siv took her hand, running his thumb along her skin. "I've picked up a different combination of responsibilities out here in the Lands Below. But I miss Vertigon."

"Me too."

They fell silent, holding hands and gliding onward as night fell. Dara knew Siv couldn't let his kingdom go. For all his efforts to step away and start a new life, it was still his mountain, and he had a responsibility to get back to it.

Dara remembered what Vine had said the other day. Would Siv make her his queen if he regained his throne? She wasn't sure how she felt about that. She wished they could stay like this: a normal couple who could ride a boat to a party without worrying that someone would kill them. Despite Lord Vex's presence in Pendark and her obligations to Wyla, she felt safer here than she had in a long time.

Red flags gave way to the midnight blue of the Garment District. A jumble of stalls selling secondhand or cheap clothing lined the outskirts. Farther in, the shops became finer and the streets and canals more sparsely populated. Tailors with quilted fabric signs advertising their services surrounded the inlet where the boat finally bumped against a dock. Siv and Dara scrambled over their nearest seatmates to disembark onto a large island.

They walked up the main street, leaving the tailors behind, and entered a residential area. Dara guessed the well-to-do garment merchants lived here. The ground sloped steadily upward, and the streets quickly became less muddy.

A woman carrying spools of thread on her back pointed them toward Khrillin's manor. They turned a corner as instructed and could no longer see any water around them. That was unusual. Most Watermight practitioners preferred to live near the shore of whatever waterways they controlled, but Khrillin had built his house as near to the center of his island as he could manage.

"Should be just around this corner," Siv said. "I recognize that green house . . . Ah. Here we are."

The manor rose before them at last. Dozens of lights glittered around the outer walls. The flickering quality of the light indicated torches of flame rather than Vertigonian Firelights. That was unfortunate. Dara would have to rely on the power in the Firebulbs in her pouch if they got into trouble.

Perhaps Siv was thinking of danger too, because he pulled her a little closer as they strode up to the gates. They were solid bronze, and the flickering torchlight made the bronze look almost like gold. He raised a hand to knock, but the door swung open before he touched it.

"Welcome to the home of the Waterlord Khrillin. Your name, please?"

"I am Sivren Amen, the pen fighter."

The door guard looked over a piece of parchment scrawled with names. Dara shifted her feet, preparing to reach for a weapon.

Siv cleared his throat. "Uh, Dellario Darting said I was—"

"Ah, here you are. Sivren Amen and a guest. Very good, sir. Please proceed to the house."

"Thank you."

Dara let out the breath she'd been holding. The guard didn't ask for her name as he waved them toward the house. Wyla hadn't specifically told her not to interact with any other Waterworkers, but she'd rather not have her attendance on record.

They strode up a crushed gravel path toward the house. Khrillin's courtyard was carefully manicured, a marked contrast to Wyla's wild garden. The hedges and pathways looked almost too perfect. The front doors of the house stood open, and music and laughter drifted out into the night. Torchlight lit the scene, casting ethereal shadows across the path.

People strolled through the garden and milled around the front doors, clad in fine coats and bright dresses in a hundred colors. Vine had been correct about the red dress helping Dara blend in with the other guests. One or two men might have glanced twice at her, but with Siv holding her tight, they soon looked away.

Most of the guests were young, exceptionally beautiful, and well dressed. The few older, uglier men in attendance had clusters of attractive younger people gathered around them, sipping wine from crystal goblets and laughing at their jokes. The men smoked long pipes, and a halo of smoke lingered above the garden.

The entryway of the manor house featured a grand fountain constructed entirely of glass. The crystalline shapes sent multihued light dancing across the entryway. Flickers of Watermight flowed through the stream like a cascade of diamonds. Dara wondered if the Waterlord himself controlled the flow, or if he employed lesser Waterworkers to create the spectacle. She trailed her fingers in the water as she passed, trying to draw some of the Watermight to her hands. She caught a hint of movement in her direction. Then she noticed the other people gathered to admire the fountain didn't dare touch the water. They watched her warily until she pulled her hands out of the fountain and dried them surreptitiously on her skirt.

Music floating from a corridor on the opposite side of the entrance hall drew the partygoers further into the house. They glided toward it as if called by a siren.

"There are more people than I expected," Dara said.

"Me too," Siv said. "This is enough people for a royal feast."

They paused partway down the corridor, where a group of women wearing wide, colorful skirts blocked their way.

"Do you see your friend anywhere?" Dara asked.

"Not yet. Let's go in and see if we can find some food."

They squeezed past the women and reached a pair of double doors halfway along the corridor, which opened into a grand dancing hall. The room was smaller than the Great Hall in Vertigon, but more people packed into it than Dara had ever seen at a royal feast. The atmosphere was less formal too. Instead of sitting at banquet tables, everyone stood, danced, or leaned on tall, round tables arrayed around the edges of the hall. Glass candlesticks lit the space, enhanced by the fanciful attire of the couples whirling past.

Serving girls carried trays of drinks and bite-size foods through the crowds. They were all dressed in wispy fabrics that made them look like fairies, or perhaps sea sprites, further evidence that spring was starting to warm the city. One of the girls, whose shimmering dress was a glistening hue that made Dara think of mist at twilight, glided up to them as they lingered by the doors.

"May I offer you a soldarberry tart?" she said. "It's a rare delicacy imported all the way from Vertigon Mountain."

Dara and Siv grinned at each other as they each took one of the treats and thanked the serving girl. The familiar burst of sweetness on her tongue made Dara think of home.

The serving girl was still standing beside them, shifting from foot to foot in her dainty slippers. "Excuse me." She blushed bright red, making her look younger than she had appeared at first. "Are . . . are you Siv the Slugger?"

Siv blinked, and Dara was sure he puffed out his chest. "Why yes, I am."

"I saw your fight against the Blade from Bell Coast," the girl said. "I thought for sure you were going to lose."

"Uh, thank you."

"But then you broke his nose!" the girl said. "It was brilliant. All that blood."

"Right, yeah." Siv tugged on the collar of his new coat.

The girl grinned at him for a moment. Then she gave Dara a quick look up and down and turned to glide back into the crowd with her platter of soldarberry tarts. "Enjoy the party."

"These Pendarkans sure like blood, don't they?" Siv said. He waved at another server, a muscular woman carrying a heavy tray of drinks.

"Did you really break someone's nose?" Dara asked as she accepted a goblet of wine. She didn't like wine, but having a drink in her hand would help her blend in with the guests.

"I barely remember that fight, to be honest. When I'm in the pen, it's like something takes over me. Turns out that something really likes to punch people."

Dara raised an eyebrow. "Aren't you supposed to be a knife fighter?"

"It's easier to subdue your opponent with a knife if you knock them cold first. Besides, this way I haven't had to kill anyone."

"At all?"

"Not in the pen." Siv rolled his shoulders. "I've done enough killing defending myself and my friends over the past few months. I don't much like the idea of slaughtering people for gold."

"But if it comes down to it, you'd kill rather than be killed, right?"

"I guess so." Siv frowned into his goblet. "When you're in the thick of things, it's hard to stop."

Dara touched his hand to show she understood. She thought of how it felt to hold the Fire, to draw in torrents of power, to never want to let go. It was harder to stop, the more power she held. Everything was more complicated for both of them than it had been back when they used to practice their dueling together. She missed those days sometimes.

"Friends, friends. Why so serious? This is a party!"

Dara started as a man strode up to them and dropped a bejeweled hand on Siv's shoulder with a thump. He was clad in white from head to toe, and he had a large, luxurious beard, with tiny jewels woven into it on fine wires of silver.

"No one comes to the home of Khrillin the Waterlord to have serious, sober conversations," the man boomed.

"You must be the man himself," Siv said.

"Guilty." He shrugged his broad, white-clad shoulders. "And *you* are Siv the Slugger. Glad you could make it."

"Thank you for the invitation," Siv said. "This is Dar—"

Dara shot him a quick look.

"Darlanna," Siv said.

"A pleasure." The Waterlord clasped Dara's hand, his grip firm and slightly sweaty. "I adore your dress."

"Thank you." Dara extracted her hand from his and dropped into a brief curtsy, hoping he wouldn't be able to sense the Work Wyla had wrought on her arm to confirm their bargain. If he noticed, he didn't let on.

"Come, come, have another drink, friends." Khrillin waved for a nymph-like servant, though their goblets were still full. "I must go greet more of my guests. We'll talk later." He clapped Siv on the shoulder again and strode away.

Dara turned to Siv as soon as he was gone. "Darlanna?"

"Sorry." He grimaced. "Had to think fast."

"Could be worse. So that was the Waterlord?"

"Seems like a sociable fellow." Siv stared after him for a moment. Then he turned back to her with a sly grin. "I know you're not going to drink that wine. What do you say we abandon these goblets and have a dance?"

Siv set both of their drinks on one of the small, round tables and pulled Dara out to the crowded dance floor. He looped an arm around her waist, pulling her close to him. She didn't know the dance, and it quickly became clear that Siv didn't either. The music was fast, and the moves were energetic, involving a lot of bouncing and spinning. The wide-skirted Pendarkan party dresses turned the dance floor into a constant whirl of colorful pinwheels.

They tried a few spins, imitating the other couples as well as they could. Dara whirled a little too fast and nearly knocked Siv over when she spun back into him. He caught her before she could spin away again, and didn't let go.

They abandoned all attempts to get the steps right.

Siv held her close against his chest, not bothering to sway in time with the music. She leaned into him, pressing her face into the side of his neck, breathing him in. He ran his fingers through her long, loose hair.

"Do you remember our first dance?" he said softly.

"The Cup Feast. How could I forget?"

"I was going to tell you I loved you then," he said. "That long ago, and I was sure of it."

"But I stormed away."

Siv chuckled, pressing his face into her hair. "I could have done a better job of communicating." He was silent for a moment. The music changed, slowing to match their pace as they turned slowly across the floor. "I'm glad I got to introduce you to my father."

Dara lifted her head and met his eyes. He looked grave and proud. Like a king.

"He was a good man," she said. "And so are you."

Siv frowned, a shadow crossing his face. "Not yet. But I think I can become one."

Dara tugged on his beard and drew his face down to hers. They kissed right there in the middle of the crowd, and the other revelers paid them no attention. Dara wished they could do this forever: dance and kiss and dare the world to bother them.

It felt indulgent. It felt like stolen time, to dance, to be together, to enjoy each other's company.

It felt too good to be true—so Dara almost wasn't surprised when her arm went as cold as ice.

"Uh-oh." She stopped, waiting for the feeling to subside.

"What is it?"

"It's Wyla again. She wants me back."

"Now?" Siv said. "We just got here."

"It has been more than an hour."

"There's no way time has gone by that quickly."

"I'd better head back to the manor," Dara said, disentangling herself from Siv's arms. "She must know where I am."

Siv caught her right hand in both of his and held it gently, as if he could draw Wyla's power from it with his touch. Even his warmth did nothing to thaw the cold of the Watermight bond.

"She can't keep doing this to you," he said.

"It'll be over in a few months."

"I'll get you away from her." He held her arm almost reverently. She'd noticed he did that sometimes, as if swearing a sacred vow on her flesh and bone. "Maybe another Waterworker—"

"I can't make her angry," Dara said. "I'm sorry. I should go."

Siv released her arm at last. "I might stick around for a few minutes," he said. "I want to find out why Khrillin invited me."

"It's not safe to leave you alone," Dara said. "I'd better stay to guard—"

"Dara," Siv said with a chuckle. "You're not my guard anymore, remember? I can take care of myself."

"But—"

"You can't watch out for me all the time." He glanced around the crowd of revelers. "Besides, I might make a friend or two here. A powerful friend."

Dara hesitated. "Vine always says that's important."

"Vine is wise. I'll see if I can find out more about Wyla from someone who isn't in her camp too."

It was hard to get used to the idea that Siv didn't need her protection—any more than she needed his, at any rate. They looked out for each other now, and she needed to trust him. "Just be careful," she said. "You don't want Khrillin to think you're Wyla's spy."

"I'll be as stealthy as a marrkrat." Siv escorted her toward the corridor, arm tight around her waist. "Unless you want me to walk you home?"

"No, you're right. You should learn what you can from Khrillin."

Siv leaned in and kissed her gently. "When can I see you again?"

"I'll send word through Vine or Rid. Don't go climbing around the manor house anymore."

"Yes, ma'am. And maybe sometime you can come see me fight."

"I'd like that." Dara stood on her toes to kiss his cheek. "See you soon."

She hurried out of the manor house as another icy wave swept through her arm. Wyla didn't like to be kept waiting.

11

THE WATERLORD

Siv watched Dara go, disappointment curling through him. He hated that she had to jump whenever Wyla threatened her with that arm-curse thing. And he hated that he was powerless to help her.

He looked around the opulent ballroom, with its crystal candlesticks and finely dressed guests. He wondered if any of them would be willing to sponsor him somehow until he earned enough gold to free her. Vertigonian duelists always got patrons to support their training. Maybe it was time the practice caught on in the Steel Pentagons of Pendark.

He meandered through the crowd, taking little notice of the colorful gowns swirling around him. None of these women could compare to Dara. He had nearly fainted when she strode up to him in that red dress, looking as ready for battle as ever. He had seen people staring at her, and he wasn't sure she even realized it. He felt like the luckiest man alive to be the one who'd gotten to dance with her all night. Or at least for part of the night.

The party didn't feel nearly as lavish without her there. He had stayed behind hoping he could get Khrillin to do something about Wyla's bond, but the man was no doubt busy entertaining his many quests. Maybe he should wait for a different opportunity to speak with him. There was still time to catch up with Dara before she boarded the canal boat.

As he turned for the door, he spotted a familiar profile through the crowd. A man of around forty with sandy-blond hair was leaning against one of the tall tables. He wore a fine red coat, and he was scanning the crowd as if looking for someone. Vex Rollendar.

Siv dove behind a nearby candelabrum. It was made of glass. *That's not helpful.* Vex's gaze swept his way. He retreated behind a group of somewhat inebriated women, who gathered in a circle toasting each other with crystal goblets. They turned to look at him, giggling madly.

He needed to get out of here. Vex's table was near the double doors. Could he sneak by in the crowd? He didn't think Vex would try anything at someone else's party. In fact, the man looked a little gray in the face. He had taken a nasty gut wound during the fight at headquarters. He must still be recovering. But he could have allies here, and Siv wasn't interested in facing them alone.

He darted through the crowd, dodging from group to group as inconspicuously as possible. He spotted Dellario across the room—too far away to be of any assistance. If anything, he might call attention to Siv's presence.

He eased closer to the doors and glanced back at the standing table. Vex was no longer there. *Damn.* The fellow was more slippery than a panviper. He broke into a jog, hand resting on his sword hilt. Almost there.

He burst through the doors into the corridor and turned for the exit. A white-clad figure stepped into his path.

"Ah, Siv the Slugger," Khrillin said. "What happened to your pretty companion?"

"She had to leave early," Siv said, trying to look as though he weren't running away.

"Shame, shame," Khrillin said. "I was about to retire to my study for a nip of my finest brandy. Care to join me?"

Siv looked around furtively. There was no sign of that sandy-blond head in the corridor. Where was Vex? Had he seen Siv trying to leave? He could be waiting to pounce the moment he stepped outside.

Khrillin cleared his throat impatiently. Siv started. It might be wise to lie low in the Waterlord's study for a few minutes. At least he'd get some decent brandy out of it.

"I'd love a drink," he said. "Thank you."

Siv followed the Waterlord as he wove among the guests lingering in the corridor, stopping often to press hands and compliment outfits. He introduced Siv to a few people, praising his recent triumphs in the Steel Pentagon. The Waterlord reminded Siv of Lady Atria. She loved to collect influential people: lords and ladies, Fireworkers, tradesmen, even the occasional duelist. Khrillin must have identified Siv as a potential jewel to add to his glittering crown of friends. Still, he wished they'd move a little faster. Vex could still catch him.

At last Khrillin led the way up a broad staircase at the back of the house to the second floor. A couple canoodling on the stairs shifted out of their way as they rounded a bend at the top. Siv wished Dara had been able to stay longer. He wouldn't have minded finding a staircase on which to canoodle. That red dress . . .

Wrapped up in thoughts of Dara, it didn't occur to Siv that it might be a bad idea to enter a room alone with this stranger until the door clicked shut behind him. He reached for his sword hilt, but Khrillin simply strode over to a massive darkwood desk. He waved for Siv to sit and poured them each a glass of amber brandy from a decanter on the desk. He pushed one of the crystal glasses over to Siv and raised the other.

"To our new friendship."

"Thanks for inviting me to your party." Siv took a sip of the brandy, which was every bit as fine as Khrillin had promised.

"My pleasure," the Waterlord said. "Now, I am a frightfully curious soul. Do tell me what it was like to be the King of Vertigon."

Siv choked. The brandy burned like Fire as it came out of his nostrils.

"I don't know what you're talking about," he spluttered.

"Come now, there's no need to play games." Khrillin smiled. "We're going to be great friends, you and I."

Siv's hand went to his blade. The Waterlord shook his head and made a tutting sound. "There's no need for that. I have skilled fighters waiting to cut you down if you lift a finger against me. You're a good fighter, but not *that* good, Your Highness. I suggest you don't risk it."

"What do you want?" Siv didn't let go of his sword hilt.

"To be friends, of course."

"Friends."

"Indeed. Friends who help each other." Khrillin sipped his brandy placidly. "I believe you and I can have a mutually beneficial relationship. If you are interested, that is."

"How did you find out about me?"

"I have my sources."

Siv frowned, wondering if Vex Rollendar was to blame. Could he have ingratiated himself with one of the most powerful Waterworkers in the city that quickly? Siv was glad Dara had left when she did. But if Vex was involved, why wasn't Siv already dead?

"What do you say?" Khrillin prompted. "Shall we be friends?"

"That depends."

"On?"

"Whether we actually have mutually beneficial interests. That's a requirement for friendship, wouldn't you say?"

"Indeed." Khrillin raised his empty glass. "Another brandy?"

Siv tossed back his remaining portion and held his glass out for another. The man clearly wanted something from him. He wouldn't poison Siv now. Besides, it was good brandy.

"Before we begin," Khrillin said, "could you clarify whether you are trying to get yourself killed in the Steel Pentagon? Our friendship will be short if you die."

"Uh, I wasn't planning on it," Siv said.

"Good, good." The Waterlord sipped from his own brandy and put his white leather boots up on his desk. "And you intend to return to Vertigon to reclaim your throne?"

Siv didn't much care about his throne. He was tempted to extract Sora from Vertigon and leave the place in the Lantern Maker's hands for good. But he had to make things right somehow—and he had a feeling this fellow was in it for the friendship of a once and future king.

"I have to return to Vertigon."

A hungry gleam flickered in the Waterlord's eyes. "Then I think our interests align. I'm still not certain why you are fighting in the pen, though, if it isn't some dramatic suicide plan. Perhaps you can enlighten me."

"My interests," Siv said, "require a fair bit of gold. This seemed like the best way to get it."

Khrillin burst out laughing. "You're doing it for the money? Oh, I like you!"

Siv cleared his throat. "Well, I would consider other means, if the exchange was fair."

The Waterlord looked pleased. "I believe research is in order before I officially back your endeavor, but consider me interested. As we get to know each other, we can discuss what form my aid might take."

"Fair enough," Siv said. "I'd better do some research of my own." He sipped his brandy, meeting Khrillin's eyes steadily. He wouldn't accept a copper from the Waterlord until he found out what it would cost him. Still, this felt like a fortuitous meeting. He kind of liked the man. Khrillin was about as trustworthy as a povvercat in a chicken coop, but he liked him.

"Shall we return to the party?" Khrillin said. "I can introduce you to another lady or two now that your companion has departed."

"Actually, I have a big training day planned tomorrow. Thanks for the brandy."

"My pleasure. I'll be in touch soon so we can discuss our future together in more detail. I look forward to our friendship."

"As do I."

Siv stood and strode for the door. His hand had just touched the knob when the Waterlord spoke again.

"One more thing, Your Highness. I don't want to hear that you've been seeking other alliances behind my back. I might have to let your little secret slip. Some of the other powers in this city would not be interested in friendship if they learned of your presence here."

"Understood," Siv said. "Anonymity suits me for the moment."

"I thought it might. And be wary of the Waterworkers. All of them."

Siv looked back at Khrillin. He hadn't moved from his desk, but beads of silver-white light had appeared at his fingertips.

"I'll keep that in mind."

The Waterlord smiled.

Siv left the manor house as quickly as he could without running—and without accidently bumping into Vex Rollendar. He had been afraid the Waterlord would put some sort of bargain spell on him as Wyla had done to Dara. He'd have to be careful not to cross Khrillin. The next Waterworker who cornered him might not let him walk away so easily.

12

FIRE AND WATER

Dara ran all the way back to the manor. Cold shot through her arm twice more on her journey, as if to prompt her to hurry. By the time she reached Wyla's district, her arm felt as if it might freeze solid and break off.

Siln was waiting for her at the manor door, a grim expression on his face.

"She is in her study," he said.

"Is she mad?"

Siln gave a dry laugh. "I would hurry if I were you."

Dara gritted her teeth and darted up the stairs, wishing she were wearing anything but a bloodred party dress. The door creaked as she entered Wyla's study. Most of the Fire Lanterns had been covered up, and the room was cloaked in shadow. Dara didn't see Wyla until she was halfway across the room.

The Waterworker was waiting beside the window, staring into the inky night.

"I'm here," Dara said. "You never told me I couldn't go out at night. If you'd given me clearer instructions, you wouldn't have to—"

"Silence!" Wyla whirled toward her, and Dara stopped dead. Wyla's eyes were solid silver, as if Watermight had filled her up and coated them completely. Her olive skin seemed to boil with the power bubbling beneath it.

"You were not simply *out*," Wyla hissed. "You went to the home of Khrillin the Waterlord."

There was no point in denying it. Dara wasn't sure if she had been followed or if Wyla could sense her exact location through her arm, but she knew better than to lie.

"Khrillin is my greatest rival," Wyla said. The anger in her voice was like a living thing, dark and solid. "Did you think you could take what you have learned of me and use it to buy favor with my enemies?"

"It wasn't like that," Dara said.

"I've experienced treachery in my day," Wyla said, "but I thought you were smarter than that. I never dreamed you would risk the use of your sword arm. I will show you what it means to betray me."

"Wait!" Dara stumbled backward as Wyla raised her hands and her fingertips began to glow. "It was just a party! My friend invited me to a party! I didn't know—"

Watermight erupted from Wyla's fingertips and streaked toward Dara. The power flew like an arrow directly toward her heart.

Dara didn't have time to think. She sucked the Fire from the Firebulb in her belt pouch and flung it up in front of her, forming it into a rough shield. The Watermight streams struck the shield, and white light exploded outward, followed by a shockwave strong enough to knock Dara back a step.

Wyla hissed in anger and sent a second volley of Watermight at her. Desperately, Dara threw up both hands to block it.

The silvery substance struck Dara's palms, stinging like needles. She gasped but kept her hands raised, trying to stop the needles from driving into her body. Both hands went cold and numb.

But the chill didn't progress any further than her palms. Sweat broke out on Dara's forehead as she pushed against what felt like a mountain's worth of pressure, sure her wrists would break.

The Watermight attack ceased. Dara kept her hands up in case Wyla tried again. The numbness hadn't abated, and she realized with a start that her fingernails were glowing silver-white.

"How are you doing that?" Wyla demanded.

"I don't know. I needed you to listen. It was just a party that I—"

"I don't care about the party." Wyla stepped closer, the anger gone from her eyes as if it had never been there. "Pay attention to what you are feeling. Describe it to me."

"Uh, I feel numb. It's only in my hands. I was trying to keep the needles of Watermight from entering my body."

"Needles? Interesting. Tell me more."

Dara answered automatically, feeling as if she were speaking through a fog. "I'm pushing against something, something as solid as a brick wall. It's not like the Fire. The Fire flows into me. It moves underneath my skin. This is like my muscles have turned to ice."

"Hold onto that feeling as long as you can." Wyla yanked the cover off the nearest Fire Lantern and bent down to scribble notes on a piece of parchment. "What were your emotions? You wanted to defend yourself?"

"Yes, and it wasn't fair. I didn't go to that manor to see the Waterlord. I wanted to spend a little time with my friend. I wasn't betraying you."

"And you felt my accusations were unjust?"

"Yes."

"Fascinating." Wyla scribbled gleefully. "Give me more."

"I don't know. I wasn't thinking that much. Wait, something's happening." The silver glow drained from Dara's fingertips, and silvery droplets of Watermight fell from her hands and sprinkled onto the floorboards at her feet.

"It's normal for it to slip away like that when you are first learning," Wyla said. "You just held Watermight, child. Do you know what this means?"

"I'm not in trouble for going out?"

Wyla barked a laugh. "I believe you didn't intend to betray me. You wouldn't have felt such righteous indignation otherwise. But you are lucky Khrillin did not know who you are. You were in danger in that house as one of my associates. I don't want you to return, or to socialize with any of his people. Is that understood?"

"Yes, ma'am." Dara hesitated, wondering if Siv counted as one of the Waterlord's people. "What about my friend?"

"This is the young man you came to Pendark to help?"

"Yes."

Wyla considered for a moment. Her expression didn't reveal anything of her thoughts. At last, she said, "He would do well to stay far away from the Waterlord too."

"I'll warn him," Dara said.

"Fine. You may return to your room. Contemplate your feelings when you caught the Watermight. I want you to capture that sensation in your memory so it will be easier to replicate. We will continue our work first thing in the morning."

Wyla strode toward the door, summoning a silvery globe of Watermight to light her way. She paused once to write down a few notes before tucking her parchment under her elbow and disappearing from view. Her fury from moments ago had vanished, dissipating faster than steam. Dara wondered if the anger had been real at all or if it was a pretext to attack her. In any case, it was an important reminder of the dangers of crossing Wyla. She shouldn't have taken the risk tonight.

Still breathing heavily from the encounter, she looked up at the Fire Lantern hanging above her. It was a Ruminor, the one depicting a Waterworker wrought in Firegold. Had she truly done it? Had she absorbed a second magical substance without damage?

She had used up all the Fire in her shield by the time she blocked the Watermight with her hands, so she hadn't wielded the two substances at once. But Wyla had been right.

A few splashes of Watermight lingered on the floor, glimmering like tiny stars. Dara crouched down, careful not to let her scarlet hem drag in the substance. She reached out to touch the power, and it clung to her fingertip, as if it were nothing more than water. Whatever mindset she'd been in when Wyla attacked her was gone now. But it was replaced with a sense of wonder. She could do it. No matter how much work it took, she was going to figure out how to take this new power—and Wield.

A week after Khrillin's party, Dara stood across the Watermight pool from Wyla yet again. Since the breakthrough that night, they had spent nearly every waking moment together. Wyla approached her research with gleeful intensity. Dara had to admire the woman's dedication. The challenge fascinated her too. For the first time since leaving Vertigon, she felt as if her power was increasing. And it was happening because of Watermight, a substance that had been as distant as a fairy tale a few months ago.

Flickering silver-white light illuminated the chamber deep beneath the manor house. The pool swirled steadily between them, the constant churn keeping the power within Wyla's control.

"Let us try again," Wyla said. "Are you ready?"

Dara rolled her shoulders and prepared herself for another attack. Attempting to wield Watermight took a lot of concentration, and it left her body as exhausted as her mind. Wyla had been right about how her dedication to dueling made her well suited for this task, if only because it required so much physical endurance.

She braced herself, waiting for the icy needles of power to assault her skin. Wyla had tried all manner of Watermight attacks in an effort to provoke the same response Dara had produced almost unconsciously the night of the party. Letting the power into her body required an exceedingly delicate balance. The Watermight didn't flow easily within her like the Fire, and she had to fight against the instincts she'd already developed in her Fireworking practice.

She barely had time to summon the memory of what she'd been feeling that night before Wyla struck. The power attacked her like a wave, rising up from the pool in a glowing torrent. Real water mixed in with the Watermight and drenched Dara's clothes as the wave broke over her head. The power slithered over her skin and dripped back into the whirlpool before she could grab hold of it.

"What do you feel?" Wyla demanded as the last of the Watermight dripped away.

"Frustrated," Dara said.

"Good," Wyla said. "Again."

She poured wave after wave over Dara's head. Each time, the power trailed over her skin, tantalizingly close. She could sense the strength, the way it hummed with an intensity that was at once familiar and alien. It wasn't the Fire, and it didn't fill her with the same thrill or the same warmth, but she recognized the potency of it. If only she could pull it in, bend it to her will.

"You are thinking too hard," Wyla said as the latest wave dripped away. Dara felt cold, even though the effort kept her blood flowing. She wished she'd brought a Firebulb down here to warm her chilled bones, but Wyla wanted her to immerse herself in the Watermight alone before they tried combining the powers.

"Let your emotions loose," Wyla said. "Get angry if you must. Imagine running me through with a sword. Use the intensity of your feelings."

"It's not that easy to fake my feelings," Dara said.

"I never said this would be easy," Wyla said. "You must work harder. I won't let your laziness keep me from proving my theory."

A hot flash of anger rushed through Dara. "I'm not laz—"

Wyla struck. Cords of power rose from the pool and shot toward Dara's chest like vipers. She threw her hands up, and the Watermight pierced them. The stream of power bent somehow, redirecting through her palms and straight up her arms. The sensation was excruciating, but Dara held on. She could push through pain when she ran, when she did squat lunges, when she took hits in practice. She could bear this. And she was *not* lazy.

The Watermight knifed deeper into her skin and flowed along her bones. It felt like ice but more malleable, as if there were a state between water and ice. She grasped the power, holding it, trying to mold it into something. She wouldn't let go this time.

Suddenly, Dara's vision sparked and flashed. She could no longer see Wyla. The whole chamber looked as if it had plunged into a silver-white blizzard. She resisted the urge to rub her eyes and instead took hold of the Watermight in her arms and forced it toward that swirling silver blizzard.

She felt more than saw the power curling out of her hands in uneven coils. It hurt, as if tiny shards of bone were forcing their way out of her fingertips. Then the coils of Watermight burst across the chamber, forcing Wyla to duck, and splattered against the far wall.

Dara's vision cleared abruptly. Wyla straightened, looking at the Watermight dripping down the wall behind her.

"That," she said, "was very interesting."

Dara's limbs shook. She lowered herself to sit cross-legged on the stone floor. She had never succeeded in forming the Watermight into anything before. It was a small step, but she was definitely making progress. She wished it weren't so painful.

"Quickly," Wyla said. "Tell me what you felt. Then we will do it again."

Dara wiped cold sweat off her forehead and obliged. When she described the way her vision had gone cloudy, Wyla got particularly excited.

"It takes years for Watermight apprentices to reach that point," she said. "I knew you'd progress quickly."

"I still can't do most of the basic tricks Watermight apprentices can, though," Dara said.

"Your skills are behind, yes, but the whitening of the eyes indicates a state of total surrender to the power. Many practitioners never achieve that state. I wondered if it would be possible for you."

"Do you think my Work with the Fire has anything to do with it?"

"Perhaps." Wyla tapped her fingers on her lips. "You are open to learning, and you have an intensity and diligence that younger apprentices simply aren't mature enough to demonstrate. You've had a taste of incredible power already, and you thirst for it."

Dara tugged at a loose thread on her poison-green skirt, avoiding Wyla's eyes. The woman meant it as a compliment, but she didn't like the idea that a deep desire for power filled her. Her father had that desire, and she didn't want to turn out like him. At the same time, she *did* want to learn. She relished the idea that she was progressing faster than Wyla's past apprentices. She had always wanted to be the best at dueling. She couldn't escape that hunger for victory when it came to Working either. But this was a lot more dangerous than sport dueling. And Wyla viewed her apprentices as expendable as long as she learned what she wanted from them.

Talk of other apprentices reminded her of a conversation they'd had when she and Wyla first met.

"Wyla, what happened to the other one?"

"Other one?"

"The apprentice you told me about back on the road that was like me. You said he learned to use Watermight later in life. Did his delayed spark mean he could access other powers?"

"We did not try. That was before I developed my theory about the Fire." She frowned across the pool. The silver-white light churned steadily between them.

"You told me before that the Watermight overwhelmed him when he tried to progress too quickly. Did his eyes also go white?"

"They did," Wyla said shortly. "But he was not disciplined. You will not let that happen to you. Is that clear?"

"Yes, but—"

"Stand up. Let us try again."

Dara gritted her teeth and stood. Why wouldn't Wyla just tell her more details? It could help her avoid the same mistakes. She was doing what Wyla wanted: training hard, doing experiments few Workers would dare contemplate. She had done everything Wyla asked. She needed more information if she was going to continue to improve. If she was going to win.

Mulling over the thought that her training was being inhibited, Dara wasn't ready when Wyla hurled Watermight at her once more.

The silvery power streaked for her knees. Dara could barely gasp before a whip of power wrapped around her legs and yanked her into the whirlpool.

She flailed, spinning wildly, unable to tell up from down. A solid wall of silver surrounded her, filled with flashes of white and blue and black and gold. Her arm scraped painfully against something, leaving it raw. She couldn't breathe. Couldn't see.

And the power. The surge of power around her was unlike anything she had ever experienced. It was a blizzard, a tornado, a riot of energy and color and pain and sound. She tried to grab hold of something, but it felt as though her skin were peeling away and her limbs were no longer connected to the rest of her body. It hurt—Firelord, it hurt—but a terrible pleasure mixed with the pain. The pure rush of power was ecstasy and nightmare as it bore through her skin and ate into her bones.

At first, she was shocked and afraid, but then anger took hold. Anger at Wyla for throwing her into this mess. Anger at her father for giving her this terrible thirst for power. Anger at herself for taking pleasure in it even as she drowned in the whirlpool of Might. Anger that she hadn't had time to practice her swimming.

But she wouldn't let them beat her.

Hardly knowing what she was doing, Dara opened her mouth and swallowed a huge mouthful of Watermight.

Her body shuddered, responded. The power spiked outward from her stomach, oozing along her bones and freezing her organs. Unlike when she tried to pull it through her skin, the Watermight in her belly didn't cut like an icicle. It melded with her form instead of fighting against it. She clutched at the sensation, let it take control. She blinked, and suddenly she could see the outer lip of the pool.

Dara swallowed another gulp of the power and launched herself toward the edge. The Watermight in her body gave her strength, helping her fight against the current. The pool couldn't contain her, not when she had Watermight within her.

Silver-white still tinted her vision, but it didn't obstruct it the way it had before. She caught the lip of the pool and pulled herself upward, using the strength of the Watermight because she had none left in her muscles.

She hauled her body over the edge and collapsed on the stone floor. She gasped in a breath, feeling the air turn to winter wind in her lungs. She felt as if her whole skeleton were coated in ice. But it wasn't brittle, and for a moment, she was sure she could smash a fist through a stone wall and her bones wouldn't break.

As she imagined what it would be like to break stone with her bare hands, curiosity overtook the anger and fear in her body. She noticed the silvery outline forming beneath her fingernails. She eased a bit of power out through her fingers and pooled it together in a glowing silver blob in the air.

Then her stomach revolted, and she vomited a rush of silver-white liquid all over the stones in front of her. She wretched, heaving every last ounce of Watermight out of her body, and lay still.

The silver-white film receded gradually from her eyes. The Watermight continued to swirl in an endless torrent beside her, a quiet rush echoing around the chamber. Her entire body shook like a leaf in a hurricane. She felt as cold as she had when she and Siv fled through the snows of Vertigon after her father took over the castle. She held onto the memory of Siv holding her tight against the cold. She pictured his arms around her as she shivered against his chest. The remembrance gave her strength, and at last she was able to lift her head.

Wyla stood over her, steel-toed boots waiting just outside the pool of silvery vomit.

"Huh," she said. "I didn't think to have you swallow it."

Dara coughed and pulled herself into a sitting position.

"What did you think would happen when you tossed me in there?"

"I had no idea." Wyla tapped a silver-rimmed nail against her lips. "We are done for the day. I must make some notes. Meet me here first thing in the morning. I'd like to try a few things before you have your breakfast."

She marched out of the chamber, not giving Dara a backward glance.

13

THE LIBRARY

Sora paced across the tall, narrow library. Light from the windows split the floor, not quite reaching the table piled with books and papers—papers she was supposed to be signing. She felt as if she spent most of her time doing paperwork these days. She was starting to understand why her brother used to sneak away for dueling practice at every opportunity.

She glanced at the door. Kel would be on duty in a few minutes, and she had the library to herself. He had taken to joining her inside whatever room he was supposed to be guarding whenever he was on duty. For official business only, of course. Such times came infrequently, but she looked forward to them, even arranging her meetings so they wouldn't interfere. It was nice to have control over her schedule again. She was responsible for most of the day-to-day operations of the castle and kingdom now. The Ruminors had set their sights on bigger prizes.

Sora chewed on her lower lip, wondering how much longer she had before the Lantern Maker made his next move. The Well was still unstable. It had been spewing an increased quantity of Fire over the mountain for weeks. Rafe had been spending more time then ever at the Well since the attack by the surviving Square Workers. As far as she could tell, instead of putting it back to normal, he was trying to repair it in such a way that it would still draw a larger supply of Fire from the mysterious Spring in the Burnt Mountains. She hadn't been able to find the rest of the old song about the true dragons and the Spring in the "burning range." It had to be a warning, but she feared it was already too late.

As Rafe's power grew, so did his disregard for caution. He edged closer to disaster the more time he spent Working above that tremendous flow of power. His allies had stepped up their work on the Fire Weapons too. Most of the increased flow was being channeled into the project, but Sora still hadn't seen the Fire Weapons in action. Perhaps it was time for another clandestine sabotage operation.

"My queen?"

Sora jumped. She'd been thinking of stealthy excursions into the Lantern Maker's domain and hadn't noticed the door opening.

"Good morning—I mean—good afternoon—I mean—hi."

Her cheeks warmed as Kel strode in and closed the door behind him. She caught a glimpse of Oat standing watch outside in case one of the Ruminors returned earlier than expected.

"You look well." Kel had an easy grin, and a handsome face that left little doubt why he was a favorite amongst the female dueling fans of the city. He was only a little taller than Sora, with a strong, wiry frame and an easygoing manner.

"Thank you, so do you," Sora said. Immediately she wished she could take back the words. Kel had proved a trustworthy ally and an uncommonly kind friend, but she didn't want to read anything into his compliments that wasn't there. She cleared her throat regally. "Is there any news?"

Kel's grin faded. "I'm afraid so. The Far Plains Stronghold has fallen."

"The Far . . . are you sure?"

"The cur-dragons just delivered the news. The Trurens held out for a few weeks, but Commander Brach prevailed in the end."

Sora stepped back and bumped into the table. She gripped it with both hands to steady herself. The Far Plains Stronghold. She was certain her mother and little sister had fled there when the Soolens first crossed the border into Trure.

"My family?"

"Your mother has been imprisoned in the Stronghold, along with Lord Valon and your relatives who were inside when the walls were breached."

"What about my little sister?"

"The message didn't mention her."

Sora felt queasy. Selivia and her mother in the hands of the invaders. They should have been safe in the Stronghold. That was where she would have sent them if she were her grandfather, King Atrin.

She frowned. That was *not* where she would have gone next after Rallion City if she intended to conquer Trure. Something didn't add up. The Stronghold was too remote to provide a strategic advantage for a conqueror. Commander Brach should focus on the towns along the High Road. A siege of the Stronghold would have left the Soolens vulnerable if the Far Plainsfolk decided to move against them. Commander Brach couldn't have expected to breach the country's most formidable fortress so quickly. Yet he had succeeded.

Come to think of it, he had decided to invade Rallion City directly instead of engaging in a long siege, as the Lantern Maker had expected him to do. That had worked too.

"Either Commander Brach is very lucky, or he really is a military genius," she muttered. And now her mother and sister were in his hands. Knots tightened in her stomach. She couldn't lose them too.

"Do you think Brach will travel beyond the Rock to take the Sunset City?" Kel asked.

Sora started. She had almost forgotten he was there. "He probably doesn't need to," she said. "All he has to do is keep a regiment at the Stronghold to discourage the Far Plainsfolk from getting involved. I don't think they'll rush to Trure's aid if Brach leaves them alone. He has to be overextended already."

Brach's risky strategies were paying off at the moment, but his winning streak couldn't continue forever. Especially when the Lantern Maker finally entered the fray. For the first time, Sora saw the appeal of Rafe's plan to bring Fire Weapons off the mountain. She pictured the Soolen forces falling before liquid flame as Vertigon's best Fireworkers advanced, eyes blazing gold. Her blood pounded in her ears as she saw them wrapping up her mother and little sister in protective arms of Fire and bringing them home. Even the legendary Commander Brach couldn't stand against Fire Weapons. How much longer before they'd be ready?

Stop. What was she thinking?

Sora crossed to the window and leaned her head against the glass. The cold, hard pressure on her forehead calmed her. She shouldn't entertain the idea of using Fire Weapons against any army, even one that held her mother and sister. Some lines shouldn't be crossed.

But what if he intends to hurt them? Would it be worth it then?

"Your family will be all right," Kel said, as if sensing where her thoughts led. "Commander Brach wouldn't hurt valuable prisoners."

"I hope not." Sora wished she felt more certain about that. She couldn't help picturing her mother and sister locked in a cell, frightened and cold.

"I wonder if there's any chance he'll hand them over to the Lantern Maker," she said. "Rafe was feeding Brach information, but they have to mistrust each other by now. Rafe wasn't happy when the Soolens breached the walls of Rallion City instead of waiting out the siege." She turned away from the window. "I wish I knew how they got connected in the first place."

"It was the Rollendars," Kel said. "Lord Von hired some of Commander Brach's men—Captain Thrashe included—and he and Rafe were still allies at the time."

"It must have soured Brach's relationship with Rafe when the Lantern Maker's wife killed Lord Von. I think it makes Rafe nervous that Commander Brach's campaign has been so successful." She looked up at Kel abruptly. "Do you think my family would be safer with the Soolens or with the Ruminors?"

Kel grimaced. "I honestly don't know."

Sora sighed, and silence stretched between them for a moment. This wasn't how she'd wanted their rendezvous to go at all. The news from the Stronghold made her feel as if things were once again spinning out of her control. Every time she thought she was making progress, something else snapped like a bridge line. Worse, there was nothing she could do to help her family. She was terrified that it was already too late. The fear took over her senses, making her want to do something reckless—such as send Fire Wielders to take the Lands Below. She wished there was a way to bottle up her fear and worry and recklessness and direct it somewhere.

Abruptly, she turned to face Kel, and they both started to speak at the same time.

"Do—?"

"I—"

"Sorry," she said, blushing slightly. "You first."

"I forgot to tell you I ran into Jully Roven the other day," Kel said. "You have quite the little spy network."

"Yes. Jully treated it like a game at first, but they understand how important all this is." Sora smiled. How did Kel know exactly what to say to comfort her? "They've been especially helpful for communicating with the nobles."

"That's true. Jully says the Nannings were speaking highly of you the other day. She reckons at least half of the noble houses are loyal to you over the Ruminors by now." Kel met her eyes, his expression gentle. "You should be proud of your little insurgents' work."

"I am," Sora said. Pride over what the young noblewomen had accomplished made her heart swell almost to the point of pain. A few months ago, she'd been a prisoner in her own castle. She wished she could focus on all the progress she'd made, but she was still fighting a losing battle. The Ruminors didn't care about the political maneuverings in Vertigon anymore. "My sis—never mind."

"What is it?"

"I was just thinking my sister would have so much fun with Jully and the others." To her annoyance, Sora's voice broke at the mention of Selivia. Kel didn't move any closer to her. She wanted to reach out to him, to seek comfort from him, but she didn't know how to communicate that. She wiped her eyes on her sleeve and tried to smile. "She loves stories of intrigue and adventure."

"She'll be okay," Kel said softly. "If she's half as smart as you, she'll scheme her way out of any trouble."

"She's clever, but her strengths are more in being adorable and charming rather than conniving."

"Well, *I* think you're adorable and charming," Kel said.

Sora laughed, but Kel didn't seem to be joking. *Now* he was moving closer to her. She felt suddenly shy. Why did he have to pick a moment when she had tears in her eyes to compliment her? She had cried on his shoulder before, but she was tired of feeling like a victim.

"I'd better get back to work," she said, looking at the papers strewn across the table.

"Do you have to? I don't get to be alone with you often enough."

"Kel . . ."

"Did I misread something?" Kel took a step closer to her.

Sora froze. "I don't know what you mean."

"You don't?" Another step. She looked down at his feet, judging the distance between the two of them.

"I mean— I know— But you— And we—" She clapped a hand over her mouth to keep from stammering.

Kel grinned. "Are you saying you don't know how you feel?"

"I do— I just— And you— It's complicated."

"It's always complicated." He took another step toward her.

Sora stared at him, his kind face, his eyes fixed on hers. She'd hoped for some indication that he wanted to be near her, nearer than a friend or a guard or an ally. He had crossed most of the distance between them, but he still stood just out of reach. If someone walked in, there would be nothing inappropriate about where they stood. She struggled for a moment. It *was* complicated, but she couldn't bear to do the appropriate thing, not when everyone she loved was in danger and the world had gone to ruin. All the worry and fear and emotion spun within her, building up. Couldn't she be reckless, just this once?

Kel's smile slipped a little when she didn't move.

"I'm so sorry, my queen." Now he was the one blushing. "I must have misinterpreted— I didn't mean— And you—"

Sora closed the rest of the distance between them, flung her arms around his neck, and kissed him full on the mouth.

If Kel was surprised at her enthusiasm, he didn't show it. He wrapped his arms around her, one hand on the back of her head, and held her so tight, it was almost painful. He held her as if it were the last thing he'd ever do. She pulled back a little to look at his face. He looked sad. She couldn't bear it. Why should he be sad now? Why couldn't he pretend, as she was, that nothing existed outside of this room?

"I'm sorry. I know it's complicated," she said, beginning to pull away. "I don't know what will happen if the Lantern Maker—"

"Sora," Kel said.

"Yes?"

"Let's not talk about the Lantern Maker."

She smiled through her tears, and he kissed her gently. Sora had never kissed anyone before. She always thought it would be nice, but she didn't anticipate the way her whole body responded to the pressure of his lips on hers. It was as though she had stepped into a waterfall, but warm rather than the icy ones created by snowmelt each spring. The waterfall seemed to rush straight through the core of her body and sent warmth all the way to her toes and back again.

She ran her fingers through the neatly trimmed hair on the back of Kel's head, tentatively at first. She needed to do something to distract her hands. All she wanted to do was pull him closer against her.

The door opened, and Captain Thrashe marched in.

Kel stepped back nimbly, his reflexes as quick as if he were dueling. Sora straightened her hair and her dress, hoping the heat and dismay rushing through her didn't show too much on her face.

They hadn't move quickly enough. Captain Thrashe surveyed both of them with his single eye. The eye patch that didn't quite hide the long scar on his face seemed to glare accusingly. He had seen them.

"Korran," he snapped. "Out."

"Captain." Kel saluted and marched for the door, his hair still slightly messy.

"What is it, Captain Thrashe?" Sora asked, striving for dignity in the face of the Soolen captain's disapproval.

"Madame Ruminor is on her way here," Captain Thrashe said.

"Thank you, Captain. That will be all."

He didn't move. "You should take more care when you arrange trysts, my queen."

"I beg your pardon?"

"You could do worse for a companion than Korran," he said. "His dueling antics are foolish, but . . ." Captain Thrashe shrugged, tugging his eye patch straight. "Madame Ruminor warned me to keep an eye on him. If you are caught, he will pay the price."

Sora gaped at the man, all pretenses of royal dignity forgotten. He was warning her to *avoid* getting Kel fired? Captain Thrashe didn't intend to reveal their secret to the Ruminors? And he approved of Kel as a . . . a companion?

Before she could say anything, the door opened again and Lima Ruminor entered. Sora was so surprised at Captain Thrashe that she didn't even feel nervous when Lima stalked toward her.

"Have you finished with those papers?" she asked without preamble.

"Almost." Sora returned to the table, wishing she'd had just a little more time alone with Captain Thrashe. Or with Kel. That would be much nicer. What had the papers been about again? "I want to check General Pavorran's latest supply order. He's requesting a lot more funding than normal. What's this about?"

Lima's lips thinned to a razor line. "Captain Thrashe, leave us."

As soon as he was gone, Lima took a seat and waved for Sora to join her. She never stood on ceremony or used honorifics with the queen. She saw little point in upholding the charade when no one else was around.

"Let me see."

Sora pushed the relevant papers across the table. Lima glanced over them then rubbed a hand across her forehead. She looked tired, and for a moment, she lost the larger-than-life aura that she usually wore like a mantle.

"Spring is upon us, child," Lima said. "You must know what that means."

"Invasion," Sora said. "General Pavorran is preparing to take the army down the mountain." She knew she should be worried about the prospect, but she couldn't help feeling a grim smugness at the chance to strike at the army that had conquered her grandfather's kingdom and imprisoned her mother and sister. The Soolens wouldn't know what hit them. "Will the Fireworkers be ready in time?"

Lima nodded. "Rafe wishes to strike before the Soolens are too entrenched in Trure. They haven't cooperated as we would have liked." She glanced at the door where Captain Thrashe had disappeared. "Brach must be dealt with."

"Is the Lantern Maker going with them?"

"Yes," Lima said. "I will remain here with you."

"Wonderful," Sora said.

"Watch your tone," Lima said, but her voice didn't hold its usual vitriol. Sora wondered if the pinch in her lips and the furrow in her brow were due to her characteristic unpleasantness—or if this was something else.

"Are you not sure this is the right thing to do?" Sora asked.

"Rafe is the most powerful sorcerer in generations," Lima said. "He deserves to seize his rightful position above Vertigon and the Lands Below. But he has been distracted since the Fire began to surge. The Well already produces enough power for all the Fire Weapons he needs to conquer Trure. But he is pushing it even further."

"And he's dangerous with too much power, isn't he?" Sora said. "Too much Fire, I mean. It changes him."

"It doesn't do anything that wasn't in him to begin with," Lima said. "Rafe was destined to rule. But he has enough now, and I worry about the consequences of disturbing the Spring and causing . . ."

Lima suddenly seemed to realize that she was confiding her fears in Sora. She stared at her for a moment then stood, knocking her chair back roughly.

"You must give the army a proper send-off when the time comes," she said. "You will express your enthusiastic support for General Pavorran and his men. Is that clear?"

"You're sending my people to die," Sora said. "Vertigon prospers without disturbing the affairs of other kingdoms. Why can't we leave the Lands Below alone?"

Lima stared at her for a moment. Something in her expression confirmed Sora's suspicion: Lima wasn't certain this was the right decision. In fact, she thought her husband was making a terrible mistake.

Without a word, Lima left the library. The door banged shut behind her.

14

HEADQUARTERS

Siv put his shoulder down and leaned in. Latch thudded into him, but instead of flipping over his back, he braced his legs against the wooden floor and kept his balance. Siv heaved, trying to hurl the fellow over his head. Latch just spread his feet and slid along the ground. Why wasn't this working? Siv would have been flat on his back by now.

"Momentum," Latch said with a grunt. "No point trying to complete the move now. You're wasting energy."

Siv abruptly changed tactics and hurled himself forward, hoping to knock Latch to the ground. The Soolen didn't budge, standing as still as a darkwood bedpost. Siv cursed under his breath. Latch was shorter than him and a bit broader in the shoulders. They were pretty evenly matched. Why couldn't he knock the guy over?

"I told you," Latch said. "Center of gravity."

"Easy for you to say." Siv pulled back and bounced on the balls of his feet, sweat soaking the neck of his shirt. "It's hard to remember all that when you're in the thick of a pen fight. You wouldn't understand."

Latch scowled and dove forward. This time, Siv was ready. He bent low, and Latch flipped directly over his back, hitting the ground with a smack that made the whole house shudder.

"Got you," Siv said.

Latch uttered a Soolen curse Siv hadn't heard before. He grinned. His friend still had a chip on his shoulder about not being allowed to compete in the pen. Siv actually felt bad for him, but that didn't mean he wouldn't use that frustration to beat Latch in a fight.

"That one was okay," Latch said at last. "I shouldn't have charged."

"You're easier to read than you think," Siv said airily.

"Humph. Not that it matters. Kres still hasn't changed his mind."

Latch lay in the middle of the pentagon painted on the floor of the house where the pen-fighting squad lived and trained. Siv flopped down beside him. Time for a break. It felt as if they'd been practicing that move all damn day.

"Are you sure he was ever planning to let you compete?"

"Maybe not," Latch grumbled.

"But he said you could when you met?"

"He knew who I was early on," Latch said. "I told him about my situation, and he was sympathetic. Said we'd be friends."

"Friendship seems to mean something different to Pendarkans than it does to the rest of us," Siv said.

Khrillin the Waterlord had invited him to dine in the Port District that very day. The message came wrapped around a bottle of fine wine. Dara had told him about Wyla's warning, but he wasn't inclined to avoid Khrillin just because Wyla didn't like him. Wyla had ensnared Dara, which put Khrillin ahead in his estimation. That didn't mean he trusted him, of course. Besides, Khrillin knew who he was, and he couldn't let that become common knowledge.

Siv wished he didn't need to court powerful friends at all, but it was becoming increasingly clear to him that he needed a lot more gold than he could earn in the pen. And he didn't want to wait another two months until Dara's term was up to leave Pendark. Rumors suggested his mother and sister had traveled to the Far Plains Stronghold before the Soolens took Rallion City—and news had just broken that Brach's army had taken the Stronghold itself.

"Hey, Latch?"

"I'll be ready for another round in a second." Latch was still lying on his back, catching his breath from the sparring session.

"I wanted to ask you about your father's—"

Latch immediately overcame his need to rest and stood to leave.

"You have to talk to me," Siv said.

"No, I don't."

"I get that you feel all angsty about your father," Siv said, getting up to follow him, "but I need information. Especially about how he treats prisoners—and how far he means to take things."

"How far?" Latch rounded on him, and Siv swore literal storm clouds formed over his head. "The man led a large portion of the Soolen army beyond its borders without the permission of the ruling family. He occupied Cindral Forest, a peaceful land that has kept to itself for centuries. He's leading a full-scale invasion of a foreign land and has already occupied its capital city, imprisoned its king, and captured its strongest fortress. And you want to know how far he's willing to go?"

Siv grimaced. He knew Latch didn't agree with his father's actions, but he needed any information he could get about Commander Brach. He just needed to wade through the surly Soolen's ire.

"Look," Siv said. "I just need to know if he would kill women."

"Women die in wars same as men, even if it's not on the battlefield."

Siv shoved him hard. "Damn it, Latch, will you give me a straight answer? My mother and sister are in danger."

Latch's shoulders slumped, and he kicked a training weight at the edge of the pentagon.

"I think he's more likely to use them than kill them."

"Selivia is fourteen, for Firelord's sake."

"Not like that," Latch said. "I mean arranging marriages or trading them for strategic locations. He's not a complete monster."

"I was starting to wonder."

"Okay." Latch sighed and sat down again. "He's not a terrible person." Every word as he spoke was like pulling teeth from a povvercat. "I thought he was noble and good until recently. Everyone did. But he got it into his head that he deserved more."

"I see." Siv was starting to get a clearer picture of Latch's issues with his father. Siv's own father had been a good man. He could understand why Latch was angered and confused to find that his hero wasn't as noble as he'd thought. Still, Siv was heartened by the portrayal. His mother and sister should be safe if they ended up in Commander Brach's hands, but he needed something more in order to secure their safety. Commander Brach wouldn't be swayed by a bit of gold from the pen, and even if he hired mercenaries, they wouldn't make it into his camp. He said as much to Latch.

"Can you think of something valuable enough to your father that he'd be willing to trade for my family?"

Latch's eyebrows drew low, and his hand crept to his sword hilt. "Kres will stop you," he hissed.

"Huh?"

"If you try it, you won't get out of Pendark alive."

"Try what?"

"You've seen Kres risk his life," Latch said. "You've seen him risk losing this season's Dances, which mean more than his own skin. You won't get away with it!"

"Hold your hell irons, Latch. What are you talking about?"

"Don't be stupid." Latch glanced furtively around the house, but no one else was home at the moment. "You think I don't know what you're getting at?"

"I'm seriously asking you for help," Siv said. "As a friend. I just want information about what your father would want enough to trade . . . Oh. Right."

It actually hadn't occurred to Siv to try selling Latch himself back to his father in exchange for the release of Siv's family. Latch may be a grump, but he and Siv had fought back to back on more than one occasion when men came after them. He wouldn't risk his life to save Latch's skin only to sell him out a month later. A friend had betrayed Siv before. He had no intention to become like Bolden Rollendar.

"You don't have to worry about that," he said. "Seriously, I'm not going to sell you out to your father."

"Even to save your little sister?"

Siv hesitated. Having the perfect ransom within reach *was* tempting. But it was no use. He intended to be a man his sisters could look up to. "I'll find another way to help them."

Latch studied him for a moment. Then he nodded.

"I'd love to know how he captured the Stronghold, though," Siv said. "That place is locked up tighter than a bullshell."

"There's something . . . that is . . . I have some information about him that could help." Latch paused and then seemed to come to a decision. "There's a reason his conquests have been so successful."

Siv didn't move, afraid he'd spook the fellow. He *knew* there had to be some reason Brach had been able to defeat the Truren army so soundly. Was Latch finally ready to tell him the secret?

Latch opened his mouth.

Then the door flew open with a squeal loud enough to wake the dead. Siv and Latch jumped. Kres sauntered inside, bringing a strong whiff of smoked fish with him.

"Well, if it isn't my two favorite protégés," Kres crowed. He strolled over to the large wooden table and tossed a battle-axe and an assortment of knives onto it.

"Hey, Kres," Siv said, fervently wishing he could shoo the man back outside for a few more minutes. "Good fight?"

"The Rockeater made me sweat," Kres said. "But I came out on top in the end."

"You always do."

"Indeed. I'm growing tired of the battle-axe, though. Perhaps it's time I switch weapons again." Kres was an all-purpose fighter. He had been alternating between the battle-axe and rapier place in the Dances depending on what substitute fighters were available. Kres eyed the two of them standing in the training pentagon. "And we need a permanent fifth soon."

Latch started to speak, but Kres forestalled him with a raised hand. "I've a bone to pick with you, Siv lad." He sat and stretched his boots out underneath the table. "Join me."

"We'll talk some other time," Latch said. He went out to sulk on the porch—one of his favorite activities. Siv made to follow, muttering some excuse about fresh air. Latch had been about to tell him something important. He was sure of it.

Kres called out before he made it three paces. "I understand Khrillin the Waterlord has taken an interest in you."

Siv froze. "You know him?"

"He's a very powerful man in this city."

"He certainly seemed rich."

"Indeed." Kres's posture was relaxed, but that didn't mean he wasn't about to attack. "I wouldn't take his interest lightly if I were you."

Siv still couldn't tell if Kres was mad or not. He sat down across from him slowly, shoulders tense.

"Does Khrillin adopt pen fighters often?"

"Only very special ones," Kres said. "You should be flattered."

"Maybe." Siv reached for a whetstone and one of Kres's knives. He watched warily for signs of anger as he cleaned and sharpened the weapon. Kres hadn't been pleased when Dellario offered to introduce Siv to powerful figures in the city. What had changed? "Do you know much about any other Waterworkers?"

"Interest from one isn't enough for you?"

"I'm just curious."

"I'll warn you to curb your curiosity, lad," Kres said. "Khrillin came out better than most in the last Watermight conflict. Now that he has shown an interest in you, it wouldn't be wise to appear too friendly with any other Workers. They are as territorial over their friends as they are over their districts."

"When was the last Watermight conflict?" Siv asked.

"Over three years ago," Kres said. "It has gotten quite boring around here lately."

"Who else came out on top?"

"Brendle of the Border District and Wyla of the Jewel District. The port lords held steady, as they usually do."

"So Brendle, Khrillin, and Wyla are the ones to watch out for?" Siv didn't need complications, but the Waterlord could end up being the only person capable of helping Dara escape Wyla's clutches.

"You should watch out for all of them," Kres said. "Just because one is ahead now doesn't mean it won't be another next time."

"Well, if I'm lucky, maybe it'll be my new friend."

"Indeed." Kres stood to retrieve a drink from a cupboard. "You seem blessed with an unusual amount of luck, Sivren Amen." He thumped a bottle of ale down on the table. "Don't waste it."

The door screeched open, and Latch returned. Tann Ridon loped in after him. Rid was a lanky young man a few years older than Siv, with brown hair and tanned skin. He carried a long staff over his shoulder and accidentally thumped it against the doorframe as he entered.

"Found this guy wandering around the stilt houses," Latch said.

"I couldn't remember which one belonged to y'all," Rid said. "I wasn't in good shape last time I was here."

"What is it?" Siv leapt to his feet. "Is Dara all right?"

"Sure. She's as busy as ever. I'm here with a message from Lady Vine." Rid looked questioningly at Latch and Kres. The latter looked him up and down, paying special attention to the way he carried his staff. Despite his slightly clumsy mannerisms, Rid clearly knew how to use the weapon.

"Hello there," Kres began.

Siv recognized the calculating look in Kres's eyes. "Let's talk on the porch, Rid," he said hurriedly. He didn't think Vine would appreciate it if Kres got his claws in her devotee.

He grabbed an extra bottle of ale, and they went outside to lean on the porch rail. The breeze carried the cloying odors of the Smokery District, along with the lush smell of new growth. Spring was beginning in earnest.

Siv opened the second ale for Rid, and they clinked bottles.

"Thank you, Your Highness—Majesty—Sire," Rid said.

"Siv is fine, really." He glanced back at the door. So far, only Latch knew that he used to be a Highness. Kres suspected enough about his true identity. He didn't need to confirm it.

"Lady Vine wanted me to tell you she found out where Lord Vex is staying."

"She saw him?"

"With her own eyes."

"Where?"

"That's the tricky part." Rid took a long swig from his ale. "Lord Vex is living with the king."

"The King of Pendark?"

"Yes, Sire—I mean Siv."

Siv scratched at his beard. "How did he manage that?"

"Don't know," Rid said. "He's awful resourceful."

"Yeah, he is." Vex Rollendar certainly wasn't wasting any time. He'd already gotten an invitation to Khrillin's party *and* an in with the king? Come to think of it, that information could prove useful. Siv had been trying to think of a way to get Khrillin to prove his trustworthiness. "He's staying in the King's Tower itself?"

"Yes. He was real injured after our fight." Rid rolled his shoulder, which must still be sore even though Wyla had used her Watermight to seal his wound and help him heal more quickly. "I reckon he has to heal up before he makes his next move."

"Hopefully, we'll be on our way before then."

"We still got two more months here," Rid said.

"Maybe," Siv said.

"You're not thinking of leaving Dara, are you?" Rid whirled

toward him, fists clenched. He looked as if he might slug Siv in the face, injured shoulder or not. "After all she's been through for—"

"I'm not leaving her," Siv said. "I want to get her away from Wyla sooner if I can."

"I don't know if that'll work," Rid said. "Lady Wyla is one mean broad." He took another swig of his ale. "All right. Count me in."

"Sorry?"

"We gotta get our ladies out of here," Rid said. "And we don't want Lord Vex getting wind of where they are either. It's up to you and me, Sire—Siv."

"All right, then," Siv said. "I'm working on a possible ally. See what you can find out about Wyla from her servants and guards. She must have some weaknesses."

"I'll do my best."

"Good. We won't let them down." He thought about the news from the Stronghold, of his mother and sisters in captivity. "But two months might be too long."

15

PORT DISTRICT

Rid's news about Lord Vex was fresh in Siv's mind when he crossed the final bridge to the Port District to meet the Waterlord. Trusting Khrillin was a risk, but thanks to Rid, he could administer a simple test before taking their "friendship" any further. And if there was a chance Khrillin could help him get Dara out of the city, he'd take any risk.

He traveled along one of the main waterways leading inland from the Black Gulf to reach the Port District. A strong breeze blew in from the coast, sweeping away the stench of the city. Well-to-do citizens and foreigners strolled along a wooden boardwalk where the river met the gulf, enjoying the cleansing sea breeze.

Siv met Khrillin in a restaurant beside the boardwalk. Built on stilts, it nestled between two larger shops with iron bars protecting their wares. The restaurant specialized in a Pendarkan delicacy: grilled eel and brindleweed. At least the Waterlord would probably pay. Siv was getting tired of eating smoked fish, stew, and brown bread.

He almost didn't recognize Khrillin without his all-white ensemble from the party. The older man lounged at a large table in the corner, looking distinguished and elegant in all black today. Siv wore the gray coat he'd purchased for the party, and he had taken extra care to shine his boots, strap a rapier to his hip, and hide a handful of knives about his person.

Khrillin remained seated when Siv approached. "So glad you could join me." He leaned forward conspiratorially, and a glint at his chin hinted at a jewel woven into the dark mass of his full beard. "Do have a seat, Your Majesty."

Somehow, the man made the honorific sound like a warning. Siv plastered on a grin and sat. "Good evening, my lord."

"Have you been to this restaurant before? It was the talk of Pendark a few years back."

"This is my first time in the Port District."

Khrillin waved for a second glass of wine. "You're going to love it, my friend."

"I'm sure I will."

Siv sipped his drink carefully, remembering with vivid clarity how it had felt to have a goblet full of Firetears drawn out of his stomach. But there would be no poisonings tonight, not while the Waterlord considered him a valuable asset.

They exchanged pleasantries about the weather, the wine, and a few of Siv's recent Steel Pentagon matches.

"What can you tell me about the King of Pendark?" Siv asked when he felt they'd made enough small talk.

Khrillin took a sip of wine, watching him over the rim of his goblet. "What do you want to know?"

"Is he dangerous?"

"Dangerous. Dangerous. It's a complicated word, isn't it?" Khrillin swirled the wine in his glass like a whirlpool. "You are dangerous, as long as you have steel in hand. I am dangerous primarily because of my power, but there's also my good looks and charm."

Siv chuckled obligingly.

"Yes, the king is dangerous, though not as much as he would like to think."

"He's not a Waterworker, right?"

"That's correct. I'm afraid many Waterworkers consider him of no consequence whatsoever."

"And what about you?"

Khrillin smiled. "He performs an important civic function. He could damage some of my investments if he had a mind. But he is a foolish man. He would have to figure out how."

"What if he had a cunning advisor?"

The Waterlord shot him a sharp look. "Such as?"

Siv wiped a sweaty palm on his trousers and played his mijen tile.

"I've heard there's a man staying with him," Siv said. "An old enemy of mine from back home. He's cunning and a lot more dangerous than I realized at first."

Khrillin tugged at the jewel in his beard. "Do you have any evidence that he's advising the king?"

"No. I think it's more likely that this enemy wants the king's help capturing me."

Khrillin studied him for a moment. Then he smiled. "You are referring to Lord Vex Rollendar, the man who trained the swordsmen who assisted in the coup against you this winter?"

Siv bit the inside of his cheek to hold in a choice curse or two. *Vex* had been the one training the secret duelists? How on earth did Khrillin know that? The man seemed to love shocking people with his revelations.

Khrillin's grin widened. "Would you like me to get rid of him for you?"

"I don't want anything," Siv said. "I figured *you'd* want to know about him given our potential alliance."

"I appreciate the disclosure," Khrillin said. "As a matter of fact, I've met this Lord Rollendar. He attended the very party where I made your acquaintance."

"Is that right."

"Lucky the two of you didn't cross paths," Khrillin said. "He was invited because I'd learned a Vertigonian nobleman was staying with the king, and I wanted to get the measure of him."

"And?"

"We only spoke briefly. When I learned about your little run-in on the day you arrived in Pendark, I made additional enquiries."

Siv sipped his wine. Khrillin sure loved telling people their own secrets. And he was well informed. Siv thought he spoke the truth in this case, though. Khrillin could easily have hidden the fact that Vex had been at his house. That he hadn't kept that detail to himself made Siv suspect he was being honest.

"I will see what else I can find out about Lord Rollendar's plans," Khrillin said. "In honor of our new friendship. I have men positioned in the King's Tower already."

"I thought you might," Siv said.

Khrillin smiled. "Ah. Here comes the food. Let's leave off this business chatter for the moment."

A procession of waiters brought huge platters of food to their table. The spread made Siv's stomach stand up and cheer. He had missed his fine foods. The simple meals had been one of the definite drawbacks of being poor and exiled. Grilled eel and brindleweed were just the beginning. Other platters featured purple prawns, bell melons, fried toadfish, and sugar mushrooms the size of his face.

As they filled their plates, Khrillin answered his questions about the exotic foods and their origins. Siv was surprised to find that he liked the man. He shared Siv's deep affection for good wine, and he had read many of the same books—including Brelling's rare travel journals. He had also traveled across the Bell Sea himself in his youth.

"A more magnificent experience I can't describe," Khrillin said. "I'd never have returned if I didn't miss having access to my power."

"Would you ever go back?"

"I have worked too hard to carve out my domain. It's never guaranteed here."

"One of the other Waterworkers would come in and take your lunch, eh?"

"Something like that."

Siv chewed on a tough piece of fried toadfish, considering the Waterlord's words. He suspected Khrillin didn't make any revelations without good reason. Perhaps he was thinking about where else he might "carve out a domain."

As if reading his thoughts, the Waterlord put another slice of sugar mushroom on Siv's plate and said, "Now then, shall we discuss what we can do for each other? Especially in regards to a certain lost kingdom."

"I think it's about that time."

Siv waited, hoping Khrillin would play his hand first. His father had taught him that the first person to speak in a negotiation always lost. He held Khrillin's eyes too. That was something he'd picked up from Dara. It seemed to help in the pen. Why not here?

Khrillin gazed back at him, apparently in no hurry. Before either of them could break the silence, the restaurant doors flew open with a bang. A sudden hush accompanied the gust of wind.

Khrillin and Siv looked over at the newcomer at the same time. Siv reached for his sword. It wouldn't be the first time he'd been attacked while trying to enjoy a drink and a meal. But he didn't know the man who crossed the restaurant toward them. He had a wide girth, with a bald head and bare arms marked with silvery tattoos not created by any ink Siv had ever seen. Despite his corpulent figure, he moved with the grace of a povvercat on a wire. His eyes glowed silver-white.

Siv tightened his grip on his sword hilt, but Khrillin caught his eye and shook his head slightly.

The mysterious Waterworker stalked across the restaurant, his heavy boots pounding on the wood floor. Every eye in the establishment turned to watch his progress. Judging by the furtive looks cast toward their own table, Siv understood that no one would have bothered to watch this man walk across the restaurant if Khrillin hadn't been present.

When the stranger was within five feet, he abruptly turned and sat at the table nearest theirs. Khrillin made a sound in his throat, somewhere between exasperation and scorn.

"Just do it, you gutterfeeder," he muttered under his breath. "I've had enough of this."

The newcomer folded his arms over his broad stomach, making the silver tattoos catch the light. He proceeded to stare directly at Khrillin while he worked his way through a full pitcher of wine and a meal equal to the one Khrillin and Siv had consumed together.

The man's presence made it impossible for them to continue discussing sensitive matters, and Khrillin grew visibly irritated. They resumed their conversation about food and foreign lands as they quickly finished their meal. As Siv popped the last piece of bell melon into his mouth, Khrillin stood and slammed some coins on the table. He strode over to the stranger's table and slammed an identical pile of coins down there as well.

"This is my favorite restaurant," he said. "You won't take it from me."

The stranger smiled, and Siv saw a bit of food clinging between his broad, white teeth.

"You're leaving first, aren't you?"

Khrillin stiffened, and for a moment, Siv thought he might hit the fellow. Instead, he waved a hand almost casually and strode toward the door. The stranger's eyes began to bulge, and a web of molten silver leaked from his eyes. He gasped, scratching at his face with his fingernails as the silver threads spread outward, wrapping around his head, squeezing tighter. Siv recoiled in horror. People in the restaurant stood up to get a better look, eager to witness the torturous progress of the silver web. Siv turned on his heel and hurried after Khrillin. He didn't need to see the rest.

Khrillin was waiting for him on the porch outside the restaurant, breathing heavily. Siv considered making a break for it, but Khrillin clearly wasn't in a mood to be toyed with right now. He waited.

After a few minutes, Khrillin's muscles relaxed.

"It's harder than it looks," he said.

"Sorry?"

"Taking Watermight from another person and using it against them. I just wanted a nice meal and a chat with my new friend." Khrillin scowled and glanced back inside the restaurant, where people clustered around the stranger. Some of Khrillin's ostentatious charm was missing, and Siv wondered how much of it was an act.

"That fellow thought he was safe because he had Watermight with him when he entered?" Siv asked.

"Correct. He should have known I will not be intimidated." Khrillin rolled his shoulders. "After all my time here, all my efforts to cultivate friendships, these upstarts still think they can challenge my position." He fixed his eyes on Siv. "I wish to leave Pendark," he said. "I've built up significant amounts of capital, and I am looking for an appropriate place to invest it where I can be assured a peaceful retirement."

"I see now," Siv said. "You think Vertigon is the place."

"Vertigon as it was," Khrillin said. "Ruled by the Amintelles. I understand you've had trouble there of late, but if you prove to be half the man your father was, I believe Vertigon can once more become a haven. If you guarantee I may live out my days with an appropriate degree of influence and comfort, perhaps with a nice greathouse overlooking the fabled Fissure and a place in your royal court, I will fund your campaign to retake it."

Siv studied the man. Had he truly tired of the endless turmoil in Pendark? Siv hadn't thought Khrillin was particularly old, but he wondered if that had something to do with his Watermight abilities. If it could seal and heal wounds, could it smooth wrinkles?

His luxurious black beard could very well be dyed. He *could* be old enough to seek a peaceful retirement in Vertigon. But did Siv believe Khrillin's story?

One thing he had said stood out.

"You said if I'm half the man my father was. Did you know him?"

Khrillin inclined his head. "I knew Sevren. Did he tell you of his travels here in his youth?" He gave a smile that could only be described as salacious.

"I suspect it was a less colorful version of the truth," Siv said. Pendark could be a raucous, debauched place for a young man of means.

"Well said, my friend, well said." Khrillin leaned against the porch rail, and his voice softened. "Actually, I considered Sevren a friend. He did me a good turn, me and another friend from my university days. I believe you know Zage Lorrid?"

Siv missed a beat. "The Fire Warden." He knew Khrillin was using these revelations for effect, but the memory of his old teacher was like a blow straight to the chest.

"One and the same. We got on well, Sevren, Zage, and I. And then there was your father's bodyguard. What was his name?"

"Bandobar," Siv whispered. He was finding it difficult to catch his breath.

"Bandobar! That's the one. Your father was in the habit of helping out unfortunate souls, no matter what danger he got Bandobar and himself into. He might be the only genuinely noble man I've met."

Siv stared at Khrillin, wanting desperately to believe it was true. He had admired his father more than anyone else in the world. Any other tests he could have administered to assess the Waterworker's trustworthiness paled in comparison to this.

A commotion came from within the restaurant as the rotund Waterworker thudded to the floor.

"We'd best move on," Khrillin said. "His friends won't like this, no matter who started it. I don't fancy being caught alone. I'll have to lay low for the next few days anyway until they decide it isn't worth jumping me and escalating things further." Khrillin sighed deeply, as if to emphasize how tired he was of the Pendarkan Watermight squabbles. "What do you say to my proposal?"

Siv held out a hand. If Khrillin had truly been his father's friend, he couldn't think of a better person to help him retake his throne. "I'd say we have a deal."

Khrillin smiled and extended his own hand. He had an honest handshake, firm and strong, like Siv's father's. And he didn't try to bind him with a Watermight curse. That was a definite vote in his favor.

Before they parted ways, Khrillin promised once more to look into Vex Rollendar's plans. Siv would wait to see what came of Khrillin's investigations before discussing Dara with him. He needed more evidence that the Waterlord would follow through on his promises before asking for aid with someone far more important than Vex Rollendar.

They said farewell at the docks, taking different paths to their respective districts. As Siv squeezed onto a boat bound for the Smokery District, he fought down the tide of emotions that rose at the thought of his father floating along these very waterways. He couldn't allow the Waterworker to use his father's memory to play him. Even so, he sincerely hoped Khrillin was telling the truth about their long-ago friendship.

16

SUNSET LANDS

Selivia chased the little purlendog through the dusty streets of Sunset City. Flashes of bright yellow flitted around the ankles of passersby. Selivia shouted apologies as she pushed past them, trying to catch up with the elusive creature. She already regretted naming the puppy Lightning Bug.

"Come back, Lightning! Wait for me!"

A strong wind blew through the streets, slowing her down. She had wrapped her scarf around her face to keep the sand out of her eyes, but the grit worked its way in anyway.

The wind didn't deter Lightning Bug at all. Selivia lost sight of him and skidded to a halt to try to get her bearings. She had turned a few times as she chased the little scamp through the streets. A riot of colorful curtains and awnings surrounded her, their patterns unfamiliar. Which way was the Tovenarov house?

Sand collected at her feet as she spun in a slow circle, hunting for her pet. She was normally good with animals, but this one was certainly keeping her guessing.

There! A tuft of bright-yellow fur stuck out from behind a tall rock at the intersection between two roads. Paintings covered the full length of the rock: fanciful creatures of red and orange. The last one had magenta flowers in a field of yellow, and the one before that had ladies in azure dresses. The one nearest Ananova's house had a vivid green dragon leaping out of a pond. Selivia thought these rocks were mile markers to help with navigation through the city, but she hadn't yet learned to interpret them.

Selivia crept up to the standing stone, hoping Lightning Bug wouldn't smell her too soon. She couldn't figure out whether he thought they were playing a game or if he simply enjoyed tormenting her. All three tails wagged enthusiastically when he popped out from behind the stone.

She snuck closer. A few more steps. Suddenly, a tall figure wearing a broad-brimmed hat appeared out of the gale and swept the purlendog into his arms.

"Oh!" Selivia stumbled back in surprise. "Um, thank you. I was just looking for him." She held out her arms for her pet.

The stranger didn't move. He had narrow shoulders and large, wrinkly hands. His hat shadowed his face, but she got a vague impression of craggy features and pale, piercing eyes. He stared down at her, holding Lightning Bug firmly around the middle.

Selivia cleared her throat. "I can take him, sir."

The stranger continued to stare.

"Sorry to be a bother," she said nervously. "I—"

"Take care where the Air leads, child."

"What?"

"The Air will tell you," he said. "Take heed when it speaks." He handed her the puppy and loped away.

Selivia frowned after him. She was starting to dislike the Far Plains Air Sensors. Why did they all have to be so cryptic? From her very first morning in the City of Wind, Air Sensors had been seeking her out. Zala's warning to be wary of their riddles didn't even begin to cover the convoluted hints and effervescent statements they made to her on a daily basis. Whenever she encountered a Sensor, recognizable by their dreamy demeanors and enigmatic words, they always warned her to listen to the Air's leading. The only trouble was the Air hadn't actually told her to do anything. She didn't understand why they were singling her out. She had tried sitting in meditation with Ananova, but it was terribly dull, and she hadn't heard anything resembling real instructions. If the Air wanted her to do something, it was going to have to speak a little louder.

Selivia's arrival wasn't the only thing to cause a stir amongst the Air Sensors. The messages they were accustomed to receiving by listening to the wind had been garbled ever since their counterparts to the south used the Air to protect Kurn Pass and the Linden Mountains border. The disruptions had gotten worse since the Stronghold fell. It must be making the Sensors antsy.

Selivia had been too busy exploring the Sunset City, training her new pet, and practicing the Far Plains tongue to worry too much about ethereal messages. It was a beautiful place, colorful and mysterious. She could live here for years without fully understanding it. She still wasn't very good at finding her way through the windy streets, but she felt safe here.

With Lightning Bug firmly in hand once more, she let the gale push her back the way she'd come. If she wandered in the right general direction for long enough, she'd come across a landmark or painted standing stone she recognized. Busy scanning nearby houses for familiar features, she didn't notice when someone fell into step with her.

"You're late."

Selivia jumped. Ivran, Zala's cousin, strolled along beside her as if he'd been there all afternoon.

"Zala has been looking for you."

"I was lost."

"How can you get lost here?" He flipped his hair out of his eyes and looked down his long, straight nose at her. "You just follow the standing stones."

"Follow them where?"

"Colors outward, symbols around. It's easy."

"Huh?"

Ivran gave her a longsuffering look. "The city is a wheel." The patient condescension in his voice made Selivia's skin crawl. "The colors on the stones go from sun-yellow in the center all the way to midnight-blue at the outskirts. The symbols are the same shooting out from the middle like spokes in a wheel. To walk to the boundary stones from the middle, you pick a symbol and follow it through all the colors of the sunset."

"That's . . . kind of beautiful," Selivia said.

Ivran shrugged and jerked his head for her to follow him. He kicked up sand with every step as he led the way back toward his mother's house. Selivia wondered if there was some way to break through his sullen exterior. Everyone else in the Far Plains had been very nice to her—well, when they weren't confusing her like the Air Sensors.

"It *is* a little unusual," Selivia said. "The colors and symbols. They use the names of historical figures and famous racehorses in Rallion City, and in Fork—"

"I don't care what they do in Rallion City," Ivran snapped.

Selivia raised an eyebrow.

"You Trurens always think you know the best way to do everything," Ivran said.

"I didn't say it was best," Selivia said. "Just different. Besides, you're more Truren than . . . never mind." Zala's extended family didn't know her identity. She was beginning to wonder if the Air Sensors did, though. Little good that did her when none of them would speak to her in straight sentences.

"I'm no Truren," Ivran spat. "It's best you figure that out now."

"Okay, okay." Selivia didn't want to get into an argument. She wasn't used to people not liking her—and she didn't enjoy the feeling. She resolved to be extra nice to Ivran. She plastered on a smile. "Thank you for showing me the way home."

Ivran glanced down at her, and she smiled wider. She'd make him crack yet.

"Whatever," he muttered, some of the aggression dissipating from his voice.

They walked in silence for a few minutes. A group of Air Sensors strolled by. One after another, they slowed to look her up and down. They continued on without speaking this time, heading toward the slopes of the Rock where they held their meditation sessions. She wished they would just tell her what they wanted.

Suddenly Ivran stopped and whirled to face her.

"I want to show you something."

"What?"

"You'll see. It's better than a silly little purlendog."

Selivia clutched Lightning Bug tighter. "Where is it?"

"In the desert beyond the boundary stones."

"There's no way I'm going out there with you." She may want to be nice, but there were limits.

"You won't regret it," Ivran said. "*Zala* will never show you."

"What are you talking about?"

"There's a lot you don't know about my cousin." Ivran sighed dramatically. "I suppose she's right not to tell you everything."

Selivia didn't want to rise to his taunts, but she couldn't help feeling curious. "What isn't she telling me?"

Ivran grinned, the expression somehow unpleasant on his fine features. "Do you want to see it or not?"

Selivia hesitated. She was desperately curious. The truth was that Zala *hadn't* told her much about what lay in the desert outside the city. She also refused to help her parse out the Air Sensors' cryptic messages. Selivia felt as if she were being coddled like a premature kitten—when she wasn't being ambushed by scary old Sensors in big hats.

"Well?" Ivran prompted.

Wind gusted in the street, blowing sand against her cheek. The Sensors had told her to follow the Air wherever it led. Was it possible Ivran could show her what the Air wanted her to know?

Her curiosity got the better of her at last. "All right, then. Show me."

"We'll leave after sunset. Excuse yourself to use the waterhouse when everyone goes in, and I'll come meet you. Don't tell anyone." Ivran flashed a puzzling grin and hurried ahead.

It was all Selivia could do to keep up with him. She tried to take note of the standing stones as they made their way back to the Tovenarov house. When they found one with a pale-green dragon, she figured they'd reached the correct street. Sure enough, Ivran turned and led her past two more leaping-dragon standing stones in successively darker shades of green before they arrived at the house at last.

Lightning Bug scrambled out of her arms and darted to join his siblings. The other purlendogs yapped happily, still trying out their immature voices. Selivia could hardly wait until they were old enough to sing.

Zala and a few of her family members were waiting for them beneath the awning. The rest bustled in and out of the house, bringing out the evening meal. Selivia liked this custom of eating together outdoors. Zala had told her there were only a few months in the winter when it was too cold for this. A sturdy screen blocked the worst of the wind, and it could be repositioned depending on the wind's direction. It made for pleasant, airy meals as they waited for the sun to set.

"How was your walk?" Zala asked as Selivia helped her arrange plates on the table.

"Interesting," she said carefully.

"Did Ivran say something to you?" Zala asked, perhaps picking up on the hesitation in Selivia's voice.

"He got offended when I said he was a Truren." Selivia thought about telling Zala everything, but she was sure to stop her from sneaking out with Ivran. She was too curious to risk missing out on that adventure. "I didn't know young people in the Far Plains didn't like being part of Trure."

"Oh, that," Zala said, sounding relieved. "Ivran can be a fool, but not about this. Some say we don't need Rallion City's leadership anymore. We've been looking out for ourselves for a long time."

"What do you think?"

Zala didn't answer. Without so much as a good-bye, she bustled off to help her aunt with the meal. Selivia sighed. Many of the Far Plainsfolk had that infuriating habit. Why did they all have to speak in riddles and fall silent when you asked a question they didn't want to answer?

They were definitely keeping something from her. Zala had been relieved that all Ivran had talked about was whether or not the Far Plainsfolk wanted to be part of Trure. That meant there was something else she didn't want Selivia to know. But what was it? Perhaps Ivran could show her the truth.

Selivia could barely contain her excitement as they ate. Her brother used to sneak out of the castle for adventures all the time. She couldn't wait to try it herself.

Sunset seemed to take hours. She didn't take the glorious vision for granted exactly, but she wouldn't mind if it went a bit faster tonight. It was all she could do to rein in her curiosity and stop her feet from tapping.

She didn't dare share her plans to go out after dark with Fenn. Her bodyguard had taken to the Far Plains with surprising grace. Selivia had even heard her asking Ananova for some paints so she could try capturing the sunset. It was nice to see her relaxed and at peace after the death of her brother. But her newfound tranquility didn't mean she'd let her young charge wander off at night. If night ever hurried up!

At last, the sun dipped beneath the horizon, taking the last drops of copper and gold with it. The family made their way indoors with their usual chatter and bustle. One of the children said something about playing table games, and the others rushed about, collecting cards and tiles and squabbling over teams. No one paid Selivia any heed when she slipped into the shadows beyond the ring of light spilling from the house.

The low music of conversation murmured from the houses around her. An unfamiliar bird called out, and a scrabbling sound indicated a mouselike creature creeping through the dark nearby. Selivia peered into the shadows, trying to catch a glimpse of a tail or a beady eye. She wondered if Ananova would let her keep the mouse if she found it. It would probably be even more likely to run away than her feisty little purlendog, though. But nothing moved in the gloom.

The Far Plainsfolk rarely ventured far from their own homes at night. Selivia hadn't thought much of it. But as she waited for Ivran in the shadows, she wondered why there weren't more people around.

Suddenly, a hand closed over her mouth. She gasped and struggled against the grip. Had the Soolens rounded the Rock? Would they capture her like her mother?

She twisted around, and Ivran's face came into view. He released her with a grin.

"Scared you."

"That was mean." Selivia pushed him away, wishing she'd bitten his hand when she had the chance.

"Here. It gets cold fast." He handed her an extra shawl he'd brought from the house. He wore a midnight-blue coat that blended into the shadows.

Selivia was surprised at the considerate gesture, but it wasn't enough to cool her anger. She pulled the shawl close around her. "Where are we going?"

"I'll explain when we're farther from the house," Ivran whispered. "Don't want anyone to hear us."

They crept down the alleyway between their house and the next, footsteps whispering in the dusty ground. Nightfall brought a deep quiet to Sunset City. Even though people would be awake for hours yet, nothing but wind and moonlight filled the streets.

Selivia didn't like creeping through the dark, but she could hardly wait to see what Ivran planned to show her. She hoped she'd find out what the Air Sensors wanted her to hear at last.

Ivran led her toward the northern edge of the city. The paintings on the standing stones got darker the farther they went.

The Rock loomed over them, blotting out one section of the stars. A rushing wind sang through the streets.

They turned onto a road where the stones were marked with birds and followed it past the city boundaries. A few houses sprawled into the plains, surrounded by little gardens and fenced enclosures for sand goats and desert fowl. They passed the last of these and kept walking.

The open desert was beautiful at night. Countless stars dotted the deep-purple sky. The wind rustled in the brush, creating a sense of movement across the wide-open land. The desert smelled of dirt and strange plants, enticing as spice cakes. Selivia almost didn't mind Ivran's company as their steps crunched softly in the darkness.

But it grew colder, and they still didn't stop walking. Selivia shivered, beginning to wonder if she'd made a mistake. Why was Ivran taking her this far outside the city? She wanted to think the best of people, but her curiosity was slowly turning to worry. She should have brought Fenn along or told Zala where she was going. She hadn't realized they'd be going this far.

Ivran was a few steps ahead of her. Should she make a break for it? She wasn't sure she could run faster than him if he tried to stop her. She had a small work knife in her pocket. Could she bring herself to stick someone with it?

Ten minutes after they left the city, Ivran stopped at last. The dark plains surrounded them, shadowy and alien. The empty beauty of the desert had grown ominous. Selivia tensed, her hand creeping toward the knife in her pocket.

"You have to swear not to tell anyone I showed you," he said. "This is a big Far Plains secret."

"I swear." Selivia was annoyed to hear the shaky tone in her voice. "Will you please tell me what's going on?"

"It's better if you see it," Ivran said.

He left the dirt path and strode into the wild scrub. Selivia followed, trepidation and curiosity warring within her. The rocks and shadows made it impossible to tell where her feet would end up next. She wondered if Ivran could see in the dark somehow. He was already outpacing her.

"Wait for me!" Selivia called, afraid she'd lose sight of him completely.

"Shh! I'm here." Ivran seized her hand, his palm sweaty. "Don't draw attention to us. I'll get in trouble."

"With whom?"

"The Air Sensors Circle."

Selivia froze, suddenly not wanting to take another step. She was supposed to be listening to the Air, not going against its wishes. Did the Air have wishes? She didn't understand. Why couldn't she have just told Ivran to go stick his head in a bowl of porridge?

"The Sensors don't want me to see this?"

"They don't know everything," Ivran said. "Don't chicken out now."

"Why are you doing this?"

"Because I think you'll like it. I swear." Ivran tugged on her hand. She had no choice but to follow him onward through the darkness. She hoped this wasn't some scheme concocted to impress her. She'd gotten the distinct feeling that Ivran didn't like her. Could she have it backward? He had another thing coming if he thought leading a girl out into a dark and scary desert was the way to her heart.

That's it. Enough being nice. She stuffed her other hand in her pocket and prepared to draw her little knife.

Ivran stopped abruptly, tightening his grip on her hand to keep her from advancing. "Careful," he said. Selivia's breath caught. They teetered at the edge of a deep crater. A bottomless black shadow filled it, and she couldn't make out any details inside.

Behind them, a soft glow nestled at the foot of the Rock. The lights of Sunset City. It was the only distinguishable feature in the vast emptiness of the plain. If it weren't for the stars, she wouldn't have been able to tell which way was up at all.

Ivran released her hand. "I'm going to turn on a light," he said. "Don't scream."

Selivia opened her mouth to ask why she'd need to do that. But when Ivran took out a Vertigonian Everlight and shone it into the darkened pit, the question died in her throat.

The body of a massive dragon lay in the crater. Shiny green scales glittered like emeralds on its hide. A ridge of spikes rose up from its spine, casting wicked shadows across its back. A long tail with a knot of hardened scales the size of a man's head at the end curved around toward the edge of the crater.

Ivran shone the Everlight along the dragon's length, revealing folded wings blacker than the finest ink from Pendark. The beam of light traveled from the wings to the powerful shoulder joints and all the way along the curved neck. Green scales covered the neck in overlapping plates, getting darker as they neared the head. At the base of the jaw, the scales were pitch black and as shiny as obsidian. The head was as big as Selivia herself. It had a thick, rounded skull, a long snout, and powerful jaws. Spikes similar to the ones lining its spine rose from the creature's head like a crown of thorns.

Selivia had never seen anything so beautiful or so sad. She couldn't imagine how the body could have been preserved in such good condition. Those scales must be practically indestructible, and the dry wind of the Far Plains probably helped as well. This was a magnificent treasure, priceless even. No wonder they wanted to keep it a secret! Treasure hunters would come from all across the world to steal scales and spines if anyone knew this was here.

The wind changed direction, carrying a deep musty smell with it. A whiff of bone and dust and smoke. Awed and silent, Selivia stared into the crater as Ivran pointed the Everlight beam at the huge scaly head. The light moved a bit. Ivran was shaking. *Why is he so nervous?*

Then the dragon opened its eyes.

17

SECRETS

Selivia screamed, a mixture of surprise, fear, and utter delight. She couldn't help herself. It was alive! A real live true dragon lay right here in a pit in the Far Plains. Of all the things she had expected to see tonight, this was not one of them.

The true dragon wasn't nearly as surprised as she was. It regarded her with eyes of deep cobalt, unlike any blue she had ever seen. It watched them calmly for a moment then raised its head and sniffed. Selivia leaned forward, admiring the way the muscles in the dragon's neck rippled when it lifted its head. The scales of its underside were a paler green than the emerald tones of its hide. The huge creature shifted its wings, revealing more of the jet-black membrane, before resettling itself and watching them warily.

Ivran was saying something about how she mustn't tell anyone, but Selivia was far too enthralled by the true dragon's movements to listen.

"Watch it!" Ivran grabbed her shoulder. She had stepped closer to the edge of the crater. It wouldn't be a good idea to tumble into the pit with the dragon, but she desperately wanted to know what it felt like to pet that huge head and run a hand over those glimmering scales. The true dragon was the most beautiful creature she had ever seen.

"How?" she said when she found her voice at last.

"He arrived one year ago," Ivran said. "Just before Zala left for Rallion City."

"Are you sure it's a boy?"

"That's what the Air Sensors say."

"What do the Air Sensors have to do with it?"

"Everything," Ivran said. "They sensed the true dragons stirring. They got curious and called one to them. I don't know how. Some powerful Air discipline that hasn't been used in centuries. It flew all the way here from the Burnt Mountains."

"He could have flown right by Vertigon," Selivia said. "I'd have loved to see him soaring over the mountain." She sighed, hardly able to process her joy at seeing a real live true dragon. Despite Ivran's company, this was the happiest day of her life. "Isn't he wonderful?"

Ivran shrugged. "Aren't you people used to cur-dragons?"

"They're so small compared to this," Selivia said. "Except for the litter that was born last . . . summer." Selivia almost toppled over as the realization hit her. A cur-dragon had borne a litter of unusually large young last summer. Her brother's pet, Rumy, was the biggest of the bunch, and surprisingly strong and intelligent. Could this true dragon have flown even closer to Vertigon than they realized on his journey to the Far Plains?

"They chained him up as soon as he arrived," Ivran said. "I don't think the Air Sensors believed a dragon would actually answer their call. It scared them something fierce. They haven't practiced communing with magical animals much."

"Whyever not?"

"They're wild beasts, Princess. Our ancestors communicated with true dragons, but the Sensors Circle couldn't control this one at all when he got here. The creatures are very intelligent, but they don't think like human beings do."

Selivia was barely listening. She dropped to her knees and leaned out over the pit, getting as close as she could to the true dragon. It stared up at her with those magnificent cobalt eyes. As she met the strong blue gaze, Selivia thought her heart would burst. How had she gotten so lucky?

The dragon shuffled its wings, pulling them closer against its side. The movement echoed that of the cur-dragons she had played with throughout her childhood. The true dragon's snout was longer in proportion to the body than a cur-dragon's, as were the spikes along its back. The colors of the scales and eyes were more vivid, even in the weak beam of the Everlight. It was as if they had a magic all their own.

"Does he breathe fire?" she asked.

Before Ivran could answer, the creature reared back on his haunches, revealing heavy iron shackles binding both hind legs. A low rumble built deep within his green-scaled chest. Selivia stared, transfixed, ignoring Ivran pulling on her shoulder.

The true dragon opened its mouth, and a burst of pure gold lit up the midnight sky. The fire spewed straight upward from its glowing throat, the flame brighter and denser than typical cur-dragon fire. Droplets fell from it, behaving more like liquid than flame. The droplets landed on its back, sizzling as they slid across its scales and pooled on the floor of the pit.

Was the true dragon spitting actual Fire? *Amazing.* Selivia wondered if all true dragons could send up a fountain of pure Fire. More importantly, had it done that as a direct answer to her question, or was it just chance? She hardly dared to hope.

"Can . . . Can you understand me?" she called softly.

The true dragon looked up at her and cocked its head to the side. Her cur-dragon pets did exactly the same thing! She grinned at the creature. As if in answer, it reared back and shot a second spurt of flame into the air. Cur-dragons loved to show off too. What other similarities were there?

She stretched out a hand. The creature shuffled nearer, dragging its claws through the shimmering puddles of liquid dragon fire. It couldn't move far with the chains around its hind legs, not even coming close to her perch on the lip of the crater. Why couldn't they make the chains a bit longer so it could fly around the pit? Or train it. Her family's cur-dragons roamed freely, and they always returned to the cave beneath the castle. Was it possible to train a true dragon?

The dragon stretched out its nose, lining it up perfectly with Selivia's hand. If she were nearer, she was sure it would let her touch it. She was so mesmerized by the magnificent creature that she didn't notice Ivran was still pulling on her arm until his harsh voice interrupted her reverie.

"We should go, Princess."

"We just got here." Selivia could happily sit here watching the true dragon for the rest of her life.

"His flame will draw attention from the city," Ivran said. "I'm not supposed to show him to you."

"Why did you?"

Ivran didn't answer for a moment. "I wanted to impress you."

"Again, *why*?"

"Because the Air . . ." Ivran kicked at a stone at his feet. "It's not my choice, Princess."

The word hit Selivia like a slap in the face. "You've been calling me princess," she said. "Why do you keep doing that?"

"I know more than you think," Ivran said.

"Tell me what you're up to."

"I'll be in enough trouble already."

Selivia leapt to her feet. "Do you want me to push you in there with him? *Tell* me!"

"You wouldn't," Ivran said. He moved to the edge of the crater and stared defiantly at the dragon in the pit, as if the majestic creature were nothing more than a bundle of brindleweed. That made Selivia angrier than anything else that had been said tonight. She entertained a brief vision of pushing Ivran into the crater to meet the true dragon directly. Unfortunately, the dragon sent up another fountain of Fire, and Ivran stepped hurriedly out of range.

"We should get home before they come check on it," he said. "We can't get caught."

"Too late for that," said a new voice.

Ivran jumped a foot in the air, and Zala stepped out of the shadows. Anger blazed in her eyes as she stared her cousin down. "What do you think you're doing?"

"None of your business," Ivran muttered, his face scarlet.

"You'd better answer me this instant."

"This isn't about you," Ivran said.

"She is my charge," Zala said. "And, more importantly, she's my friend. When your mother hears what you did—"

"She won't care, not now that you're back." Ivran kicked the dirt. The true dragon raised its head at the noise, perking up like a hunting hound. "Perfect Zala and her little princess," Ivran muttered. "She never listens to what I have to say."

"Will you two *please* explain what's going on?" Selivia said. "Why did you bring me out here, Ivran? And why didn't you tell me there's a *true dragon*, Zala?"

Zala grimaced. "It's complicated."

Ivran opened his mouth, but Zala shot him a death glare, and he closed it again.

"Changes are happening all over the continent," Zala said. "We have to protect the Far Plainsfolk."

"From what? Soole?"

"The Other Lands," Zala said. "All of them. The Sensors hear whispers of threats to our people on the Air. Soole's invasion is just the beginning."

Selivia still didn't understand. The Far Plains were part of Trure. Trure had a long-standing alliance with Vertigon. So why were the Plainsfolk worried about *all* the Other Lands and not just Soole?

"Let me get this straight," Selivia said. "You think the Other Lands are a threat to the Far Plains, so the Sensors called the true dragon here for protection?"

"That's correct."

"Can they fight with it?"

Zala shook her head. "The true dragon hasn't been as easy to control as the Sensors hoped."

"So you just left him chained up down there?" The true dragon ruffled his wings as if in response to Selivia's query. Poor thing. And he'd been here a year?

A crunch of footsteps sounded as Ivran walked closer. The shadows from the dispersing dragon fire made him look ghoulish.

"I had a better idea."

Zala tensed. "Ivran, don't—"

"You."

Selivia blinked. "Me?"

"You're a princess of the royal families of both Trure and Vertigon," Ivran said. "If anyone can control it, it's you. I *told* them, but no one believed me."

"Why?"

"Because he's wrong," Zala cut in. "The Sensors have discussed it. They've already agreed the song has nothing to do with you, Sel."

"What song?"

"Some of the Sensors aren't so sure," Ivran said. "Fodorov listened to my theory. He thinks the Air has a plan for her."

Zala rounded on him. "Did you tell Fodorov you were bringing her out here?"

"No," Ivran mumbled. "I wanted to prove it first."

"Prove what?" Selivia stamped her foot, even though it wasn't especially princess-like. "What song?"

"'There's an old rhyme about true dragons," Zala said. "It's etched in a chamber deep in the Rock—the one we came through when we left the tunnels, actually. The Sensors thought the true dragon could save us, but now they think it was the wrong choice to call it here. If more of them wake and the Other Lands think we did it . . ." She shuddered. "No one can know."

Selivia felt queasy, as if the stars hanging above the vast plains had begun to spin.

"How does the song go?"

Zala took a deep breath, and her voice rose, sure and sweet.

In burning range, let not the wild Spring break
Lest Fire spread across the land
And bid true dragons wake.

In drowning land, let not the dark Earth quake
Lest Water bind us in its hand
And bid true dragons wake.

In sighing rock, let not the harsh Wind take
Lest swift Air catch us in its band
And bid true dragons wake.

Listen for the child of fire and rain,
Betwixt the mountain and the plain.
Gold will crown her and blood will claim.

Listen, for the child of fire and rain
Will bind the dragon to save the land
And all will fear to speak her name.

Zala's voice faded away, leaving only the rustle of the wind on the plains and the low, heavy snort of the true dragon's breath.

"You think it means I can control the dragon?" Selivia said at last. She met Ivran's eyes for an instant and quickly looked away, worried he'd see the hope in them.

"'Child of Fire and rain, betwixt the mountain and the plain.' That stuff about a crown. You're a half-Vertigonian, half-Truren princess. And no one will say your real name around here." Ivran shot a triumphant look at his cousin. "Some of the Sensors think the Air led you here to save us from the Other Lands."

"No, you think that," Zala snapped. "No one else does. Not even Fodorov. And you weren't supposed to show her the dragon. Wait until your mother finds out."

"I had to try," Ivran said. "You don't scare me."

Selivia frowned. The crown part made sense, but the rest? Trure could be a rainy place, but it was a stretch to say someone from Trure was a "child of rain." And what was all that about spring breaking and the earth quaking? The song could be interpreted any number of ways. It didn't mean she was destined to befriend this particular dragon, did it? It looked as if the Sensors had taken the binding part literally. Those chains on the poor creature's hind legs made her so mad.

She shook her head and focused on Zala. "Do you really think your people will end up fighting mine?"

The light from the lingering Fire in the pit revealed Zala biting her lip. "The Air has been suggesting it for some time now."

"What about your secret plans with my mother?" Selivia said. "She hired you to look out for me, right?"

"You weren't supposed to know our lands might end up on opposite sides," Zala said.

Selivia went cold. "You were going to betray me?"

Zala sighed. "I care about you, Sel. But if it comes to a question of you or the Plainsfolk, I'll choose them. I didn't want you to have to worry about it at all. We could be wrong."

"But if our countries go to war, you'll use me as a hostage anyway, won't you?"

"Sel—"

"At least Ivran thinks I could actually do something to help. You just want to use me. So much for friendship."

"It's for everyone's safety."

Selivia snorted. "You have your dragon. Your chained, enslaved true dragon. You can't have me too."

She set off walking across the plains. She didn't have to accept this. She wouldn't be used as a hostage in a conflict against her own people. She may not understand the song or the Air, but she understood betrayal.

Zala and Ivran accompanied her back toward the glowing city lights in silence. Selivia wanted to walk the other way, to set off into the desert where no one could use her for their own ends. But she needed to gather supplies and make a plan for her escape. When she left, she intended to take that poor true dragon with her—whether the song was about her or not.

18

THE POOL

"Skin!" Wyla crowed.

"What?" Dara dug the heels of her hands into her eyes, still not quite awake. She had lost count of how many early-morning research sessions Wyla had demanded of her since discovering she could control Watermight if she swallowed it first. Instead of meeting in the bright, Fire Lantern-filled study, she descended deep into the dank cavern to Work above the whirlpool each morning.

"I have a theory that may help you with both powers."

"My skin?"

"It's preventing you from easily drawing in the Watermight," Wyla said. She waved a piece of parchment covered in notes. She didn't seem to have gone to bed since their last practice session. "I believe your skin may already be too attuned to the sensations of the Fire to draw it in. But you absorb the Watermight easily enough through your stomach."

"I wouldn't call it easy," Dara grumbled. She had quickly grown tired of swallowing gulps of liquid magic in an attempt to replicate her most recent breakthrough.

"Skin and righteous indignation." Wyla cackled like an ancient witch. "You are always defending yourself when you manage to take in the Watermight, and you usually feel some sense that you are being treated unfairly. You describe it differently at times, but I believe that's the crux of it."

"So my skin can work the Fire, but my gut can work the

Watermight?" Dara rubbed her temples. "That doesn't make sense."

"No need to describe it in such a crass fashion," Wyla said. "I believe your skin responds so well to the Fire that it tries to fight against the Watermight unless something else occupies your attention, such as anger."

"So if I get it past my skin, I can control it?"

"That is my working theory." Wyla pulled out a knife that was almost as long as her forearm. The light from the Watermight pool glowed on the curved blade. "Care to test it?"

"Wait." Dara stumbled back a few paces. "I'd rather stick with drinking the stuff for now."

"I'm curious about how your blood responds to direct contact with the Watermight," Wyla said. "You've described how the Fire runs through you like blood, so I hadn't thought the Watermight would behave the same way."

"Yes, that's right," Dara said. "No blood." Her hand strayed to her Savven blade. The warmth reminded her with a jolt that it had been days since she last practiced with it or even did footwork. The Work was consuming more of her time and energy every day.

"But if we are wrong, the potential—"

"Forget the potential!" Dara said. "You're not cutting me up until we know more about this whole blood and skin and gut connection."

"Perhaps I'm being unfair," Wyla said. A truly evil smile split her face. "Quickly! Drink this!"

She dipped a stone goblet into the whirlpool and shoved it into Dara's hands.

Dara scowled at her over the rim. Wyla had played her. Threatening to cut her without a good enough reason just to get her riled up. Well, it had worked. Dara drained the goblet in one gulp.

For a heartbeat, nothing happened. Dara glared at Wyla and wiped a silvery droplet from her lips. Then she felt it.

The magic surged in her stomach. Ice filled her, spreading outward. The cold power crept along her bones, making her strong. She balled her hands into fists, and a bit of silver appeared at the edge of her fingernails. It was working! She concentrated on the way the magic moved within her. She might be able to draw the power out, give it form.

Then her stomach tightened as if she'd been punched, and she hurled. The Watermight splattered at Wyla's feet, some of it splashing over her steel-toed boots.

"Drink more," Wyla said.

"Give me a minute to—"

"No time to waste!" Wyla shoved another goblet of Watermight into Dara's hands.

She choked it down. This time, the Watermight came up immediately. She spit out curses alongside the liquid power.

Wyla was waiting with another goblet.

They did it over and over again. Dara gulped down Watermight, Wyla urging her on. She wanted to slow down, to be more careful. Wyla shouldn't be making her do it like this. She was going to be overwhelmed.

Her stomach and throat felt raw. Tears streamed down her face, mixed with shimmering bits of silver.

Still Wyla served her more.

"That's enough!" Dara tossed back one final goblet of Watermight. The power surged within her. Her bones creaked with cold power. Instead of throwing up, she threw the goblet against the wall, and the stone shattered into a thousand pieces.

Dara turned on Wyla. The woman didn't even step back. She watched eagerly, pen poised, as Dara advanced on her.

Not sure what else to do, Dara Wielded exactly as she would have with Fire. She spooled threads of Watermight out of her fingers, wincing at the pain, and shot them toward Wyla. The cords wrapped around her wrists and ankles like shackles. Almost before Dara knew what she was doing, she used the Watermight to yank Wyla off her feet and lift her into the air.

Wyla hovered, suspended above the stones for one heartbeat. Two. A mixture of surprise and glee flashed across her face. And fear. The moment Dara saw the fear, her control collapsed. She just managed to lower Wyla down again before she keeled over and expelled the last of the power out of her body.

She knelt on the stones, breathing heavily, attempting to regain control.

Wyla stepped up beside her, already chatting in a brusque, scholarly fashion. As usual, she asked about Dara's feelings and probed her for details to add to her notes, but it was too late. Dara had seen it. For a brief moment, Wyla had been terrified of her.

Dara heaved again, wanting to get the last of the foreign substance out of her body. At last, she straightened and met Wyla's eyes. A touch of silver edged her lashes. Wyla was holding onto Watermight herself.

"Are we done?" Dara asked.

Wyla smiled, and for an instant, Dara saw that flash of fear once more. Wyla didn't release any of the power she held. "We are just getting started."

Dara's whole body was shaking when the session ended at last. She didn't even attempt to follow when Wyla climbed the stairs, leaving her lying on the cold stone. She could die right there. She was a little surprised she hadn't died already. Wyla was getting useful information out of her, but Dara knew with utter certainty that the Waterworker wouldn't even blink if she drowned, or froze to death, or was swept into oblivion by an overwhelming torrent of power.

She forced herself to stand and climb the stairs, still shivering. She had to clutch the wall as she eased out of the underground chamber. She was tempted to try swallowing a bit more Watermight to give her the strength to make it to her room, but her body couldn't handle it right now.

She leaned against the heavy wooden door at the top of the staircase to open it, almost falling into the entryway. Wyla's bodyguard, Siln, approached from deeper in the house.

"She asked me to make sure you made it out of there," he said.

"Could have used help getting up the stairs," Dara said.

"She's a tough instructor." Siln made no move to help Dara as she shuffled carefully toward the kitchen. "You'll be stronger for it."

"I've had strict teachers before," Dara said. "But she's just experimenting with me. I don't know if *she* even considers herself my teacher."

"Learn from her in any case," Siln said. "I wouldn't be the Wielder I am today if not for her."

"The what?"

Siln chuckled. "You didn't know I'm also a Watermight practitioner?"

"I . . . no." Dara had gotten along well with Siln on the journey through the Darkwood, but they had mostly talked about dueling. It was rare to find a fan of the sport in the city of the Dance of Steel.

"That's why it was just the two of us when we picked you up in Fork Town," Siln said, falling in beside her as they entered the large kitchen. It was empty of servants. Wyla only required a handful to keep her manor running, and she hated having potential loose mouths running around. "She'd never travel with only one powerless bodyguard for protection. Wyla has too many enemies."

He pulled a loaf of bread out of a cupboard and set it on the rough wooden table in the middle of the kitchen. A dark shape moved beneath the table. Rumy the cur-dragon was snoozing beneath it. No wonder the servants had cleared out.

"Who are Wyla's enemies?" Dara asked, dropping into a chair by the table and reaching for the bread.

Siln gave her a warning look. "Anyone outside this household is an enemy, no matter how friendly they seem."

"It's not like she lets me outside of the household much anyway," Dara said.

"That's true." Siln set a kettle on the cast-iron stove and tossed some logs through the door, sending up sparks from the glowing coals at the bottom. "She finds you fascinating. You should be proud."

The clang of the kettle on the stovetop caused Rumy to start up from his sleep. He shuffled over to Dara and laid his head in her lap. It was warm and heavy, and she stroked his nose as he snuffled contentedly. She *did* like that she was making progress, but she wasn't sure if Wyla's admiration was something to be proud of.

"What's your Watermight specialty?" she asked Siln.

"Combat."

"Yeah? Are you good?"

Siln grinned, flexing the muscles beneath his tattoos. "I owe Wyla too much to branch out on my own, but even the most powerful Waterworkers are wary of me."

"And here I thought you just liked sport dueling."

Siln rummaged in the cupboards for a pair of mismatched tea mugs. "I think you'll find that your fencing skills will help if Wyla decides to teach you to fight."

"Could you teach me?" Dara asked.

Immediately, Siln's friendly demeanor disappeared. "I will do nothing unless she wishes it," he said. "You would do well to remember that."

"I didn't mean behind her back," Dara said quickly, though that was exactly what she had meant. "But if you're that skilled, I just wondered if she might assign you to coach me."

Siln studied her for a moment, an earthenware mug in each muscular hand. She stroked Rumy's nose, trying not to appear tense. At last Siln relaxed.

"Perhaps she will," he said. "And you can show me your dueling moves. If you weren't so valuable to Wyla, I'd like to see how you'd do in the Steel Pentagon."

"Do you watch pentagon matches often?" Dara asked.

"When I can." The kettle on the stove shrieked as the water reached a boil. Siln picked it up to silence the screaming. "Black or green tea?"

"Black. Thank you."

Dara was still shivering. She thought about drawing on Rumy's Fire to warm herself, but it might not be wise in this state. Tea would help, and Rumy's head on her lap warmed her plenty. She had spent far too much time Working of late. As any good athlete knew, downtime was necessary to allow her muscles—not to mention her mind—to recover between practice sessions. She needed a break.

"Do you think I could come with you to watch a pen match? If Wyla says it's okay, of course."

Siln shrugged, focusing on his tea preparations. "I don't see why not. I'm going to a Dance this Turnday. A league match. There are some strong teams this year."

"Is it common for Waterworkers to take an interest in pen fighters?" Dara asked.

"You are wondering about your friend The Slugger and Khrillin the Waterlord?"

Siln handed Dara a heavy earthenware mug. She wrapped her hands around it, savoring the warmth and considering how to respond. Siv believed this Khrillin would pay for the fighting men he needed to retake his castle. They'd mostly communicated through Rid lately, but she could tell he'd already pinned his hopes on the prospect.

"That's right," she said at last. "What can you tell me about him?"

"He has always been full of surprises," Siln said. "That is one of the reasons I'm going to this match."

"To spy on Khrillin?"

"To get a sense of his plans," Siln said. "Wyla believes he may be using your friend to get to you."

Dara blinked. "Me?"

"It worked, didn't it?" Siln sipped his tea, his lean muscles flexing. "You walked right into Khrillin's house."

"But he didn't know who I was or that I'm connected to Wyla." Dara didn't add that Khrillin had more than enough reason to be interested in Siv alone. Rumy nuzzled her hand, and she hugged him a little tighter.

"Khrillin is crafty," Siln said. "He may be playing a long game. He could court your friend for a year before he ever asks him about you."

"We won't be here in a year," Dara said.

Siln smiled. "If you say so. It's not easy to walk away from Wyla—and what she can teach you. In any case, I'm curious what Khrillin will do if you appear right under his nose at your friend's match. I'll speak to Wyla about giving you a Turnday off. Perhaps I can spot something that was hidden to you at the party."

"Mmm."

Dara and Siln sipped their tea for a few minutes. She wasn't sure if she'd call the silence companionable. She mulled over Siln's story. He must have a highly compelling reason to stay in Wyla's service if he was as powerful in his own right as he claimed. Dara wondered what Wyla had over him.

Siln was the first to break the silence. "Kres March's team has been causing a stir this season. Your friend is quite popular—and nice to look at, I hear. He was also a duelist in Vertigon, correct?"

"Yes, he was." Dara kept her eyes on her tea. Siln would have to try harder than that if he wanted information about Siv. Wyla still hadn't pressed her for details about him, but Khrillin wasn't the only one capable of playing the long game. She considered Siln's words: *It's not easy to walk away from Wyla—and what she can teach you.* She didn't like the implication.

In truth, Dara wasn't in a hurry to leave. The more she learned about the Watermight, the more she felt she should be able to use the two powers together. Her father wouldn't be daunted by the kind of basic tricks she knew so far. She needed to be able to use both if she had any hope of defeating him. And there was still the problem of actually getting the Watermight to Vertigon.

Wyla's power was intriguing, thrilling even, but unless she could figure out a way to transport it over long distances, it wouldn't help against her father's Fire. She had seen him in combat, and if Zage Lorrid hadn't been able to defeat him, she wasn't sure how she could either. She still had so much to learn. For now, Wyla was the only one who could teach her, even though her help came with strings and barbs.

She would worry about that later. Right now, she wanted to finish her tea, curl up under some blankets, and sleep for a month.

19

THE STEEL PENTAGON

Dara met Siln in the manor house entryway on Turnday. She wore trousers and a black blouse instead of Wyla's poison-green colors today. She had buckled her Savven blade around her waist and tucked a few Firebulbs into her belt pouch. After some consideration, she filled a wineskin with Watermight from Wyla's supply and hung it from the other side of her belt. Watermight didn't travel well, but it ought to last through the day. She hoped she wouldn't need it. They were supposed to be observing Khrillin, nothing more. And enjoying the fighting, of course.

Siln proved to be a pleasant companion as they walked to the Steel Pentagon. It took almost an hour to get to the venue, which was located near the Royal District. Along the way, Siln regaled her with tales of his Watermight battles. Dara listened carefully, hoping to pick up something she could use. Siln had probably cleared it with Wyla before bringing up the topic. He was utterly loyal, as far as Dara could tell, and he wouldn't teach her anything without Wyla's permission.

After spending so much time Working in Wyla's basement, Dara was surprised to find that spring was in full bloom in the city. The creeping vines and ground moss that were brown and withered when they'd arrived had turned brilliant green. Water lilies bloomed on the slow-moving estuaries, and tiny frogs hopped from leaf to leaf. It had rained recently, and the damp ground felt ripe, ready to break open at a touch. Even the salt wind off the sea smelled fresher than it had when they first arrived. Many people had abandoned shoes and stockings in favor of leather sandals. The feral children that always seemed to pop up in crowded areas ran barefoot through the mud and chased furtive creatures through the shallows.

Dara felt as if she could finally thaw out after her weeks in the dungeon-like Watermight chamber. Actually, months. Dara stopped short at the thought. She had been in Pendark for nearly two months. She didn't have too much longer until Wyla removed the bond on her arm. And Wyla still hadn't told Dara what she owed her for helping save Siv's life during the fight in the Smokery District.

"What is it?" Siln asked.

"Huh? Oh, nothing." Dara caught up to him, and they continued through the city. "I thought I saw a salt adder."

"If you spot it again, let me know," Siln said. "They're delicious."

"Aren't they deadly?"

"Only to touch. Their skin secretes a poisonous slime. But Watermight has its uses. I can catch and filet a salt adder in three seconds flat. My friends and I used to race when we were first learning the Might."

Siln picked up the pace as they approached the crowd surrounding the extra-large Steel Pentagon. Stands as high as two-story buildings rose around the arena. The rocky foundations supporting the stands sank slightly under the weight of all the spectators. The crowds gathering outside were rougher and rowdier than typical dueling spectators. Vertigonians could be rabid fans, but they didn't start fistfights in the audience or shout vicious profanities at each other.

Dara and Siln pushed their way through the tumult and climbed the stands on the western side of the pen. They had a good view of the Royal District from here, including the King's Tower, a single column spiking into the sky with a balcony encircling the top like a crown. So that was where Vex Rollendar had taken refuge—at least according to Vine's most recent intelligence.

Vine herself had decided not to attend the Dance. She'd located an Air Sensors manor in Pendark, a somewhat forlorn operation compared to the one they'd visited in Rallion City. She planned to spend the day meditating in hopes that she might communicate with her friends in Trure. It took a long time to accomplish anything with the trace amounts of Air in Pendark, but they needed to know what was happening in the rest of the world.

Dara and Siln found seats a few rows from the barrier. The arena's obstacles were more elaborate than Dara had expected. Siv had described barrels, logs, and assorted broken-down conveyances. This Steel Pentagon featured a wood-frame castle, complete with a moat dug deep around it. The castle was built in three tiers and was taller than a house. The wooden frame had no walls, leaving the interior exposed. The spectators would have a full view of the action within the skeletal structure.

As Dara examined the island and moat in the center of the pentagon, an unsettling sensation wormed through her stomach. She quickly scanned the crowds for any sign of Vex Rollendar. She wouldn't be surprised to find he enjoyed the blood sport. But Vex was nowhere to be found amongst the spectators, many of whom were getting steadily drunk as they waited for the fights to begin.

Dara rolled her shoulders uneasily, unable to shake the feeling that something wasn't right. The wood-frame castle kept drawing her attention.

"It's new," Siln said when she asked about the structure. "The league will do anything to keep their ticket sales up."

"You don't approve?" Dara asked.

Siln examined his well-cut fingernails. "I like the Dances now and again, but they lack a certain elegance."

Dara quickly saw what he meant when the first fighters were called into the ring. The two heavyset men wielded battle-axes in a brief contest of intense, gory action. Both took wounds, and they christened the new wooden castle with their blood.

Siln sighed in disapproval. "They always start with brawlers."

Despite his words, Dara noticed the way Siln leaned forward to follow the trail of blood as the two competitors limped out of the arena. He may enjoy the elegance of Vertigonian dueling, but he liked the brutality of the Pendarkan sport more than he let on.

"Aren't there supposed to be ten fighters?" Dara asked.

"They always hold a few solo rounds before the melees," Siln said. "The audience needs time to get drunk and place their bets for the Dances."

A rapier bout came next. The fighting style reminded Dara of Berg Doban's training as he prepared the New Guard to defend the king with real steel. She missed her coach's steady presence. He berated his students all the time, but she had been close to him for many years. Compared to Wyla, he was positively cuddly.

The duelists made better use of the castle obstacle than the battle-axe fighters had. They crossed the deep trench that passed for a moat on a plank bridge and darted around the wooden frame to avoid each other. It did make the fight more dynamic. The fighters knew better than to actually climb into the castle, though. It would be difficult to wield a sword within the constricted space.

One of the swordsmen was lighter on his feet than the other, and he leapt back and forth across the moat, taunting his opponent. The crowds jeered and laughed as he danced out of the other man's reach. At last, the larger man took up a position on the island and bellowed a challenge at the smaller fighter.

The spry swordsman leapt off the island again and strutted around the edge of the pentagon. He raised his arms to the audience, calling on them for more cheers, more applause. The stands shuddered as the audience obliged, drumming their feet on the rickety wood and filling the spring air with their voices. The other fighter remained on the island, glowering at his showy opponent.

After whipping the crowd into a frenzy, the smaller swordsman gave a dramatic bow and darted back to the center of the arena. He jumped back across the moat to resume the fight on the island.

The cheers turned to gasps in an instant.

While the spry little fellow had been strutting for the crowd, the other swordsman had stayed alert. He advanced as his opponent jumped across the moat, timing the movement carefully. His blade came up at precisely the right moment, and he skewered the jumping man through the heart.

The spry swordsman froze, teetering on the edge of the trench with steel protruding from his back. Then his opponent put a boot in his belly and shoved. The smaller man fell backward into the ditch. The body disappeared from view completely, the moat deeper than it first seemed.

Siln tutted beside her. "See what I mean? No elegance."

All around them, people rose to their feet, hollering, banging on their thighs, stamping. Dara remained seated, gaze fixed on the thin line of blood tinting the victorious fighter's rapier. She had been in a deadly battle before. She would never shake the memory of the fight beneath the blue house on stilts where Siv had been attacked. She had killed that day. It had been necessary, and she hadn't hesitated. But this? Why couldn't these fighters use blunted weapons as they did in Vertigon? They could still use obstacles and fight in the round to keep it interesting. Why did it have to be this way?

But as the crowds roared, she understood that they weren't here for a sportsmanly contest of skills. They were here for the blood.

Two women fought the next bout. One was the saber-wielding Gull Mornington. She was skilled and efficient, and she made quick work of her opponent, finishing the fight with her blade at the other woman's throat without even going near the central obstacle. The crowds cheered for her, but their response to Gull's fight wasn't nearly as enthusiastic as it had been to the previous deadly bout.

"She has talent," Siln said, watching Gull salute all five sides of the pentagon and stride out of sight. "But she should have dragged it out for longer."

Dara didn't answer. She had just spotted Siv waiting at the edge of the arena. He was up next.

The announcer finished singing Gull's praises and called the assembly to order.

"Friends!" he shouted, voice carrying over the din. "Our next fight features a newcomer to Pendark who has already stolen the hearts of many. He slices with zeal, but it's when he slugs it out in the mud that he really shines. I give you Siv 'the Slugger' Amen!"

The crowds rose to their feet, cheering wildly. Women tossed handkerchiefs and wildflowers toward the arena. Dara looked around in surprise. She hadn't realized how popular Siv had become over the past weeks. He may have actually been modest when he'd described his successes. How unlike him.

As Siv strutted into the pen, Dara was reminded of the arrogant young prince she had first met last summer. His coat hung open, and he moved with an easy grace suggesting he wasn't remotely worried about the deadly contest. Dara couldn't help smiling. He'd had to become so serious after his father's murder. But there once more was the lad who'd shrugged off warnings about the plots against him and spent his time drinking, dueling, and sneaking out to watch her matches. He had grown up a lot lately, but he was still the same Siv.

He punched the air a few times before removing his coat and striking a casually elegant pose. With the rough shadow of his beard, his strong cheekbones, and the confident charm of his movements, Dara could see why he had become so popular. It made her stomach flutter to know that she was the one he wanted to be with, the one who actually got to kiss him.

The crowds were still cheering so loudly, the announcer had trouble being heard as he introduced Siv's opponent.

"Sounds like your friend has a few fans," Siln said.

"Is this normal?" Dara asked.

"Pentagon spectators love anything new and shiny. They will calm down soon enough. He'll lose a few matches, and they'll see he's a man same as any other. Eventually, another up-and-comer will take their fancy."

"Let's hope he doesn't lose," Dara said.

"Everyone does eventually," Siln said. "Knife fighters tend to outlast most pen combatants, though, so long as they keep their heads in the Dance."

"Do knife fighters often face broadswords and battle-axes directly in the melees?"

"Depends on the strategy," Siln said. "The heavier weapons are unwieldy. A nimble knifeman can hold his own with proper planning."

Dara didn't like the idea of Siv facing off against larger weapons with nothing but a knife. It struck her as more risky than it was worth. He had claimed (through messages dutifully carried by Rid) that he wanted to keep earning money in case Khrillin proved untrustworthy, but Dara wondered if he liked the attention a bit too much. He was certainly getting plenty of it. He strutted around the arena, waving to the crowds, as his opponent made his entrance.

"No need to look so worried," Siln said, nudging her with his elbow. She realized she had squeezed her hands into tight fists. She tried to relax. "Kres the Master is a well-known strategist. He doesn't lose members of his team very often."

"What else do you know about Kres?" Dara asked. She wanted to keep talking to take her mind off the coming fight. She couldn't think of anything worse than watching Siv fall in the arena after all they had been through. She flexed her fingers to get the blood flowing to them again.

"He's a strategist outside the pen as well as in," Siln said.

"What does that mean?"

"Kres has powerful friends," Siln said. "He's discreet, but he has ties to some important people."

"Important people? Like Waterworkers?"

"Perhaps."

"Khrillin?"

"I've seen hints," Siln said. "But I don't know for sure."

Siv hadn't mentioned a connection between Khrillin and Kres March, but it had been a long time since she'd spoken with him directly. Sending messages back and forth with Rid just wasn't the same.

Dara and Siln fell silent as Siv and his opponent, who was called the Terrerack Terror, assumed their guard stances below. It felt so strange to be the one sitting in the stands while he competed. She didn't like it. She dug her fingernails into her palms. Siv had better not get himself killed.

"All ready?" The announcer's voice rose above the crowd. Dara's stomach plummeted like a stone falling from a bridge. The Terrerack Terror crouched low, knife glinting in his large fist. He was a beefy man, and he looked like a bit of a slugger himself. The announcer stepped out of the way. "Let us dance!"

The Terror rushed at Siv, still in a crouch. Siv slipped aside, allowing the Terror to barrel past him. The man spun and charged again. Siv stepped out of his reach. Again.

They moved around the arena, never actually making contact. The Terror launched assault after assault, but Siv didn't allow him to come within reach. After the first few attacks, Siv made a show of putting his knife away in his belt. The crowds jeered.

Then Siv danced. He moved swiftly, even elegantly, as he stayed out of the Terrerack Terror's range. They circled around and around the pentagon, and the Terror grew angrier by the minute. His face turned dark red, and he roared in frustration as Siv led him on a merry chase around the arena.

"He moves well," Siln said.

Dara didn't dare respond. Didn't dare breathe. It would only take one slip, one misjudged step, and the Terror would obliterate him.

Suddenly, Siv darted for the central obstacle, leaping across the moat to the island and hoisting himself up the skeletal castle. The crowds cheered as he balanced at the top, strutting like a cat along the narrow wooden beams.

The Terror bellowed a curse and advanced toward the moat. Siv taunted him from atop his perch. A dull glint shone in his hand. He had taken out his knife again. That was a relief. The showing off made Dara nervous. It was time for Siv to finish this.

Apparently, the Terror thought so too, because instead of crossing the moat, he dug his hands into the dirt piled beside it and pulled out a handful of fist-sized rocks. He proceeded to hurl these at Siv, who had all he could do to keep from falling off the castle as he ducked to avoid the rocks.

The crowds hollered. Siv's foot slipped, and he nearly toppled off the wooden structure. Dara leaned forward, heart sputtering like a candle. Siv recovered his footing—just in time to dive out of the way of another rock. Still he taunted the larger man and danced along the razor edge.

The Terrerack Terror was getting angrier, his curses completely incoherent. The crowd began to grow restless. They shouted for the combatants to cross the moat and finish the fight. Siv shook his head, gesturing for the Terror to come at him.

The Terror was too agitated to make a clean jump. He took an ungainly leap and landed on the edge of the little island, feet scrabbling against the edge of the trench as he tried to keep from falling. Dirt fell away from his boots as he dug his toes into the side of the moat and climbed onto the island, leaving deep scores in the muddy wall.

While the Terror was busy trying not to fall into the ditch, Siv quietly climbed down from the wood-frame castle. When the Terror got to his feet at last, Siv was waiting. He landed a neat punch to the man's jaw. The Terror toppled backward into the moat.

The crowds leapt to their feet, screaming and cheering. Dara did the same, her legs shaky. He had won. And he didn't have a scratch on him.

She had to admire Siv's strategy, the way he timed his taunts to enrage his opponent and then finished the fight with a clean blow. The Terror would have a nasty headache when he woke, but there had been no bloodshed at all. And the fight had been interesting enough to keep the crowds engaged.

She was glad to see he could hold his own in the arena, but he wasn't out of danger yet. Siv's team was scheduled for a Dance of Steel today. He would face a group of five next, all armed with bigger weapons than either his knife or his fist.

Siv turned at last to face their side of the arena. Dara waved frantically until he caught sight of her. A wide grin split his face, and he waved back. Flush with victory, he looked truly proud of his performance.

Movement flickered near his ankle. Dara barely had time to shout a warning before a grubby hand grabbed Siv's leg and pulled him into the moat.

The Terrerack Terror was still conscious. The fight wasn't over yet.

The sound of fists meeting flesh echoed through the arena, competing with the screams of the crowd. Dara dug her fingernails deeper into her palms. She couldn't see them. The moat was too deep. One of the fighters threw the other against the wall of the trench, and a huge chunk of mud gave way and slipped out of sight.

Judging by the flailing limbs and the crunch of fist against bone, neither of the fighters had kept hold of their knives when they fell into the moat. It was a brawl, not a duel.

The spectators grew hoarse, whipped into an even greater frenzy by the new development. It was hard to see the action in the ditch, but most people were too excited that the fight was still going on to complain. They drowned out any grumbles in a torrent of cheers.

Abruptly, Siv's head appeared above the edge of the trench. His lip was bleeding, and a pair of huge hands wrapped around his throat. The Terror held him up against the muddy wall of the moat, trying to choke the life out of him. Siv's hands scrabbled at the vise around his neck, his face turning purple.

Dara dug her hand into her pouch for the Firebulb. She'd promised to let him take care of himself, but he wasn't going to die for the amusement of the crowd.

Before she could draw the Fire from the metal and shoot it across the arena, Siv reached forward and dug his fingers into the Terrerack Terror's eyes. The man bellowed in pain. His grip loosened, and Siv gasped in a breath. Dara did the same, as if she were breathing for the first time.

Despite the pressure on his eyeballs, the Terror still didn't release Siv entirely. He slammed him against the wall as hard as if he were made of straw.

Siv held on to the Terror's face. The Terror shoved him into the dirt wall again and again, but Siv kept digging at his eyes with his fingernails. The Terror roared, the sound shaking the very earth of the Steel Pentagon. Still, Siv held on, scratched, gouged. At last, the Terror released his grip, and Siv toppled out of sight.

The Terror clapped his hands over his bleeding face, howling in fury. Before he could move more than two steps, Siv popped into view again and put a newly retrieved knife to his throat. It was over.

When the Terror realized what had happened, he bellowed a curse and lurched away from Siv to climb out of the pit. Siv waved his knife above the rim of the trench, showing that he was still okay, as the announcer called out the results for those who couldn't see the action.

Siv turned to the dirt wall the Terror had been slamming him against and hauled himself out of the pit, moving with a little less alacrity than before. Dara released her death grip on the Firebulb at last, letting the power ease back into the metal. That had been too close. She didn't much like watching him fight after all.

Siv strutted along the edge of the little island, hamming for the crowd once more. He would have a swollen lip and a black eye—or two—but he had survived. He looked a little unsteady from the beating he'd taken before clinching the victory. The newly constructed island had taken a beating as well. The dirt had loosened considerably when Siv was being slammed against it. As he whirled on his heel, a huge section of the mud wall crumbled into the moat.

Siv kept his balance and leapt lightly away from the patch of ground as it gave way. But it wasn't his precarious position that caught Dara's attention as the chunk of earth fell into the trench. The slide of the dirt revealed an impression in the island that had been carved out during the construction of the moat. It was as if there was a pocket of air inside it that the repeated battering with the Terrerack Terror's heels and Siv's body had broken open.

Except that the pocket wasn't filled with air. Dara stared, transfixed, as a fountain of Watermight spewed forth in the center of the arena.

20

THE VENT

The silvery Watermight spewed from the ground like water from a fountain, except with a lighter, liquid-gas consistency. Without the constraint of a whirlpool or the direction of a Waterworker, the magical substance burbled and swelled of its own accord. This was Watermight in its rawest, purest form. Dara's body reacted to the rush of power like a twanged bowstring.

"Is that—?"

"A new vent," Siln cried. "Quickly. Follow my lead."

He dove forward through the stands, clambering over the benches and spectators standing between him and the arena. A few people moved out of his way, but most were transfixed by what was happening at the center of the pentagon.

Siln wasn't the only person in the audience who had figured out what was going on. Others were hurrying forward, knocking people out of the way. Suddenly, it was a mad dash of Waterworkers trying to lay claim to the power spilling out of the vent and filling the moat with silvery-white magic.

Dara was more worried about Siv than the fresh Watermight supply as she followed Siln over the barrier. He was still on the island, staring in surprise as a dozen people—none of them pen fighters—charged toward him.

He had the sense to climb onto the skeleton castle, getting himself a bit farther out of the way as the Waterworkers raised their hands and began calling streams of power toward them. Even the weakest ones wanted to collect as much as they could before someone claimed this vent.

Siln was faster than most, and his eyes were already glowing silver-white by the time he skidded to a stop near the moat. He lashed a whip of Watermight toward the nearest Worker, a woman with wild red hair, a dress of jet black, and several knives strapped about her person. She defended against Siln's attack with waving hands and vicious shrieks. She took control of the whip of Watermight, molding it with deft movements. Siln cursed as the power he'd thrown toward her settled in front of her in the form of a silver shield.

But he was already calling more of the Watermight from the moat, spinning it faster than Dara thought possible. She gasped as a silver stream whipped toward her and forced its way between her teeth.

Dara swallowed. Her first instinct was to fight it, but she knew Siln would push the power down her throat if she didn't comply. He didn't even look at her, directing three different attacks at other Waterworkers trying to establish themselves around the arena.

Dara spluttered as she gulped down the power. The Watermight took hold in her body almost instantly. Angry at how Siln had forced the stuff down her throat, she managed to keep from coughing it back up again. She stood still for a few heartbeats as the power coursed through her, icing her bones and lending her strength.

Battle raged around her, far more frantic than the pen fights had been. All the Waterworkers in the audience had been taken by surprise, and at least two of them looked as if they'd spent a few hours getting drunk in the stands before all this began. They lurched about, flailing razors of Watermight around, barely keeping their feet.

Siln showed in a matter of seconds why Wyla prized his combat skills. He spun spheres of Watermight from his palms, sending them out to engulf the heads of his opponents. The spheres clung to their faces like raindrops capturing ants. Some managed to break the spheres or draw in the power, but at least one man panicked and sucked the Watermight into his lungs. Apparently, that wasn't as safe or effective as swallowing it, because his eyes rolled back in his head and he fell to the ground.

Dara didn't know what to do. She reached instinctively for her Savven blade, but that wouldn't be much help here. Neither would the bit of Fire in her belt pouch. Why couldn't Wyla have started her combat instruction a few days sooner?

She recalled when her father and Zage Lorrid had fought in the Great Hall. They'd used the Fire to create metal weapons. These Waterworkers couldn't melt metal into spikes, but they could move things. Within minutes, they turned the arena into a churning sea as they lifted objects up on waves of power and hurled them at each other. They swept some opponents off their feet with fountains of silver and forced others to sink into waist-deep mud.

Some Waterworkers had brought bodyguards with them into the ring, and these fighters bore the brunt of the Watermight attacks. Harming another magic wielder was a lot more difficult than drowning a mundane fighting man trying to protect his liege. Dara had barely gotten her bearings before a man flew across her path, borne on a narrow wave of power, and crashed into the wooden castle. Siv was still perched at the top, hanging on for dear life as the structure shuddered from the impact. She had to get to him.

Dara fought for control of the icy torrent of Watermight in her core. She managed to seize it just as the first attack launched against her. A beam of wood the size of a man hurtled toward her on a violent wave. She raised both hands to protect her face, and the beam crashed into her with a sickening crunch. Splinters and Watermight rained down around her.

Dara froze, fearing the bones in her arms had been shattered. But the Watermight coursing through her body made her strong. She felt pain, but the beam didn't do as much damage as she had expected. She looked up to find the wild-eyed redhead staring at her in surprise.

Dara took a step toward the woman, and a silver-white veil fell across her vision. She felt that incredible strength she had experienced when she'd tried to swim out of the whirlpool. Before she could think better of it, she closed the gap between them and lifted the woman into the air with her bare hands. The woman shrieked a curse as Dara heaved her across the arena. She tumbled end over end, red hair flying, came to a stop at the base of the railing, and lay still.

Dara stared at her hands, awed at the way the Watermight made them supernaturally strong. She wondered what else she could do. *Worry about that later.*

She quickly took stock of the savage melee raging in the arena. Siln hurled ice daggers at one of the more intoxicated Waterworkers, who threw them back with much less dexterity. Siln worked with an efficiency and grace that Dara would have admired in any duelist. She could certainly picture him skinning and filleting a salt adder in a matter of seconds. A pair of non-wielding fighters lay bloodied at his feet, with more darting away from him.

The crowds beyond the barrier had thinned drastically. The Pendarkan masses may enjoy a good brawl, but even they knew when an altercation had the potential to boil out of control.

Siv was still hanging onto the wood-frame castle as it teetered dangerously over the newly opened vent. Several combatants had used pieces of the frame as weapons in the fight. Siv would be lucky if the whole thing didn't collapse. Dara charged toward him. She had to reach him before anyone mistook him for a Waterworker. This wasn't his fight. It wasn't really hers either. She was barely more than an apprentice.

But as Dara hurried toward the center of the pentagon, a familiar figure caught her eye. Khrillin the Waterlord was striding across the muddy ground toward Siln, clad all in red. He hadn't joined the fray initially. Now that some of the Waterworkers had taken each other out, he made his entrance.

Siln was still occupied with the drunken ice-dagger thrower, and he didn't see the Waterlord stalking toward him, quietly gathering a stream of Watermight from the vent. His eyes already glowed silver-white.

Even in the chaos, Dara knew Wyla would hear of what she did here. If Khrillin defeated Siln, Wyla would know that Dara hadn't stepped in to help.

"Siln!" she shouted. "Look out!"

She couldn't draw on any more power herself, but she still had some in her wineskin. She drained it in one gulp and ran toward Khrillin, the Might coursing along her bones. The power gave her speed as well as strength. She barreled into the Waterlord, using the momentum to knock him off his feet.

Khrillin cried out in surprise. Dara leapt up, not letting him grab her. She forced a jet of Watermight out of her fingertips and blasted the Waterlord at close range. He threw up his hands to protect his eyes. When he lowered them, a dangerous grimace stretched across his face. He stood.

Dara darted out of his reach. The delay had been enough. Siln finished off the drunken Waterworker with an ice dagger to the heart and strode to Dara's side. He spared her a brief nod before advancing to meet the Waterlord.

Siln and Khrillin stared each other down. Watermight built around them as they each gathered mighty waves and prepared to do battle. Death danced in the Waterlord's eyes, but Dara's distraction had made him lose some of his reserve of power. His wave wasn't building as quickly as Siln's. He was going to be overwhelmed, and he knew it.

Siln raised both hands, preparing to launch a devastating attack. Khrillin would be dead in seconds. But the instant before the power could burst from Siln's hands, a figure darted between him and Khrillin, waving frantically.

"Wait!" It was Siv. He stood directly in Siln's way, hands raised.

A memory flashed before Dara's eyes: Siv standing before her father, a golden cage of Fire closing in on him. She hadn't had the skills to stop that attack. All she could do was try to distract her father before he killed the man she loved.

Dara's heart squeezed tight. Siv was in danger again, and her magical skills were *still* inadequate. She couldn't defeat her father's Fire, and she couldn't stop the Waterworkers either. Desperately, she ran forward and grabbed Siln's arm.

"Don't hurt him!"

"Get back." Siln shook her off with a curse. She grabbed him again, digging her nails deep into his tattooed flesh. Siln ripped out of her grip, not even wincing at the deep gouges she left in his skin. He turned back to his adversary.

But Siv's action and Dara's reaction gave Khrillin enough time to recover. He stepped out from behind Siv, eyes blazing white, and called more of the power from the vent. He raised his hands at the same time as Siln.

Dara tackled Siv into the mud as the two attacks met in the middle with a savage crack. Her Watermight-strengthened body protected Siv from the worst of the impact as the waves of power crashed over their heads. Silver magic thundered down around them like hailstones.

Not waiting to see if Siv was all right, Dara rolled off him and crawled sideways out of the conflict. He scrambled through the mud after her. When they were far enough away, they turned back to watch Siln and Khrillin duel.

A mighty tempest raged across the arena. The few people remaining in the stands ooed and ahed as the two Waterworkers wielded their power against each other in a violent torrent of attacks and counterattacks, parries and feints. The glow of Watermight lit the pentagon as if a giant star had settled at its center.

Siln and Khrillin were both expert fighters. It was clear there would be no easy victory here. Dara could barely breathe as she watched the Watermight contest. The sheer power was magnificent, and it drew her eyes like a lodestar. She yearned to be able to control a fraction of that brilliant storm of silver.

"You're freezing," Siv said in her ear. He put his arm around her and drew her close. She was struck by the overwhelming sense that it had been too long since they had last touched each other. She shivered, suddenly feeling as if she were lying exposed on a mountainside in the depths of winter. She wished she could pull on a bit of Fire, but with Watermight still coating her bones, she thought she might combust.

"Why did you jump in like that?" she said.

"I need him," Siv said. "He's going to fund my campaign to retake Vertigon."

Dara shivered harder. The fight might have been over quickly if Siln had succeeded in taking control when he had the advantage. But Dara had prevented Siln's certain triumph in order to protect Siv. She was going to be in trouble if he didn't win.

"You could have been killed," she muttered.

Siv pulled her closer against him. "I knew you wouldn't let him hurt me."

"What if I wasn't fast enough?" Dara hissed. "I can't use the Watermight to stop him if he decides to kill you."

"I'm alive, aren't I? It worked."

Dara resisted the urge to smack Siv with her Watermight-enhanced strength. His still-bleeding lip and swelling eye were the only things stopping her. And the fact that her body was warming in his arms and she suddenly, desperately wanted to kiss him. She pulled him—none too gently—farther toward the edge of the arena until they sat against the wooden barrier. The important thing right now was not to draw attention to themselves. Still, she couldn't help entwining her fingers with his and pressing against him again while they waited out the fight.

The battle for the vent raged on. The Waterlord could control larger quantities of Watermight than Siln, but Siln was the more skilled combatant. He made up for his lesser strength with swift movements and fine-tuned attacks. His razors of power could have sliced the skin off a soldarberry. He favored forming weapons—such as icicles and razors—out of the power, while Khrillin preferred to bludgeon his opponents with heavy objects.

Dara had no idea how they were going to resolve this contest. Neither fighter could injure or distract the other long enough to take control of the fountain burbling from the island. The prize was priceless: access to a new Watermight vent, a new source of power that would destroy the balance in Pendark once more. By digging into the earth to create a more interesting obstacle for their spectators, the pen-fight organizers had unleashed a new source of turmoil onto the city.

For one wild moment, Dara thought of taking the vent for herself. She could do anything with her very own Watermight source. But she wasn't skilled enough to hold onto it yet, and she was in Wyla's thrall for another month. She couldn't get involved in the Waterworkers' fight for power.

Siln began to gain the upper hand at last. He forced Khrillin farther from the vent, strengthening his hold on it with each assault. The Waterlord appeared to be tiring. Any moment now, Siln would drive him from the arena. It was almost over.

A silvery flicker of movement caught Dara's eye beneath a section of the stands that had been destroyed earlier in the fight. Khrillin was only stepping back as a pretext. While he continued to hold off Siln's attacks, he was gathering a pool of Watermight beneath the mess of jagged wood.

Dara leapt to her feet. Siln was so busy spinning weapons of ice across the arena that he hadn't seen the threat. Siv needed Khrillin, but she couldn't let him kill Siln. Wyla would drown her in the whirlpool for that, and probably throw Vine, Siv, and Rid in for good measure.

She ran along one edge of the pentagon. She had to get there before Khrillin sprung his attack. Siv shouted her name and chased after her. But she had enough of a head start.

As she ran, Dara recalled the Work the red-haired woman had performed. She forced the last of the Watermight out of her hands. It hurt as it slid through her skin, but for once, the substance responded to her commands. She formed the Watermight into a rough shield and thrust it in front of Siln—and not a second too soon.

Khrillin's wave rose beneath the pile of rubble and hurtled forward. Broken wood hammered into Dara's shield like arrows, the jagged weapons sinking in as if the shield were made of putty. Not a single one reached Siln's flesh. Khrillin stared at her in surprise. She had halted what could have been a final, decisive attack. Then his eyes widened even further.

"You," he said slowly. "I've met you before. *This* is an interesting development."

Dara didn't respond. It was taking everything she had to hold back the wave with her shield of Watermight. Then Siln sent a hundred Watermight razors shooting around her shield.

Khrillin dove for cover. He took refuge behind the ruined stands, narrowly avoiding being sliced into little pieces. Before Siln could press his advantage, a dozen men charged into the arena, all wearing crisp uniforms in Khrillin's particular shade of midnight blue. They advanced toward the combatants, gathering Watermight from the vent.

Siln surveyed this new threat with the eyes of a practiced battle strategist.

"We have to go," he said to Dara as Khrillin's reinforcements drew nearer.

"But the vent—"

"It's too late. They won this round."

Watermight still issued from the island beneath the remnants of the wooden castle. The Waterlord's men moved to surround it, but they couldn't contain it all. Silvery power flooded the arena and trickled out to stream through the city in all directions.

"We'll have another chance," Siln said. "Wyla won't let him keep all that power, and neither will the others."

"What does that mean?"

Siln gave her a grin that was every bit as bloodthirsty as that of the most rabid pen-fighting fan.

"It means war."

He turned on his heel and ran for safety on the opposite side of the arena. Dara had no choice but to follow. She had shown herself to the Waterlord. She had assisted Siln twice. If Khrillin hadn't known she was working for Wyla before, he would now. And being a known ally of a specific Waterworker just became a lot more significant.

She vaulted over the barrier to exit the arena. As her boots hit the mud, Siv ran up and caught her by the arm.

"Dara, are you—?"

"I have to get out of here," she said.

"Come stay with me," Siv said, tightening his grip on her arm. "I'll protect you from Wyla."

"It doesn't work like that," Dara said.

"Khrillin can help us." Siv nodded at the men who had come to the Waterworker's aid. "Maybe he can help you break the bond."

"I have to finish my time," Dara said. Siln was already out of sight, but he'd be back if she didn't follow him soon. She pulled her arm out of Siv's grip and reached up to touch his battered face. "Stay away from the Waterworkers until things calm down."

"Dara—"

"I have to go."

Siv grimaced then pulled her into his arms. The kiss made heat flare through her, as intense as cur-dragon Fire, but it was far too short. She wanted to clutch his coat, pull him closer.

Instead, she disentangled herself from his arms and shoved him toward the exit. As soon as she was sure he was leaving, she turned to flee. She had a sinking feeling that it would be a while before she saw him again. Siv had declared himself to be a Waterworker's ally today too. He had defended Khrillin for all to see.

A new Watermight contest had begun, and Dara and Siv were on opposite sides.

21

AFTERMATH

Siv made his way through the chaos outside the arena. The Waterlord's men had officially taken over. Spectators and fighters still milled around the grounds—a safe distance from the Waterworkers. The agitated crowds shouted about the Watermight interruption, sounding every bit as excited as they had about the Dance of Steel itself.

Siv reunited with his team, and they dragged him off to get drunk and tell them what had happened.

"You had the best seats in the house, lad," Kres said, pulling him along the canal bank to the nearest alehouse.

"I'll say. My clothes are still damp from all that water flying around."

"Wasn't much actual water," Gull said. "It's rare to see pure Watermight flowing free like that."

"I think I've seen enough to last me a lifetime," Siv said.

Truth be told, he hadn't known Watermight was that powerful. And Dara had been using it herself. He couldn't wait to ask her more about what it had been like to wield magic in battle. He hoped he hadn't put her in danger by forcing her to intervene, but he needed the Waterlord. Stepping in to save his life might inspire Khrillin to help his cause. And it was what Siv's father would have done. Sevren would have protected his friends.

"Hey, what happened to the Terrerack Terror?" Fiz asked.

"I have no idea, actually," Siv said. "He must still be in there. He'll be shiny as a sea snake by the time he swims out of that moat."

"Might do him some good," Fiz said. "He looked pretty heated by the end of your fight."

"Yes, it was well fought," Kres said. He eyed Siv up and down, his expression guarded. Siv wondered if the boss had seen how involved he'd gotten at the end.

"Where are we drinking tonight anyway?" Fiz said. "Or should I say this afternoon?"

"Anywhere," Siv said.

"You sure you're up for it?" Gull asked. "You took quite a beating."

"I could down a whole barrel of badlands liquor," Siv said. "Though my head hurts a little." He touched his lip, and his hand came away bloody. "How's my eye?"

Fiz thumped him on the shoulder. "That punch improved your appearance, all things considered."

Siv shoved the larger man back, producing almost no response whatsoever. Fiz Timon was not easily moved. But Siv forgot all about making a clever comeback when a trickle of silver caught his eye. A thin trail of Watermight meandered through the canal beside them, draining slowly away from the battleground they had left behind.

"Is that—?"

Suddenly, a slim figure darted across their path and splashed straight into the canal. The figure—a girl of eleven or twelve—waded toward the thin stream of Watermight. The little girl dipped her fingers in the silver strip, and the power flowed into her. The silver glow in the canal muted as she drank up the Watermight as quickly as she could.

A terrific splash made her look up. A teenage boy crashed into the water from the opposite bank and charged toward the little girl.

"This is my territory now!" he shouted. "Get lost."

The girl jumped nimbly out of his reach and fled, carrying her measure of Watermight with her. The teenager cursed at her before taking her place and gathering up Watermight for himself. He was blindsided when another boy leapt onto his back from the shallows and whaled away with his fists. Soon, spurts of unnaturally silver water cut through the air as the boys fought inexpertly with the power.

Siv started toward the canal. "Should we break it up?"

"Best leave them to it," Fiz said.

"They're just kids."

"Trust me," Fiz said. "We don't want to be here when the real Waterworkers show up."

"Would they hurt them?"

"Only if they stand in their way."

Kres and Gull had already gone on ahead, but Siv lingered, feeling conflicted. The boys fought until one of them broke away, holding onto a cut on his arm. The other remained to gather up more Watermight from the canal.

"What are they going to do with the power?" Siv asked when he caught up with the others.

"Sell it for food," Gull said. "Some urchins with the ability might be lucky enough to get picked up as apprentices, but most will hand over whatever they have to whoever will pay."

"They're lucky," Kres said. "It has been a while since Watermight flowed free in the city. The little vagrants will eat well tonight."

"I wish this had happened while we were out of town," Fiz muttered. "We're in for a nasty couple of months."

"Why?" Siv asked.

"The Waterworkers will fight over that vent until half the city drowns."

"I thought Khrillin and his men won it fair and square," Siv said.

"He has but won the first round," Kres said. "There will be more. Khrillin is not the only Waterworker with an army of thugs. The others will be along soon enough to try and take it from him. And a lot of power runs free. We'll see a hundred smaller fights apart from the main contest."

"Let us dance," Gull muttered.

"I'll drink to that."

Siv frowned. He was worried about Dara. He wasn't sure how today's events would affect the remaining month of her sentence. He half hoped Wyla wouldn't have time for her dangerous research anymore. Dara had seemed different in the brief moments they had together. She'd shown the intensive focus she ordinarily reserved for dueling, apparently treating her "research" with Wyla like training for the biggest tournament of her life. But she'd also lost weight and muscle, as if her body was paying the toll for her increasing power.

He should trust that she knew what she was doing. She had been an athlete and a fighter for far longer than he had. Of course she'd throw herself into her Watermight training with this single-minded intensity that he'd always admired about her. But he worried that the situation was spinning out of control.

He thought about the silent vow he'd sworn on Dara's sword arm after he learned of her bargain with Wyla. He had vowed to protect her with every movement, every thought, every breath. He'd vowed to do whatever it took to earn the loyalty she'd shown him. He was doing it the only way he knew how, but he feared it wouldn't be enough.

Siv rolled his shoulders. He was becoming as gloomy as Latch. Speaking of which, where was the surly Soolen? He asked the others about their fifth.

Fiz shrugged. "He took off."

"When?"

"When the chaos started, I reckon."

Siv frowned. Why would Latch have disappeared when the Watermight conflict began? It would have been the most exciting thing he'd seen in a while.

"Did he say anything about—?"

"Latch is fine," Kres interrupted. "You'd best prepare your most dramatic telling of what you saw out there." He took Siv's arm and led the way into one of their usual taverns. "You're getting your drinks free tonight."

"Now you're speaking my language," Siv said.

Latch and his secrets didn't worry Siv too much. Things could have turned out worse for him, all things considered. He was pleased Dara had seen him fight—and win, though the victory wasn't as clean as he would have liked. He hoped she'd worry about him less now that she'd seen him hold his own in the pentagon.

He figured Khrillin would come out on top in this conflict. He'd gain more power and riches—riches he could use to help Siv pay his team of mercenaries. Wyla's man would have seen where Siv's allegiances lay, but with any luck, Khrillin would make short work of anything Wyla threw his way. Maybe he'd even take her out in the process. Yes, Siv could see this turning out very well for him indeed.

His optimism lasted for a whole two hours. Then Tann Ridon found them surrounded by pen fighters at the second—or was it third?—tavern they'd been to that evening and delivered a message that changed everything.

"It was the scariest thing I ever saw," Rid said. He dropped into a seat in front of Siv with an extra-large ale, looking as if he'd seen a marrkrat in a cradle. "Siln told Lady Wyla what happened to y'all, and her eyes went all white and shiny. I swear the room got as cold as a mountaintop."

"What exactly did Siln say happened?"

"It was kinda garbled." Rid took a long sip of ale. "The important bit was about Dara interrupting him when he almost had that other fellow. Krellfish, is it?"

"Khrillin."

"That's the one. Anyway, Siln reckons he would have won if Dara hadn't stopped him."

Siv's stomach lurched, and he felt like throwing up all the free ale he'd been drinking. "Is Dara okay?"

"Oh yeah. She faced the witch down like she planned to stab her with her eyeballs. That's when Wyla said she was extending Dara's bargain."

"What?"

"She says Dara betrayed her, and she'll keep that bond on her arm until she decides otherwise."

"You mean she's not letting her go at the end of the three months?"

Rid shrugged one shoulder, the other apparently still giving him trouble. "That's what she says."

"Did Dara fight her?"

"Begging your pardon," Rid said, "but Dara is too smart for that."

Siv grimaced. So Wyla was angry enough about Dara's intervention on his behalf that she was extending her term indefinitely? She must want to keep Dara in her service until the end of the Watermight conflict—or longer. He wasn't going to let her get away with that.

He tapped his empty tankard on the table, considering his options. "You're sure she wasn't hurt?"

"No, sir," Rid said. "She was still standing there like a linden tree when Wyla kicked me out."

Siv looked up, distracted. "She kicked you out?"

"Practically hurled me out on my ear." Rid rubbed his freckled nose. "She knows I've been carryin' your correspondence, you see. I reckon she doesn't like Dara being tied to anyone but her. The messages weren't doing any harm before, but she changed her mind now."

Siv's hand went to his knife hilt, almost unconsciously. So his only link to Dara had been severed, just when things were getting heated in Pendark.

"Do you have somewhere to stay?" he asked Rid.

"I was hoping to stay with you, to be honest. I can offer my services as a general errand runner."

"Can you fight?" Kres asked suddenly. Siv jumped. He had completely forgotten they weren't alone. Kres had been sitting there in silence throughout Rid's tale. Now he studied the young man with a look of mild interest.

"I'm handy with a staff," Rid said.

"Ever tried a battle-axe?"

"No, sir."

"You're in for a treat, then." Kres grinned, sizing up the young man. Rid was tall and gawky, but he was reasonably thick around the shoulders. "You may stay with us at headquarters until you find other lodgings."

"Thank you kindly." Rid looked back at Siv. "I need to make sure Lady Vine is okay first."

"Was she there during all this?"

"No. She's very busy with Air stuff lately. She reckons she should be able to talk to people in Rallion City. It's this witch—I mean—Sensor thing."

"Really?" Siv was momentarily distracted. He was desperate for a reliable news source. He hated that he didn't know what was going on up north while he planned his return.

"I can bring her to headquarters if you want to ask about it."

"I think it's best if she stays with Dara," Siv said. "I don't want her to be alone there."

"Fair point, sir, but I don't think Wyla much cares to hurt Dara. She's worth a lot to her."

"Are you sure about that?"

"Well, I don't know about now that she's not so sure she can trust her. That's one of the things she said, that Dara ruined her trust by fighting for her enemy."

"It was a defensive move," Siv said. *She was defending me.* "She didn't fight for Khrillin."

"Still, Wyla has gotten a lot of useful knowledge out of Dara," Rid said. "She is valuable, but she's also dangerous. Not sure how much longer the wi—the Waterworker will put up with that. Reminds me of when Farmer Wells's foreman fired the farrier 'cause he was more popular with the hands than him. Reckon he was worried about his job."

Siv fell silent as Rid launched into a drawn-out account of what the farrier had done after being dismissed. He took out a knife and twirled it between his fingers, considering his options.

Rid's assessment was actually quite insightful. Dara *was* dangerous to Wyla. A young, strong, and capable Wielder would always threaten a woman like that. And Dara had shown her willingness to step out of line today. Wyla may claim she valued Dara's service, but if she ever posed too much of a threat, no amount of useful information would save her.

Wyla wasn't going to let Dara walk away. Simple as that. It was time for Siv to take back the woman he loved. He only knew one person capable of helping him do that. Fortunately, Khrillin now owed him a favor.

Siv went to see the Waterlord the very next day. His head pounded from a combination of the ale and the beating he'd taken yesterday. Every muscle grumbled in protest as he returned to the scene of the incident.

Khrillin had set up a temporary camp in the Steel Pentagon near the Royal District. His men patrolled the grounds around the new Watermight source, alert for attacks from other Waterworkers. They had dismantled the rest of the castle obstacle and used the timber to build barricades around the arena.

The Waterlord himself stood before the infamous vent, clad all in black with glittering chips of obsidian woven into his beard. He was carrying on a rousing argument with the owner of this pen-fighting venue. Watermight simmered in the moat beside them, not looking that different from real water beneath the bright morning sun. It still burbled from the rent in the earth, showing no sign of slowing.

"You must leave before the next match," the pentagon owner was saying as Siv walked up. "This is my property." Despite his brave words, the fellow kept a healthy distance from the Waterworker.

"The vent isn't going anywhere anytime soon," Khrillin said. "I have work to do yet before I can contain it."

"I shall petition the king!"

Khrillin smiled. "And what will the king do for you?"

"He has soldiers," the man said, his shoulders hunching perceptibly. He knew how ineffectual soldiers would be against the Watermight Wielders.

"Friend, friend. I shall compensate you for your property," Khrillin said. "You can purchase another pentagon ground."

"I've hosted pen fights here for forty years. If you think I'm just going to let you have it—"

Khrillin named a figure that made even Siv's eyes bulge.

"Fine," the owner said at last. "I'm tired of cleaning up blood anyway."

"Of course. My associate will arrange payment. Good day." He noticed Siv waiting beside him. "Ah, Siv, my friend. So good of you to join me."

"Khrillin."

The former proprietor gave Siv a curious look before one of Khrillin's men directed him firmly out of the arena. He clearly recognized Siv from the fights. Make that one more person who knew about his association with Khrillin. Word would spread quickly.

"I owe you my thanks for yesterday," Khrillin said. "It was foolish to step between two Waterworkers, though."

"That's what friends are for," Siv said lightly. "I hope I bought you a bit of time."

"Indeed, indeed. It was most effective." Khrillin moved a little closer, studying his face. "You didn't tell me your lady friend was a Waterworker."

"She's more of an apprentice," Siv said.

"For Wyla of the Jewel District."

Siv shrugged, hoping Khrillin would say more about Wyla—and their relationship. His men kept busy around him, apparently working to control or contain the flow of Watermight from the vent. Streams occasionally made a break for freedom despite their efforts.

Khrillin drew Siv away from his men so they couldn't overhear the conversation.

"Wyla is a dangerous creature," he said.

"But you defeated her man," Siv said.

"Temporarily." Khrillin glanced at his team of Waterworker thugs, his expression wary. He didn't trust his own men. Very interesting. "How do you know her apprentice?"

"Dar—lanna?" It took Siv a split-second to remember the false name he had used before. "I've known her since before I came to Pendark."

"Ah. I thought she had a Vertigonian look about her."

"Mmm."

"She couldn't have learned to use Watermight in Vertigon." Khrillin's gaze was as sharp as the teeth on a burrlinbat. "The Watermight doesn't travel well." He paused. "Unlike Fire."

"She must have spent time here when she was younger," Siv said, his voice carefully neutral. "I met her less than a year ago."

"Hmm." Khrillin fixed him with a shrewd stare. "Intriguing."

Siv fought to stay calm. He couldn't let Khrillin find out that Dara could Work with both Fire and Watermight. That could make her even more valuable to Khrillin than the former King of Vertigon—son of his old friend or not. Siv would not expose Dara's secret, but Khrillin was still his best chance of getting her out of Wyla's clutches.

"She's why I'm here, actually," Siv said at last. "She works for Wyla, but I don't think she enjoys it much. Would you be interested in offering her your . . . friendship?"

"Someone who is already apprenticed to Wyla herself? I'm afraid I can't do that."

"Please," Siv said. "I have to help her."

"It's not worth it, son."

"But—"

"Wyla causes me enough trouble already," Khrillin said. "I have no wish to poach her people unnecessarily."

He started to turn away, but Siv seized his arm. "Will you do it for my father's sake?"

Khrillin raised an eyebrow. "This Darlanna must be more than just a pretty companion to you."

"She is."

"I don't see that you need me," Khrillin said. "Can't she resign her apprenticeship?"

Siv hesitated, still not sure how much he could reveal. "She would, but there's a problem."

"Go on."

"She made a bargain with Wyla. I don't know all the details, but Wyla put some sort of Watermight curse on her arm. If she goes beyond the boundaries of Pendark, her arm will freeze." He watched Khrillin for any sign that he recognized what had been done to Dara. His face gave nothing away. "It was supposed to be for three months, but after she distracted Wyla's man to help me yesterday, Wyla extended her term indefinitely."

Khrillin fiddled with the obsidian in his beard, studying Siv pensively. "I begin to understand why you need me."

"Can this Watermight thing Wyla did to her arm be reversed? Now?" Siv wasn't willing to sit around waiting for Wyla to tire of Dara. With the eruption of the new Watermight vent, Pendark had become significantly more dangerous. The sooner they were out of the city, the better.

"What you ask won't be easy," Khrillin said. "I will need time."

"But my friend—"

"I understand your concern." The Waterlord laid a hand on Siv's shoulder. "This kind of bond is delicate. I need to study it before trying to break it. Will you bring your charming lady friend to see me?"

"Not unless you're sure it will work," Siv said at once. "If anyone sees her with you before the bond is broken, freezing her arm will be the least painful thing Wyla will do to her."

"Unfortunately, this is not a simple matter," Khrillin said. "Wyla is not the strongest Waterworker in this city, but she is the most innovative. Most of us can place bonds on people, but hers are a good deal more intricate and powerful. She may have included a few surprises. I don't take your friend's safety lightly, especially because she is apparently so valuable to Wyla." He stroked his beard, giving Siv a piercing look. "She doesn't chain every apprentice in this manner, you know."

Siv kept his face expressionless. Let Khrillin fish for information. He didn't like putting Dara at his mercy, but it was better than leaving her with Wyla. And he wouldn't give away any more of her secrets than necessary.

"I can see she is important to you," Khrillin said when Siv didn't respond. "And you did stand up for me yesterday. However, I have a lot going on at the moment." He waved at the vent burbling erratically beside them.

"We have to help her now." Siv's hand strayed to his knife, even though it would be worse than useless next to Khrillin's power.

The Waterlord saw where Siv was reaching and shook his head. "You must think this through," he said. "If Wyla bonded your friend, do you think she'll let her go easily?"

"I don't care. I'll do whatever it takes."

Khrillin sighed heavily. "I will see what I can discover and get back to you." He raised a hand when Siv began to protest. "That's all I can offer right now. It may be impossible for me to break a bond placed by another. You must be prepared for that."

Siv contemplated hitting Khrillin over the head and dragging him to help Dara. Could he do it before the army of Wielders turned him into silver jelly? He would not accept failure. But one thing was certain: he would only have one chance to get this right. Dara had exhausted any mercy Wyla might have shown her otherwise. They had to break the bond on the first try. He hated that he couldn't help her right away, but he couldn't take risks with her life either. Khrillin was still his only hope.

At last, even though it made his teeth ache, he said, "Thank you, sir. Please let me know when it is convenient for you to help."

Khrillin smiled, already turning back to his work with the vent.

"Wait," Siv said. "When can we set out for Vertigon?"

"I can't spare the resources until things settle down here."

"I was afraid of that."

"Have no fear, my friend," Khrillin said. "I won't forget about you."

Siv walked away, anger stiffening his muscles. Why couldn't that

Watermight have stayed in the ground? He didn't need this complication. But he needed Khrillin's power to save Dara, and he needed his money to save Sora. He had no choice but to trust him. Hopefully, both Dara and his sister could hold on a little while longer.

22

THE QUEEN'S SPEECH

Sora strode solemnly across Thunderbird Square. Men packed it from end to end, shouldering closer together to open a channel for the queen. She nodded at people as she passed and occasionally paused to pat an arm or squeeze an outstretched hand. The journey across the square felt longer and larger than the whole of Vertigon Mountain.

She knew the men lining her path. Young nobles she'd danced with at royal feasts. Duelists who'd entertained the city with their competitions and rivalries for years. Bridge workers. Miners. Traders. Servants. Beyond the rows of able-bodied men waited the very old and the very young. Women and children. Her friends and subjects.

The Ruminors waited for her across the square, standing in the shadow of House Zurren with General Pavorran. They hadn't bothered to greet the men, perhaps knowing that those gathered here today were more interested in Sora's approval anyway.

She met the eyes of yet another young man. He couldn't be any older than her—eighteen—and he looked as if he should be preparing for his first big Vertigon Cup. He stood straight and saluted, the buttons glinting on his uniform. Every man in the square was similarly attired. Every man a soldier. The newly expanded army had gathered to receive the blessing of the queen before marching to war.

Things had gotten terribly out of hand. Sora was supposed to be looking out for her people. She was supposed to be working against the Ruminors. But they had moved too quickly, and their ambitions were about to be realized. General Pavorran and the army were about to march down the mountain to invade the Lands Below.

Every eye followed Sora's stately progress across the square. She wore a royal-purple gown and an ash-gray cloak, which she'd pushed back out of her way. She hardly needed it. Spring had finally reached Vertigon. Her curly hair fell loose around her shoulders like a second cloak. The Amintelle crown sat atop her head, heavy and cold, Firejewels glittering in the band. She clenched her hands in her skirts as she neared House Zurren.

Rafe nodded approvingly when she reached the end of her slow procession. Lima's approval came in the form of slightly less pursed lips. Sora walked past the Ruminors without acknowledging them, a sinking sensation in her stomach. She was doing exactly as they wanted. She had made their jobs easier. True, she had kept all-out civil war from breaking loose after the Fire surge the night of her birthday, but now she was about to exhort her people to begin a far worse war in foreign lands.

The terrible part was that Sora was almost glad to send the soldiers on this mission. The Vertigonian army might be the only thing that could stop the marauding Soolen horde. And her mother and sister were imprisoned in the Lands Below. Sora wanted to choose peace over war, but she couldn't help the sneaking feeling of vindication that rose within her as she marched among her men. Her people were about to show the Soolens what happened to anyone who attacked her family's lands.

At the door to House Zurren, Sora motioned for her escorts, Oat and Yuri, to wait below with the Ruminors and General Pavorran. Telvin Jale stood at the craggy old general's side. Telvin, her bodyguard and friend, had reenlisted in the army, not wanting his former comrades in arms to march to war without him. She wasn't the only one who was being seduced by this perilous campaign.

Sora entered the greathouse alone. She ignored Lord Zurren's obsequious bow and Lady Zurren's insincere greeting and climbed the grand staircase to the rooftop. A spring wind blew sharply across the flat roof, a space designed for drinking and dining in a peaceful kingdom that no longer existed.

She crossed to the railing and looked out over the assembly of fighting men. She had insisted on doing this alone. She was about to exhort her people to descend and conquer in her name. She would do it without allowing her enemies or the allies who had given up so much to stand at her side.

A curved terrerack bullhorn was waiting for her on the balcony railing. It was hollowed out and polished smooth, ready to amplify her voice. The crowd looked up at her expectantly. She wondered for a brief, reckless moment if she should call on them to rise up against the Fireworkers once and for all. They would do it for her. But they wouldn't succeed, even with this huge army. Vertigon was about to see why the triumph of the Fireworkers was inevitable. Rafe Ruminor had one more mijen tile to play, and today, everyone would see the truth.

Sora raised the horn to her lips.

"Good afternoon," she called. "I am honored to stand before so fine a company today. My family has served the people of Vertigon for a century. We have been proud to call ourselves kings and queens of this great land." She tried to make eye contact with as many soldiers as possible, noticing the way their faces brightened when she met their eyes. Noting the grave pride.

"After today," she said, "the entire continent will know your worth. Men of Vertigon, it is time for you to depart our mountain and spread our dominion across the Lands Below. Today, you will make history." She stopped and swallowed. She had always wished she could witness the great deeds of the kings and queens of old. She wondered if those ancient queens had felt so conflicted when sending their people to war.

"I ask that you carry our banner with pride," she continued. "I ask that you fight with bravery. Show the world what it means to be from Vertigon. I know you will make your country proud."

Applause thundered across the square. The people filling the rooftops and terraces of the surrounding greathouses cheered almost as loudly as the soldiers themselves. Feet drummed the earth, and Sora wondered if they could let loose another Fire surge with the pure force of their enthusiasm. The scars of the last one were still visible: burn marks on the stone, withered trees, half-healed injuries.

They were going to see something more dangerous than a surge today. Sora raised her hands, waiting for the crowds to fall silent.

How many of the cheers were faked? Did her people truly want to see Vertigon reigning over the continent? Surely she wasn't the only one who objected to the Ruminors' plans. But too many of them had decided to appease the Ruminors out of fear—including her. And now it was too late to stop them.

When the last shouts faded away, Sora raised the horn to her lips again. "My people. You will not be going alone into the Lands Below. You are brave, and your swords will swing true, but you carry with you an even greater weapon. For the first time in living memory, you will bring Vertigon's greatest power into the Lands Below. You will take our strength, once used only for production, for trade, for practicality, and you will achieve glory unlike anything the continent has seen before. Today, you carry our Fire into the world."

Murmurs spread through the crowd, nervous and eager in equal measures. Jully had told her rumors were rife about this aspect of the planned campaign. Today was the first time everyone would see it.

"Rafe Ruminor, our Fire Warden and Chief Regent, will accompany you to Trure. He and his Fireworker colleagues will fight beside you using their own weapons, Weapons of Fire, weapons that will make the armies of Soole tremble before you. Together, you will show the world what Vertigon can do."

Sora pointed toward Fell Bridge, which spanned Orchard Gorge at the opposite side of the square. Eight Fireworkers had quietly gathered there during her speech. The soldiers turned as one to face them, the thud of their boots echoing over the mountain. The Fireworkers stood shoulder to shoulder and raised their hands.

Gasps rippled through the crowd as two massive structures rose from the gorge, carried on cords of Fire. The soldiers stepped back as the structures floated forward and landed heavily on the cobblestones.

Assault catapults. Sora had only seen them in pictures. The ungainly instruments of war were little use on the steep slopes of Vertigon, but the catapults would perform well on the flat plains of Trure. They would help the army take Rallion City back from Soole—and that was only the beginning. Each catapult was loaded with a white-hot ball of concentrated Fire.

The Fireworkers didn't wait for Sora's nod of approval. They released the catches on the weapons, and the fiery balls soared through the air, arcing over the soldiers' heads as if they were twin comets. Sounds of awe and fear rose from the assembly, drowning out the hiss of the Fireballs' passage.

The fiery spheres landed on the bare rooftop behind Sora and exploded. Droplets of Fire splattered across the roof. The Fireworkers had figured out how to condense the Fire so the Fireballs would be hot enough to cause serious damage when they struck their targets. The droplets of Fire would cling, melt, burn, destroy.

The glow of power spread, consuming the building. Sora didn't move as the rooftop melted behind her. The people would see their queen silhouetted in a glorious halo of Fire. Shocked silence greeted the display as the onlookers realized one by one that these were not ordinary lumps of Fire. Nothing could dowse these flames. Nothing could stop the army that wielded them.

That was when the cheers began.

The people clapped, shouted, stomped their feet. Eyes brightened as the truth dawned. With these Fire Weapons, this would be no ordinary war. From her post atop the burning building, Sora witnessed the exact moment when the Vertigonians realized they were going to win.

The roof shuddered, on the verge of collapse, but she had to stay. She had to see.

The Fireworkers on the bridge let loose a second type of Fire Weapon, spools similar to decorative Fireblossoms that would spin directly into an enemy's body. The Workers used straw dummies placed along the bridges to show the effects. The straw men exploded one after another in a shower of sparks, flames, and ash. Sora could only imagine what that would look like if the bodies were made of flesh.

The cheers grew louder, more frenzied. Soon, the soldiers and spectators were chanting.

"Vertigon! Vertigon! Vertigon!"

"Long live Queen Sora!"

Sora stood above them, listening to their adulation as the Fire blazed across the rooftop behind her. Bits of burning straw floated on the breeze like fireflies. Smoke thickened over Orchard Gorge. She knew she should feel horrified, but the cheers rippled through her, warming her like Firetears. The Vertigonians were going to achieve glory unlike anything the continent had ever seen. And they would do it shouting her name.

The demonstration finished with an eruption of fiery razors whirling from the Fireworkers' hands and spinning into the sky like stars. The people ooed and ahhed as if they were at a festival. They must know that with these weapons, the armies of Vertigon would be unstoppable. Soole, Trure, even Pendark itself would never stand against them.

Sora made her exit while the final spectacle drew the attention of the crowds. She crossed the burning rooftop between the pools of Fire eating holes in the stone and descended through the house. On the ground floor, Lady Zurren was watching the smoking holes in her ceiling with a sour expression on her hawkish face. The Zurrens had eagerly offered their greathouse for the demonstration. No doubt they believed this would solidify their status as the Ruminors' favorite noble family.

Lady Zurren seized Sora's arm as she left the burning house.

"Are you sure about this, my queen?"

"What?"

"Invading the Lands Below with Fire Weapons . . . putting all those young men at risk." Lady Zurren glanced around to make sure no one could hear. "I wonder if it's really necessary."

"It's not necessary," Sora said, "but the soldiers won't be in too much danger with the Fireworkers on their side."

"But, my queen, perhaps you could—"

Lima appeared in the doorway, and Lady Zurren immediately fell silent. Naked fear flitted across her face for the briefest instant. So her loyalty to the Ruminors didn't run as deep as it appeared.

"Hurry," Lima said. "The roof will not hold long. You are not yet finished."

Sora followed her out, avoiding Lady Zurren's eyes as they left the burning greathouse together.

Sparks were falling outside from the Fireworkers' display. Sora hoped the fiery remnants wouldn't damage the orchards filling the slopes beneath the bridges. They needed the sustenance the trees provided more than they needed dominion over the Lands Below. But she couldn't help thinking that it was useless to worry. They may defeat the Soolen invaders of Trure. They may take new land for themselves. They may grow stronger. But the Peace had been destroyed. Vertigon was dying.

And still, the sounds of the cheers sang through her.

Sora offered a final exhortation from the steps of the greathouse. She repeated the words exactly as Lima had given them to her.

"This is but a taste of the Fire Weapons our Chief Regent has worked so hard to develop. The Lands Below will not stand against Lantern Maker Ruminor's power. They have no magic and no strength to rival ours. It is time to take our rightful place for the glory of Vertigon. Farewell, and may your bravery carry you home again."

The soldiers cheered, shouting Sora's name to the heavens, making the citadel shudder with the power of their voices. They had seen the truth. The Fire Weapons would make them unstoppable.

On General Pavorran's order, they began the long march down the slopes of Vertigon. The invasion of the Lands Below had begun.

Sora felt as if she were carved from marble when she returned to her tower bedroom. Warmth from the repaired Fire Gate filled the room, but she didn't bother to remove her cloak. She had made a terrible mistake. She had encouraged Rafe to focus on his projects so he'd be less dangerous to those around him. And now she'd seen the results of that focused work. The moment she'd decided keeping the peace was more important than removing the Ruminors from power, they had triumphed.

She wished she felt something besides this terrible numbness.

The door flew open. Sora spun around as Kel strode in, the door banging shut behind him. His hair stood on end, and a reckless intensity shone in his eyes.

"What's wr—?"

Kel swept her into his arms and kissed her. It was so unexpected that she stood utterly still for a few frantic heartbeats before throwing her arms around his neck and kissing him back. Her numbness receded, if only a little.

He set her back on her feet.

"Let me take you away from here."

"What?"

"You refused before, but you can't stay here any longer."

"If I hadn't stayed, the people would have tried to attack the Lantern Maker, and he would have—"

"I know." He put a hand on her cheek, brushing a finger over her lip where it had split the very last time Lima hit her. "You were right, but it's different now. You've become the Ruminors' weapon. Please let me save you from that."

Sora disentangled herself from Kel's arms and stepped back. "Their weapon?"

"You saw the way that crowd was cheering. The Ruminors pointed you like a blasted Fire Arrow, and the people followed. You're playing into their hands." Kel glanced back at the door. "Oat and the others agree with me."

Sora folded her arms. "Do they."

"You've done a great job of keeping everyone calm," Kel said. "Maybe it's time to let things fall apart a little bit."

"It isn't that simple," Sora said. It didn't matter that she had been lamenting the way she'd helped the Ruminors moments ago. She walked a razor's edge. And there were other people involved besides her.

"They're taking advantage of your popularity to get you to—"

"Commander Brach has my family," Sora cut in. "Don't forget that. Maybe I'd have pointed *my* armies to the Lands Below even without the Ruminors. I'd take the Fire Weapons all the way to the Soolen peninsula if that's what it takes to save them."

Kel walked toward to her, voice softening. "I know you're worried about them. But we all want what's best for the kingdom, Sora."

She winced at the way her name on his lips sent a warm rush through her. She wished her numbness would return. She didn't want Kel to whisper sweet nothings in her ear. Did he think to manipulate her, to take advantage of her affections to get his way? She'd had enough of that.

"Why are *you* here, if Oat and the others agree with you so much?" she demanded. "Did you think a kiss would convince me to abandon my duty?"

Kel halted, staring at her as if she'd slapped him. Then he reached a hand toward her face. "In all fairness, last time, you kissed—"

"Stop," Sora said. "Please don't." She turned her back on him. Why hadn't she seen it sooner? Kel and the others had probably gotten together to figure out how to convince her to do what they wanted all along. All those hand touches and secret glances. Had Kel really instigated those, or had they decided to make use of the fact that she kept making eyes at the handsome dueling heartthrob?

Kel's footsteps tapped out a question on the floor as he moved closer to her.

"Please hear me out," he said softly.

Sora whirled around, the hem of her skirt brushing over the toes of his boots.

"I bet you'd prefer it if I ran off, wouldn't you?" she said. "Then you wouldn't have to worry about me anymore. You could join the army like the rest of the duelists, go fight for glory, and forget you ever met an Amintelle."

"I could never forget you," Kel said. "But I can't stand by while they use you to start a war."

"Please don't tell me how to run my kingdom."

Kel blinked. "I'm not. Let me take you away from here. I'll make it so you never have to frown into your notes or tug on your hair or hide your tears anymore. You deserve better than this."

Sora couldn't stop the tears from forming. She wished it were that simple.

"Where would we go?"

"We could cross the Bell Sea," Kel said. "Or even the Ammlen Ocean. We could visit the East Isles and do nothing but eat exotic fruits and lie on the beach. You could read, and I could snooze. No one would ever know who we used to be."

"I can't," Sora said softly. She put a hand on his cheek. "We still have a chance to work against them from the inside. Captain Thrashe will help us for sure now that they're moving against his people. Maybe he can—"

"Captain Thrashe is dead."

"What?"

Kel's shoulders slumped, and he took a few steps away from her. "I'm sorry. That's why I ran straight here. The Ruminors brought Captain Thrashe and the remaining Soolen swordsmen out to Thunderbird Square after you left. They executed them all."

"Just now?"

"Madame Ruminor announced that Thrashe's men killed your father and brother. I think they did it to convince any remaining holdouts of the justification for moving against the Soolen army.

And to send a message to anyone who was thinking of transferring their allegiance to you."

Sora's allies were falling left and right. Who would be next? Berg Doban? Jully Roven? Kel himself? How much more could she take? Mercifully, numbness flooded her body once more.

"You think they realized Captain Thrashe was becoming loyal to me?"

Kel inclined his head. "Thrashe's men have expressed their admiration of you. I've encouraged it whenever I could. Someone must have given them—us away."

Sora noticed anew that Kel's hair stood on end. He'd run in here hoping to sweep her away, hoping to flee at last. He had just seen the executions of men he'd lived and worked with over the past few months, men he himself had tried to turn to her side. He had been in danger every single day since he stopped Lima from hurting her. She didn't truly think he was manipulating her with his affection—but that didn't mean she could walk away. Not even with him.

"I'm not leaving," she said. "But you should. They'll come for you next."

Kel searched her face for a moment. He didn't deny her assertion.

"I heard the soldiers talking," he said. "They are absolutely rabid in their support of you. 'Long live Queen Sora, the First Great Queen.' Before you know it, they'll be calling you Empress."

Sora stared at him. Empress? The First Great Queen. She was almost afraid to admit that she liked the sound of that. An empress didn't rule a single nation. She ruled lands. She sent magic wielders to do her bidding. The idea curled through her, tantalizing, seductive. She'd be lying if she said she didn't care that she was becoming so popular. She could be stronger than her brother or father had ever been.

"What's your point?" she said hoarsely.

"The Ruminors started a war with a queen," Kel said. "What do you think they'll do with an empress? I can't leave you to that fate."

Sora looked away, fiddling with the edge of her ash-gray cloak. She didn't see it quite the way Kel did. The Lantern Maker may be using her, but couldn't she use him as well, him and his power? The people looked to her more than him. And thanks to these new Fire Weapons, she was on the verge of becoming more than a queen. The Lands Below wouldn't stand a chance against them. How could she walk away now?

She met Kel's eyes. "You should go."

He shook his head. "I pledged my life to you. Let me take—"

"I wouldn't want to leave with you anyway," she lied. "I can release you from your pledge."

"No, Your Majesty. It doesn't work like that." The formality of Kel's tone made Sora feel as if her insides were breaking to pieces.

"Maybe it's best we don't see each other alone anymore." The Ruminors knew Kel was on her side. They would use him to control her, even if he didn't try to do it himself. A queen couldn't allow herself such weaknesses. Not in a time of war. "I don't want you to get the wrong idea."

Kel offered her a polite bow, not quite quick enough to hide the hurt scouring his face.

"Very well. Will that be all, Your Majesty?"

"I'll call if I need you."

Kel returned to his post outside her door, his casual saunter missing. She wished she could have been less cold after he offered to throw everything away for her. But it was better this way. They should never have allowed themselves to get this close.

23

MESSAGES

Selivia and Zala climbed the winding staircase up the side of the Rock. Their destination was only halfway up the side, but it felt much higher. Selivia's legs shook as she looked back down the steep pathway. The Sunset City spread below her like a quilt. A very small and faraway quilt.

"Almost there," Zala said.

"I'm not tired." Selivia clutched the steps in front of her, scrambling up like a kitten. "Or s-scared."

"Only a few more steps."

Zala meant to be soothing, but Selivia couldn't bring herself to thank her. Things had been different between them since the night she met the true dragon. Zala had intended to betray the promise she made to Selivia's mother and use her as a hostage. Not even her excitement over the dragon could quite temper the feeling that she had been used.

They reached a flat plane at last. Selivia flattened herself on the ledge and looked back. The path was so steep that she couldn't see parts of it below. Other ledges poked out here and there, interrupting the steep cliff face. The desert stretched out past the city. Rocks, brush, and sand merged together into one shimmering, sunlit sea.

The wind howled, strong and swift against the side of the Rock. They had climbed to where the Air Sensors communed with their ethereal power. A larger concentration of Air flowed up here, and Selivia suspected it issued from the ancient Rock itself.

The Air Sensors themselves sat cross-legged on the bare stone ledge, swaying gently in the wind. Ananova was among them, along with several familiar faces, Sensors who had cornered Selivia to hint at the Air's plans for her. She wondered if they'd ever heard from the Air at all, or if they were trying to figure out if she was the "child of fire and rain" who was supposed to help them with their little dragon problem. It would have been so much easier if they'd just talked to her about it. On the other hand, they didn't agree with each other about their interpretations of the Air, the old song, or even whether any of it was connected to current events at all. She didn't know how anyone got anything done around here.

She frowned at the Sensors. The nearest one shuddered as if he could sense her disapproval. Or perhaps he was receiving a message of some kind. Zala had explained how the Sensors used the Air to communicate with people far away. That was why they had made the climb to this high ledge today. Selivia was hoping the Air Sensors would have news of her family.

"The Air has been less cooperative since the Soolen invasion began," Zala had warned her before they made the climb. "The Air Sensors to the south used the power to protect the border. They called on great quantities of Air, leaving less of it to whisper through Rallion City. Our Air Sensors are doing what they can to gather information, but they are subject to the whims of the Air and the wind."

The Sensors didn't even look up when they approached, so focused were they on the whims of the wind. Zala and Selivia found seats on nearby rocks and settled in to wait. Selivia splashed some water on her face from a water skin she'd carried up the Rock and took a long, refreshing drink. Zala had warned her this could take all day, so they had come prepared with refreshments, including a lunch of rubbery pink feather cactus and flatbread with honey for later.

They had a nice view for their picnic. The late-morning sun stood sharp above the desert, making the colorful décor of the city look more vibrant than ever. The people moved like bright beetles through the streets. From this height, the rainbow pattern of the standing stones was clearly visible, lighter in the center, growing dark toward the outer ring.

Beyond the city boundaries, Selivia could just make out the dark shadow of the true dragon's pit in the shimmering expanse. She snuck outside the city boundaries to visit him whenever she could. She loved watching the magnificent creature stretch his wings and circle the narrow confines of his prison. So far, she hadn't worked up the courage to climb into it with him. As much as she wanted to be a long-prophesied dragon tamer, she didn't trust Ivran's interpretation of the old song.

In the meantime, she was studying when the dragon's keepers came to feed and tend him so she could plan their escape. It was desperately sad that the creature had awoken from his long slumber, answered the Sensors' call, and ended up trapped. She would do whatever it took to free him, whether she had been chosen for it or not.

She wished she had the abilities of her Amintelle ancestors, who had been Firewielders in the old days. At least they would have been safe from the dragon flame. She'd have to rely on her more mundane affinity with animals and whatever information she could gather about the true dragon as she planned their escape. She hoped the Sensors could find out what was going on in the rest of the continent in the meantime so she would know where to go first.

Suddenly, the nearest Sensor shuddered far more violently than before. Selivia froze, fearing he had somehow read her thoughts. It was the craggy-faced fellow with the broad-brimmed hat who'd picked up her purlendog the day Ivran showed her the dragon.

His quivering intensified. Then the other Sensors reacted too, bracing themselves as if they had been hit with a huge gust of wind that Selivia couldn't feel.

"What's going on?" she whispered to Zala.

"I don't know." Zala clutched the scarf protecting her head, watching the Sensors strain against the invisible pressure. She focused on her aunt at the opposite side of the circle. Ananova's face was as white as a newborn furlingbird. She seemed to be in a trance.

"There has been an attack." The craggy-faced Sensor spoke, voice distant and eerie. It made Selivia's blood run cold.

"Yes, the fighting," Ananova whispered.

"The pain!" said another.

"An attack," the man repeated. "An attack on Rallion City."

The other Sensors in the circle repeated the words, voices murmuring like a breeze through the plains grass.

"The Soolens took Rallion City months ago," Selivia whispered to Zala. "Are they receiving an older message?"

"I don't think so," Zala said. "Listen to Fodorov."

"They were proud," the male Air Sensor said. "They thought their victory was complete. Too proud."

"The pain," another Sensor wailed again. "The heat."

"So much heat!"

"They cannot stand against it."

"The Air screams. It screams," Ananova cried. Suddenly, she toppled forward. A few other Sensors shuddered as if they had been slapped. The man with the craggy face—Fodorov—leaned over his knobby knees as if he might be sick.

"Oh, the heat," called another Sensor. "It is too much."

Selivia started up, wanting to help, but Zala grabbed her arm, still watching her aunt intently. Every Sensor in the circle seemed to be hearing the same terrifying message. It was awful to sit there, unable to hear what the Air was saying, unable to help.

At last, the strong wind that seemed to be blowing amongst the Sensors quieted. Their desperate quaking subsided, leaving them pale and trembling.

Slowly, Ananova sat up, wiping a shaking hand across her brow. "The balance is destroyed," she said.

Fodorov inclined his head. "Yes, it is worse than we feared."

Ananova got to her feet, slowly, as if her bones were creaking, and came over to where Selivia and Zala waited. Her graying hair fell loose from her dusty-rose scarf, and her face was grave.

"Rallion City is under attack," she said.

"By the Soolens?" Selivia asked. "I thought they captured it ages ago."

"They thought they'd won," Ananova said. "No, they are the ones defending the walls this time."

"I don't understand."

Fodorov came over to join them, casting a long, thin shadow over the shorter women.

"It is Vertigon," he said.

Ananova bowed her head. "Yes, but not Vertigon."

"The pain is almost too much to bear."

Selivia felt dread creeping through her. "What do you mean?"

"We accepted a message from our friend Meza. She shepherds a Sensors Manor in Rallion City. She saw so much . . ." Ananova shuddered. "She struggled greatly to calm herself enough to speak to us."

Selivia slipped a hand into Zala's, their earlier quarrel forgotten.

"Meza has seen weapons," Fodorov said. "Terrible weapons of Fire and power. They are burning everything, destroying anyone who stands in their way. Trure is burning, and Vertigon holds the torch."

"Vertigon? You mean the Fireworkers are attacking?" Selivia stared between them, wondering when the world had gone mad. "Are they trying to save Trure from the Soolens?"

"Alas, no," Ananova said. "Trure is under attack once more, her and the Soolen soldiers within her. She is a battleground, a terrible, burning battleground."

Selivia fought the urge to cry, tears welling up anyway. She didn't understand how this had happened. Why were her people attacking Trure if not to help their long-term ally? Vertigon was supposed to be peaceful. The Fire wasn't meant for war.

Suddenly, a wailing rose from two Sensors who had resumed their meditations. They seemed to be receiving a second message.

"Oh, it burns. The pain! The land burns."

"They call her name," another Sensor wailed. "Her name. Her name."

"Whose name?" Selivia asked.

Ananova listened for a moment, eyes closed and body swaying.

"The queen," she said at last. "The invaders are fighting in the name of the queen. The Lantern Maker couldn't rally them, but the soldiers fight for Queen Sora. The Fireworkers fight for Queen Sora. They will burn the plains for Queen Sora."

"She wouldn't do that," Selivia said. "That's our grandfather's land."

"Your grandfather is dead," Fodorov said.

Ananova winced, as if she had planned to share this information more delicately, but Fodorov barreled on. "King Atrin has fallen and his city with him. Commander Brach has fled into the plains. He fights still, but can he stand against the Fire?"

Another Sensor shrieked, long and loudly. "The land burns!"

Selivia couldn't take it anymore. She couldn't stand the screams, the idea of the magical Fire turned into a weapon. She fled down the side of the Rock, heedless of the danger. Why couldn't the Fireworkers continue to create beauty and warmth? Vertigon had thrived for a hundred years as the Workers made Fire Lanterns and sent pretty Fireblossoms spinning across the sky. But now they were bringing Fire and destruction to the Lands Below. How could Sora let them do this?

Selivia ran all the way to the boundaries of the city. A strong wind whipped around her, and she imagined it carried ash and death across the plains. She wished she'd never climbed the mountain to hear the Sensors' words.

She didn't stop running until she reached the pit where the poor true dragon lay, captive and sad. She dropped to her knees beside his prison. He had soared all the way through the Burnt Mountains, wild and free and beautiful. And now he was trapped, like her poor sister. It wasn't fair at all.

"Hello there," she called. "Can you hear me?"

The true dragon lifted his magnificent head and fixed her with a single cobalt eye.

"I need your help."

The true dragon merely stared.

"I want to free you from your chains," Selivia said. "But I need you to carry me back to the mountains. You can go home from there. Will you help me?"

The true dragon snorted. Suddenly, his entire body moved, the muscles rippling like water. Selivia tumbled backward. But he simply settled down in a new position, still watching her.

"Will you . . . will you promise not to eat me?"

The dragon looked up at her. Then he smiled. Okay, maybe he just sort of opened his mouth, but she was sure the true dragon was smiling at her. She swallowed her fear and swung her legs over the rim of the pit.

"Are you insane?" A harsh grip closed on her shoulder just before she slipped over the edge. It was Ivran.

"Get away from me!" she said.

"You're going to unchain the dragon," he whispered, horror in his eyes. "You're mad."

"He shouldn't be tied up here, and I have to help my sister. Let go of me."

"He will eat you," Ivran said. "You're the same size as the sand goats we feed him. The brute probably can't tell the difference."

A terrific snort came from within the pit, making Ivran topple backward in surprise. Was that how dragons laughed?

"See?" Selivia said. "He understands."

"That doesn't mean he won't eat you," Ivran said. "And what makes you think he'll go where you want even if you manage to get the chains off without turning into barbecued princess?"

Selivia hesitated. She looked down at the true dragon. It looked back, cocking its head to the side and lashing its tail as if it were a cat. The effect would have been a bit more innocent if the lashing didn't emphasize the head-crushing knob of scales at the end of the tail.

"My sister needs me," Selivia said. "I have to do something."

"I don't think she'd want you getting yourself killed," Ivran muttered. "Let's go back. My mother and Zala are looking for you."

Selivia ignored him. She studied the true dragon, his striking green and black scales and his wondrous black wings, wondering what it would take to get him to work with her.

After a few minutes, Ivran spoke, his voice lower than usual. "You really think you can help your sister with that dragon?"

"I have to try."

"Then I won't stop you," Ivran said.

Selivia looked up, surprised. "Why not?"

"Look, I don't much like you," Ivran said. "But it'll be bad enough for the Far Plains when the Other Lands find out we called on the dragons. We don't need them thinking we kidnapped you. I'll help you get away if I can."

Selivia studied him, still skeptical. Ivran was not a nice boy, and she didn't trust him for a second. He had some ulterior motive that she couldn't see. Still, he did seem to care a lot about his homeland. She believed he wanted to keep trouble away. And she believed he was telling the truth when he said he didn't like her.

"How can you help?" she asked.

"My mother has an old book about the magic wielders who used to work with true dragons. She got it out when they lured him here. At least have a look before you do something stupid."

"That . . . would be useful, actually. Thank you."

Ivran shrugged. "Don't tell anyone. The sooner you and the true dragon are gone, the better."

Selivia looked back at the true dragon, wondering if she should try making a break for it now anyway. She didn't think he would eat her, but it would be good to learn more about him. And maybe the Sensors could help her get a message to Sora somehow. If they could talk to Meza, maybe they could communicate with someone in Vertigon. It was a shame Vine Silltine had run off with Dara.

Selivia froze. Vine was with Dara. And possibly with Siv. She might be able to talk to them with the help of the Sensors. Then they could work on a plan to help Sora together!

She was sorry to leave the true dragon in captivity for another day, but if they ran away together, she would have no hope of communicating with anyone. She had to stay with the Far Plainsfolk a little longer. For now, they were her only link to the rest of the continent. And it sounded as if everything was falling apart out there.

"Hang on a little while longer," she whispered to the true dragon. "I'll be back for you."

24

PATROLS

Every Waterworker in Pendark wanted the new vent. Dara had never seen a fiercer competition. It only took two days before the first major assault launched against Khrillin and his men. A lesser Watermight practitioner rallied a dozen others—including three who'd previously worked for Khrillin himself—to attack the Steel Pentagon. They overcame the Waterlord's guards and directed a huge wave of Watermight out of his control. Then they turned on each other. Half the conspirators ended up dead, and Pendark ran with blood and Watermight.

Every day, more Workers joined the contest, taking drastic measures to capture the free-flowing power for themselves. Floods burst through the streets at random. Islands were destroyed and reformed as Watermight practitioners set up their own petty kingdoms, further altering the landscape with every clash. The flag makers did brisk business as the districts shifted their allegiances again and again.

Siln directed Wyla's battle operations, and he often took Dara with him when he patrolled the streets for vulnerable pockets of Watermight or potential challengers. Siln was colder toward Dara than before. He wouldn't forgive her easily for preventing him from killing Khrillin. He had received a harsh rebuke from Wyla after the ill-fated pen fight.

Wyla's anger over Dara's intervention had been even worse than she feared. Dara was honestly surprised she survived the reprimand. If she hadn't made so much progress in her Wielding, she was sure Wyla would have killed her for her insolence.

Instead, Dara's worst fear had come to pass. Wyla refused to let her go at the end of her three-month term. Dara was Wyla's servant now unless she wanted to lose her sword arm. She considered it, but she knew Wyla wouldn't stop at maiming her—and everyone she loved—if she tried to escape.

She was forbidden to see Siv. Wyla had thrown Rid out of the manor so he couldn't facilitate their communication. As the Watermight war intensified, she had precious little free time, but she watched for a chance to sneak him a message. Siv had to leave Pendark. There was no use in him waiting for her now. He should take the gold Khrillin had promised and return to Vertigon.

Despite the souring of their relationship, Wyla wanted Dara out in the streets as much as possible while the conflict raged. Every day, she woke before dawn and went out with Siln. With Wyla's blessing, he taught her to fight with the Watermight at last. They strode through the streets together, spinning ice daggers and drowning spheres at rival Waterworkers or sending great waves rushing along the canals to wash out their hideouts. Dara still had to swallow the Watermight, and it hurt to push it through her skin, but she was making progress.

She carried Firebulbs in her belt pouch too, but it had been a long time since she had tried Wielding the two powers together. Wyla didn't push her as quickly on that front now that Dara was in her service for good. They'd have plenty of time for all kinds of experiments—if Dara survived the war.

Wyla herself had grown more irritable since missing out on a clean defeat of Khrillin, whom she considered her greatest threat. She hated how messy everything was becoming. She rarely stepped out to fight herself, preferring to let Siln and Dara act on her behalf.

Vine, meanwhile, spent less time in Wyla's manor than ever. She was using the disorder to investigate Lord Vex's presence in the King's Tower. They still weren't sure why he hadn't attacked Siv again. The longer it took him to act, the more Dara worried he was preparing a bigger scheme behind the scenes.

Vine also made regular trips to the Sensors Manor in hopes that they'd eventually break through the communication barrier between Pendark and the rest of the continent. It had been too long since they last had word from Trure and Vertigon. Most people were too distracted by the Watermight conflict to notice, but the silence was becoming eerie.

"The Air will grant me the gift of contact one day," Vine always said, patient as ever. "I must continue to ask."

By the second week after the opening of the vent, utter chaos reigned in Pendark. The vent changed hands again and again. During each fight, a little more power disappeared into the secret storage facilities the various Waterworkers used, and the rest escaped to run loose in the streets. But the vent just kept producing more power.

"They don't always keep going like that," Siln explained as he and Dara marched through the Jewel District one day, keeping watch for enemy Waterworkers. "Some vents only have a bit of juice in them. It gets divided up, and then everything goes back to normal."

"Wyla has had her main vent for a long time, right?"

"It's one of the deeper ones." Siln glanced around their green-flagged surroundings. "You'd best not speak about it on the street. Not everyone knows its form or its location."

"How do other Waterworkers hold their power?"

"Usually in pools, fountains, or underground streams. Wyla's whirlpool system is particularly effective. I've heard rumors of people keeping the power in stone for a time, but I don't believe it's possible. It needs to be active, or it drains away."

"Why is it so hard to store and transport the power?"

Siln shrugged. "Always has been. If someone figures out a better way, they'll become the most powerful Waterworker in the city overnight. They could rule the continent itself. Pendark could be so much greater if not for the Might's limitations."

"And if people stopped fighting each other over it."

"True enough," Siln said.

Dara nodded toward the King's Tower rising in the distance. A haze hovered over the swampy land, obscuring the lights that always burned in the tower windows.

"Does he ever try to control the Watermight practitioners?"

"It would be pointless," Siln said. "The king serves as a buffer for the mundane people of this city. He can dispense justice and protection to them while the Waterworkers are otherwise engaged."

"Why doesn't one of the Waterworkers become king or queen?" Dara asked. "The first Amintelle king in Vertigon was a Fireworker. He set up a distribution system to prevent this sort of anarchy."

Siln snorted. "Yes, well, the Fire has suffered for it, don't you think?"

"Suffered how? Vertigon's Fireworks are coveted all over the world."

"Trinkets and lanterns and a handful of Fire Blades. Can you imagine what the Fire could do if it weren't so limited? If those Workers spent their time on something besides basic craftsmanship?"

Dara didn't answer. That came a little too close to her father's beliefs. He had always wanted to do away with the limitations on his power. She may be curious about what else the Fire could do, but that didn't mean she was comfortable with the implications. Unlike Watermight, Fire could be transported and solidified. The Fireworkers could rule the world if they ever tried.

Dara prayed that would never happen—and that Wyla and the others would never figure out a way to transport the Watermight for longer than a week. She wondered if that was why Wyla wanted to study how she used the Fire. She might one day figure out how to create a comparable containment system. The powers were fundamentally different from each other, but if Dara could use both, they might have more in common than anyone believed.

Of course, she still couldn't use the Fire and the Watermight at the same time. Her ability to use the Watermight would do her little good in a confrontation atop Vertigon Mountain, hundreds of miles from the nearest Watermight source. And she might never leave Pendark anyway.

Dara and Siln approached a bridge leading from one of Wyla's islands to another. Suddenly, a pair of teenagers leapt from behind a nearby gem shop. Most of the shops on the street were boarded up, their owners taking shelter until the violence subsided.

"Halt!" one of the boys shouted. "You can't walk here."

"Yes," said the other, his voice squeaking. "We are the Waterlords of this place."

The boys were perhaps a year or two younger than Dara, ill-fed lads who positively shook with power.

"Do you know who I am?" Siln said softly.

The boys exchanged nervous glances. A glimmer drew Dara's attention to a small pool of Watermight floating in the shadow of the bridge. The power cache that made them brave.

"We don't care," the older boy said. "This is our territory now. We'll drown you if you come any closer."

"This district belongs to Wyla," Siln said.

"Not anymore." To his credit, the boy's voice didn't shake as he faced down one of the most skilled Watermight combatants in Pendark. Dara had to admire the ferocity in the boys' faces as they tried to claim a bit of the city for themselves.

"Why don't you take these two?" Siln said, turning to Dara. "It'll be good practice."

Dara stood frozen for a moment. She didn't want to hurt these gangly young fellows. They were just trying to carve out a place for themselves. But if she didn't deal with them, Siln would. And Wyla would hear of yet more disobedience.

"We aren't afraid of you," the boy said.

Siln chuckled. "You should be. Dara?"

Dara tipped back her head and swallowed a measure of Watermight from the wineskin at her side. She advanced on the boys, the power icing her bones and giving her strength.

The fight was over quickly. She neutralized the boys by whirling a spool of Watermight around their heads and obscuring their senses. The boys soon gave up and took off running across the bridge, still trying to free themselves from Dara's entrapment. Siln tutted in disapproval, but she didn't care. She wasn't killing anyone for Wyla.

Vine was pacing across their bedroom when Dara returned from patrol. She'd eaten a quick meal with Siln then stumbled upstairs to find her friend waiting, dressed in a light dress and sandals for the southern spring clime. Dara was still cold and shaking from her latest dosage of Watermight. She pulled an extra blanket from the wardrobe and put on her coat before sitting on her bed.

"The Sensors have picked up increased levels of Air in the city," Vine said, dancing across the floorboards. "They think there's a break in the barrier between Pendark and Trure."

"With more Air, that means—"

"Yes! We can communicate with the Truren Sensors. I may even be able to reach someone in Vertigon!"

Dara wasn't sure whether to feel happy or nervous about that. They had relied on rumors in the streets to keep track of events in the north, but with the outbreak of the Watermight conflict, the city gossips had more important topics on their lips. More than the war in Trure, Dara was nervous about what her parents had been up to since seizing power in Vertigon. How long had it been since she'd heard anything of them? She wondered if it would be possible to communicate with them directly. Not that she had any idea what she'd say.

She pulled her blanket tighter. Her muscles ached as if she'd been alternating push-ups and sprints all day, and she had a dull stomachache, a side effect of swallowing the Watermight.

"Was there anything else?" she asked.

Vine didn't answer. She had stopped pacing, and she was frowning at the wall as if she could see through it to the far side of the city.

"Vine," Dara said. "Are you all right?"

Vine turned toward her, face glowing in the moonlight from the window.

"Oh Dara, what is it?"

"I just wondered if there was any more news." Dara frowned at the faraway look in Vine's eyes. "You seem worried."

"No, that's all the news I have for now . . . Only . . ."

"What's wrong?"

Vine bit her lip. "You've been busy with the Watermight, and I haven't had a chance to talk to you. I'm worried about Vex. I've been dreaming about him every night."

"Still?"

"I'm afraid so."

"You think it means something?"

"It's complicated, Dara." Vine sighed. "I saw him leaving the King's Tower again a few days ago, and I felt a . . . connection to him. I'm sure it had something to do with the Air. The moment I felt it, he turned around and looked straight toward me. I dove behind a flower cart, so I don't think he saw me, but it was uncanny."

"Do you think he got some sort of spell or curse done that would link him to you?" Dara held up her sword arm. The idea that

Vex still had power over her friend made her angry. She should have stabbed him during that fight months ago.

"It's possible." Vine fell silent for a moment, chewing her lip. "But what if that's not it? Why would the Air bring me dreams about Vex? He ought to be the least of our worries right now. Information about Vertigon would be vastly more useful."

"Are you sure it's the Air?" Dara asked. "Could something more mundane cause the dreams and whatever you felt when you saw him?"

"What do you mean?"

"You and Vex spent a lot of time close together on our journey," Dara said. "I'm sure you had intense feelings related to him. Fear. Anger. It makes sense that you'd have a strong reaction to seeing him again."

Dara thought of the visceral response she'd had when she saw her parents after learning they were murderers. They haunted her thoughts still. She'd even had a vivid dream about them in the Air Sensors' manor back in Rallion City. Her mother standing over her, wielding a ball of Fire. Dara had plenty of anger and fear and emotion when it came to her mother.

Vine must have thought the theory had merit, because she was quiet for a long time. Dara watched her friend twirl a dark curl around her finger, wondering whether she should mention the dream about her mother. She still found it difficult to talk about her parents, even with her best friend. But Vine had always been there for her. She would understand.

Suddenly, Vine gave a sharp intake of breath. "You are so right, Dara." She whirled around. "I should have talked this over with you sooner. I should have known you'd help me figure out the truth."

Dara blinked. "What truth?"

"That I'm attracted to Lord Vex, of course."

"I— *What?*"

"That's what you meant, isn't it?" Vine said. "Intense feelings. Being close together. It's no wonder you figured it out."

Dara wondered if she was dreaming right now. "What are you *talking* about, Vine?"

Her friend didn't seem to hear her. "I never thought of him that way in Vertigon, but then I didn't take much notice. Now if I'd seen him duel . . . Who knew he was so skilled? And then our journey together." Vine smiled slightly. "I do wonder whether the connection outside the King's Tower was related to some vibration of the Air or if it was simply our feelings for each other manifesting in a tangible way."

"Feelings for each other?" Dara said faintly.

"You do think he has feelings for me too, don't you?" Vine said. "He tried valiantly not to whilst we were his captives."

Dara stared blankly at her, wondering if she was falling for a prank. She certainly hadn't seen this coming. Vine simply looked back at her, eyes hopeful, maybe even a bit misty. She wasn't joking.

Dara figured out what she wanted to say at last. "Are you insane?"

Vine chuckled. "What *are* you talking about?"

"Vex Rollendar kidnapped us so he could kill Siv. He'd have killed us in a heartbeat to achieve his goals. You can't possibly like him, and he . . . he . . ."

Dara wanted to say he definitely didn't share Vine's feelings, but she had noticed Vex being quite solicitous of Vine. She recalled when he had bought her a pair of boots and laced them up himself with unexpected gentleness. They had talked a lot throughout their journey, and when Vine and Rid joined the fray at the pen-fighters' headquarters, Vex had looked almost pleased to see her. Dara could see Vex being infatuated with Vine quite easily now that she thought about it. But that didn't change the fact that he was dangerous—probably more so than ever—and Vine had no business whatsoever having feelings for him.

"He what?" Vine prompted.

"He's too old for you," Dara said weakly.

Vine gave a tinkling chuckle. "'Age is merely a measure of days.' Haven't you ever heard that saying?"

Dara shook her head, contemplating how to shake sense into her friend. She wanted Vine to find happiness, but not with one of their mortal enemies. If she had to pine after an older man, why couldn't she have chosen Siln? Or one of the pen fighters? Or one of the dozens of safer men that fell in love with her on a daily basis?

"You're not thinking of acting on these feelings, are you?"

"I'm afraid I'll need more information before I do that. I may very well be in love—"

"In lo—?"

"—but I'm never rash. Perhaps we can use this development to our advantage." Vine kicked off her sandals and skipped over to her own bed. "I am so curious what I'll dream tonight. Thank you for helping me figure out my feelings, Dara. Good night."

She climbed into bed and was asleep before Dara could summon a coherent word.

Dara burrowed beneath her own covers, wondering how to get Vine to come to her senses. Her friend had a tendency to do exactly as she pleased. That her schemes usually worked out was beside the point. Connection or not, it was only a matter of time before Vex tried to kill Siv again.

Vine sighed in her sleep, apparently dreaming peacefully. Could Vex have done something to her in order to lure her to him? Dara flexed the muscles in her sword arm, trying to sense something of the bond Wyla had left there. What else could magic do to link people together? Induce feelings? Vine wasn't *really* attracted to Vex . . . was she?

Dara hoped Vine was right about the increased Air presence at least. Something must have changed in Trure to allow it through. They needed to know what Siv faced if he ever got out of Pendark alive. And the sooner she got Vine out of here, the better. Wyla may never let Dara herself go, but she'd do whatever it took to make sure her friends escaped unharmed.

25

SENSING

Selivia sat beneath the shaded awning of Ananova's house with Zala. Fenn worked on a new painting nearby. Rain had fallen over the past few days, and the desert bloomed around them. Pink blossoms decorated the cacti like fanciful hats, and the earth smelled of warm clay. Selivia had a book spread on her knees, but she had abandoned it in favor of listening to the spring breeze and the buzz of insects.

Stealing a moment of quiet was hard these days. News of the Fireworker attack on Rallion City had spread quickly. The Plainsfolk packed the popular spots for Sensing to listen for additional information. The latest news was that the barrier between Trure and the southern lands no longer held. No one knew if that was because the Sensors were focused on the events to the north or if the assault of the Firewielding Vertigonian army had caused a rift in the Air barrier.

The more people listened to the wind, the more they worried about Commander Brach's next move. After being driven from Rallion City, he had disappeared into the plains. His men still held the Stronghold, and the Far Plainsfolk feared he would turn his attention west. Selivia was more concerned about what would happen to her mother if the Stronghold fell.

The Fireworkers had laid waste to the lands surrounding Rallion City. By all accounts, the city itself had been reduced to ash and mud. Selivia hated to think of it: the flowers trampled, the Azure

Lake soiled, her grandfather's palace burned. They stood no chance against the Fireworkers. The Lantern Maker's men burned gleefully, recklessly, as if making up for the past hundred years.

It was more important than ever for Selivia to get in touch with her family. They were responsible for Vertigon—and the Fireworkers. Their people had been corrupted, sent by the Lantern Maker to conquer in the Amintelle name. They couldn't let it continue.

Zala had warned Selivia not to bother the Sensors when they were listening to the Air, but she was growing impatient. She couldn't sit here doing nothing for much longer. Unfortunately, Zala and Fenn watched her more closely than ever. Fenn seemed to think the Far Plains was the safest place for her, hostage or not. Selivia hadn't had a chance to visit the true dragon again.

Ivran had come through for her, though. He'd dropped the book about magical creatures in her lap without so much as a hello. He had also kept his promise not to tell anyone about her escape plans. She still couldn't figure out what he was up to, but she'd take any help she could get.

The book lay open on her knees now, its pages crinkly and faded with age. It was written in an older version of the Far Plains language. She had entreated Zala to help her translate it, insisting she was just curious about the true dragon.

"Are you sleeping?" Zala said.

"What? No."

"Read me that passage again."

Selivia fidgeted with the corners of the book. "Can't you just tell me what it means?"

"Your accent still needs work," Zala said. "If you're to live here, you should really improve."

Making Zala think she planned to stay was the easiest way to research the dragon in peace, but Selivia didn't like lying to her friend. She wasn't very good at it. She shifted on her chair and read aloud from the book once more.

In ancient days, the Air Sensors spoke with animals—especially magical ones like true dragons—but that aspect of the discipline hadn't been practiced much recently. Unfortunately, the book assumed its readers would know the basic art of dragon taming. All too soon, Selivia faltered over a confusing word used in a complicated phrase, and Zala had to interpret for her.

"Communion," she said. "That's what that word means. It's talking about the communion between a magical creature and the human who works with it."

"Is that like communication?"

"It's more than that." Zala took the book from Selivia's hands and ran her fingers over the ancient words. "Communion implies a deeper connection than mere words. It's when you have an empathetic relationship with someone."

"Like a friendship?"

"Sort of. But you can be friends with someone without truly communing with them." Zala rubbed the toe of her dark-green slippers along the dirt. She wore a matching dark-green scarf to protect her hair from the ever-present dust. "Like us," she said. "We're friends, but I'm willing to hold you here to protect my people, and you don't really understand why. We're not really in communion."

Selivia bit her lip. She wanted to reassure Zala that she understood. At the same time, Zala was keeping her from helping her own family. The things they needed smashed against each other like two fighting bullshells. That must have been what Zala meant. Communion wasn't possible when they had different needs.

Selivia wondered if her big brother shared communion with Dara. They were desperately in love, but Dara's father was a mountain-sized problem. She had taken Siv's side to protect him, yet she still felt bad about disappointing her parents. Selivia wondered if it was even something they could overcome. She had always thought love would be enough, but Dara had still been terribly sad and confused the last time they talked about it. The world was a lot more complicated than Selivia had once thought. She wondered if that meant she was growing up.

For her part, she had communion with her sister at least. She didn't understand why Sora had allowed the Fireworkers to leave the mountain to fight in her name. The treacherous Lantern Maker must have forced her to do it. Selivia felt uneasy over the fact that her sister was going through something she couldn't fully understand—and possibly making decisions she couldn't agree with.

She shifted in her chair. She should worry about things she could control. She didn't know if that included the true dragon yet. She had always felt a connection with animals. Even creatures other people called grotesque were living beings with quirks and personalities. She and the true dragon both wanted to escape the Far Plains. She hoped that would be enough to keep him from eating her for breakfast. The question was whether she could convince him to carry her where she wanted to go.

Shuffling footsteps announced Ananova's return to the dwelling. Selivia leapt to her feet, upsetting Lightning Bug, who had been snoozing by her ankles. He yelped and darted around her feet in a frantic circle.

"Ananova! Is there any news?"

"The Air struggles," Ananova said. She went over to Zala and rested a hand on her shoulder. It wasn't clear whether she meant to comfort or lean on her niece for support. The cheery, talkative woman who had welcomed them to Sunset City was gone. Deep circles shadowed Ananova's eyes now, haunted by pain and weariness. "It carries so much pain, but it is no longer restricted. Our brothers and sisters to the south have stopped calling upon it for their barrier."

"Why?" Zala asked.

"We are not sure. The attacks may have stretched farther than we imagined."

Selivia knew she should be worried, but she felt a burst of hope. "So there's not a barrier anymore?"

"No, child."

"There's something else," Zala said, studying her aunt. Selivia wondered if Zala had a touch of the Air Sense herself.

"Fodorov and some of the others believe the Soolens are fighting the Vertigonians with a magical substance."

Zala gasped. "Is that possible?"

"I do not know. But the fighting has been so terrible . . . The Fireworkers didn't just sweep in and destroy the Soolens, as they should have with their power. They took them by surprise, but now the Soolens are fighting back."

"With Fire?" Selivia said.

"Perhaps. There are blinding flashes and explosions on both sides. It's possible the magic clashes caused the barrier to fall."

"Could . . . could the Soolens defeat the Fireworkers?"

The Vertigonians must have believed they'd win an easy victory. Selivia feared for Sora. Her sister couldn't have known that the army was in real danger when she let them leave Vertigon. Who'd have thought the Soolens had magic too?

"It is too soon to say," Ananova said. "I came to find you for a different reason, child. The other Sensors believe you can help."

Selivia glanced at Zala. Here it was. They were going to use her to protect themselves, friends or not. Perhaps it would work out for the best.

"Help how?"

"The Sensors Circle believes the Amintelles have the power to stop the violence."

Selivia blinked. The power? Not as a hostage, then? She thought of the song about the "child of fire and rain, betwixt the mountain and the plain." Could it be talking about Siv instead of her? Or even Sora? They were all scions of both Vertigon and Trure. She could see why the Sensors weren't sure. But she didn't have to rely on old songs. Her brother and sister would fix everything.

"Are . . . Are you going to help me talk to my family?"

Ananova gave a tired smile. "We can ask the Air if it will assist us. Now that the barrier has fallen, it should be easier. Come. I'd welcome a distraction from the ash and destruction."

"How does it work? Do we have to climb the Rock? When can we start?"

"Easy, child," Ananova said. "We will meditate together. It may take some time."

"I'm ready." Selivia clutched Ananova's hand. "Who should I call first? My sister?"

"Vertigon is a source of terrible pain," Ananova said. She grimaced, and Zala squeezed her hand. "Communication is difficult there. But we may petition the Air to carry your voice to other realms."

"Siv, then," Selivia said. "But I don't know where he is. Can the Air help me find him?"

"We may ask," Ananova said.

They ascended the Rock together. They didn't climb all the way to the ledge where Selivia had seen the Sensors Circle before. All they needed was a flat plane above the hubbub of the city. They found a suitable spot and sat cross-legged on the stone.

"You must be patient," Ananova said, taking Selivia's hands in hers. "Empty your mind. Hold only the image of your brother in your thoughts. I will ask the Air to give me a channel."

"How will I know if he can hear me?"

"You will know."

Selivia and Ananova waited, sitting on the Rock far above the plain. They didn't speak, didn't move. Only breathed. A strong breeze wafted the vibrant smells of the blooming desert around them. The hair rose on Selivia's scalp. She still wasn't sure whether the wind carried the Air around or if the substance moved by itself. The way the Sensors talked about the Air giving gifts and speaking and leading, it was almost as if a person directed it. Would it speak to her?

Whatever they were listening for, within minutes, Selivia was certain she had never been more bored in her entire life. Emptying her mind was incredibly difficult. She kept wondering what Siv was doing and whether Dara and Vine had found him yet. She'd ask Ananova to help her talk to Vine next. It ought to be easier because Vine meditated with the Air herself. She could be trying to gather information in the wind just like the Far Plainsfolk! Not that Selivia should be thinking about that right now. Right. She had to be calm.

But every time her mind began to empty, she found herself going over what she and Zala had read about dragons or reviewing the new Far Plains vocabulary she had learned. She wondered if there was any truth to the theory that the Soolens were fighting with magic too. That would be crazy. She thought about Ivran for a bit, but the image of his sneering face only made her blood boil. Next, she thought about the Far Plains dress she was learning to sew and the paintings Fenn had been working on as they settled into their exile.

At one point, Ananova opened her eyes and breathed deeply and pointedly, as if to remind Selivia she should be calming herself. Oops. She could probably tell Selivia wasn't very good at this. She hoped Ananova couldn't hear the rather uncharitable things she'd been thinking about her son.

Selivia returned to thoughts of Fenn's paintings. Her bodyguard had achieved a level of serenity that Selivia found both admirable and terribly dull. She couldn't stand this quiet existence when there were so many exciting and horrible things going on in the world.

But Fenn had found solace in art, turning the colors of the desert into beautiful images that rivaled the paintings on the Rock itself.

Thinking of the paintings evoked too many memories in Selivia's mind, too many images that weren't her brother waiting somewhere for her to make contact. That wasn't helpful.

So she focused on the colors.

She thought of Fenn mixing her paints to create new ones, how the hues swirled slowly together, becoming something new. Scarlet, amber, emerald, teal. It was mesmerizing, somehow managing to both calm and stimulate at the same time. Pearl, azure, ochre. Burnt umber. Deep lilac. Gold.

Suddenly, a whooshing sound filled Selivia's ears, as if she'd stuck her entire head inside a tornado. The sensation made her dizzy. She fought for the calm Ananova had talked about. It was the most difficult thing she had ever done. She wasn't a calm person. The world was a wonderful, exciting place. She loved bright colors and romance and intrigue and adventure. She had no interest in being calm when the world was so brilliant.

She forced herself to breathe slowly, imagining the colors of the rainbow shifting before her eyes, mixing like paint. Mixing and blending, distinct and cohesive, just like her family. She had to do this for them.

The wind quieted gradually. The rush of color surrounded and swallowed her. Then, contact. She still sat atop the ledge, but she sensed another presence now, uttering the deep, slow breaths of sleep. Somehow, she knew it wasn't Ananova. The person whose breath she heard on the wind was very far away indeed.

"Siv?" she said. "Can you hear me?"

26

LATCH

Siv was deep in a dream. He'd taken Dara to a secluded waterfall on Square Peak. The spring snowmelt had turned the usual trickle into a flood. The water cascaded over a rocky cliff into a crystal-blue pool. It was twilight, and a Fire Lantern rested on a large rock beside the waterfall. The Firelight transformed the water into a flood of diamonds and Firejewels.

Siv stood beneath the waterfall, his feet inches from the icy water. Dara sat on the rocks above him across the stream from the Fire Lantern. The glittering light and soft shadows made her look like an ancient Fire goddess. She was the most beautiful person he had ever seen.

"Jump!" he called to her.

"I can't swim."

"Yes, you can. I'll catch you!"

"You won't." Dara frowned, the magical light flickering in her eyes. "You're the reason I'm here. Wyla would never have trapped me."

Suddenly, in the way of dreams, Siv was sitting beside Dara on the rock. Mist from the waterfall sprayed their faces. It was the same silvery shade as Watermight. He touched her sword arm, the one that kept her confined to Pendark. It felt like ice.

"I vowed to protect you."

"You've vowed things before." She shifted away from him, suddenly appearing on the opposite side of the waterfall. She picked up the Fire Lantern and held it high. "My parents were right about you. They were right about everything."

Siv shook his head. He'd always known Dara would have to make a final choice: him or her parents. The decision hung like a specter behind their every conversation. But he couldn't believe she was choosing their side. Not now.

She continued to stare at him, the Firelight playing on her skin, and Siv wished he could wake up. At least he knew it was a dream.

Suddenly, his sisters were there, standing in the icy pool beneath the waterfall.

"Siv, can you hear me?" *Selivia called.*

"Of course," Siv said. "I'm right here."

Selivia looked around, not acknowledging him. Water seeped into her bright-yellow skirt. Sora stared straight at him with solemn, accusing eyes.

Selivia called out again. "Sivarrion Amintelle, can you hear me?"

"Yes. I'm here, Sel."

"Siv?"

Sora folded her arms and surveyed him. "Honestly, Siv, do you intend to sleep all day?"

"Huh?"

Selivia was beginning to look distressed. "Siv, can't you hear me? Blast. Why isn't this working?"

"Siv," Sora said, still not looking at her sister, "wake up."

Siv sat bolt upright. He was in his room at headquarters. The first rays of dawn were peeking through the window. The details of his strange dream faded quickly. Dara had been there. What had they said to each other? Something about a choice? And Selivia had been searching for him even though he was right in front of her.

What did that mean?

"Siv! It's Selivia. Can you hear me?"

Siv jerked backward, banging his head painfully on the wall. Latch stirred in the next bed, grumbling softly.

The voice came again. "Siv, are you there?"

He had to be dreaming. But the bump on his head hurt! His legs were sore from yesterday's training session, too. And that voice . . .

"Sel?" he whispered.

"Yes!"

"Where are you?"

"The Far Plains!"

Siv rubbed the back of his head, wondering if he'd hit it harder than he thought. "I must be going as crazy as a bullshell on a ship."

"I'm using the Air." Selivia's voice was as clear as if she were standing at the foot of his bed. "Or my friend is using it to make a channel I can use to speak to you. Isn't it magnificent? I'm staying in the Far Plains. It's the most astonishing place. They have purlendogs and sand dancers and—" There was a muffled sound in the background. It didn't come from within Siv's room. "Right, sorry, the news." Selivia cleared her disembodied throat. "I don't have a lot of time. We've had news from the Sensors in Rallion City. The city has been captured."

"I thought the Soolen army occupied Rallion City months ago."

"They did. They were attacked. It's the Fireworkers, Siv. The Lantern Maker led the Fireworkers off the mountain, and they're using Fire Weapons in battle."

"*What?* Why?"

"They mean to conquer the Lands Below. They've already killed Grandfather Atrin. The fighting is dreadful. You have to stop it."

Siv wanted to leap up and pace, but he wasn't sure if that would break the connection with his sister. He could hardly believe this was possible. Fire Weapons. What had Ruminor done?

"Is Mother with you?"

"No. She stayed behind in the Stronghold." Selivia's voice broke. "I couldn't get her to leave with me."

"What about Sora?" Siv asked. "Have you heard from her?"

"The Fireworkers say they're fighting in her name. But Sora wouldn't allow that, would she?"

"She must be a prisoner," Siv said. "That damned Lantern

Maker . . . I'm going to help her. I'm gathering resources to return to Vertigon."

"I knew you'd help!" Selivia said. "But you need to hurry. These Fire Weapons are awful. They've already had the most horrible battles with the Soolens and the last of the Trurens. No one will tell me the exact details." Selivia sounded both annoyed and relieved that she had been spared the gory details. Siv could imagine enough.

"I'll be there as soon as I can," he said. "What about you? Are you safe?"

"Oh yes. The Far Plainsfolk are delightful!" Something in Selivia's tone sounded forced, but he wasn't sure if that was just the effort of speaking through the Air channel.

"Good. Are you staying with—?"

"Oh dear. I didn't catch that." There was a muffled sound. Then Selivia said, "We are losing the wind. This Air communication isn't always stable. I still have to tell you about the Soo—"

"Sel?" Siv called. "I couldn't hear that."

"Magic . . . heard . . . not just . . . might . . . awful!"

"I can't hear you so well anymore. Can you say that again?"

"Siv . . . connection . . . later."

"Try to contact me again!" he shouted. "And don't even think about leaving the Far Plains until I send for you!"

There was no answer. The connection was gone. Siv waited for a few seconds, questioning whether he had hallucinated the whole thing.

"What are you doing?" Latch asked.

Siv jumped. His roommate was sitting up and staring at him, his expression stony. Siv wasn't sure whether or not Latch had heard the other voice in the room or if that had all been in his head.

"Talking to my sister," he said at last.

"Uh . . ."

"Don't ask me how. Some sort of Air thing."

"That hasn't worked for months," Latch said. "There was a barrier between Pendark and Trure."

Siv gaped at him. "How did you—?"

"It doesn't matter. What did she say? What's the news?"

"The Fireworkers are attacking," Siv said. "They left the mountain armed with Fire Weapons, and they're trying to conquer the Lands Below. They already took Rallion City away from your father's army."

Latch's face went gray in the dawn light. "Are you certain?"

"That's what she said." Siv felt queasy at the thought of his people becoming pillagers and conquerors. The power of the Fire would be a catastrophic weapon. This was what his family had worked against for generations.

"Can Fire beat Watermight?" Latch asked, his voice taking on a strange tone.

"I don't know. But I can't believe they'd come all the way here. I don't think they'll be conquering Pendark anytime soon." *At least not too soon.*

"It's not Pendark I'm thinking of," Latch said. "It's my father and his army."

"Sounds like they've already had skirmishes. I'm sorry, but I can't imagine the Soolens will last long against Fire Weapons."

"They'll put up a fight."

"I'm sure your countrymen are very brave," Siv said. "But *they* don't have magic."

The most peculiar expression crossed Latch's face. Siv frowned. "They don't have magic, do they?"

Latch didn't answer.

And another piece of Latch's puzzle whirred into place.

"Wait a minute." Siv leapt to his feet and began pacing back and forth across the small room. "You asked me if Fire can beat Watermight. But you weren't talking about Pendark." He stopped and stared at Latch for a moment. The Soolen met his eyes stonily. "Are you saying there's Watermight in Soole? It's close enough to the sea. I suppose you could have secret vents."

Latch maintained his sullen silence. Siv resumed his pacing. There was one more missing detail. Pendarkans, despite their famed violence and ambition, had never tried to take over any of the northern lands because Watermight was too unstable to be moved long distances. That meant . . .

"You can transport it!" He whirled to face Latch. "Your father figured out a way to bring Watermight north and used it to conquer Trure!"

Latch's mouth tightened. Then he nodded.

Siv could hardly believe it. He *knew* there had been a reason his grandfather's army was defeated so quickly. But this? This was insane. This meant Watermight and Fire could even now be clashing on the battlefield in Trure.

"Can you do it yourself? Are you a blasted Waterworker?"

Latch sighed. "It's a family trait. I didn't choose it."

No wonder Latch's father had sent mercenaries after him in Fork Town. He must know how to transport the Watermight. That secret would be even more valuable than the life of his prodigal son. Commander Brach might have let Latch go his own way if he didn't carry such vital information.

"If you tell anyone, I'll kill you," Latch said.

"You can't just sit on this secret," Siv said. "This is bigger than . . . than . . . I can't even think of anything this big."

"I'm not telling you how to do it. You realize your people are fighting against mine now, don't you?"

"Yours invaded first," Siv said. "But I don't want my people trying to expand Vertigon's boundaries, and I certainly don't want a bunch of Pendarkan Waterworkers joining the fray. You've told me before you don't think your father should have done it with Soole either. We have to make things right again."

"Do what you want," Latch said. "I don't want to be involved."

"You have to be. You can't just look the other way after what your father has done. You have a chance to stop him." Siv sat and began putting on his boots. "I'm not letting my people continue this Fire Weapon insanity."

"It's not my problem," Latch said.

"You're worried about your father," Siv said, waving a boot at him. "I know you are. If I take back my kingdom, I can call back the Fireworkers. They'll kill him if I don't."

"Don't underestimate the strength of my father's Watermight arsenal."

"He's already torn apart my grandfather's army," Siv said. "I get that he's dangerous. But Trure had no way to fight back. The Fireworkers will do more damage before the end, to your people and to themselves. It's up to us to stop this war."

Latch was quiet for a long time.

"I'll think about it," he said at last. "But you have to swear not to tell anyone."

Siv halted. Could he promise that? This secret was worth more than both of their lives, and he didn't want to make promises about it lightly. But if he and Latch were going to save their peoples from destruction, they had to be straight with each other.

"I'll be as quiet as a morrinvole."

Latch nodded then rolled over with his back to Siv. Somehow, Siv doubted he would go back to sleep.

He finished dressing and collecting his knives, his head buzzing with all this new information. With Latch's knowledge, Siv and Dara could bring Watermight to fight against Rafe Ruminor's Fire. Even if Dara wasn't as strong as her father, maybe she really could do something with both powers to overcome him. Now that the Lantern Maker had invaded, it was more urgent than ever to get her out of Pendark. They needed to get to Trure before there was nothing left but ash.

27

THE LIGHTHOUSE

A familiar squawking drew Dara's attention when she and Siln returned to the manor house after another day of patrols. Rumy perched atop the gates like an overgrown gargoyle. They had kept the cur-dragon out of sight as much as possible since their arrival in the city. Too many Pendarkans would happily capture and sell him. He was sure to fetch a high price beyond the Bell Sea.

"I still can't believe how large he is," Siln said as they entered the gates and Rumy flew down to meet them on the other side. "Are you sure he's an ordinary cur-dragon?"

"No, I'm not sure." Dara scratched Rumy's scaly head, feeling the warmth emanating from his body. He scratched at her boots with his blunt claws, drawing her attention to a parchment tied discreetly to his ankle.

"I'm going to spend a little time with him," she said to Siln. "I won't leave the manor grounds."

"See that you don't," Siln said. "You're in as much danger from the other Waterworkers as you would be from Wyla if you cross her again."

"I've learned my lesson."

"I certainly hope so," Siln said. "She taught me that lesson long ago. It wasn't pleasant."

Dara wandered along the garden path with Rumy at her side while Siln went into the house. Guards patrolled the walls. Trying to leave would be foolish even if Siln weren't watching from the windows.

When they reached a hedge she could comfortably hide behind—the same one Siv had used the day he threw pebbles at her window—she sat down and pulled Rumy's head onto her lap. He snorted and purred as she scratched him under the chin with one hand and pulled the note from his ankle with the other. The note was written in a familiar elegant hand.

D,

I didn't think it would be possible to miss you any more than I did after my unplanned departure from Trure. Shows what I know. It's excruciating to be in the same city when I can't see you. Not to be too sentimental or anything, but I can hardly sleep for thinking about you. I want to see your intense eyes and touch your beautiful mouth. Honestly, if all I could do was look at you, I'd probably die happy.

I've learned some important information that could change everything. Can you meet me by the beach where you learned to swim tomorrow after nightfall?

I remain yours for as long as I draw breath.

S

P.S. You should burn this letter when you're done. Preserving my eloquent prose wouldn't be wise in our current predicament. I swear to write you better love letters when all this is behind us. Also, did I mention I love you?

Dara traced every word with her fingers before asking Rumy to burn the parchment. She couldn't risk sending him back out with her answer. Siln would watch for something like that. Siv would go to the beach even if she didn't respond.

The note turned to ash in her palm, and heat trickled through her body. She held onto the dragon Fire as she considered the message, enjoying the way it flickered within her, more wild and unpredictable than the Fire of the mountain. Siv's note had been oddly spare of details. The information must be important indeed if he'd use Rumy to carry it but wouldn't actually write it in the note.

She wouldn't risk sneaking out ordinarily, but tomorrow night, Wyla and Siln planned to attack Brendle of the Boundary District, a powerful Waterworker who'd raided the new vent last night. Dara was originally supposed to accompany them, but Wyla had changed her mind that very morning. Dara would have the night off.

She drew Rumy's Fire from her body, letting the liquid gold pool in her hands. Meeting Siv would be risky, but she couldn't stand not seeing him anymore. He lived within walking distance, yet it felt as though she were back in the wilderness, wondering if she'd ever get to see him again. She had to go. She had to tell Siv to leave the city. They walked a dangerous tightrope here, and he couldn't stay any longer.

Still, she couldn't help wondering if the information involved a way to free her. She Worked the Fire into a wheel and let it spin across the garden, feeling a burst of hope for the first time in a long while.

Vine agreed to cover for her the following evening.

"Are you sure I can't retrieve the information?" she said. "Wyla doesn't care what I do."

"He must have asked for me for a reason," Dara said.

"I can think of a reason or two, honey, but that doesn't mean it's wise," Vine said.

"Wyla and Siln are busy," Dara said. "I might not get another chance to see him."

It probably would be better if Vine went in her place, but Dara hadn't been able to sleep the previous night at the thought of her rendezvous with Siv. She had to take the risk, or she might combust for not seeing him.

When darkness fell at last, Dara armed herself with her Savven blade and a hefty measure of Rumy's Fire before slipping over the manor-house walls. The guards weren't as diligent as usual with the lady of the house out for the evening. They were playing cards when Dara scaled the tree beside the wall and dropped quietly over the side.

The Fire hummed under her skin as she crept through the streets. Few people were out this evening. Most thought it prudent to stay indoors while the Waterworkers warred over the districts. Still, she pulled a cloak over her head in case anyone recognized her.

The hot night reminded her that it would be summer soon. With the warmth of the evening, the weight of her cloak, and the Fire running in her veins, Dara was surprised she wasn't glowing.

Heat didn't affect her the same way it did other people, but she was still sweating by the time she reached the coast.

The rocky beach was deserted, and sentries strode back and forth along the walls of the nearby manor house. The Waterworker who lived there—one of the port lords—was taking no chances with everything happening in the city. Dara waited in the deep shadows beneath a stilt house by the beach for Siv to arrive. She was sure he would be there even though she hadn't sent Rumy back to him with her answer. He'd have to hurry, though. As much as she was looking forward to this reunion, she couldn't stay long. She intended to be asleep in her bed by the time Wyla and Siln returned to the manor.

Darkness surrounded her, tense and eerie. Sweat crawled down her scalp. The gentle waves muted the city noises. Pendark felt as if it were poised on a cliff, waiting to see whether or not it would fall.

A hand landed on Dara's shoulder. Her Savven blade was halfway out of the sheath before she confirmed that it was Siv. She released the sword with a soft rasp. Siv put a finger to his lips and nodded toward the sentries guarding the nearby manor. Another pair strolled along the waterline, watching for threats from the night-dark waves. She hadn't noticed those two before. Siv pointed to the far end of the beach about halfway to where the shoreline curved around to encircle the Gulf. A long, narrow stretch of land reached a finger out into the water. It appeared to be a rocky jetty. Dara nodded, preparing to follow him out there.

Before they moved from their hiding spot, Siv seized her jaw in his hand and kissed her. Her body blazed like the sun as his lips met hers. Firelord, she had missed this. She clutched the front of his coat, barely able to think for the heat and the Fire spiking through her. He released her too soon, grinning like a schoolboy, and set off into the darkness. She followed on shaky legs.

The beach was longer than Dara remembered. Lone figures appeared sometimes, picking up shells or walking amongst the beachfront stilt houses. The two sentries still patrolled the waterline. Dara and Siv flitted carefully through the shadows, hiding under the stilt houses to avoid being spotted. Dara found herself assessing the larger patches of shadow to see if they could stop for another quick kiss. Or a slow kiss. She shook her head. *That's not why you're here.*

Siv clearly had a specific destination in mind. When they reached the jetty, he paused for a few heartbeats to make sure no one was coming then darted across the beach to the rocky structure. He clambered up the slick stones and started out onto the causeway.

Dara hesitated. Wyla's mission tonight *should* keep her occupied, but Wyla's house was relatively close to their beach meeting place. If she went out onto that long jetty, she could activate the curse in her arm and alert Wyla that she'd left the house.

As if sensing her concern, Siv came back to her and whispered, "The spot is within the city boundaries. I checked." He brushed a kiss on her ear before heading out onto the jetty.

Dara followed. She had nearly forgotten about whatever information Siv needed to impart. She needed him, and every brush of his lips on her skin and touch of their hands reminded her of it. Their time apart had only intensified her longing. She wanted nothing more than to disappear into the dark with him.

They walked in silence. A sliver moon rose above the city, and the sea wind blew sharply across their cheeks. It cooled Dara's face, doing nothing to dispel the heat building within her body. A few more seconds, and they would finally be alone together. Her breath quickened.

A dark shape emerged ahead. A slim tower jutted out from the end of the jetty. As they drew nearer, Dara realized it was an old lighthouse. A much larger one overlooked the channel where the Gulf opened into the Bell Sea. A brilliant Fire Lantern—one of the largest ever exported from Vertigon—warned ships away from the rocks peppering the mouth of the Gulf. This smaller tower must have been used for a similar purpose once, but now the glass-encased top was dark.

"Let me check inside," Siv said. He crept to an opening in the base of the old tower. The wooden door had mostly disintegrated, and more pieces fell away as he pushed it open and disappeared inside.

Dara waited, hand on her Savven blade, and studied the barren strip of land around the tower. It felt as if they had left the city, but her arm felt completely normal. Siv must be right about the boundaries of Pendark. Still, she felt as if she could breathe a little easier here, cooled by the wind rushing across the gulf, sweeping away the cloying scents of the city.

Siv poked his head through the doorway and called out in a normal voice, "All clear. You coming?"

"I can't stay long."

"I know. But it has been too long since I got to spend time with you. I thought we could check this place out." Siv took her hand and drew her through the doorway. "I've been told it's very romantic."

"In a dark and scary sort of way," Dara said. "Good thing I brought a light."

She eased the Fire from her veins to pool in her palm then formed it into a glowing lantern shape and lifted it into the air. The Firelight cast a golden hue over the inside of the tower, revealing broken furniture and a pattern of mildew on the walls.

"Maybe it's more romantic in the dark," Siv said, wrinkling his nose at the mildew.

A ladder on one wall led into darkness above them. Dara sent her Fire slowly up its length until it reached an opening at the top.

"Shall we see if it's nicer upstairs?"

"I'll go first," Siv said, advancing to the ladder.

"You don't want to risk injury," Dara said. "You're a professional athlete now."

"I guess I am." Siv laughed. "And you're a very important person to the powers that be. Look at us changing places."

Dara grinned. "Are you going up there or not?"

Siv climbed carefully, the ladder creaking under his weight. Just before he reached the opening, Dara sent the Firelight through ahead of him. She wished she could use it to project her field of vision somehow. She suspected it was possible to do something like that with Watermight, but Wyla hadn't taught her yet. Fire had greater tangible advantages given how transportable and versatile it was, but Watermight had an interesting relationship with the mental and physical aspects of the human body. It could clean and seal wounds and take root in one's bones to secure a bargain. She wouldn't be surprised if it could be used to enhance sight too.

Why are you thinking about the Work now? She used to get like this with dueling sometimes. If she let it, the Work would consume her. She had much more pleasant things to focus on for once.

Siv scanned the upper level of the tower then pulled himself through the hole.

"Floor seems sturdy enough," he called.

The rungs felt rough under Dara's hands as she climbed the ladder. Every movement echoed strangely in the tall, narrow space. She clambered through the opening to the upper level where Siv waited. The circular room was empty of furniture, save for a solitary chair by the far wall, leaving plenty of space for them to move around comfortably.

A bronze apparatus hung from the ceiling. It must have once held the light for the lighthouse, which could have been a Fire Lantern or a more mundane flame. Dara floated her conjured Fire Lantern up to rest on the bronze casing. They wouldn't be here long enough for it to matter if anyone noticed the glimmer at the top of the tower.

High windows were set in the top of the wall. Dara stood on her toes to see out of them. The windows were open to the air, and glass crunched under her boots as she moved closer. Glass shards clung to the window frames as well. It must have been a long time since they were broken, perhaps blown in during a storm.

The tower offered a magnificent view of the inky surface of the Gulf. The water roiled, restless in the wind. Pendark glittered beyond it, looking remarkably calm despite the turmoil of recent weeks. Within a few seconds of watching it, Dara spotted glimmers of silvery light where Watermight skirmishes must be breaking out. She wondered if one of the contests involved Wyla and Siln. The thought reminded her that she shouldn't linger.

"What did you want to tell me?" she asked Siv, who had come over to join her. He didn't have to stand on his toes to admire the view.

"Just a minute." He wrapped his arms around her from behind and pressed his cheek against hers. "Let's just enjoy the peace and quiet. I've missed you."

Dara leaned back against his chest, breathing him in along with the salt wind off the gulf.

"I missed you too."

"Has Wyla been making you fight?" he asked. "I've been worried."

"I'm learning Watermight combat from Siln," she said. "I still have a way to go before I'll be really dangerous."

"Have you tried using Fire against any of the Waterworkers?"

"No. As soon as I ran out, I'd be vulnerable. I'm no match for them with the Watermight yet. It would be like a beginning duelist throwing a rock at a champion swordsman and then trying to duel them immediately after making them mad."

"Understood."

"I'm making progress, though. I should be able to hold my own after a few more months of practice."

"I don't think we can wait a few months," Siv said.

"Wyla won't change her mind," Dara said. She held tight to Siv's arms around her, wishing they could have gone a little longer without discussing Wyla. "Especially with everything going on in the city."

"I have a better plan," Siv said. "Khrillin can help break your bond."

"The Waterlord?" Dara stiffened. "You told him about me?"

"He reckons Wyla's bargains are tough to unravel, but he's willing to give it a go with enough research."

"At what cost?"

"I saved his hide, didn't I? And we're working together."

"So I hear." Dara pulled away and turned to face him.

"What's wrong?"

"You're a known ally of the Waterlord. Wyla already knows you're connected to him, and I'm connected to you. She's going to be angry when she finds out you told him about our bargain."

"You'll be free by then."

"Wyla won't be defeated that easily," Dara said. "You might have just gotten me killed. Why didn't you talk to me before going to Khrillin?"

"I'm not even allowed to see you." Siv kicked a boot through the broken glass on the floor. Then he caught her hand in his. "I told you I would find a way to get you away from Wyla."

"I didn't think you'd share my secrets with one of her biggest enemies."

"It makes sense, doesn't it? Get the cullmoran to eat the povvercat."

Dara pulled her hand out of Siv's grasp. "How do you know Khrillin is the cullmoran?"

"He's the only Waterworker I've got," Siv said. "I'm not saying I trust him completely, but if he's going to fund my attack force, I reckon it's not too much to ask him to free my lover first."

"You don't understand. Wyla does things no other Waterworker can do. She's an experimenter. An inventor."

"He mentioned something about that."

"And Wyla has been experimenting with me and my abilities in a way that no other magical practitioner has, as far as I know."

"So what?"

"So I'm unique." Dara paced across the tower. "What I can do is unique—at least for the moment. And it's supposed to be secret. If the Waterlord finds out I'm a Fireworker who can wield Watermight too—which he will as soon as we step foot in Vertigon—I could become more valuable to him than even you are. You shouldn't have told him a single thing about me."

Siv threw up his arms. "What choice did I have? Wyla has you fighting her little war. She won't let you go. I can't wield magic against her, but I had to try something."

Dara stomped back and forth across the small space, considering the best way to handle this. How much did the Waterlord guess already? If word got out that he knew about her bond, Wyla would assume Dara had conspired with him. It would be worse if he tried to break the link on her arm—and failed. She didn't know enough about the Waterlord or his abilities to trust him to try. If the attempt didn't kill her, Wyla would.

Besides, she *was* unique. Through what seemed to be a fluke of circumstance, she was learning to do something no magic wielder in living memory had done. Dara *wanted* to learn more from Wyla. She still hadn't managed to wield the two powers together, but she was determined to reach that elusive goal. She could rise above every Fireworker and Waterworker on the continent, more powerful than all of them. She couldn't just walk away.

"You have to tell Khrillin to leave me alone."

"She'll never let you go, Dara," Siv said. "Don't you see?"

"And what if I don't want to go back to Vertigon?" Dara snapped. She turned to face Siv, standing in the center of the tower beneath the conjured Fire Lantern. "That's your fight. I told you a long time ago that I didn't want to kill my own parents."

Siv stared at her as if she'd slapped him.

"It's not just my fight."

"It's your kingdom."

"It's not about the crown anymore," Siv said. "I have to tell you my news. Your father led a force of Fireworkers off the mountain. They're attacking the Soolen and Truren armies—with Fire Weapons."

"What? How do you know?"

"It's a long story."

Fire Weapons. Dara had seen enough fights between Waterworkers to imagine what that would be like. Fire clinging like water, melting everything it touched. Hot metal spinning out of control. Men roasting in their boots. Cities burning to ash. She remembered what Siln had said about the full potential of the Fire, the danger and destruction it could unleash. In her father's hands, the Fire could raze the world.

She looked up at Siv. "I can't stop an army of Fireworkers."

He took a step toward her. "But you might be able to stop their leader."

"He's my *father.*"

"Exactly." Another step. "You can't wash your hands of your parents, Dara. It'll eat away at you for the rest of your life. It's the right thing to do."

Dara shook her head. "My skills—"

"You're better than them," Siv said. "I know you are. You can do it."

His confidence made her heart creak painfully. He truly believed it. He couldn't know how inadequate her Wielding abilities were. She still had so much to learn.

"I can do something unique," Dara said gently, "but it's not the same as being better than them. The Fireworkers of Vertigon have years of experience. The only thing that makes me special is the Watermight, and I can't use that unless the fighting comes a lot farther south."

"Right. That." Siv frowned and scratched at his short beard. He seemed to be struggling with something. Was there more to the information? Had he planned to tell her something else tonight?

He rolled his shoulders as if adjusting something heavy. "Please, will you at least come with me to see Khrillin? We don't have much time."

Conflicting emotions pulled at her like a mighty current. She wanted to stop her parents. Their ambitions could destroy Vertigon—and the Lands Below. Did her father really wish to be a conqueror? In a flash, she pictured him striding tall across the plains of Trure as armies burned around him. She forced away the image with a shudder. She wasn't strong enough to stop him.

"I can't," she whispered, wishing she and Siv had waited longer before speaking. She'd have been happy if they didn't talk at all. "You have to leave the city without me."

"You can't stay forever." Siv closed the remaining distance between them and grabbed her hands. "Fight her, Dara. Figure out a way to use Wyla's magic against her, or bash her over the head. I don't care. Just don't give up."

His gaze bore into her with the intensity of a whirlpool. Dara avoided it.

"We should go," she said. "We can't be seen together."

"I'm not letting you change the subject," Siv said, his hands tightening on hers. "Please let the Waterlord break the bond so we can go back where we belong. Together."

"It won't work," Dara said.

"You can't accept that," Siv said. "Vertigon needs us. It's our home. You're a Fireworker. You may be able to use this Watermight stuff, but don't get caught up in their fight. You should be on the mountain, blazing like the sun. Not sitting here letting some slimy Pendarkan witch tell you what to do."

"Siv . . ."

"They need our help."

Dara's throat constricted. Siv couldn't stay here while his family and his kingdom were in peril. She wanted to go with him. She had promised to defend him until her last breath. But she wasn't strong enough yet.

And she wanted the power. She wanted to Wield as no magic user had before. She wanted to show every magician, Worker, Wielder, practitioner, Sensor, and Artist on the continent that she could defeat them all.

The Fire above her flickered, as if it could sense her agitation. It made the tower glow like the inside of a lantern. Siv pulled her closer, as if he could sense the conflict within her. Or maybe he couldn't wait to hold her any longer.

"Please," he whispered, pressing his forehead against hers. "*I* need you."

Dara's heart felt as if it were being stretched out, pulled in two different directions. It was excruciating. The only thing holding her together was Siv's body pressed against hers. She didn't want to spend their precious moments together arguing. She didn't want to say another word about Khrillin, or her father, or the war.

Apparently, Siv didn't either, because he bent his face to hers and kissed her at last.

The kiss was earnest, intense. It had been far too long.

He wrapped his arms around her, held her tighter. The kiss deepened, intensified.

"Siv," she breathed against his lips.

He seemed incapable of speech. His hands found her waist, and he tugged her shirt loose from her trousers. He ran his fingers over the skin of her stomach, her back. Dara burned like a lantern. She wanted this so much.

Hardly knowing what she was doing, she drew the Fire back toward her. It sang through her veins, passionate, burning, as Siv's touch set her skin alight. Dara arched her back, pressing against him, her mouth still captured by his. He spread burning shivers along her body with his fingertips.

The Fire in her blood sang in time with the heat. She had forgotten how much she loved this, loved the Fire. She needed the heat and the intensity and the power. And she needed him.

As Dara glowed like a torch in Siv's arms, she detected a flicker of something at the edge of her senses. Something with the same intensity, the same power, but freezing rather than burning.

Then a massive wave of Watermight hit the lighthouse with the force of a thousand terrerack bulls.

28

THE POWER

Watermight thundered over the tower, pouring through the windows and cascading around them. It moved like a living thing, like a torrent of vipers threatening to swallow them whole.

Dara glowed with Fire and heat and need. There was no time to release the Fire before battling the Watermight trying to drown them. Still holding onto Siv, she opened her mouth and pulled down huge gulps of Watermight, gasping as the ice met the flame.

Excruciating pain swept through her. Her bones screamed with the intensity of the power. She couldn't move, couldn't breathe. Siv held her in his arms, his head buried in her neck to protect his eyes from the rush of silver-white magic. She thought he shouted her name, but she couldn't hear anything for the screaming of her own body.

She was going to be overwhelmed. The Fire and Watermight would meet, combust, destroy her and Siv and everything within a hundred miles. She felt the powers swirling in her body, dancing around each other like knife fighters. She couldn't take it much longer.

"Fight it," Siv hissed in her ear. "Fight it, Dara. You can do it."

She couldn't do it. No one could. The powers couldn't work together. This was folly. Wyla was wrong. She couldn't.

"Fight. Dara. You can beat this."

So Dara fought.

She remembered the Watermight giving her strength. She pulled it close to her body, her bones. She held onto it like a bridge in a storm, forcing it to keep her together while whoever was directing it tried to tear her apart. Then she reached for the Fire, for the sensations that were familiar yet still wild and all consuming. The Fire rioted in her veins, oozed out of her skin like sweat.

Focus, Dara. Fight it.

She focused on the two powers, twins and enemies, fighting within her, giving her strength. She *would* control them both. She would bend them to her will. She couldn't lose now.

Slowly, the Fire and Watermight stabilized in her body. They whirled together, a terrifying cacophony of power—but they didn't combust. The pain lessened, though it didn't dissipate entirely.

Then she had it. For one perfect moment, she found a balance.

She seized the riot of power with all her strength, rode it like a kite on the wind. A wave of force rose within her, building, building.

Breaking.

The stone walls of the tower shattered like glass as the power exploded from her. The concussion pushed against the Watermight torrent. The Fire, even in this small quantity, amplified her power. It forced back the attack and sent a wave traveling away from them in a perfect circle, Watermight bedecked with flickering tongues of Fire. A shrieking sounded around her, and Dara thought her eardrums would burst.

She kept her eyes open despite the blinding pain. The wave of power reached the city, shattering windows and making houses tremble on their stilts. It swept through half a district before finally losing its power, dying out like a spring wind.

An abrupt silence followed. Then chattering filled the air as birds took flight and streaked away from the source of the concussion, fleeing for the Bell Sea. Screams and shouts of anger and confusion rose from the city. Every face in Pendark was no doubt turning toward the terrible explosion of power.

Dara and Siv stood at the center of the chaos. The concussion had burst the top of the tower like a bubble, but the lower part remained intact, if more rickety than before. Neither one moved. Dara feared the burst of power had killed him, the concussive wave turning his brain to mush in an instant. He wasn't moving. Why wasn't he moving?

The power was completely gone from her body. She still had strength left, but she was utterly terrified of what she would find if she moved.

Then Siv lifted his head and looked at her, eyes wide.

"Is it over?"

"I don't know," Dara said.

"That . . . that was you, right? The explosion part at the end?"

"Yeah. I guess that's what happens when you get Fire and Watermight to work together."

"Mother of a cullmoran." Siv stepped back from her. Their light was gone, but so was the roof of the tower. Moonlight revealed the color draining from his face. "That was incredible."

"We need to go before they attack again."

"I doubt whoever sent that wave will be attacking anything anytime soon," Siv said. "I'd be surprised if they're still standing. I'm surprised *I'm* still standing."

"You'd better be ready to run," Dara said. "We can't be seen here."

"You're always looking for new ways to get me to go running, aren't you?" Siv turned for the hole in the floorboards. "Looks like the ladder couldn't handle the pressure. Give me a second."

He swung his legs through the opening and dropped into the darkness. Dara approached the hole cautiously. She felt shaky, but not as much as she would have expected now that the pain was gone. She was mostly surprised and a little scared of what she had just done. If Wyla realized just how powerful the Fire and Watermight could be together, she would never let Dara walk away.

"Ladder's in pieces," Siv called. "Go ahead and jump. I'll catch you."

"It's okay. I don't want to kick you in the head." She waited until he was clear before dropping to the ground. She landed hard, but Siv was there to steady her before she stumbled. He stared at her for a few heartbeats, a strange expression on his face. She thought it was wonder.

She started to speak. He raised a hand to quiet her.

"Shh. Someone's coming."

The sound of rocks shifting on the jetty announced the approach. They drew their swords, ready to defend themselves. Dara tried to pull on trace Watermight. The wave had left nothing behind. She was surprised not to feel utterly drained. Using the two powers had been incredibly painful, but it hadn't taken her energy in the same way that overloading on the Fire could. Interesting.

They waited in front of the tower as the steps drew closer. Confused shouts rose in the distance. Lanterns bobbed at the end of the jetty, more people coming to investigate.

A pair of young boys reached them first, one of them wearing a familiar orange bandana.

"You see anything, Tel?" his companion said, voice shaking slightly.

"Nothing."

"What do you reckon happened?"

"Must have been a Fire sorcerer," said Tel, the boy in orange.

"Fire sorcerer?"

"Like they have in the north."

"You're crazy," his friend said. "It's just one of them Waterworkers trying out a new trick."

"I don't think so," said Tel. "This was diff—"

"Shh! Someone's there!"

"Where?"

"By the old lighthouse."

"I don't see anything."

Dara jumped as Siv nudged her arm. He put his sword in its sheath and stepped out of the shadows.

"Ho there!" he called.

The scrambling footsteps stilled.

"Who's there?" Tel called. "We got weapons."

"You won't need them," Siv said. "We're just looking around. Wanted to see what that big explosion was all about."

"Oh." The boy sounded relieved. "Us too."

The two ventured near enough that they could make out more details about them in the dark. They wore the tattered clothing of street urchins, and they carried muddy sticks in their hands like swords. Both had been among the swimmers they met at this beach a few months ago.

"You seen any Fire sorcerers?" asked the younger boy.

"The tower was empty when we got here," Siv said. "If there was a Fire sorcerer, he's long gone."

"Too bad," the boy said.

"We'd best be getting back to the city." Siv looped his arm through Dara's. "Good luck with your investigation."

He hurried her past the boys. They kept their faces down and in shadow. With luck, they wouldn't report back to anyone about the couple they had found at the center of the explosion.

"Hey! Wait a minute!"

Dara winced. She felt Siv's arm tightening around her. Tel caught up to them before they had gone three paces, a shrewd look on his face. "You're Siv the Slugger, aren't you?"

Siv plastered a huge smile on his face. "Why yes, I am."

"I've seen you fight," the boy said excitedly. "I saw you in a gutter match against the Rockeater of Soole!"

"I hope it was fun to watch," Siv said.

"I'll say!" Tel shoved his friend. "Wait 'til we tell our friends we met Siv the Slugger!"

"Uh, maybe you shouldn't mention it," Siv said. Dara could sense the tension in his arm. "It can be like a fun secret."

"What fun are secrets? I met Siv the Slugger!"

Dara tugged urgently on Siv's arm. They couldn't linger here. The boys had seen them already. The damage was done. She wondered if they should pay him something so he wouldn't tell anyone. She was about to suggest as much when Siv saluted the boys and gave them another smile.

"Well, it was nice to meet you both," he said. "Careful in that lighthouse. I don't think the walls are stable."

"Sure thing."

"Bye, Siv the Slugger!"

Dara and Siv hurried onward toward Pendark, keeping their heads down to avoid being recognized again. More people were venturing out to explore the devastation wrought by her wave.

"Think we should have paid him to keep quiet?" Dara asked when they were far enough away from the two boys.

"No," Siv said quietly. "Those boys will tell their friends what they saw, but it might not occur to them to take the story to anyone more dangerous unless they know the information is valuable."

"Let's hope they're not already in the payroll of someone dangerous," Dara said, thinking of Tel's bright-orange bandana.

"Yes."

"We should split up," Dara said. "We don't want anyone seeing us together."

"Will you be all right?" Siv looked at her anxiously. "That . . . thing you did couldn't have been easy."

"It's not far. I have to get back before Wyla does."

Siv still didn't release her arm. His face was cloaked in shadow, and she couldn't read his expression.

"That wave," he said after a minute. "Do you think you could do it again?"

"Maybe," Dara said. "I'm not sure why it worked this time. Wyla always tries to get me in the same mindset or emotional state when she wants me to repeat something I've done before."

"Same mindset, eh? I don't know about that, but could it be the thing you've been looking for: a way to defeat your father?"

"It doesn't matter. He's not coming here, and I can't take the Watermight there."

Siv opened his mouth and closed it again. Once again, she got the sense that there was something he wanted to tell her, but he decided against it.

"Maybe you could stay with Wyla another few days . . . see whether you can learn to do it again."

Dara frowned. "You're okay with me staying now?"

"Only for a few days." Siv looked around swiftly. "I understand you're doing important work. But be careful."

"I will," Dara said slowly. He seemed to be hiding something, but she couldn't imagine what it was. And where was the urgency to leave immediately that he'd shown earlier?

"I'll make contact again soon," he said.

"All right." Dara kissed his cheek, forcing a cheery tone. "Tonight was fun. We should do it again some time."

Siv grinned. "Maybe next time we won't get interrupted."

Dara was still thinking about his words as she made her way through the streets. She needed to isolate exactly what she had done to control the two powers at once. The sheer power of that wave had been nothing short of shocking.

The houses near the waterline were badly damaged. Sand coated the walls on the sea-facing side, and hundreds of shingles had been torn loose from the roofs. Every window in the path of the wave was empty of glass. Debris from the beach littered the streets for several blocks inland.

What had been different this time to produce such devastating results? She'd been surprised and afraid, of course, but that often happened when Wyla attacked her during their research session. What else had she been feeling? She blushed at the memory of Siv's hands trailing across her stomach beneath her shirt, his fingers tracing circles on her back. There had been *that.* But would that kind of emotion help her bind the two powers together?

Broken glass crunched in the street as she hurried back to the manor house. She picked her way through an extra large pile of shards, which glittered like diamonds beneath her feet. When she looked up again, Wyla was standing before her.

29

PLANS

Siv went straight to Khrillin's manor in the Garment District, still a little unsteady on his feet. He had felt surprisingly calm during the attack. He'd known Dara would protect them. But the significance of what she'd done dawned on him as he strode through the aftermath of the wave. Dara had accomplished something no other Wielder could do. She had Wielded Fire and Watermight together, revealing the incredible potential of their union. Dara had power, the kind of power that armies and kings couldn't replicate. And her power wasn't just an oddity. It was a weapon.

They didn't have a moment to lose. It was stunningly clear to Siv that Dara needed to leave Pendark immediately. Wyla would never let such a valuable weapon slip out of her grasp. And as soon as she learned how to do the trick, she would kill Dara. Wyla wasn't a teacher or a mad scientist or an artist. She was a woman of power, and she would never let an apprentice challenge her position.

Well, damned if Siv was going to let that happen. He knew Dara didn't want him to trust Khrillin. He didn't intend to tell the man what she could do. That would be just as bad as if Wyla learned the truth. But he also wouldn't stand idly by while Dara was in peril. He had only suggested they wait a few days to keep her from protesting. He wasn't waiting even a few hours.

Siv paused at the gate to the manor. What would happen if Dara returned to Vertigon with that power? It was actually possible now. Latch could teach her to carry the Watermight.

For the first time, Siv truly pictured it. Dara could wipe out his usurper with a single blow. She could send the marauding Soolen army back where it belonged. She could march the Fireworkers back to their shops on the mountain, never to venture forth again. If he asked, she could obliterate his enemies so thoroughly, they'd never dare challenge him or his family. She would be invincible. She would make *him* invincible. With her power, they could challenge every army on the continent.

"Don't be stupid," he muttered. "You're not going to be that kind of king."

"What kind of king are you going to be?"

Siv started as Kres March walked through the gates of Khrillin's manor.

"I'm just babbling," Siv said. "What are you doing here?"

"Very interesting babble, lad." Kres stepped closer, ignoring the question. He faced Siv nose to nose, eyes sharp. "Tell me: what kind of king do you intend to be when you return to Vertigon?"

Siv froze. Kres's face was always hard to read, and in the darkness, he seemed like nothing more than a pair of glittering eyes in the shadows.

"Have you been drinking, Kres?"

The man burst out laughing. Okay, maybe that hadn't been the best thing to say.

"Siv lad," Kres wheezed. "I know everything. A dozen armed men attacked you in my front yard. You didn't think I'd just forget about it without asking any questions, did you?" Kres chuckled, wiping tears out of his eyes. "Who do you think told Khrillin?"

Siv blinked. "I thought Dellario—"

"That buffoon? Yes, he got you the invitation to the party, but he didn't know anything. He thought you were just a shiny new pen fighter." Kres dissolved into chuckles once more.

Siv didn't speak, not wanting to give anything else away. He still didn't know why Kres had been at Khrillin's manor.

"You and Khrillin have hit it off," Kres said when he had exhausted his mirth. "I'd say that alone is worth something. Not to mention how I've taken you in and protected you as a member of my squad."

"I'll always be grateful," Siv said slowly, waiting for Kres to get to the point. "You do look out for your team."

"Aye," Kres said. "Between you and Latch, my team has turned out to be quite the retirement plan."

Siv let out a breath at last. "You want money."

"Of course I want money," Kres said. "I've put away gold from the pen, but I'm getting too old for this. Soon enough, I'll be done risking my blood for someone else's entertainment."

"What about Latch? You protected him against me for a long time."

"I didn't know your identity then," Kres said.

"But you let me fight in the pen still. Whereas Latch—"

"You are valuable dead or alive—you'd probably be worth more dead, in fact. Latch carries information in that lumpy head of his that will be gone for good if he dies. I've gone to a great deal of trouble to make sure it stays attached to his shoulders."

Suddenly, Kres's hand shot out, and he pulled Siv close enough to reveal the lines around his eyes. The whiff of drink on his breath revealed that Siv's first question hadn't been so far off after all.

"I don't care if it's you or Latch," Kres slurred. "I expect to be well taken care of for my troubles."

"You will be," Siv said. "If Khrillin helps me retake my kingdom, I will reward you handsomely for the introduction. Even if he doesn't, I'll repay you for your assistance on the road. I can probably offer you a greathouse in Vertigon itself, if you feel like retiring."

Kres studied him for a moment. Something flickered in his eyes. If Siv didn't know better, he'd say Kres looked almost . . . wistful. He wondered how many times people had refused to keep their promises to him before.

"I'll take the money." Kres barked a laugh. "I love this festering cesspool of blood and death. I can speak my name with pride here. Keep your greathouse."

"I don't know how things will turn out," Siv said. "But if you ever change your mind, I reckon Vertigon could use a knife-fighting league . . . preferably with blunted knives."

Kres released Siv's shirt and straightened the collar for him, chuckling. "Perhaps it could. I'll consider your offer, lad."

"Good night, Kres." Siv pushed through the gates, leaving Kres humming to himself as he disappeared into the night.

Siv was admitted to the Waterlord's study at once. Kres wasn't the only person who had been drinking here tonight. Khrillin—clad all in blue today—sipped brandy with his feet up on the darkwood desk, eyelids drooping.

"King Siv!" he called. "Just the man I wanted to see. Sit. Sit and have a drink with me."

"I can't tonight. Have you made any progress on your research into my friend's curse?"

"Research? Oh, for the pretty young Waterworker, you mean?"

"We have to break Wyla's bond. Tonight."

Khrillin raised an eyebrow and dabbed at a drop of brandy in his beard. "Calm yourself, son. These things take time."

"I've waited long enough. You and the Waterworkers can throw Watermight back and forth until the true dragons wake if you want. But if you're going to help me, it has to be now."

"I can't tonight." Khrillin lifted his empty glass, hands wavering. "Come back in the morn—"

Siv crossed the room and thudded his fists on the darkwood desk.

"Want me to stick your head in a bucket to sober up?" He loomed over the older man. "Does that work with Watermight users?"

Khrillin didn't even flinch. "It's not my state of intoxication, though that is advanced," he said. "I can't break Wyla's bond."

"What do you mean?"

"I've made a few discreet inquiries. Anything I do will kill your friend. It's impossible."

"I can't accept that," Siv said. "If your friendship with my father meant anything to you—and if you want a future in Vertigon—you have to do this. Dara is the key to getting Vertigon back."

"I'm telling you it can't be done, Sivarrion. The bond would fight against me, likely doing irreparable damage in the process. There's simply no possibility that I could break it."

Siv thought of the very worst curse he knew and spat it at Khrillin.

Khrillin sipped his brandy. "That's no way for a king to talk."

"I'm not a king. But when I am, don't you dare come to me for favors. You can stay in Pendark and burn for not helping her."

Siv turned on his heel and stalked to the door.

"Wait a minute," Khrillin called.

Siv paused, but he didn't turn around.

"Unless you're agreeing to help, we have nothing to talk about."

"*I* can't break the bond," Khrillin said, "but it's possible *she* can. It would take an immense amount of power. If she was behind that explosion tonight, she might be able to do it herself."

So Khrillin knew about the explosion—or guessed enough. Siv didn't have time to worry about that.

"How?"

"I don't know," Khrillin said. "But she has a better chance than I do. If she can find the edge of the bond, harness whatever she did to create that wave of force, and strike while Wyla is distracted, she might manage it."

Fire. Dara had combined Watermight and Fire to create that force. Siv didn't intend to reveal that part to Khrillin, but he knew she was capable of incredible power. If Khrillin thought enough power could break the bond, Siv would do everything he could to give her a chance to use it.

"Thank you," he said shortly. He considered apologizing for his outburst, but the truth was that Khrillin had done precious little to prove his loyalty to Siv beyond keeping his secret. He needed action right now, not diplomatic words. He left Khrillin's study, the door banging shut behind him.

"Latch, I need your help." Siv burst into the bedroom he shared with the Soolen, who was reading a tattered novel.

"What kind of help?" Latch asked.

"I need to get Dara out of Pendark."

"This is news?" Latch turned back to his reading.

"I mean now. Like, tonight."

"What do you expect *me* to do?"

"I want to use your Watermight secret to rescue her."

"Excuse me?"

"Just as a diversion." Siv had spent the canal-boat journey from the Garment District formulating his plan. It was risky, but they didn't have much time to strategize. The other Waterworkers would want to know who had produced a Work of such pure concussive force on the jetty. He did *not* want to be forced to fight through the entire Watermight-capable population of Pendark to get Dara.

But for his plan to succeed, he needed Latch's cooperation.

"You can show off your secret Watermight containment thing and promise to teach Wyla your trick on the condition that she releases Dara from her bond. The moment she's free, Dara can blow Wyla to smithereens."

"Um, since when can Dara do that?"

"She's got this power," Siv said. "She's magnificent."

Latch rolled his eyes. "I get that you're in love. But what you're suggesting—"

"She's strong, Latch, beyond anything I've ever heard of. I think she could defeat Wyla without the bond. But we have to make sure she's released before we try anything. We can't risk her getting hurt."

Latch carefully placed a ribbon in his book and set it beside him on his cot. An instant later, Latch's knife was pressed up against Siv's neck. He didn't even have time to feel surprised.

"Okay, I get it," Siv said quickly. "Bad idea to suggest using your—"

"That information," Latch said, every word slow and deliberate, "is a secret so precious to my family that there isn't a man among us who wouldn't die to protect it. Let me impress upon you the seriousness of what you are suggesting. You want me to reveal a secret that better men have died for to one of the most dangerous magic wielders on the continent so you can take your girlfriend home with you."

"Wyla won't live long enough to tell anyone," Siv said, conscious of the steel at his throat. "Dara will take care of her as soon as she's free." He didn't know if Dara was willing to kill her erstwhile teacher, but if she hesitated, Siv would do it himself. "Wyla is never going to let Dara go if we don't help."

"You're probably right about that," Latch said after a moment. "She's conniving, and you should never trust a Pendarkan." He directed a glare toward the window—and Pendark in general. "I can't risk that secret, though."

"The truth will get out anyway," Siv said. "Your father used it to conquer a powerful nation. It's only a matter of time before everyone knows Watermight was involved. The Waterworkers will travel to Soole en masse, torturing Brachs until they find one who will talk."

"Eat rocks," Latch muttered.

"We can stop this war," Siv said, "but only with Dara's help."

Latch didn't move. The blade was perilously close to cutting into Siv's neck, but he wasn't afraid. This wasn't even the first time they'd been in this position.

"You once told me you ran away because you believed your father's actions were wrong," Siv said. "He deceived thousands of men and betrayed your country to further his own ambitions. You tried to join the noble pen fighters in the Dance of Steel, but now you don't even get to do that. Kres is counting on a reward for keeping you alive. He'll never let you compete." Siv knew it was risky to list Latch's most sensitive points with a knife at his throat, but he had to use every weapon he possessed right now. "This is your chance to be noble, despite what your father has done. If we end the war, you can save your father, his men, and your country."

"What makes you think we can end the war?"

"Dara," Siv said. "It's not just her power. Her father leads the Vertigonian Fireworkers." Siv swallowed, the knife bobbing against his neck. "He's . . . he's the one who usurped me and killed my father."

Latch's stoic mask slipped a bit, his eyes widening. All their secrets were out in the open at last.

"Dara can stop her father," Siv said. "She's the only who can. And you can help to stop yours."

Latch removed the blade from Siv's neck to scratch at his chin with the tip, a frown wrinkling his forehead. Siv held his breath.

Then Latch said, "Fine. I'll help you, you Vertigonian bastard."

"Great." Siv grinned, not quite managing to hide his utter relief. He rubbed at the spot on his throat where Latch's knife had been. "What do you think about my plan?"

"I've heard worse," Latch said. "You're offering Wyla pretty much the only thing that could be as valuable to her as your girl: the knowledge of another magic wielder."

"A unique magic wielder," Siv said. "She doesn't much care about Vine's knowledge, even though she can do a bunch of Air things."

"Yeah, Air is useless," Latch said. "My father doesn't value the Air Sensors either."

Siv shook his head. The arrogance of these wielders never ceased to amaze him. Why were they all so convinced that theirs was the only power that truly mattered? He figured Wyla was onto something by trying to combine the magical substances. But even she wasn't impressed by Air.

"So Dara has a unique ability, and I have a secret ability." Latch met his eyes steadily. "You really think she'll take the trade?"

"It's the only idea I have at the moment." Dara might be able to break the bond herself, but Siv would only risk that if he couldn't get Wyla to release her. The attempt could kill her.

Latch turned his knife in his hands, considering. "And you want to do this tonight?"

"We have to act before Wyla finds out Dara was behind the explosion on the jetty."

"We'd better wait until morning, then," Latch said. "If you go tonight, she'll know it's connected to the explosion. We won't have a chance."

Siv didn't want to wait another minute. He was already cursing the delay going to Khrillin had caused. But Latch was probably right. They only had one chance. And waiting until morning would give them time to pull together the final crucial elements of his plan.

"Okay, tomorrow it is. We'll need to stage it just right, though. She'll be suspicious of ambushes. There aren't many places she'd be willing to meet us."

"Where does Dara think we should do it?" Latch asked.

"Oh, Dara doesn't know about any of this."

"Say again?"

"I haven't shared the plan with Dara," Siv said. "There's no time. Besides, if we take her by surprise, it'll be easier for her to pull off the magic thing she needs to do. That's how it worked, as far as I could tell. Something about being in the same mindset or emotional state."

Latch stared at him as if he had gone insane. "So she hasn't even said whether or not she thinks she can defeat Wyla?"

"I know she can, even if she doesn't," Siv said. "Tonight, she was surprised, under attack, and trying to protect me. I reckon that's a pattern we can replicate."

"You have a lot of faith in her."

"Why wouldn't I?"

Latch opened his mouth then closed it again.

"Anyway, are you sure you're in?" Siv said impatiently. "Can we get on with the planning?"

"Tell me what you have in mind."

Siv didn't treat Latch's involvement lightly. The man was taking a terrible risk with his family's secret. But Latch had been itching to be useful for a while now. He would finally get his day in the arena.

30

THE MANOR

Panic shot through Dara when she saw Wyla waiting for her in the street. Should she make a break for it? How had Wyla gotten here so fast? She and Siln were supposed to be off in the western Boundary District. If Dara started running now . . . a brief shooting cold in her arm warned her to think better of it. Wyla beckoned for her to follow.

She knows.

The thought tumbled around in Dara's head as they walked. Passersby ducked into shops and made sudden turns out of their path when they saw Wyla coming. Dara couldn't blame them. Wyla strode through the streets as if she were a goddess reclaiming her dominion with thunder and fury. Every thud of her steel-toed boots was a death knell.

She knows it was me.

Dara wracked her brain for an explanation as they marched through the chaotic streets. It may not matter what she said. Wyla knew.

They pushed open the iron gates and entered the overgrown garden courtyard. The bushes had exploded with flowers over the past few weeks, some of which only bloomed after midnight. Wyla turned, her boots crunching on gravel, and skewered Dara with a cold stare.

What could she say? Had Wyla seen Siv? Could she know how entangled they had been during the attack? Perhaps she'd sent a spy to follow them while she was busy with Brendle in the Boundary District. Speaking of which . . .

"Where is Siln?" Dara asked. "Did the attack on—"

"Siln is dead," Wyla snapped.

"What?" Dara felt as if she'd been punched in the gut. "How? I thought he was stronger than Brendle." She had enjoyed the man's company, even though he would have killed her without hesitation if Wyla ordered it.

"Brendle didn't kill him," Wyla said. "You did."

Icy dread filled Dara's stomach like a gallon of Watermight. Siln had been her friend. And he had been unmatched by any Watermight fighter in the city.

"I—"

"You figured it out," Wyla said softly. "You bound the powers together. I knew it would be explosive. I knew you could do it."

"But Siln—"

"What was it, child?" The gravel crunched as Wyla stepped closer. "Tell me quickly. The surprise? The fear? The method of the attack?"

Dara stared at her. Wyla's face held no anger at all now. No disappointment that Dara had disobeyed her instructions to stay in the manor. No sadness at the loss of her longtime bodyguard and loyal ally.

"It was you," Dara whispered. She felt as if a plug had been pulled, draining all the blood out of her body. "You attacked to get me to react with both of the powers."

"Of course." Wyla waved an impatient hand. "Or more accurately, Siln attacked you. He threw his very best at that tower tonight."

Dara stared at her in horror. "He died when I defended myself."

"You've made remarkable progress. We haven't had as much time for our research lately, but I haven't forgotten you."

"But you made Siln take the backlash," Dara said. "There was a risk I'd succeed, and you didn't even have the strength to attack me yourself." It occurred to Dara that Wyla hadn't wielded Watermight against her since the day Dara lifted her into the air beside the basement whirlpool. "You're a coward."

"Berate me if you wish," Wyla said. "But you must tell me more about what you experienced when you responded to the attack."

"I'm not telling you anything."

"You are still beholden to me," Wyla said. Icy pain shot through Dara's arm, and this time, the sensation didn't fade away. "Tell me. Was it the surprise? Or perhaps"—a cruel grin spread across Wyla's face—"it was the presence of the man you love."

Dara's jaw went rigid with horror.

"I thought so," Wyla said. "When I learned of your tryst, I wondered if this might be the breakthrough you needed."

"You knew we were going out there?"

"Of course. Your light in the tower helped Siln direct his attack with better accuracy. He was going to flood the whole jetty. I wonder if the directness of the attack made your response more powerful. Hmm . . . I will have to devote more study to it."

Dara's brain felt as if it were packed with wool. The only thing lending clarity to the situation was the sharpness of the pain in her arm. "Aren't you sorry for getting Siln killed?"

"Why would I be? He served me well. Besides, you are the one who killed him, not me."

Dara stared at her, unable to hide the hatred radiating from her face. Wyla used people and discarded them, no matter how loyal they had been to her. Siln had served her despite his own strength. Dara had never learned what Wyla held over him—and now he was gone.

"Let's go in," Wyla said. "No need to stand in the garden like street urchins. It will rain soon."

Dara didn't move.

"Have it your way." Wyla climbed the steps to the manor house. She stopped at the door. "Oh, I've decided how you will repay me for my assistance saving that fourth life months ago."

Dara stayed rooted to the spot, knowing what was coming.

"You will bring your lover here," Wyla said. "I have need of him and the power you can create in his presence."

"No."

"Refuse me if you like," Wyla said. "Rant and rage. Try to kill me. But you will do this. Your debt compels you. Bring him to me, or I will have him dragged here."

"What will you do to him?"

"I don't care about him." Wyla waved a wrinkled hand. "I care about what you can do with him. Aren't you curious to see if you can replicate what you did tonight?"

"Not enough to bring him within a thousand feet of you."

"Come now," Wyla tutted. "You needn't deny it. You are as intrigued by the power as I am." She stood on her threshold, her white hair seeming to glow in the light from the torches. "We are alike, Dara. You want to know as much as I do. You've always wanted to be the best."

Dara stared at her, mouth ajar. She did want to know. Hadn't she pictured what it would be like to be the greatest magic wielder of them all? Hadn't she been tempted by the possibility of victory unlike any other, a victory that Siv's presence could bring within her grasp?

"You know it's true," Wyla said. "So, you will bring him to me, and we will see what else you can do." She entered the manor house, not waiting to see if Dara followed.

A clap of thunder announced the onset of a storm. The wind picked up, and the torches on the walls flickered erratically. Dara's arm still felt as if a blade of ice had replaced the bone. She had half a mind to run anyway. She needed her sword arm, but not as much as she needed to keep Siv safe.

But Vine was still inside the manor house. Rumy was likely on the grounds as well. Wyla wouldn't hesitate to kill them both if Dara ran. She had to make sure her friends were safe. And, Firelord take her right to his realm, she was curious about what else she could do with her abilities. The explosive wave was just a hint. With that kind of power under her control, she could level cities and armies. She could return to her father as a force far stronger than his greatest imaginings. And she and Siv could work together to do it. He brought out the power in her somehow.

Rain began to fall, and Dara hurried into the manor house. Maybe Wyla was right. She could bring Siv here, keep him by her side while Wyla taught her to use the incredible strength in the unification of Watermight and Fire. There might be no limit to what she could do.

Vine was waiting up for her in their room.

"Are you all right?" Vine asked, hurrying to hug her. "When I heard that explosion, I feared . . . never mind. You're safe. What happened?"

Dara changed into dry clothes as she told Vine everything, including the part about the intense passion she'd been feeling the moment the attack hit. She had to assume the desperate intensity of the kiss contributed to what she'd done, even if she wouldn't tell Wyla that.

"I think it's the breakthrough we've been waiting for," she finished.

"Does Wyla know?"

"She suspects enough. The thing is, she's probably right." Dara drew her Savven blade and turned it in her hands, tracing the intricate metalwork on the night-black hilt. "My power has always been connected to Siv. My best Works have resulted from trying to help him."

"That's not entirely true," Vine said. She sat cross-legged on her bed, her posture almost meditative. "You defended Rid, Rumy, and me back in Fork Town. That twirling statue was quite magnificent."

"That was done with Fire alone," Dara said. "I'd been practicing a lot by then. And I learned to Work from Zage Lorrid, who wasn't the most passionate person around. It's the link between Fire and Watermight that needed a catalyst."

"And you intend to make use of this discovery?"

"You should have seen how powerful it was," Dara said. "The explosion. If I could take back a fraction of that power, no one could keep us out of Vertigon. We'd be sure to win it back."

"If there was even a Vertigon left to claim," Vine said.

"I'll learn to control it," Dara said.

"And then what?" Vine's position didn't change, but her presence seemed to grow and intensify somehow. "You'll teach more Fireworkers how to Wield Watermight and more Waterworkers how to Work the Fire? Some of them are bound to do both eventually."

"I haven't really thought—"

"You have to think that far, Dara. What you and Wyla have been doing is incredibly dangerous. Are you sure this is a door you're willing to open?"

Vine had dropped her usual singsong tone entirely. She looked very grave, and for a moment, she reminded Dara of her sister. Renna would have been Vine's age if she had lived. Dara had come to think of Vine as more than a friend. They'd been through more peril than most sisters by now. But she had never specifically felt like the younger sister before.

She sat down on the opposite bed, still clutching the warm hilt of her Savven blade, and faced her friend as lightning flashed through the room.

Vine leaned forward, meeting her eyes earnestly. "Dara, you have to answer the question. Not tonight, maybe, but before you take this power beyond the boundaries of Pendark."

"Maybe we don't have to worry about it," Dara said. A crucial detail remained, one that would be an automatic check on any world-changing skills she developed. "The Watermight can't be contained long enough to bring it all the way to Vertigon. It might not matter."

Vine studied her for a long time, seeming to struggle with whether or not to reveal something.

"What is it?"

"I've learned some very interesting things in my meditations over the past day or so. Something has definitely changed in the Air."

"Oh." Dara almost chuckled. Since she'd begun Working with Wyla, she couldn't help thinking all the hours Vine spent waiting for some hint of vibrations in the wind had been wasted. Air was nothing compared to the power of Fire and Watermight.

"You can scoff if you wish," Vine said calmly. "But that tells me how unprepared you are."

"Unprepared for what?"

"It's possible there's a way to transport Watermight," Vine said at last. "I don't know for sure how it works yet."

Dara stared at her, flabbergasted. "You can preserve Watermight?"

"I said it's possible."

"Tell me what it is." Before Dara knew it, she was on her feet. She couldn't believe Vine was thinking of holding this back. Vine was supposed to be her friend. If Dara could transport Watermight as well as unite it with Fire, she would be unstoppable. "Tell me."

"Dara Ruminor, look at yourself," Vine said.

"What?"

"Look at what you've let the power do to you already," Vine said. "You are better than this."

Dara blinked, confused. Then she realized she still had the

Savven blade in her hand. She had been brandishing it as she urged Vine to talk. The tip hovered mere feet from Vine's face.

Dara dropped the sword on her bed at once as lightning flashed again, followed by a peal of thunder. She hadn't meant to threaten Vine. She had forgotten she was holding the sword. Yet she still felt the urge to force Vine to tell her everything. She needed to win, to be the one to make this breakthrough first. And she had been angry—at least for a moment—that Vine had figured out the trick before her.

"I'm sorry," she said, feeling stunned and ashamed.

"It's all right," Vine said. "Actually, I'm less nervous to face you with a sword than I would have been a month ago. When was the last time you did footwork? Or went for a run? Or actually practiced dueling? You haven't been yourself lately, Dara."

Dara slumped onto her bed. She touched the blade sitting beside her, feeling the familiar heat in the metal, but she didn't pick it up. Vine was right. She had never gone this long without practicing before. What was happening to her?

The wind picked up, driving rain against the windowpane and howling around the manor. She swore specks of Watermight appeared in the droplets sliding down the glass. Her eyes felt hot and scratchy, and she wished the window were open so the gale could cool her face.

When she didn't speak, Vine unfolded her legs gracefully and came over to sit on Dara's bed. "You're hardly the first person to be driven off course by a taste of power."

"That's my father," Dara said. She couldn't look at her friend, remembering Vine's eyes when Dara had waved a weapon in her face. She took a shuddering breath. "All I wanted was not to be like him. And that's what I've become. Another power-hungry Wielder who doesn't care about the consequences to the rest of the world as long as I triumph." She laughed hollowly. "It didn't take long."

Vine didn't answer. She must realize Dara was right. She must see the parallels.

"He was always working to improve his Fire Lanterns," Dara said. "I admired him so much as a child. Even though I couldn't Work, I wanted to be as dedicated as he was. And now . . ."

"Dara, you're not him." Vine took her hand and squeezed it tight. "But you are like him. You have his dedication, his talent, and yes, some of his weaknesses. But you know where to draw the line.

And you have put your life in danger countless times to protect the people you love. You won't turn into him as long as you continue to draw those lines. Besides, you have people to hold you accountable. He has your mother urging him on. Forgive me, but I believe she's as ambitious as he is and with a cruel streak in the mix. If there's one thing you don't have in you, it's cruelty."

Tears filled Dara's eyes as Vine spoke, hot as ember, but she didn't let them fall. Her parents had left her a heavy legacy. She wanted to overcome it, she really did. But she also needed to overcome them and take away the power they had seized in Vertigon. To do that, she had to step a little closer to that line.

"Wyla wants me to call Siv here," Dara said. "She wants me to use him to become more powerful."

"Are you going to do it?" Vine's question was soft, almost lost in another roar of thunder.

"No."

She may lose her arm for it. She may lose her freedom for it. But Vine was right. There was a line, and she couldn't cross it. She would not use the man she loved to turn herself into a weapon.

"You have to leave the manor," Dara said. "Find Rid, and get out of Pendark. I'll try to find a way to break with Wyla, but you need to be out of the way."

"We can do that," Vine said. "I've been making friends here for a reason, after all."

"Good."

"Shall we take Rumy?"

"If you can." His Fire would be useful when she confronted Wyla, but she didn't want to get him killed either.

"Very well." Vine stood and made to return to her bed. "We should get some sleep. There will be time to run in the morning."

Dara shook her head. "Wyla will anticipate this. You should go before she has time to act."

"As you wish." Vine went to their wardrobe and pulled out a pair of saddlebags, already fully packed. Of course she'd be prepared. She was Vine Silltine. Within seconds, Vine was dressed in traveling clothes, complete with a cloak and a sturdy pair of boots. She gave Dara a tight hug, her soft hair falling over Dara's hands as they embraced. "The Air Sensors will direct you to me if you have any trouble finding us. The channels are open once more."

As Vine skipped to the door, Dara called out to her.

"Will you tell me what you heard? About who can preserve the Watermight?"

Vine looked at her serenely. "Are you sure you want to know?"

Dara sighed. "No, you're right. It's best if you wait until I'm out of Wyla's clutches."

"A wise decision. Take care of yourself, Dara."

Dara felt terribly lonely when Vine left. They had been looking out for each other for a long time. Vine would pull Dara back from the brink when no one else could. But Dara was the only who could solve this problem. And she couldn't let anyone else get swept up in the storm.

At last, Dara lay down for a night of fitful sleep, interrupted by the howling wind. She clutched the pendant Siv had given her as she drifted off, hoping it would help her remember why she couldn't become like her father.

But before she could tell Wyla she would never comply with her demands or put Siv at risk for the sake of the power, Siv came to see them himself.

31

THE BARGAIN

Siv and Latch knocked on the iron gate of Wyla's manor house first thing in the morning. In the end, they'd decided bringing the fight straight to Wyla would be easier than convincing her to meet them somewhere. The uniformed doorman tried to usher them into the courtyard, but they insisted on waiting outside the stone walls. They weren't going to walk into the cullmoran's nest if they could help it. Siv knew exactly what that was like.

He had been up all night arranging the pieces of his plan as if they were mijen tiles. Latch had helped, and he was far less surly than usual. He must have been awfully bored since arriving in Pendark. He even smiled when it was time to leave headquarters to head to Wyla's.

Siv had warned Kres, Fiz, and Gull there was going to be trouble over breakfast. Rid was nowhere to be found. Siv urged the others to stay safely away from Wyla's district that day.

"I don't like my two insurance policies walking off together," Kres said.

"We'll be safe as gutter turtles in a burrow," Siv said. "Besides, if we pull this off, I'll have to leave the team anyway."

"Team? Come now. We're family." Kres stood and began strapping weapons around his person.

Siv gaped at him. "What are you—?"

"We have your back," Fiz said as he followed Kres's lead. "Whatever trouble you're in, I reckon we can get you out."

Siv didn't want to get anyone else involved in his fight. He turned to Gull. "Can you talk some sense into them?"

But the swordswoman was testing out the sharpness of her saber, her battle stare already in place. "That ever worked before?"

Latch gave a dry chuckle. "We probably shouldn't turn up with too much armed backup. She might think we're not there to talk."

"That's true," Siv said. "Look, I appreciate this, but my plan requires a bit of diplomacy."

"Well, aren't you fancy?" Gull said.

Fiz thumped Siv on the shoulder hard enough to hurt. "He's a regular little diplomat, our Slugger."

"I'm serious," Siv said. "She can't think we're attacking."

"Very well, lad," Kres said. "There's a decent stilt tavern in the Jewel District. We'll be close if you need us."

"Thank you," Siv said. "I promise to repay you if I ever get my position back."

"What is your position exactly?" Gull asked. "All the hints are getting boring."

"Kres can tell you all about it," Siv said. Kres raised an eyebrow, then a glass. Siv knew he would enjoy telling that particular tale.

"And what's Latch got to do with it?" Fiz asked.

"That's an even better story," Siv said. "But we'll have to keep that one under wraps for a bit longer."

"A shame." Kres sighed. "That one's my favorite."

They all left headquarters together. Kres, Fiz, and Gull settled themselves within shouting distance of Wyla's manor while Siv and Latch proceeded to her gates. Siv hoped he wouldn't have to call on the pen fighters, but it was nice to know they were nearby.

It was still early when Siv and Latch reached Wyla's place. The morning felt fresh, clean. The sun cast a sharp light over the canal running alongside the manor. The muggy scents of the city had been washed away by the torrential rains of the night before. The canals grew more pungent than ever as the temperature rose.

Despite the early hour, sweat trailed down Siv's face as he waited for the doorman to fetch the lady of the manor. He feared Wyla wouldn't let Dara join the conversation, but when the gates opened at last, Dara followed the Waterworker out of the manor. She looked tense and suspicious. And surprised. If anything, Dara looked more taken aback than Wyla to find Siv at their gates. Good. They needed her to be surprised.

The two women stopped in the stone gateway where they could easily retreat behind the walls if necessary.

"Good morning, Lady Wyla." Siv offered a courtly bow.

"You must be the young man I've heard so much about."

Wyla was shorter than he'd expected and old enough to have entirely white hair. Her lined face was animated, and she looked at him as if he were a curious sea creature that had washed up on the beach.

"It's a pleasure to meet you." Siv gestured to his companion with a flourish. "This is my friend Latch Brach."

Wyla's eyes widened. Latch stood back a few feet, arms hanging loose at his sides. He'd better be ready for this.

"Brach," Wyla said at last. "This is interesting."

"Yes, ma'am," Siv said. "I see you know the Brach family."

"By reputation only." Wyla gave Latch a hungry look. Siv was relieved the fellow didn't take off running in the other direction. That was what he would do if Wyla looked at him like that.

"He is the son of Commander Brach, the leader of the Soolen army attempting to conquer Trure."

"They had succeeded, the last I heard," Wyla said.

"They ran into a complication." Siv could still hardly believe his own people had marched on the nation that had once been their closest ally. His relatives were imprisoned. Selivia was exiled. His grandfather was dead. No word of Sora or his mother had reached him in months. He would finally be able to help them now. *If* this worked.

Wyla raised an eyebrow. "A complication."

"My friend Latch here can tell you all about it. It's one of the many things he has to offer."

"Offer?" Wyla's voice sharpened like a knife. She shot another appraising look at Latch.

"Yes. But first, I want you to free Dara from her bargain."

"*What?*"

The exclamation came from Dara, not Wyla. Siv hurried on before she could put an end to the entire proceeding.

"I want you to remove the bond on her arm and let her leave Pendark. You'll relinquish all debts and claims to her services and grant her unconditional freedom this very day."

Wyla chuckled. "Oh, you must have something very valuable indeed if you expect me to agree to that."

"I offer you Latch," Siv said. "He will replace Dara in your service."

Dara stared at him as if he'd gone as mad as a povvercat in the rain. Fear and fury crossed her face in equal measures.

"I'd offer myself," Siv said, "but I think you'll find Latch is more useful than me."

"More useful than my *very* talented apprentice *and* the King of Vertigon? He must be special indeed."

Siv choked. From the bulge of Dara's eyes, he knew that she hadn't realized Wyla knew his true identity either. Did the whole damn city know who he was?

"Yes," he said, recovering his voice with only a small hitch. "More useful than both of us." He nodded to Latch, who hadn't moved during the exchange. "Allow my friend to demonstrate. I think you'll find his talents are worth bargaining for."

Wyla gave a curt nod and turned to Latch. Judging by her reaction, Siv suspected Wyla knew a lot about the Brach family, perhaps more than Latch himself realized. She probably wouldn't even be surprised by what she was about to see. Or at least the first part.

Latch advanced a step and halted, staring at the lintel above Wyla and Dara's heads. He didn't move his hands or give any indication that he was doing anything. Wyla leaned forward. Siv held his breath. He didn't dare look at Dara.

Latch's limbs began to tremble. Sweat broke out on his forehead. Then a trail of silvery Watermight rose from the nearby canal and snaked through the air toward the wall. It touched the stone gateway and melted into it as if it were the surface of a pond.

A loud crack split the air, and a large stone broke away from the top of the gateway. A shiny glimmer revealed a layer of ice where the stone was once attached to the wall. It drifted through the air and landed neatly at Wyla's feet.

"What—?" Dara began.

But Latch wasn't done. Two more stones lifted away from the wall and sailed high into the air. An instant later, they plummeted to the ground and smashed on either side of Wyla, scattering ice like broken glass. She didn't even flinch.

"More," she whispered.

Another stream of Watermight spurted from the canal. Siv had spent most of the night acquiring a supply of the substance for this demonstration. He'd searched out street urchins and gutter dealers, anyone who was holding onto a bit of Watermight while they waited for prices to go up. It had cost him every last coin he had saved from the Steel Pentagon.

The stones on either side of the gateway began to explode, one after another. Shards of rock flew through the air. Latch was sweating freely. He looked happier than he had the whole time Siv had known him. Who knew the Soolens could be as gleefully violent as the Pendarkans themselves?

Wyla certainly enjoyed the show. A film of silver-white covered her eyes, and she quivered with glee as Latch demonstrated his skills. Siv prayed she wouldn't strike too soon. They couldn't let her bind Latch in one of her bargain spells before they could get power into Dara's hands. *Just a few more minutes.*

The largest stone yet exploded in a shower of dust, leaving a gaping hole in Wyla's wall. Siv raised a hand.

"Now that you've seen what my friend can do," Siv said, "I'd like to trade his knowledge of the secret Soolen Waterworkers in exchange for Dara's freedom."

Wyla smiled, the expression grandmotherly. Siv wouldn't have been surprised to see her take out a pair of knitting needles.

"Your skills are impressive," Wyla said. "But Dara can destroy walls too. I think you have something still more valuable to offer me, don't you?"

Latch hesitated and looked at Siv. Their eyes met, but Siv didn't say the words himself. This was Latch's secret to offer. It was up to him to reveal the truth. *Please, help me out here.*

Latch didn't speak.

Wyla took a step closer, making Siv and Latch jump. It was amazing how such a sweet-looking old lady could make them so nervous.

"It's true, isn't it?" she said. "Your father has brought his secret supply of Watermight to Trure, hasn't he?"

Dara looked between them, clearly confused.

Latch inclined his head, jaw tense.

"Do you know how to do it?" Wyla said softly. "Can you preserve the Watermight so it can be carried far from the sea?" She almost quivered with anticipation. Oh, this was valuable information indeed, especially since Wyla apparently already suspected the secret resided with the Brach family. She was going to agree to the trade. This had to be the one thing she wanted even more than Dara.

Latch squared his shoulders and nodded. Siv held his breath.

Wyla opened her mouth to say more.

Then Siv felt a tickle of wind at the back of his neck, an unnatural stirring sensation.

And a gigantic wave crashed into them.

Water and power swirled around them like a tornado, shrieking, chaotic. Siv lost all sense of direction. He couldn't see the others, couldn't see Dara. A chill colder than a mountain blizzard surrounded him, freezing him in his boots. What was going on? Where had this attack come from?

Suddenly, a razor line cut through the tornado, forcing it to stop spinning. Water and Watermight thundered down, soaking the earth. Siv found himself on his knees. Dara crouched on the ground a few feet away, taking cover in the gateway. Wyla herself remained standing. She looked utterly furious.

"You think you can ambush me in front of my own home?"

"Wait," Siv said. "This wasn't our—"

Suddenly, a canal boat sped up to them, moving unnaturally fast. A dozen men piled out—men Siv recognized as Khrillin's Waterworker thugs. What were *they* doing here? This wasn't part of the plan. Wyla had been about to agree to the trade!

Wyla hissed, and water swelled up around her. She was gathering power, preparing to hurl it back at her attackers. She wasn't fazed by the surprise attack, but she was outnumbered, and Latch had destroyed a large section of her wall during his demonstration.

Khrillin's men advanced, hands raised to seize control of the Watermight raging through the air. There were at least a dozen of them. Would it be enough?

Wyla called out a command, and armed guards in poison-green uniforms poured out of the manor courtyard. One grabbed Dara and tried to pull her back inside. Siv called out desperately to Latch. An instant later, the rest of Wyla's wall exploded.

A concussive wave knocked Siv backward. Dust, rocks, and ice fell around him. Siv flung up a hand to protect his eyes and charged toward Dara. She freed herself from the guard in the confusion and stumbled forward to escape the others, who were already climbing to their feet. Siv wrapped her in his arms before she regained her balance. So much for their big plan. Dara was going to have to break the bond herself.

As his arms closed around her, a second wave of Watermight hit. The rush of water and power knocked them off their feet, but Siv kept his grip.

"What are you doing?" Dara said, struggling against him.

"It's time to fight, Dara."

"They won't win." She was right. Khrillin's Waterworkers were already being forced back. Wyla was a hurricane of power and rage. A pile of rocks exploded nearby—Latch doing his part to add to the chaos—but Wyla appeared to be gaining the upper hand quickly. Firelord, she was powerful.

"It doesn't matter," Siv said. He refused to let go of Dara, even though she nearly twisted out of his grasp, fury granting her strength. That was good. She was surprised and angry, he held her tight, and the power whirled around them—hopefully the same conditions as last time she'd managed a Work of incredible power. And quite a bit more Watermight raged around them than he had been able to afford thanks to the intervention of Khrillin's men. Time for the final ingredient.

"Quick," Siv said. Keeping one arm around Dara, he pulled a Firebulb and all the Everlights and Firesticks he had been able to afford out of his pockets. "Use this to break the bond while she's busy."

"Are you insane?" Dara hissed.

"You have to do it now," Siv said. "Only the person in bondage can break it and only with a huge amount of force. You have to use the Fire and Watermight together."

"This isn't going to work."

"You're stronger than her," Siv said. "Don't let her keep hold of you."

Dara stared at him incredulously. He stared right back. He knew she could do it. Dara was tough. She had never backed down from a fight. She had to do it to save herself.

The Watermight fight raged around them. Bits of power flew their way. Siv hoped it would be enough for Dara to use. Droplets of the silvery substance slid over her skin. Had she gotten any into her system? He held her tighter.

Wyla's non-magic bodyguards had recovered from the latest wave. They advanced toward Khrillin's men, steel bared. The Waterworkers were focused on Wyla. Vulnerable.

That was when Kres March uttered his battle cry. The pen fighters leapt into the fray. They fought to keep the guards away from Khrillin's Workers, allowing them to focus on fending off Wyla. And they'd brought backup. Siv saw Dellario the Darting Death darting amongst the combatants. The Rockeater of Soole took a stand in front of Latch while he fought with the Watermight. Even the Pendarkan Panviper was there, getting his gangly behind kicked by one of Wyla's guards. Siv could hardly believe it. Where had all these pen fighters come from? And why were they risking death on his account?

Another wave of canal water drenched them, carrying blood and slime along with the Watermight. Siv pulled Dara farther from the action. He sat down in the mud and pulled her onto his lap. They had their own fight to worry about.

But Dara still wasn't doing anything. She stared at Siv with an expression bordering on catatonia. He hoped he hadn't gone too far with the whole taking her by surprise thing.

"Dara," he said. She shook herself, and their eyes locked. "You can do it. Fire and Watermight together—and find the edge. That's the key."

She grimaced, her eyes burning into his. He put a hand on her cheek, ran his fingers through her golden hair. He wished he could help her with this fight somehow.

Suddenly, a silver-white film slid over her eyes, so opaque that he couldn't see her irises anymore. Then the Firebulb in his other hand winked out. *Yes!* The Everlight was next. Dara quivered like a leaf. Siv held her as she drew in the Fire he had brought her bit by bit. Her body grew warmer, like a living ember in his arms. He pulled her closer, trying to lend her whatever strength he could.

Her right arm went cold under his hand. The contrast between the ice in her arm and the Fire in her body was so shocking that he almost let go. But he'd never do that, not for as long as he drew breath. Dara had given up so much for him. He may not be able to fight Wyla directly, but he would help Dara fight her—and win.

But Dara's arm remained cold and stiff.

Siv tore his gaze away from Dara's to survey the battlefield. The pen fighters were gaining the upper hand against the bodyguards, some dueling within the ruined walls of the courtyard itself. But the true battle was the one being fought with Watermight. Latch had taken cover in the canal along with the Rockeater. He stood waist deep in the water, filling things with ice to make them explode left and right. He looked positively gleeful. But Khrillin's Waterworkers were being pushed back once more, and too many lay still in the mud. Wyla drove the survivors before her, wrapped in towering wrath. She was even more powerful than Siv had realized. How could she hold her own against so many at once?

Dara began shaking uncontrollably on his lap. She was still staring at him through those moon-white eyes, but the ice in her arm hadn't thawed at all. If anything, it had grown colder. He kissed her forehead, smearing the mud and water that coated them both. He whispered encouragement in her ear, the words barely coherent. She had to fight it. They would all die if she didn't break through somehow.

Wyla directed a massive torrent of Watermight from within her ruined walls. Silver power rushed around them, thunderous as a waterfall. Siv held on to Dara as the storm tried to rip them apart. The non-magic fighters took cover from the flood behind fallen chunks of stone. Then Wyla lifted the canal boat on the wave of silver power and hurled it at the enemy Waterworkers, forcing two to dive out of the way and crushing two others.

Holding back the last of the attackers with a solid wall of water, Wyla turned, victorious. Her face went dark when she saw Siv holding Dara on his lap. Her apprentice shook with power, with *both* powers, making no move to help in the battle. She must know what was going on at last.

Dara screamed then. *No. Not now.* The pain in her voice cut Siv deep—deeper than anything save his father's death. She screamed as if her arm was not only being frozen, but sliced into tiny pieces. And there was nothing Siv could do about it.

Well, almost nothing. He couldn't fight with magic, but he could still fight. No one would hurt the woman he loved anymore. He let Dara slide to the muddy ground, placing the last of the Firesticks in her palm, and launched himself toward Wyla. He drew his knife as he ran, knowing it wouldn't do any good, his other fist swinging. That wouldn't be enough either. He was already dead. But he would fight with everything he had left to give Dara more time.

The first attack slammed into him. He hit the ground hard, his back sliding ten feet through the mud before he came to a stop. He was on his feet a second later, running at Wyla again. This time, ice blades cut toward him, spinning like wheels. He ducked some, taking cuts from the ones he couldn't avoid.

He got within two feet of Wyla before the Watermight knocked him off his feet again.

He climbed up, blood spurting from his wounds, and attacked again.

Ice daggers. Torrents of water forcing into his lungs. Waves falling like mountains. Every time he attacked, Wyla threw him back. His blood mixed with the water. His pain was a distant thud at the back of his brain. The only thing he heard was Dara screaming. He thought he heard his name in the cry.

He lurched to his feet for another attack.

Wyla was angry now. She'd have killed him in the first instant if she weren't still trying to keep Khrillin's Waterworkers from entering her manor through the ruined walls. But she'd have killed Dara if he weren't still trying to stick a thorn in her side. Either that, or she was toying with them both, inflicting maximum pain to teach them a lesson before the end.

He lunged again, knowing it was his last chance. He couldn't win this fight. But as he launched himself forward, a patch of earth exploded directly beneath Wyla's feet, ice filling the debris. She hissed and stepped back. Silently thanking Latch for the distraction, Siv hurled himself into her.

They hit the mud with a splash. Siv had lost his knife, so he pummeled Wyla with his fists. She would recover any second. She'd send an ice blade through his heart or sweep him off her with a wave. But with every strike, he bought Dara extra seconds. She had to break free. He just had to give her a little more time.

Then something smashed into his head, and the world went black.

32

THE BOND

Colors swirled across Dara's vision. Silver-white and gold. Flashes of black and emerald and cerulean and bronze. The pain was excruciating. An agonizing panic rattled her, made it hard to think. And then there was the fury. Wyla was going to win. Pure, gold rage exploded in Dara at the thought. She wouldn't let that happen. Wouldn't let the surprise or the fear or the confusion defeat her.

She had to break the bond. The moment Siv said it, she knew it was the only way they'd both get out of this alive. They were already too far into this fight. She was angry with him for surprising her, but he was also the only thing holding her together. She needed him to work this magic. Needed him to help her break free.

She started drawing in the Fire he had brought her, but she was still a tangle of rage and fear. He meant to surprise her, the way they'd been surprised before. He meant to put himself in danger, the way he'd been in danger before. But she wasn't ready. She didn't know how to work this kind of magic. Last time had been self-preservation, a wave of pure force exploding out of her. How could she use that to break Wyla's bond without destroying herself in the process?

Siv believed provoking her would help, but that didn't mean she could do this. Her skills were inadequate. She hadn't trained enough. It was impossible.

Focus, Dara. She'd mixed Fire and Watermight in her body once before. It had been a breakthrough, but she hadn't come close to mastering it. She struggled for balance, for control—and failed.

The two powers tore through her body. She felt like a piece of fabric being picked apart at the seams during a violent storm. If she let go of a single thread, the wind would rip her asunder.

She tried to remember Siv's words. Something about finding an edge.

She flailed, still riding that wave of power, searching for something to grab. This wasn't working. *Focus!*

For a second, she sensed a change. What was it? A shift in the power? A tug on her arm. There was something there. Something like an edge in her arm.

But the swirl of the two powers made it impossible to concentrate. She needed to isolate them. What had it been? Watermight in her gut and Fire in her blood? Or was it the other way around? She couldn't do this. The power was spinning out of control.

Suddenly, she became aware of something warm and solid at her back. Beneath her. Surrounding her. Something holding her tight. Holding her together. *Siv.* He pulled her onto his lap, wrapped his body tight around hers. He spoke to her, the words lost in the howl of the power.

She felt that edge again, scraping at her senses like a fingernail on her skin. She reached for it, straining against a cyclone of fear.

There! She found the edge, prodded at it, first with her mind, then with a bit of Fire. This sent pain through her arm so intense, she almost passed out. She tried Watermight next, choking more of it down whenever it drenched her. She nudged the edge in her arm with Watermight, and it moved. This hurt too, but less than the Fire had. She could work with this. The Watermight had some effect, but it wasn't strong enough. Maybe if she used the Fire to make the Watermight push harder? Could she twirl them together somehow and try again?

Before she could do anything, blistering cold burst through her arm. Pain on top of pain. It was in her bones, in her soul. The tenuous control she'd achieved evaporated. She was vaguely aware she was screaming.

Then she felt a shift, as if the ground had tipped under her. She blinked, trying to clear her vision and figure out what was happening around her. She couldn't see more than shapes in the blizzard. Chaos. Cold and damp beneath her.

Siv had set her down. The anchor that kept her steady as she worked at the bond was gone. She squeezed her eyes shut and opened them again, trying to see through the swirling madness of color and blackness and light.

A figure moved through the confusion, barely more than an outline. She knew it was Siv as surely as she knew her own name. He launched himself into a roaring column of silver-white light. Wyla herself appeared as a pure blaze of power to Dara's silver-lined eyes. She screamed, knowing it was too late, knowing he could never stand against all that power.

Siv flew backward, away from the tornado. He couldn't do anything against Wyla with that much power!

But Siv got right back up again and lunged forward for another attack. Dara screamed, long and loud, the sound trapped within her brain. He couldn't fight this. He was going to die.

She couldn't let this happen, but she couldn't move. Her arm felt as heavy as if it were made of iron. The bond held her down in the mud, not yet breaking the bone but not allowing her to rise.

Siv threw himself forward again. He wasn't going to give up. He would keep attacking until Wyla killed him.

Dara screamed his name and hurled everything she had at the iron weight in her arm. Once again, she nearly passed out from the pain. But she fought against the darkness, fought against the silver-white Might and the blazing Fire and the raging pain.

Blood ran down Siv's body. He threw himself toward Wyla again.

Idiot. He was going to get himself killed. He was fighting a power far greater than he could possibly understand. It was stupid and brave, and she loved him for it. She loved him with a fierceness and desperation far beyond anything she could comprehend. She loved him more than the power, more than the power, more than the whirl of confusion and pain turning her brain and her body into mush. He was fighting for her. He was hurling his life down for her.

Dara could no longer think, no longer process. So she held onto that wave of love and passion and fury and fear and focused it on the edge in her arm. She sent every ounce of it into that bond, into the shackle Wyla had placed on her. Wyla wanted to turn her into her father, wanted to use her and use Siv to further her own aims no matter who got hurt in the process. Dara wouldn't let her do that, and she wouldn't let her kill Siv.

The bond in Dara's arm moved. She pushed harder against it, knowing she might shatter her dueling arm after all.

Siv attacked Wyla yet again. He swung his fists, trying to defeat one of the most powerful magic wielders on the continent with flesh and blood and bone.

Dara fought. The pain made her delirious. She was sure the intensity would sweep her under at any moment. Silver-white coated her eyes, then pitch-black, then gold. She saw her father, blazing with power. She saw Zage Lorrid, standing up to take in the Fire when she couldn't control it. She saw her mother, bitter and proud and filled with sadness so intense, it cut her to shreds. She saw Siv, standing and fighting when all was lost. She saw Vine and Rid, felt them as if they were laying hands on her shoulders and telling her to keep fighting. Telling her to take control.

Suddenly, one of Dara's father's sayings came to her: *You are my flesh and blood and Fire.* It was a statement of allegiance, a statement of loyalty deeper and wider than magic and ambition. It was the kind of loyalty she and Siv had shown each other again and again. It was blood. It was Fire. It was love.

Dara pushed against her bond with the Watermight, lending it strength with the Fire, focusing with all her training, then letting it go in a powerful torrent of love for Siv.

There was a terrific crack. Instead of pain, Dara felt the most delicious warmth in her arm, like the first days of summer. She flexed her fingers as her vision cleared. Watermight dripped from her fingertips and disappeared into the earth. She was free. It had worked.

She clenched her hand into a fist and got to her feet.

The chaos of the Watermight battle had ended. The attackers had retreated from Wyla, but the woman herself was on the ground. She looked winded but conscious. Siv lay crumpled beside her, dripping with blood, unmoving.

Dara advanced on Wyla, clutching for more Watermight. Plenty of the power drenched the ground around her. The Waterworkers had provided a distraction, but they'd also given Dara what she needed to make her final stand. She called the Watermight to her—

and it answered, flowing obediently to her hands. It still pricked like needles, but she forced it through her skin anyway.

Dara stood over Wyla, hardly daring to look at Siv. She didn't know whether he still lived. She couldn't face the answer yet.

Wyla's lip was bleeding, and she looked more furious than Dara thought possible. Her pitch-black rage would have sent Dara running mere months ago. Now Wyla was on the ground—and Dara held the power.

But she didn't want to kill Wyla. She had never wanted to kill her. Wyla had taken her in and taught her to be powerful. Dara had been willing to see out her bargain and repay Wyla for her help. But Wyla hadn't honored the agreement. She would have kept the bond on Dara's arm forever. And she had sent Siln to his death for the sake of her experiments. She had lorded her power over her subordinates, knowing she could play with their lives—and dispose of them if she wished.

Well, now Dara was in control, and Wyla knew it. Fear laced the rage in her eyes. Dara had expected a fight, but Wyla only stared at her, waiting for something.

Then Dara realized the truth: Wyla was terrified. She had seen Dara's Fire and Watermight combination kill her best fighter. She knew Dara was capable of destroying her with this dangerous new mix of powers. So she didn't attack, waiting for Dara to make the first move.

Dara held out a hand.

Wyla stared at it, disbelieving.

"Let me help you up," Dara said.

"You've won." Wyla didn't take Dara's hand. "You're free from your bond."

"You tricked me," Dara said. "But you also helped me. I won't hurt you, but I've repaid my debt."

"And now you'll go straight to Khrillin with what *I* taught you," Wyla said. "I'm not stupid. I don't know how you coordinated this attack, but I know who's behind it. Tell him to beware. I won't relinquish any ground. If he thinks he can use your power against me, he is sorely mistaken."

"I'm not working for Khrillin," Dara said.

Wyla scoffed. "You may think so, but you're a fool to trust him. He is a dangerous man—almost as dangerous as me."

"I'm leaving Pendark," Dara said. "It doesn't matter."

"You are too naïve, child," Wyla said. "You will regret this day."

"I don't want to be your enemy," Dara said. "But I can't be your slave either. I have responsibilities back in Vertigon."

"Go, then. Take your fallen king." Wyla nodded at Siv. Dara's heart did a painful flop at the sight of his prone, bleeding form. "But you are not ready. This power you've claimed will overwhelm you. Mark my words. You still have a lot to learn about being a Wielder."

"I know I do," Dara said, "but power isn't everything."

"Touching. Very touching," said a voice behind her. "I must agree with Wyla on this point, though. You don't know anything about true power."

Dara turned to find a man with a large beard standing where the entryway to Wyla's manor had been, clad in silver from head to toe. Watermight swirled around his ankles. Khrillin.

"See," Wyla said softly. "I knew you were working for him."

"I'm not—"

"You'd best see to our friend," Khrillin said. The Watermight supply around him was growing larger, fed by a trickle from the manor house. "Wyla and I have unfinished business. Stand aside."

Dara didn't move.

"What are you going to do to her?"

"As much as I'd love to turn her loose in the gutter so she can live with the knowledge that I control her prized whirlpool vent, I think it would be wiser to kill her. Don't you?"

"Wait!" Dara said. "You can't—"

But as Dara took a step toward Khrillin, Wyla screamed. One of his men had slipped behind Dara and sliced a knife across Wyla's throat. She gurgled, clutching at the bright-red gash on her neck.

"There," Khrillin said. "That's done. Why don't you accompany dear Sivarrion into the manor?"

Dara ignored him. She dropped to her feet beside Wyla and tried to seal up the bloody gash with Watermight. This was the first Work she'd seen Wyla perform on the day they met. But the cut was too deep, and her efforts were clumsy. They had spent so much time fighting and experimenting that she hadn't learned how to heal.

"I'm sorry," Dara whispered.

Wyla locked eyes with her. For a moment, her gaze shone

silver-white, and a fierce smile split her face. Then her body relaxed under Dara's hands.

Dara sat back, her hands bloody. But she had no time to mourn—if that was even the right response for the woman who had been both mentor and jailer. She scrambled over to Siv. He bled from dozens of cuts, though his wounds appeared shallower than Wyla's. Dara lifted his head gently into her lap and called upon the last of the Watermight. She hadn't been fast enough to help Wyla, but maybe she could stop the worst of the bleeding.

Khrillin made no move to help with the inelegant healing job. He stood behind her, waiting for her to finish her Work and follow his order to bring Siv into the manor.

The task was difficult, and it required more delicacy than she could muster after her struggle. Her hands shook badly, and she feared she was making Siv bleed too much as she cleaned his wounds. He groaned softly, his eyes remaining closed. *Please hold on.*

Then a splash sounded nearby, and Latch Brach emerged from the canal covered in mud. He dropped to his knees beside Dara and Siv and took over the healing job without a word. He concentrated on his friend, pasting seals over the cuts one by one. Dara met Latch's dark eyes briefly, her thanks unspoken for now. Between them, blood red turned to silver until the marks covered Siv like shooting stars. He was going to be all right.

They weren't out of danger yet, though. Dara didn't like the way Khrillin loomed over them. She didn't want to turn around and put herself under his control, even though he had helped Siv in the past. Wyla's words stuck with her: *you'd be a fool to trust him. He is a dangerous man—almost as dangerous as me.*

"Shall we go in?" Khrillin said softly.

Siv trusted the man, but she couldn't put herself in another Waterworker's hands. She suspected Latch wouldn't like being under Khrillin's power either. They needed a refuge, somewhere separate from the Waterworkers and their bargains and promises.

"I'd rather not."

"No?"

Dara cradled Siv's head in her lap as Watermight sealed over his last wound, searching for an escape route. The pen fighters were busy tending their wounded. Kres March appeared at Khrillin's right hand, sharp eyes on Dara. It was clear whom he worked for now. She couldn't count on any of them to help her except Latch.

"Are you going to fight me?" The hungry look in Khrillin's eyes was all too familiar. He took a step forward. "Perhaps create an explosion like the one last night?"

"I will if you come any closer," Dara snapped.

"Is that any way to speak to your rescuer?"

"We need time to rest and recover," Dara said. "I'm happy to discuss how to work together later."

"Later."

Dara shivered at Khrillin's flat tone. She had run out of Fire when she broke the bond. If Khrillin attacked her, Dara would never defeat him with Watermight alone. She reached for the Savven blade at her hip.

Suddenly, a warm breeze blew over them, sweeping Dara's hair back from her face. The wind seemed to carry a message, a promise that they would be all right. She was free, and it was time to move forward. Time to go home.

Khrillin took another step.

Latch leapt to his feet and lifted an entire pile of rubble into a wall around the Waterlord, encasing Khrillin and Kres entirely. They shouted, voices muffled behind the rocks. No sooner was the wall in place than a canal boat pulled up beside them, and armed men hopped out of it. Strangers.

Latch glanced at Dara, a blaze of Watermight coating his eyes. Dara nodded at him and hugged Siv closer as they prepared to defend him once more.

"Is he alive?" A shadow fell across them. Dara looked up to find Vine standing over her. The tightness in her chest eased at last. They were saved.

"Yes."

"And your bond?"

"Broken."

"Lovely work, Dara," Vine said. "I think it would be wise for us to relocate as soon as possible if you're feeling up for it."

"Good idea."

"I've arranged alternate lodgings for us." Vine gestured to the canal boat. "Come, gentlemen. Let's get our friends to safety."

Two men hurried over to assist Vine. One, as expected, was Rid. The other was Vex Rollendar.

Dara started up, gripping the Savven blade. Her sword arm was shaky, but whole. She had one more fight in her.

But Vine stepped in front of Vex and raised a placating hand. "It's all right. Vex here has decided to see things our way."

"What are you talking about?"

"He's on our side now."

"*Vine.*"

"We can explain when we are out of danger," Vine said. "Vex has arranged a hiding place for us until this Watermight business blows over."

"A hiding place?"

"Indeed. Come along. I believe he will give us exactly the help we need."

Dara couldn't believe what she was hearing. Had Vex enchanted Vine somehow, found a way to make her think he was on her side so he could kill Siv at last? But the Rollendar lord carried no weapons, a fact that Vine was quick to point out.

"I will explain everything, Dara. You must trust me."

Dara didn't move. Vex had crossed the continent to kill Siv. He had kidnapped her and Vine, used them to get what he wanted. She didn't believe for a second that he wasn't doing the same thing now. He must have put a spell on Vine. All those strange dreams. All that talk of being in love. Dara should have looked into it sooner. Like Wyla, she had dismissed the worries as more of Vine's effervescent obsession with the Air. And now her friend was trapped.

"I can see this won't be easy," Vine said. "Come, my friend, I am trying to help."

"But he's a Rollendar."

"Yes. And we are out of time. I'm terribly sorry about this."

Vine closed her eyes and breathed deeply. Dara felt a whisper on her skin, a spring breeze building to a gale. Suddenly, the breeze stiffened, becoming a physical force on her skin. And Dara could no longer breathe.

She stared at Vine, eyes bulging, and pulled frantically for power, any power. But she had exhausted all the magical substances in the vicinity. Except for the Air, apparently.

She pushed against the force, trying to get closer to Siv. She still couldn't breathe. She couldn't concentrate, couldn't fight against it. Why was Vine doing this? Could her friend have betrayed her?

Vine waved Vex forward. "You will have to carry Siv. Rid, you take Dara. She'll be less likely to kill you when she wakes."

Shock pounded through Dara as the men moved to obey. She couldn't see Latch. Would he defend his friend? She clutched frantically for Fire, for Watermight, for anything, but it was too late. It had been too long since her last breath. Dark spots overtook her vision, and she slumped to the ground.

33

ATTACK

Selivia awoke at dawn to Fenn shaking her shoulder.

"Get up, Princess. We have to hide."

"What is it?"

Before Fenn could answer, a strong wind gusted through the house, forcing back the curtains and carrying the warning straight to them in urgent, Air-guided whispers. *Danger. The Sunset City is in terrible danger.*

Selivia leapt up, hurrying into her clothes as Fenn dressed and strapped on weapons beside her. Zala appeared at the door.

"The Soolen army snuck around the Rock," she said breathlessly. "No one saw them coming."

"The Soolens? Are you sure?"

"They must be looking for a new base now that the Fireworkers hold Rallion City," Fenn said.

"Why didn't the Sensors hear them coming?" Selivia asked.

"I don't know," Zala said. "Bring whatever food and water you can carry. We must hide."

"Where?"

"The Rock. We will wait in the tunnels until it's over."

Zala darted away to make sure the rest of the house was on the move.

"Won't we be cornered in the tunnels?" Selivia asked as she stuffed her feet into her shoes and grabbed her cloak.

"Better than being captured in the open," Fenn said. Her Far

Plains serenity had evaporated. She was a severe Vertigonian bodyguard once more. The change in her demeanor made fear spike through Selivia's stomach.

They hurried out of Ananova's house with the rest of the family. Every face was pale, every jaw tense or trembling. Dust blew around them, the wind carrying a frantic warning through every street. *Danger. Terrible danger.*

The older Plainsfolk remained calm and organized groups to usher the children east toward the Rock. Men and boys gathered weapons and farming tools, hands shaking as they turned the tools into instruments of war. They formed up with their neighbors and rushed north to meet the attack. Selivia spotted Ivran among them. He wore a look of grim determination, and he carried a club. He was only two years older than Selivia. He shouldn't be going to war. Was there any hope the Far Plainsfolk could keep the Soolens at bay?

Fenn and Zala joined a group heading for the Rock, sheltering Selivia between them. Her heart pounded as they fled through the gray drawn. With every turn, she was sure they'd meet the dreaded Soolen army at last—the men who had killed her grandfather and imprisoned her mother. Now they were here for her. She curled her hands into fists and prayed for bravery.

They had to take a roundabout way to try to reach the Rock. The Soolens advanced on the city from the north, occupying spokes of the wheel one by one, heading toward its heart. If they didn't reach the tunnels soon, they'd be cut off for good.

"Faster," Zala said, urging her onward as death marched on her city. "We have to go faster."

They heard the soldiers before they saw them. The thud of boots on the hard-packed desert earth was like a thunderstorm rolling over the mountain and echoing along the Fissure.

"Faster."

Selivia caught glimpses of the enemy soldiers as they ran from house to house, seeking shelter behind the humble mud walls. Stony faces and brilliant teeth gave the soldiers an unearthly quality. Boots pounded. Steel flashed. The colorful awnings shuddered ominously, caught in the wind and the thunder of footsteps. She couldn't believe she had once thought it would be exciting to be in a city under attack. This was terrifying.

It also wasn't fair. The Far Plainsfolk were peaceful. They didn't even have a standing army. The men and boys were only taking up arms to give the women and children time to get away. They didn't stand a chance.

Suddenly, a spike of silver shot through the street. It looked like a snake winding through the dust until it reached a nearby standing stone. The silver entered the stone, lining the cracks. Then the standing stone exploded.

Selivia dove to the ground, and Fenn landed on top of her. The larger woman grunted at the impact. Selivia felt too squashed to grunt. Fenn was on her feet a second later, dragging Selivia into the shelter of a nearby house.

"Where's Zala?" Selivia asked.

"There." Fenn pointed to a house across the way. Zala popped out briefly to gesture for them to wait, then disappeared from view. And not a moment too soon.

A company of Soolen soldiers tramped down the street. Their leader's eyes glowed silver-white in his dark face. He drew the silver snake back toward his hands. Selivia could hardly believe it. The rumors were true! How could the Soolens have magic without anyone knowing?

She and Fenn huddled beside the strangers' house, waiting for the soldiers to pass. More explosions erupted around the city, dull booms followed by a clattering like hailstones. What kind of magic was this? It didn't look like Fire. And from the sounds of things, it was devastating. She understood now why the Air Sensors trembled when they listened to reports of the fighting in Trure. The Fireworkers of Vertigon against these stone-crushing Soolens? It must be horrible.

The Rock loomed ahead, but Selivia felt torn. Now that she'd seen what these Soolen fighters could do, she knew they couldn't be allowed to keep fighting the Fireworkers. The magic conflict would spread destruction across the land, and innocent people like the Far Plainsfolk would pay the price.

Her family had to stop this. They were responsible for Vertigon—and for the damage its people wrought. It was up to them to end the conflict. And that meant it was time for her to go.

"Fenn," she whispered. "This group is almost past. Let's run to Zala on the count of three."

"Agreed." Fenn readied herself, her strong body poised like a runner's. "Stay close to me."

"One. Two. Three."

Fenn darted across the dirt road, diving to join Zala in her hiding place.

Selivia ran the other way.

She didn't dare look back to find out if the others had seen her escape. She hurried north, darting from house to house, hoping the soldiers would ignore her in favor of the more threatening men. She hated to leave Fenn and Zala behind, but if the Soolens caught them, they'd be safer without the enemy princess. And she had a job to do.

She followed the colors of the wheel outward. Many standing stones had already been destroyed by that strange power, but enough fragments remained to guide her. The rising sun shone harshly on the shards of ice in the dust. How much longer before the Soolens took over?

A few blocks from the city boundary, Selivia came upon a group of Air Sensors. She ducked behind an overturned cart to avoid being seen. But the Sensors weren't looking at her. They sat perfectly still in an open square, surrounding a standing stone painted with ladies in dark-green dresses. The Sensors stared forward, eyes open and unseeing, serene as ever. Fodorov sat at their head, leading them in the oddest form of combat Selivia had ever seen.

On the opposite side of the square, a company of Soolen soldiers formed up, weapons glittering in the early-morning sun. The soldiers looked so dangerous compared to the Air Sensors that it was almost comical. But as they attempted to advance on the Sensors, something held them back. Something invisible but tangible gusted up the street, impeding their progress. The soldiers on the front line appeared to be having trouble breathing. Every step forward looked labored, even painful.

Then Fodorov uttered a sound Selivia had never heard before, like a hurricane captured in a whisper, and the invisible force strengthened. The lips of the foremost soldiers stretched back from their teeth, as if they were running incredibly fast into a strong wind. The others bent low, shielding their eyes from the driving sand.

The Air Sensors shook under the pressure of this feat. Even their shuddering was perfectly in sync. Veins stood out on Fodorov's forehead, evidence of his incredible concentration.

Then, slowly at first, the Soolen soldiers began to drift backward. Heels scraping the dirt, feet scrabbling for purchase. They cried out angrily as the wind pushed them back. One man hurled a knife into the gale, and it flew back, slicing through a comrade's ear.

The Air Sensors were winning the fight! Selivia could hardly believe it. She had no idea the Air was this strong. She was so transfixed by the scene that she almost forgot she was supposed to be fleeing. She still needed to get around the skirmish. Her destination lay to the north.

Before she could move from her hiding place, a new player entered the contest. The Soolen officer was tall and distinguished, with a hint of gray at his temples. He had the most beautiful brown eyes Selivia had ever seen. Or at least they were brown at first. Within seconds of the officer's arrival in the square, the brown leached out of his eyes, replaced by a solid silver-white. He raised a hand, and a thin razor of silver sliced between the seated Air Sensors and the retreating Soolens.

At once, the soldiers stood up straight. The silver razor had cut through the attacking wind. The soldiers formed up, preparing to advance.

The Air Sensors renewed their assault. That terrible gale gathered once more. Sand rose and settled in the street, glimmering in the morning sunlight.

Before the Sensors could build enough strength to push the soldiers away, the Soolen officer sent a whip of silver toward Fodorov. The tip solidified into ice the instant before it reached him. The icy dagger sliced directly across Fodorov's throat then skittered away across the dirt.

Selivia gasped, the sound lost in the commotion as the Sensors reacted. Naked shock and horror painted their faces as their leader toppled forward, scarlet blood leaking into the burnt-umber dirt. The surviving Sensors tried desperately to resume their concentration, but the Soolens broke rank and darted among them, weapons flashing.

Selivia ran, staying to the shadows. She had to get out of sight before anyone saw her. As she darted across the edge of the square, she spotted something shiny on the ground. Not thinking, she stooped to pick it up, her fingers closing on a cold, hard object. It was the icy dagger the Soolen officer had whipped forward to kill Fodorov. A thin line of blood marred the iridescent shard.

Resisting the urge to drop it, Selivia clutched the shard of icy magic tight. She had only her tiny work knife in her pocket. She might need this before she made it out of the city.

The Soolens closed in on the helpless Sensors as Selivia left the square behind, running as fast as she could.

Chaos reigned in the streets. It took three times longer than it should have to reach the outer boundaries. She darted from house to house, hiding behind sand screens and colorful curtains, a stitch catching in her side. Her hand went numb from clutching the dagger, but it didn't melt as quickly as ice normally did. It was still wider than her palm by the time she crept from the shadows of a boundary house and charged onto the plains.

She stumbled, stunned by what she found. A huge Soolen force gathered in the desert, amassing in the shadow of the Rock while the vanguard dealt with the resistance in the city. This must be the entirety of Commander Brach's force! Selivia prayed most of the Far Plainsfolk had made it to the tunnels. She spotted a few brightly clad figures fleeing across the plains, but the Soolens didn't seem interested in chasing after stragglers. There was nowhere for them to go out here.

Selivia stayed well away from the soldiers as she hurried into the wilderness. Pollen hung thick over the plains, and aromas bloomed around her as she crushed wildflowers in her haste to reach her destination. Her dress was soaked through with sweat, and her breath came in gasps. She hardly dared contemplate what she was about to do. She focused on the swirling colors beneath her feet and the ice in her hand. She couldn't let fear stop her now. This was her only chance to escape. The Soolens would never let her near the true dragon again if they succeeded in taking the city.

A different smell overpowered the scent of crushed flowers as she arrived at the true dragon's crater: charred flesh. Someone had reached the dragon before her. Two bodies lay on the sloping wall of the pit. They had climbed down to attack the captive creature and been roasted for their troubles.

The true dragon himself looked more like a wild beast than ever. He snapped his jaws angrily, pacing about with his shackles rattling. A feral light burned in his cobalt eyes. Selivia appreciated how dangerous he truly was for the first time as he stalked across the crater floor, pulling at his chains, tail lashing like a mace. She wished she could abandon her mission when she saw how agitated he was. But there was no turning back now.

How could she get close to his chains? He didn't look as if he'd be calming down anytime soon. Then Selivia spotted the source of his fury. Someone—one of the charred soldiers probably—had stuck a spear into the softer scales on his belly. It didn't go in too deep, but the angle of the spearhead made it impossible for the creature to grasp it with his teeth and pull it out.

The true dragon bellowed, and Selivia's heart cracked at the sound of his pain. He spit a jet of Fire toward his own body, attempting to melt the spearhead, but he couldn't quite reach. He was growing frantic with pain and rage. He had to calm down before he hurt himself. Or attracted more soldiers.

"Hey," she called.

A furious spurt of Fire answered her. She dove out of the way as the liquid magic drenched the spot where she'd been standing, heat coming off it in waves.

It took Selivia a minute to recover her courage enough to peek over the edge of the crater again. She had startled him. That was all.

The dragon sat on his haunches, watching his Fire trickle down from where he'd tried to roast her. She took a deep breath and called out again. "Hello there! It's me. I'm your friend."

The dragon snorted, but he didn't spurt Fire again. He looked up at her and ruffled his wings angrily.

"I know," she said. "I'm sorry this happened to you. I'm glad you got those guys though."

She nodded at the charred figures, trying not to look directly at them.

The dragon snapped his jaws, apparently proud. Then he let out a keening sound and presented his breast, where the black spearhead stood out against his pale-green scales.

"That looks dreadful," Selivia said. "Will you let me help you?"

The true dragon cocked his head to the side.

"I'll take it out if you promise not to breathe Fire at me. Is that okay with you?"

The true dragon huffed. Then he made that expression that she was certain was meant to be a smile. She took another deep breath and swung her legs over the edge of the crater.

"Here goes nothing."

She slid on her bottom down the side of the pit, staying well clear of the corpses. She kept her eyes on the true dragon's cobalt ones, watching for any hint that he had changed his mind. But the dragon simply watched her as she scooted nearer.

She approached cautiously, trembling hands raised. She shouldn't make any sudden movements or get close too quickly. *Easy.* He had to get accustomed to her presence. *Easy there.*

Suddenly, the dragon lowered himself toward her and presented her with his injured belly, imposing and insistent. It happened so fast that she squeaked and fell to the ground. The dragon simply hovered with the spearhead directly within her reach. Okay, so he didn't want to wait while *she* grew accustomed to *him.*

Before fear could overwhelm her, she reached out and laid a hand on the true dragon's scales. They were hard and exquisitely smooth. The belly scales reminded her of the softness of a baby cur-dragon. She stroked the true dragon gently and tugged on the spearhead with her other hand.

It didn't budge. The true dragon roared, the sound a mixture of pain and impatience.

"Be quiet, you big baby," she said. "I need a better grip."

The true dragon snorted, but it settled lower, making it easier for her to grasp the wicked black metal.

She gave one sharp pull, and the spearhead slid out.

The dragon shuddered. His scales seemed to rearrange themselves to protect the tender wound—but not before she saw a shocking sight: the dragon's blood was pure silver. She ran a finger over the silver staining the spearhead, wondering at the sheen. In the second she was looking down, the true dragon shifted around, and suddenly his cobalt eye was even with her face.

Selivia jumped, dropping the spearhead, as the dragon brought his head within inches of her. It really was the size of her body. The morning sunlight slid over the obsidian scales on his nose as if they were made of glass. She stared back into that glorious cobalt eye.

"You're beautiful," she whispered. She was sure the true dragon chuckled, his hot breath huffing around her.

Then he shot out a quick spurt of Fire and melted the offending spearhead into a smoldering lump.

"It deserved that," Selivia said.

The true dragon pulled back to look her over. She accepted his scrutiny, figuring it would be a good idea for them to get to know each other.

"My name is Selivia," she said. "I'm a princess. Aren't princesses and dragons supposed to be friends?"

The true dragon tipped his head sideways.

"Okay, I don't know either. But I want to be your friend. I think we can help each other. We don't have a lot of time. Can we escape now and get to know each other later?"

The dragon snapped his jaws within an inch of her face. The sudden movement almost made her heart stop, but she thought it meant yes.

"Okay, then. Let's see about getting you unchained."

The true dragon huffed then pointed his massive nose at the lump of melted metal that had once been the spearhead.

"It won't hurt you anymore," she said.

The true dragon shook his head and pointed at the metal again, shuffling his feet beneath him.

"I don't understand."

"He can't melt the chain."

Selivia's surprise at the new voice was nothing compared to the dragon's. He leapt up and sent another jet of Fire roaring toward the rim of the crater. It went on for a long time, and Selivia feared there would be nothing left of the newcomer before she even knew who it was.

"Will you tell him to stop?" the voice called after a minute. "I'm trying to help."

"Ivran?"

"Yes! Tell him not to roast me."

The dragon was still merrily spitting Fire at the rim of his prison, the liquid gold running down the walls in shimmering waterfalls. She tapped on his scales.

"Would you let him talk?" she asked. "He's a friend. Well, not a friend, really, but I don't think he'll hurt us."

The true dragon stopped expelling flame at last and sat back.

"Promise you won't hurt him?"

The true dragon sighed heavily then shuffled back even farther, somehow managing to look as innocent as a kitten. The shift in his position revealed the chains on his ankles, which appeared to be made of iron. Fire was supposed to melt iron, wasn't it?

"Ivran? You can come down now."

"No way," Ivran said, creeping to the edge of the crater and poking his head into view. "I'll stay up here, thanks."

"Fine," Selivia said. "What were you saying about the chains?"

"There's an Air spell on them to keep Fire from getting through. That's why he didn't melt through them his first day here."

"Can it be broken?"

"I can do it," Ivran said. "But only if you promise to stop the Soolens."

"Stop them how?"

"Use the true dragon. If the beast will do what you say, you should go out and roast the invaders in their boots."

Selivia looked up at the true dragon. He gazed back steadily.

"I think we're friends," Selivia said. "But I don't think he'll do what I say."

"Then you're not flying him out of here," Ivran said. "You can't abandon us."

Selivia looked up at the rim of the crater and folded her arms. "I don't owe you anything, and neither does he. You kept him a prisoner for a year!"

"It was only so he could protect us," Ivran said. "Now's the time."

"You can't just order him to fight for you," Selivia said. "You have to work together. Commune."

Ivran's jaw set. It was amazing how ugly such a good-looking boy could be. "If you won't promise, then good luck breaking that Air spell."

"Please, Ivran."

"They're coming!" He looked over his shoulder then back at the pit. "Get out of there before they see you."

"Ivran, wait!"

He disappeared from view once more. Selivia couldn't believe it. He had said he would help her! She understood he wanted to protect his people, but they couldn't enslave others to do it. It wasn't right.

But it was too late. Ivran was gone, and the steady beat of footsteps announced he was telling the truth. The Soolens were coming.

Selivia clutched at her skirt. What was she going to do? She couldn't use the Air. How would she break the spell on the dragon's chains? Then her fingers brushed something in her pocket. Something cold and hard.

"The shard!" She pulled out the bit of Soolen magic she'd picked up in the square. It had melted some, but a sliver as long as her hand remained. She looked up at the true dragon.

"It's worth a try. Hold still."

She crept beneath his belly, trusting he'd allow it. Neither of them had much choice right now. The Soolens would never let such a dangerous creature live.

The true dragon had a shackle around each hind ankle. Knowing she might only have one chance, she broke the ice shard in two pieces, each one shorter than her pinky finger. She crept to the true dragon's side and jammed the first one into the lock. It slid in cleanly. The Air spell didn't keep out the Soolen magic—whatever it was. She worked the shard back and forth, trying to spring the lock.

It was no use—the ice seemed to meld into the lock, but it didn't release it.

She heard voices. The Soolens were getting closer. The dragon shuffled impatiently. Feeling frustrated, Selivia left the lump of ice in the lock and moved to the other ankle. She worked the second piece back and forth, trying once again to get it to work.

Suddenly, there was a burst of heat nearby. The true dragon spit a jet of Fire at its ankle, directly at the lock where she'd left the shard.

"Wait! I might be able to use that to—"

It was too late. The Fire hit the lock. Even if the Air spell protected the iron, it was sure to melt that bit of ice. It would be useless.

Instead, the shard popped like a bubble, forcing the lock to spring open with a flash of white light. The true dragon gave his ankle a mighty shake, and the manacle clunked to the ground.

"You did it!" Selivia shouted. "Quickly, let's get the other one."

She forced the last bit of hardened magic into the lock as the first of the Soolen soldiers reached the pit.

"Blasted rock-eating goddess!" a man shouted. "Look what I found!"

"Is it one of ours?"

"Does it look like it to you?"

The first man's response was muffled as Selivia dove behind the true dragon's tail, hoping they hadn't seen her.

"There's someone down there with it."

"Blast," she whispered.

The true dragon grunted and gave her an impatient look. She stared back at him for a second before she understood. Then she grabbed hold of his hind foot and used the remaining shackle to climb onto his back.

The instant she was secure, the true dragon blasted another jet of Fire at the shard in the second lock. It burst open in a shower of metal and white light. The true dragon gathered his strength, spread his jet-black wings, and launched into the air.

Selivia screamed. The dragon scales were hard and slippery. The beat of the wings threatened to send her falling to the earth with every stroke. She was too stunned to take in her surroundings at first. She knew only the heave of the wings and the light of the morning sun on the jet scales protecting the dragon's head. The sharp crown of spikes cut into the blue sky beyond. They were flying! Actually flying!

She was riding a real live true dragon! She had never been more scared or happy in her entire life.

The dragon banked sharply, and Selivia tightened her grip on its neck to keep from tumbling off. It was much harder to keep her grip than she would have expected. Warm wind whistled around her, ripping her scarf from her hair and making her skirt fly up around her thighs. She didn't care. Nothing mattered but the glorious rush of the sky and the dragon and the utterly terrifying feeling of being in the air.

The true dragon tested out his strength after his year in captivity. He flew in a wide circle, the black membranous wings almost transparent in the sunshine. He didn't seem to be in any hurry to leave the sunset lands just yet.

Selivia worked up the nerve to look down. The sight made her stomach plummet, but they weren't too high up yet. The true dragon's crater passed beneath them, and the soldiers gathered at its edge looked as small as cats. They stared at the dragon soaring overhead with wide eyes and open mouths.

The dragon turned, and they glided toward the city. Flashes of silver appeared below, and stones continued to explode. People darted around in groups, but the Soolens had occupied most of the eastern border, blocking their access to the Rock. The Far Plainsfolk were trapped.

As she soared high above the chaos, Selivia felt a tinge of regret. She couldn't just leave them. Yes, the Far Plainsfolk had planned to use her as a hostage, but they had also offered her refuge. She counted Zala and Ananova as friends still. Plus, Fenn was down there. Her bodyguard would be safer without Selivia at her side, but she still felt uneasy about leaving her. She wondered if she and the true dragon could even the score before making their escape.

Before she could ask, the true dragon let out a vicious roar and banked so sharply that she almost fell off his back.

"What?" she gasped. He probably couldn't hear her above the rushing of the wind. She looked down, stomach lurching when she realized how high they had climbed now. She spotted the source of the dragon's cry. A Soolen officer stood in an open square, gathering a coil of that silvery power. He hurled it at the dragon, trying to lasso him as he soared overhead.

Selivia shrieked as they swooped to avoid the silver rope. She kept her arms wrapped tightly around the true dragon's neck. It was folly to think she could control the creature. The true dragon would do exactly as he pleased.

Heat built within him suddenly, his scales becoming so hot, it hurt to hold on. An instant later, Fire spewed from his mouth in a deadly fountain and engulfed the Soolen officer. The officer screamed, sharp and short. A blinding flash of light filled the square.

The true dragon shrieked in triumph. Selivia had no idea whether the destruction pleased him or if he was just happy to breathe Fire and soar through the sky. He banked sharply and spat a jet of Fire over a group of Soolen soldiers. He didn't seem to care that these soldiers weren't the ones who'd held him captive.

The dragon's rampage drew the attention of more Soolens. The soldiers ran toward him, throwing glittering spears and trying to shoot him with silver arrows. Selivia clung to his neck, body rigid with terror. But fear and confusion filled the eyes of the soldiers too. Every company focused their efforts on the true dragon. As they tried to shoot him down, more Far Plainsfolk slipped through their grasp.

The dragon wheeled for another pass, boiling a trio of soldiers where they stood. But more were coming, arrows nocked, and at least two additional magic workers were now sending ropes of silver high into the air to try to catch him.

He roared and climbed higher, sailing away from the carnage he had wrought. He must have decided he'd had enough excitement for one day.

Selivia's arms tired quickly from holding on, but she didn't dare shift into a more comfortable position. Her dragon hadn't flown for a year. He must need rest soon. She was still rigid with exhaustion and rank terror.

Just when Selivia feared her arms would give way for good, the true dragon landed with a mighty thud. Dust bloomed around them, obscuring the sky. When a brisk wind blew the dust away once more, they stood on a plateau with no sign of Sunset City or the Soolen army in sight.

Selivia slid off the dragon's back and fell flat on her bottom, every limb shaking. The dragon lumbered a few feet away and collapsed too. His heavy breathing sent up dust all around him.

Selivia looked around, feeling disoriented. There was nothing but flat desert all around her. Had they gotten that far from the city so quickly? She knew they'd been flying fast, but she expected to see the colorful awnings or the leftover smoke from her dragon's exploits in the distance.

And where was the Rock? That should at least tell her what direction they had gone. She turned in a full circle, noting that the sun still hovered over the eastern horizon.

And that was when she figured it out. They hadn't flown far away from the Rock. They were standing on top of it. The true dragon had carried her to the crown of the ancient land formation. And now the only living beings in sight were she and the first true dragon to leave the Burnt Mountains in centuries.

34

THE TOWER

Dara awoke in an airy room. Bright afternoon light poured over her from a tall window. Silk curtains fluttered in the breeze, which was warm and scented with salt and a hint of flowers. Her head hurt, but she couldn't remember why.

She felt a cool hand on her brow and looked up to find Vine staring down at her.

Dara jolted upright, reaching for a blade, a bit of Fire, a drop of Watermight.

"It's okay, Dara," Vine said, her voice a familiar singsong. "I'm sorry I had to knock you out back there. I'm still on your side."

"Where are we?" Dara demanded, ducking the soothing hand Vine attempted to place on her forehead. "Where is Siv?"

"I'm here."

The voice came from beside her. She lay on a massive bed covered in silk blankets and dozens of pillows. Siv sat upright next to her, looking somewhat the worse for wear thanks to his silver-sealed cuts and bruises. But his eyes were bright, and he grinned at her.

"Welcome back to the land of the conscious."

"What happened?" Dara demanded.

"I had to put you to sleep for a little while to get you safely here," Vine said. She stood beside Dara's side of the bed, trying to dab her forehead with a cool cloth. Dara knocked it away.

"I woke up when we were halfway here in a canal boat," Siv said. "Had the surprise of my life when I saw Vex Rollendar standing over me."

"Vex!" It all came back to Dara in a rush. She scanned the room quickly, but there was no sign of the Rollendar lord. They were in an elegant bedchamber. The silk curtains and silk sheets were only the beginning. Plush carpets covered the floors, and fine paintings decorated the walls. A crystal tea set awaited them on a low table, along with plates piled with cakes and fruit. Dara's Savven blade leaned against a porcelain vase inlaid with gold. "Where are we?" she said again, already guessing the answer.

"The King's Tower," Vine said. "I can't wait to show you around. The King of Pendark is ever so lovely."

"He's been harboring Vex and his men."

"Well, Vex doesn't really have men anymore," Vine said. "His associates abandoned him after his recent change of heart."

"Change of heart?"

"He has left the service of his former liege. Also, he's desperately in love with me. Isn't it delightful how things turn out?"

Dara stared at her, waiting for her to say it was all a joke. Vine gazed back blandly, ignoring the absurdity of what she was saying.

"We are free to come and go," Vine said. "I suggest you rest for a little while, take the king up on his generous offer of hospitality. This is the only place in Pendark where we will be completely protected from all Waterworkers. I'll leave you two to talk."

Vine smiled at them both and skipped across the room. "Vex and I will be dining with the king. I do hope you'll join us." She gave them a sunny smile and disappeared through the door. As if to demonstrate that they were free to go, she left it open a crack.

Dara and Siv looked at each other.

"She's finally lost it," Dara said.

Siv shrugged. "Maybe. On the way over here, Vex didn't seem interested in killing us, though. I reckon there's more to the story."

"You don't believe what she was saying about being in love, do you?"

"I gave up on trying to understand Vine Silltine a while ago," he said. "Has she ever let you down before?"

"No," Dara said. "But she's also never knocked me out with Air before."

"I must have missed that part." Siv settled back on the silk cushions, grimacing slightly. "Can't argue with the accommodations, though."

"How do you feel?" Dara asked. She moved closer to him and touched one of the sealed cuts on his arm to make sure the Watermight was still firmly in place. His skin was warm against hers.

"I've taken worse beatings in the pen," Siv said. "How's your arm?"

"I think the bond is gone." Dara turned the limb in question back and forth, sensing for any hint of ice or broken bones. Then she poked Siv in the ribs. "What were you thinking? You could have warned me about your plan, seeing as the whole thing relied on me breaking the bond in time."

"I had to take you by surprise," Siv said. "Also, I really thought bargaining for Latch's Watermight knowledge would work."

"What if it hadn't? Wyla would have killed you, and Latch would have ended up tied to her too."

"I knew you could do it," Siv said simply.

"But—"

"And I was right." Siv caught her hand before she could poke him again. "You should just admit it. I'm always right."

"It was too much of a risk," Dara said.

"It wasn't," Siv said. "I trust you, Dara. Those aren't just words."

Dara sighed, some of the anger draining away. Siv had shown utter confidence in her today, even though he was putting his own life in peril. A hot coal flared to life in her chest as Siv tightened his grip on her hand. It was irritating that he had been right, too. As if he sensed her thoughts, he grinned, and the coal became a flame.

"Fine," she said. "You were right. Thank you for your help."

Siv's smile widened. "Any chance I could get a kiss along with that thanks?"

Dara grinned back and leaned in.

They walked together to meet the king, both unsteady on their feet after their ordeal. A serving woman in a white dress met them at the door to show them the way. The king's private dining chamber was empty, and they found the king and his guests lounging on a balcony through vast double doors.

The balcony was located near the top of the King's Tower, the tallest building in Pendark. The view was incredible. The sun sparkled on the Black Gulf, making the water glimmer like a star-brushed sky. From way up here, the city looked almost peaceful. No sign of the conflict that had raged in the streets over the past month disturbed the tableau.

Vine hurried forward to greet them from where she'd been whispering with Vex Rollendar. The elusive lord had a cruelly handsome face, with sandy-blond hair and sharp eyes that reminded Dara too much of his nephew Bolden. Vex's movements were powerful and lithe, hinting at his talent as a swordsman.

Dara was sure Vex had found some way to enchant Vine, but she saw no evidence of it. In fact, Vex was the one who appeared to be enchanted. He watched Vine's dancing movements as if she were made of Fire and magic. Dara didn't trust him, but at least he didn't seem to be planning to stab anyone here and now. He must be playing a longer game. Dara would find out what it was before he hurt her friend.

Vine drew them toward a table for six covered with a delectable spread of food at one end of the terrace. Dara's stomach rumbled. The dishes were a mix of local favorites and delicacies from across the Bell Sea. He may not have much power here, but the King of Pendark certainly lived well.

The man himself sat at the head of the table. He was older than Dara had expected, with deep wrinkles and wispy hair that glowed silver in the sunlight. His hair was the exact color of Watermight, and Dara had to remind herself forcibly that this man couldn't Wield. She felt no power in the vicinity, Watermight or Fire. The king may not be able to use the magic substances, but he knew how to protect himself from them in his tower far above the city.

"Welcome to my home," the king said. "I understand you've had an adventurous visit so far."

"Pendark lives up to its reputation," Siv said. "It's nice to meet you, Your Majesty. My father spoke highly of you."

"I am sorry for your loss."

Siv inclined his head.

"Please sit and eat," the king said. "You must regain your strength."

"Lady Silltine believes you mean to help us," Siv said, not moving toward the chairs. He appeared calm, even grave, reminding Dara of how much he'd matured over the past year.

"I will do what I can," the king said. "You must know the limits of my power here, if you did your homework as a boy."

"I've read Merlin Mavril's histories," Siv said.

The king chuckled. "I'm afraid Mavril paints me as a bit more bloodthirsty than I am."

"I understand Pendarkans like that sort of thing."

"They do indeed," the king said. He reached for a tart from the rich spread before him. "They like you as well. I've heard of your exploits in the Steel Pentagon."

The king nodded pointedly at the chairs, clearly wanting to continue the conversation over a meal. Siv remained standing.

"How long have you known I was in the city?"

"Quite some time. I learned of you from my friend Vex here." The king nodded toward the Rollendar lord, who had moved closer while they were speaking.

Siv stiffened, and Dara put a hand on her Savven blade. Vex gazed at them impassively, staying on the opposite side of the table. Dara met his eyes, daring him to make a move. She remembered all too well when he had thrown a knife into her shoulder.

A breeze whipped around the balcony, ruffling the tablecloth, but no one moved. Dara watched Vex. Siv watched the king.

Then Vine skipped over to Vex and looped her arm through his.

"He has promised not to tell anyone else," she said. "Let's not get distracted. Do sit. We're all going to be friends."

"Wait," Siv said. "Khrillin told me you were the one who trained the swordsmen for your brother's coup. Is that true?"

"Yes," Vex said. He still held Dara's eyes while he answered Siv's query. "Von shouldn't have trusted the Lantern Maker. My men would have won him the crown." Dara glared back at him. He shouldn't be so confident. Her Castle Guard had been a match for Vex's swordsmen.

"Many of the swordsmen were Soolens," Siv said.

"That's correct." Vex broke Dara's gaze at last and turned to Siv, facing him across the table. "My brothers formed an alliance with Commander Brach of Soole. I left the mountain to liaise with him. I was in his company when my brother was murdered." His eyes cut to Dara again. Right. Her parents had killed his brother Von, betraying their tenuous alliance. She wondered if he knew that his nephew had been in on it.

Vex's attention returned to Siv. "Brach sent me to find you after you escaped his men in Trure. He doesn't like loose ends."

"You traveled across the continent to kill me," Siv said. "And now you want to sit and chat over soldarberry tarts. Why?"

"Well, my Lady Vine—"

"Why else?" Siv said. Dara was glad to see he didn't buy the story of Vex's infatuation, no matter how charming Vine could be.

"Revenge," Vex said softly. "I'll ally with whoever defeats the Lantern Maker. Based on the latest reports, I'm no longer sure Brach is the man to do it."

Siv rubbed a hand across his chin. Dara watched him study Vex, his expression thoughtful. She knew he'd be pacing if he didn't have to play the dignified king right now. He must be thinking of revenge too. Revenge against the man who killed his father. Siv and Vex had an enemy in common. Dara's father.

Uneasiness wormed through her stomach. She agreed that they had to stop her father—especially now that he was using Fire Weapons—but she didn't like the idea of working with someone who hated him so completely.

She glanced at Vine and caught an unexpectedly shrewd expression on her friend's face. It was gone so quickly that Dara wondered if she had imagined it. Vine was already back to gazing admiringly at Vex. Interesting. Was Vine working on a deeper scheme here? Dara wanted to trust her, and Vine's strategic mind was second to none. Maybe she wasn't the one who'd been enchanted here.

Suddenly, the king stood up, making everyone start.

"Friends, I think we have an opportunity to set things right and establish a new era of peace." He was positioned between the two pairs staring each other down across the table, and he raised his arms as if to encompass them all. "I wish to help the Amintelle family regain the throne of Vertigon."

"Why?" Siv asked. "If I may say so, Your Majesty, it doesn't really have anything to do with you."

"Not yet." The king took a piece of parchment from his pocket and handed it to Siv. Dara peered over his shoulder as he read the message.

Rallion City has burned to the ground. The Fireworkers are too strong. They march on Soole next.

"I see," Siv said. "You know if the Fireworkers continue their rampage, they'll come for Pendark eventually."

"They must be contained," the king said. "And there's more. The Air Sensors have recently regained contact with their counterparts in Trure. I received word this morning that Commander Brach's remaining forces have taken the Sunset City of the Far Plainsfolk."

"The Far Plainsfolk?" Siv said. "My little sister is with them."

"I'm afraid I have no word of her," the king said. "But the Sensors should establish contact again in good time."

"I didn't know you had such good relations with the Air Sensors," Siv said.

"I practice the discipline myself," the king said. "The meditations help me sleep, and I'm a regular visitor to Pendark's only Sensors Manor. That's where I met Lady Vine and arranged for her to reconcile with Lord Vex."

Dara glanced at Vine, who was still gazing at Vex. So the Air had connected them after all. Vine hadn't told her she'd met the king. What was she planning? No matter what happened with Vex, the King of Pendark could prove to be exactly the ally they needed. She doubted Khrillin would be as eager to leave Pendark now that he'd taken control of Wyla's vent. Firelord, he'd just become the most powerful man in the city by a significant margin. She wondered how important his friendship with Siv's father would seem now.

Siv met the King of Pendark's eyes steadily. "So you want me to go north and clean up the mess Brach and Ruminor have made and keep everyone away from your city. The Soolens will go back to Soole, and the Vertigonians will go back to Vertigon. Is that a fair summary?"

The king nodded. "I wish to have balance in the continent. If I have learned anything after ruling Pendark, it is that we must have balance."

"And you're willing to help me do it."

"I will give you whatever assistance you require to turn the tide against the Lantern Maker. The Amintelles must reign once more—and they must rein in the power of the mountain. The Fire is too dangerous to blaze unchecked."

Siv glanced at Dara, clearly wanting her opinion. She could tell he wanted to agree. It was unclear whose side Khrillin was on now, and they were running out of time to set things right in their homeland. She held his gaze for a moment, and then she nodded. A faint smile flitted across Siv's lips.

"In that case," he said, advancing to shake hands with the older king, "I think we can work together. Now, shall we have a seat and enjoy this excellent food while we get to know each other?"

The King of Pendark smiled. "An excellent suggestion, King Sivarrion."

As the five of them sat to eat, Dara couldn't help feeling troubled. Who was this man to say what the Fireworkers could do with their power? The king may want checks on the magical substances, but Fire and Watermight were the only things that could stop her father. And perhaps Air. It was proving to be more powerful than she'd realized. Could the answer to her troubles be found in all three substances?

She remembered what she and Vine had discussed the other night and leaned over to whisper to her. "You said someone figured out how to transport Watermight."

"Oh yes!" Vine said. "That reminds me. Where is dear Latch?"

"Ah," the King of Pendark said. "I believe young Brach was taking a rest, but he—"

"I apologize for my tardiness." Latch strode out onto the terrace then. He was clad in a fine Pendarkan coat, looking every inch the young lord. Rumy the cur-dragon prowled at his side. "It has been a while since I had access to a proper bathing chamber."

"Latch here knows the secret," Vine said. "I wasn't sure if you figured that out during the chaos."

It had certainly been a surprise to see the young Soolen wielding Watermight that morning. She still didn't know him very well.

Latch took the final seat at the end of the table. Rumy settled between him and Siv and began poking at the food on Siv's plate. Latch gave Vex Rollendar a wary nod before filling his own plate.

"Thanks for your help today, Latch," Dara said.

Latch grunted. "Siv thinks you're our only hope."

"I . . . really?"

"He'd better be right."

"King Siv isn't the only who believes you are the key, Lady Dara." The King of Pendark leaned forward. "Lady Vine assures me you can be trusted. She says you will do what needs to be done, but you will not let the power corrupt you."

Dara looked between Vine and the king. Then she turned to Siv. He was busy sampling delicacies and feeding bits of food to Rumy. When he noticed her looking at him, he grinned reassuringly. Warmth spread through her stomach at the confidence in his smile. She wasn't at all sure she could defeat her father or keep the power from getting to her. She was afraid she'd let her friends down. She was afraid she wouldn't be strong enough. But she had to try. The fate of the continent depended on it.

She turned to Latch. "Will you teach me your secret?"

He met her gaze, brown eyes solemn. He seemed to be sizing her up, like a duelist studying a potential training partner. Then he nodded.

"It's a magnificent trick." Vine gave her a sunny smile. "Your swallowing incident should have been the first hint of how it works."

"Even if I drink a gallon, it won't last through the whole journey," Dara said.

"You won't be the one drinking it." Latch laid a hand on Rumy's head. The overgrown creature was still chomping away at Siv's dinner. "Soolen Watermight Fighters Work with the power, Dara, but true dragons carry it."

Dara blinked. Had Latch been hit over the head during the fight that morning? But Siv laughed.

"I knew it! Sorcerers always have dragons in the stories." He poured himself a glass of wine, still chuckling. "They're magical beings. Of course they can carry magical substances."

"Hold on," Dara said. "Where did the Soolen army get true dragons? Aren't they fast asleep in the Burnt Mountains?"

"A rare species lives deep in Cindral Forest," Latch said. "It borders my family's land. That's why my father's army spent so much time there before invading Trure."

"They were rounding up dragons?"

"There are only a handful," Latch said, "and they have to return to the vents in Soole to retrieve more Watermight every once in a while. My father must be running out if the Fireworkers are winning the war."

"So in addition to my power, we need a true dragon to help us carry enough Watermight to push the Fireworkers back to Vertigon?" Dara shook her head ruefully. "I'm not sure how that knowledge helps us."

"We have Rumy," Siv said.

"He won't be big enough," Latch said. "We need a real true dragon."

"No need to look so grim, my friends," Vine said. She looked around the table with a beatific smile. "Ever since the Air channels have opened, I've had the most interesting conversations. I happen to know someone who has a true dragon of her very own."

EPILOGUE

Sora stood at her bedroom window, looking out over the mountain. It was unusually clear today. She could see all the way to Trure if Village Peak weren't blocking her view. Smoke rose in the distance, far beyond the crown of the peak, as it had for days. Her people had wreaked havoc on the armies of Soole in their bid to take their prize away from them. The surviving Trurens had endured worse.

But the Lantern Maker had made a critical miscalculation. She looked down at the note in her hand, delivered by cur-dragon that very morning.

Soole has magic too.

Those four words spelled doom. The Lantern Maker had begun his assault assuming the Lands Below would stand no chance against him. He had brought her people into danger, and she had let him do it. She had exhorted them, urging them to fight in her name. Now, they were locked in a deadly contest from which they might never return.

Sora felt sick. She had appeased the Lantern Maker to protect her people, and now her soldiers were caught in the midst of a magical contest the likes of which the continent had never seen. She had tasted power, danced to its seduction. And now everything had gone to ruin.

She marched across her room and threw open her bedroom door. Kel and Oat stood guard. She had barely been able to look at

Kel since refusing his offer to carry her away. Well, she may not be wise all the time, but she was willing to admit when she had made a mistake.

"I've changed my mind," she announced. "Bring me Berg Doban. It's time to fight back."

ACKNOWLEDGMENTS

This book and this series wouldn't exist without the help and encouragement of a lot of people. First and foremost are the readers who continue to express enthusiasm for Dara's story and share it with their friends. Thank you for reminding me why I do this on a regular basis.

Special thanks go to Marina Finlayson, Laura Besley, and Ayden and Julie Young for your help on this book in particular (and for cheering for the dragons). The writers of Hong Kong—those currently living here, those who've moved on, and Willow, who came back—are a wonderful source of advice, encouragement, company, and inspiration. I'm thankful for Author's Corner, which runs on pure inspiration and all the jokes. I couldn't do this without you people.

I'm grateful to Susie and Lynn at Red Adept Editing and Kitten and Kim at Deranged Doctor Design. Thank you for polishing this book and helping it shine.

My agent, Sarah Hershman, and Tantor Media have done wonderful work on the Steel and Fire audiobooks. Narrator Caitlin Kelly brings the story to life in the most spectacular way. Thanks for taking me on.

My husband and my family continue to be my biggest cheerleaders. Thank you for talking me through moderate amounts of writerly angst this time around.

Thanks again, readers, for all the rest. I'm diving into the fifth and final book in the series right now. Wish me luck!

Jordan Rivet
Hong Kong, 2016

ABOUT THE AUTHOR

Jordan Rivet is an American author of fantasy and science fiction. Originally from Arizona, she lives in Hong Kong with her husband. She is the author of the post-apocalyptic *Seabound Chronicles* and the *Steel and Fire* fantasy adventure series. She fenced for many years, and she still hasn't decided whether the pen is mightier than the sword.

Also by Jordan Rivet:

Steel and Fire
Duel of Fire
King of Mist
Dance of Steel
City of Wind

The Seabound Chronicles
Seabound
Seaswept
Seafled
Burnt Sea: A Seabound Prequel

CPSIA information can be obtained
at www.ICGtesting.com
Printed in the USA
BVHW032140180420
577900BV00001B/42

9 781541 240056